P9-BYK-549

Praise for the Novels
of Lauren Willig

The Deception of the Emerald Ring

"Heaving bodices, embellished history, and witty dialogue:
What more could you ask for?" —*Kirkus Reviews*

"Willig's latest is riveting, providing a great diversion and lots of
fun." —*Booklist*

"Eloise Kelly continues her research of early nineteenth-century
spies in the smart third book of the Pink Carnation series. . . .
Willig—like Eloise, a PhD candidate in history—draws on her
knowledge of the period, filling the fast-paced narrative with
mistaken identities, double agents, and high-stakes espionage. . . .
The historic action is taut and twisting. Fans of the series will
clamor for more." —*Publishers Weekly*

The Masque of the Black Tulip

"Clever [and] playful. . . . What's most delicious about Willig's
novels is that the damsels of 1803 bravely put it all on the line for
love and country." —*Detroit Free Press*

"Studded with clever literary and historical nuggets, this charming historical/contemporary romance moves back and forth in
time." —*USA Today*

"This is a genre-bending soup of mystery, romance, and espionage, laced with wit." —*Taconic Press*

continued . . .

"Willig has great fun with the conventions of the genre, throwing obstacles between her lovers at every opportunity . . . a great escape." —*The Boston Globe*

"Delightful." —*Kirkus Reviews*

"Willig picks up where she left readers breathlessly hanging. . . . Many more will delight in this easy-to-read romp and line up for the next installment." —*Publishers Weekly*

"Terribly clever and funny . . . will keep readers guessing until the final un-Masquing." —*Library Journal*

The Secret History of the Pink Carnation

"A deftly hilarious, sexy novel." —Eloisa James, author of *Taming of the Duke*

"A merry romp with never a dull moment! A fun read." —Mary Balogh, *New York Times* bestselling author of *The Secret Pearl*

"This genre-bending read—a dash of chick lit with a historical twist—has it all: romance, mystery, and adventure. Pure fun!" —Meg Cabot, author of *Queen of Babble*

"A historical novel with a modern twist. I loved the way Willig dips back and forth from Eloise's love affair and her swish parties to the Purple Gentian and of course the lovely, feisty Amy. The unmasking of the Pink Carnation is a real surprise."
—Mina Ford, author of *My Fake Wedding*

"Swashbuckling. . . . Willig has an ear for quick wit and an eye for detail. Her fiction debut is chock-full of romance, sexual tension, espionage, adventure, and humor." —*Library Journal*

"A juicy mystery—chick lit never had it so good!"
—*Complete Woman*

"Willig's imaginative debut . . . is a decidedly delightful romp."
—*Booklist*

"Relentlessly effervescent prose . . . a sexy, smirking, determined-to-charm historical romance debut." —*Kirkus Reviews*

"An adventurous, witty blend of historical romance and chick lit . . . will delight readers who like their love stories with a bit of a twist." —*The Jamestown News* (NC)

"A delightful debut." —Roundtable Reviews

THE DECEPTION OF THE
Emerald Ring

Lauren Willig

NEW AMERICAN LIBRARY

New American Library
Published by New American Library, a division of
Penguin Group (USA) Inc., 375 Hudson Street, New York, New York 10014, USA • Penguin Group
(Canada), 90 Eglinton Avenue East, Suite 700, Toronto, Ontario M4P 2Y3, Canada (a division of Pear-
son Penguin Canada Inc.) • Penguin Books Ltd., 80 Strand, London WC2R 0RL, England • Penguin
Ireland, 25 St. Stephen's Green, Dublin 2, Ireland (a division of Penguin Books Ltd.) • Penguin Group
(Australia), 250 Camberwell Road, Camberwell, Victoria 3124, Australia (a division of Pearson Aus-
tralia Group Pty. Ltd.) • Penguin Books India Pvt. Ltd., 11 Community Centre, Panchsheel Park, New
Delhi - 110 017, India • Penguin Group (NZ), 67 Apollo Drive, Rosedale, North Shore 0745, Auck-
land, New Zealand (a division of Pearson New Zealand Ltd.) • Penguin Books (South Africa) (Pty.)
Ltd., 24 Sturdee Avenue, Rosebank, Johannesburg 2196, South Africa

Penguin Books Ltd., Registered Offices:
80 Strand, London WC2R 0RL, England

Published by New American Library, a division of Penguin Group (USA) Inc.
Previously published in a Dutton edition.

First New American Library Printing, September 2007
10 9 8 7 6 5 4 3 2 1

Copyright © Lauren Willig, 2006
All rights reserved

Cover painting: Detail of *The Marquise of Montebello* (1855) by Franz Xavier Winterhalter. Château de
Compiegne, Oise, France/Bridgeman Art Library.

 REGISTERED TRADEMARK — MARCA REGISTRADA

New American Library Trade Paperback ISBN: 978-0-451-22221-3

The Library of Congress has cataloged the hardcover edition of this title as follows:

Willig, Lauren.
The deception of the emerald ring/Lauren Willig.
p. cm.
ISBN 0-525-94977-1
1. Napoleonic Wars, 1800–1815—Fiction. 2. Ireland—Fiction. 3. Women spies—Fiction. I. Title.
PS3623.I575D43 2006
813'.6—dc22   2006025304

Set in Granjon
Designed by Leonard Telesca

Printed in the United States of America

Without limiting the rights under copyright reserved above, no part of this publication may be reproduced, stored in or introduced into a retrieval system, or transmitted, in any form, or by any means
(electronic, mechanical, photocopying, recording, or otherwise), without the prior written permission
of both the copyright owner and the above publisher of this book.

PUBLISHER'S NOTE

This is a work of fiction. Names, characters, places, and incidents either are the product of the author's
imagination or are used fictitiously, and any resemblance to actual persons, living or dead, business es-
tablishments, events, or locales is entirely coincidental.

The publisher does not have any control over and does not assume any responsibility for author or
third-party Web sites or their content.

The scanning, uploading, and distribution of this book via the Internet or via any other means without
the permission of the publisher is illegal and punishable by law. Please purchase only authorized electronic editions, and do not participate in or encourage electronic piracy of copyrighted materials. Your
support of the author's rights is appreciated.

To all my grandparents, with love.

Acknowledgments

Some books are a joy to write. Fluid lines of perfect prose unroll across the computer screen, the plot unfolds without holes or wrinkles, and all the characters go exactly where they're told.

This was not one of those books.

I would like to extend my heartfelt gratitude to all those people who patiently repeated, "Yes, the book will get done. No, your career isn't over," and didn't push me into the Charles River, no matter how much they might have wanted to. Sincere thanks go to both my editors, Laurie and Kara, who were angels of forbearance over missed deadlines and an outline that changed about once a week; to my family, who didn't disown me; to Nancy, Claudia, Liz, Jenny, and Kimberly, who undertook the monumental task of keeping me sane through the long, dark months of struggling with simultaneous law school and book deadlines; to Weatherly, who made sure I got my monthly recommended allowance of alcohol; and to Emily, who went to Globalization so I didn't have to. An extra special thank-you goes to those readers who generously took the time to e-mail with words of praise and encouragement. Those e-mails kept me writing when even caffeine failed. Thank you all, so much.

As for everyone else, I haven't been deliberately avoiding you, honestly. I really have been meaning to return that phone call/e-mail/singing telegram. And I will. I promise. Just as soon as I get started on Pink IV....

THE DECEPTION OF THE

Emerald Ring

Prologue

A watched phone never rings.

At least, my phone wasn't ringing. The same, unfortunately, could not be said of the man sitting in front of me, whose mobile kept shrieking with all the abandon of an inebriated teenager on a roller coaster. Each time his phone shrilled out "Danger Zone" from *Top Gun*, I lunged for my bag. After a mere ten minutes on the bus, my abs had gotten more of a workout than they had in months.

I hauled my computer bag up onto my lap for easier access and slid my hand into the front pocket, just to make sure that the phone was still there. It was. Further inspection revealed that the ringer was on, the volume turned up, and all the little bars indicating signal strength blinking merrily away. Damn.

Sticking the phone back in my bag, I listened to the man in front of me recite his weekend's activities for the fifth time. They seemed primarily to involve adventures in alcohol poisoning, and an encounter with a burly bouncer that grew more elaborate with each retelling. Craning my head toward the window, I checked the progress of the traffic ahead of us. It hadn't. Progressed, that was. The bus sat as steadily immovable as an island in a tropical sea, placidly parked behind a string of other, equally immobile buses. It didn't improve the situation that the light was green.

I knew I should have taken the tube.

There had been all sorts of good reasons to choose the bus that morning, as I set out from my Bayswater flat towards the British Library. After all, the tube always broke down, and it couldn't be healthy to spend that much time underground, and the fact that it was actually not raining in England in November needed to be celebrated. . . . And the bus had cell reception while the Underground didn't. I glowered in the direction of my phone.

Life would be far more pleasant if I were better at fooling myself.

One day. It had only been one day by the calendar, two years in terms of agonized phone staring, and about half an hour in boy time. It is a truth universally acknowledged that time moves differently for men. There was, I reminded myself, no reason why Englishmen should differ from their American counterparts in this regard.

There was also the fact that Colin didn't have my phone number. But why let reality interfere with a good daydream? And my daydreams . . . Well, they weren't really the sort of thing one could get into on a public bus, even if other people—I scowled at the man in front of me, who had progressed from barhopping to amorous adventures—had no such scruples. Besides, if Colin wanted my phone number, he knew how to find it.

After a sleepless night alternating between daydream and denial, I had finally admitted to myself just how much I really hoped he wanted it. Colin was, not to put too fine a point on it, the first man who had made my pulse speed up since a breakup of massive proportions the previous winter.

Admittedly, when we'd first met, the emotion quickening in my veins hadn't been attraction. Irritation was more like it, and that sentiment, at least, had been entirely mutual. What it all boiled down to was that I was going through his family's archives and he didn't want me to.

It wasn't prurient interest that drove me to Colin's family papers, but academic desperation, the sort that sets in at some point after the third year of grad school, as the bills begin to mount, teaching bored undergrads loses its luster, and the coveted letters "Ph.D." continue to dance a mocking jig just out of reach. No dissertation, no degree. I had nightmares of becoming one of those attenuated grad students who lurk in the basement of the Harvard history department, surrounded by books so overdue that the library has long ago given up toting up the fines. Every now and again, you'll encounter one of them making the long trudge up the stairs to the first floor, and wonder who on earth they are, and how long they've been down there.

I refused to become one of the forgotten basement dwellers of Robinson Hall. Among other things, the vending machine down there had a very limited selection.

Unfortunately, the dissertation topic that I had chosen with such naive optimism at the end of my second year proved to be just like its subject: elusive. I was after a trio of spies, the Scarlet Pimpernel, the Purple Gentian, and the Pink Carnation, those daring men in knee breeches and black cloaks who twirled their quizzing glasses in the face of danger and never failed to confound the agents of the French Republic.

Unfortunately, they also confounded me. There was, I discovered, a reason that no one had written a book on the topic. The material just wasn't there. True, we knew who the Scarlet Pimpernel and Purple Gentian were, and even much of what they had done, but the Pink Carnation's identity remained shrouded in mystery, the only evidence of his existence a series of contemporary accounts in newsletters and diaries, each recorded exploit more improbable than the last. Some scholars, sitting in the security of their twentieth-century studies, had decreed that the dearth of corroboratory evidence could mean only one thing.

The Pink Carnation was a creature of myth, a deliberate fabrication invented by the British government to buoy their beleaguered nation through a prolonged and desperate struggle.

They were wrong.

I enjoyed a good little gloat over that. There's nothing like a little "I told you so" to make one's day. On a rainy day the previous week, Mrs. Selwick-Alderly, an elderly descendant of the Purple Gentian, had admitted me to a virtual Ali Baba's cave of historical documents, the diaries and letters of the Purple Gentian and his half-French bride, Miss Amy Balcourt. Then there was Amy's clever cousin, Miss Jane Wooliston—better known as the Pink Carnation. As a dashing spy, she was an unlikely choice. Whoever heard of a spy named Jane? Or Wooliston, for that matter? The very name suggested fleecy sweaters and woolly hats, a frizzy-haired Miss Marple puttering about the village green. It was the sort of discovery that had "tenure" written all over it.

Unfortunately, like Ali Baba's cave, this one came with a catch. Instead of forty thieves, my treasure trove came complete with one very irate Englishman. Mr. Colin Selwick didn't much like the idea of strangers rooting about in the family archives, and he became positively apoplectic at the prospect of the publication of his family's papers. He was also definitely, undeniably possessed of more than the ordinary measure of good looks. After a couple of late-night encounters, the sparks he was emitting weren't all of the negative variety.

Two nights ago, there had been a little incident involving a dark room, an arm above my head, and a deliberate movement forward that might have been about to turn into a kiss, when . . .

Brrring!

Ringing! It was ringing! I lunged for the bag and snatched out the phone, hitting the green RECEIVE button before the caller could think better of the enterprise. "Hello?" I breathed.

"Eloise?" Instead of a masculine murmur, the voice had the crackly quality of old film.

Damn. I deflated against the nubby upholstery. Served me right for not checking the number before I hit RECEIVE.

I settled the phone more firmly against my ear. "Hello, Grandma."

Grandma wasted no time on trivialities. "I'm so glad I've caught you."

I stiffened. "Why? Is something wrong?"

"I've found you a man."

"I wasn't aware I had lost one," I muttered.

Of course, that wasn't entirely true. To say I'd lost him might be a bit extreme, though. In the first place, I wasn't sure that he was mine to lose. In the second place . . .

In the second place, Grandma was still talking. With an effort, I dragged my attention back to the phone, just as the bus started to crawl slowly ahead. "—in Birmingham," she was saying.

"What about Birmingham?" I asked belatedly.

Over the headrest, the man in front of me gave me a dirty look. "Would you mind?" he said, gesturing to his phone.

On the other end, Grandma was clamoring for attention. "Darling, have you been listening to a word I've said?"

"Sorry," I muttered, slinking down in my seat. "I'm on the bus. It's a bit noisy." As if in retaliation, the man in front of me upped the volume.

With a hint of a huff, Grandma started over. "As I was telling you, I was at the beauty parlor yesterday, and who should I see but Muffin Watkins."

"Really! Muffin!" I exclaimed with false enthusiasm, as though I had any idea who she was.

"And she was telling me all about her son—"

"Dumpling?" I suggested. "Crumpet? Scone?"

"Andy," Grandma said pointedly. "He's a lovely boy."

"Have you met him?"

Grandma ignored that. "He just bought the loveliest new apartment. His mother was telling me all about it."

"I'm sure she was."

"Andy," declared Grandma, in the ringing tones of a CNN correspondent delivering election results, "works at Lehman Brothers."

"And Bingley has five thousand pounds a year," I murmured.

"Eloise?"

"Nothing."

"Hmph." Grandma let it go. "He's very successful, you know; only thirty-five, and he already has his own boat."

"He sounds like a regular paragon."

"So I've given your number to his mother to give to his younger brother, Jay," Grandma concluded triumphantly.

I took the phone away from my ear and stared at it for a moment. It didn't help. I put the phone back to my ear. "I don't get it. You're setting me up with the inferior brother?"

"Well, Andy's mother tells me he's just started seeing someone," Grandma said, as though that explained everything. "And since Jay is in England, I don't see why you can't just meet for a nice little dinner."

"Jay is in Birmingham," I protested. "You did say Birmingham, right? I'm in London. Not exactly the same place."

"They're both in England," countered Grandma placidly. "How far away can it be?"

"I'm not going to Birmingham," I said flatly.

"Eloise," Grandma said reprovingly. "You have to learn how to be flexible in a relationship."

"And we're not having a relationship! I haven't even *met* him."

"That's because you won't go to Birmingham."

"Grandma, people don't go to Birmingham; they go away from Birmingham. It's like New Jersey."

The man in front of me let out an indignant "Oi!" but whether it was addressed to my rising volume level or the slur to the northern metropolis was unclear.

"I just want to see you married before I die."

"We'll just have to keep you around for a good long while then, won't we?" I said brightly.

Grandma changed tactics. "I met your grandfather when I was sixteen, you know."

I knew. Oh, how I knew.

"Not everyone is as special as you, Grandma," I said politely. "Oh, look, it's my stop. I have to go."

"Jay will call you!" trilled Grandma.

"I've heard that one before," I muttered, but Grandma had already rung off. Undoubtedly to phone Mitten, or Muffin, or whatever her name was, and break out the celebratory champagne.

Grandma had been trying to marry me off, by one means or another, since I'd hit puberty. I kept hoping that, eventually, she would give up on me and switch her attention to my little sister, who, at the age of nineteen, was dangerously close to spinsterhood by Grandma's standards. So far, though, Grandma stubbornly refused to be rerouted, much to Jillian's relief. I would have admired her tenacity if it hadn't been directed at me.

I hadn't been entirely lying about it being my stop; the bus, imitating the tortoise in the old fable, was slowly inching its way past Euston station, which meant that I would be the next stop up, across the street from one of the plethora of Pizza Expresses that dotted the London landscape like glass-fronted mushrooms.

I stuffed my phone back in my bag and began the torturous process of navigating the narrow stairs down from the upper level of the bus, consoling myself with the thought that with any luck, this Jay-from-Birmingham would be as reluctant as I was to go on a family-assisted setup. I could think of few things more ghastly than sitting across the table from someone with whom the only thing I had in common was that my grandmother shared a beauty parlor with his mother. Anyone who had seen Grandma's hair would agree.

Swinging myself off the bus, I scurried through the massive

iron gates that front the courtyard of the British Library. The pigeons, bloated with the lunchtime leavings of scholars and tourists, cast me baleful glances from their beady black eyes as I wove around them, making for the automatic doors at the entrance. It was early enough that there was a mere straggle of tourists lined up in front of the coat check in the basement.

Feeling superior, I made straight for the table on the other side of the room, transferring the day's essentials from my computer bag into one of the sturdy bags of clear plastic provided for researchers: laptop for transcribing documents; notebook in case the laptop broke down; pencils, ditto; mobile, for compulsive checking during lunch and bathroom breaks; wallet, for the buying of lunch; and a novel, carefully hidden between laptop and notebook, for propping up at the edge of my tray during lunchtime. The bag began to sag ominously.

I could see the point of the plastic bags as a means of preventing hardened document thieves from slipping out with a scrap of Dickens's correspondence, but it had a decidedly dampening effect on my choice of lunchtime reading material. And it was sheer hell smuggling in tampons.

Toting my bulging load, I made my way up in the elevator, past the brightly colored chairs in the mezzanine café, past the dispirited beige of the lunchroom, up to the third floor, where the ceilings were lower and tourists feared to tread. Perhaps "fear" was the wrong word; I couldn't imagine that they would want to.

Flashing my ID at the guard on duty at the desk in the manuscripts room, I dumped my loot on my favorite desk, earning a glare from a person studying an illuminated medieval manuscript three desks down. I smiled apologetically and insincerely, and began systematically unpacking my computer, computer cord, adapter, notebook, arraying them around the raised foam manuscript stand in the center of the desk with the ease of long practice. I'd done this so many times that I had the routine down.

Computer to the right, angled in so the person next to me couldn't peek; notebook to the left, pencil neatly resting on top; bag with phone, wallet, and incriminating leisure fiction shoved as far beneath the desk as it could go, but not so far that I couldn't occasionally make the plastic crinkle with my foot to make sure it was still there and some intrepid purse snatcher disguised as a researcher hadn't crawled underneath and made off with my lunch money.

Having staked out my desk, I made for the computer station at the front of the room. I might know who the Pink Carnation was, but I stood a better chance of making my case to a skeptical academic audience if I could definitively link many, if not all, of the Pink Carnation's recorded exploits to Miss Jane Wooliston. After all, just because Jane had started out as the Pink Carnation didn't mean she had remained in possession of the title. What if, like the Dread Pirate Roberts, she had handed the name off to someone else? I didn't think so—having worked with several of Jane's letters, I couldn't imagine anyone else being able to muster quite the same combination of rigorous logic and reckless daring—but it was the sort of objection someone was sure to propound. At great length. With lots of footnotes.

I needed footnotes of my own to counteract that. It was the usual sort of academic battle: footnotes at ten paces, bolstered by snide articles in academic journals and lots of sniping about methodology, a thrust and parry of source and countersource. My sources had to be better.

From my little dip into Colin's library that past weekend, I had learned that Jane had been sent to Ireland to deal with the threat of an uprising against British rule egged on by France in the hopes that, with Ireland in disarray, England would prove an easy target. Ten points to me, since one of the daring exploits with which the Pink Carnation was credited was quelling the Irish rebellion of 1803. But I didn't know anything beyond that. I didn't have any proof that Jane was actually there. In the official histories, the failure of the rebellion tended to be attributed to a more mundane series of mistakes and misfortunes, rather than the agency of any one person.

According to the Selwick documents, Jane wasn't the only one to be dispatched to Ireland. Geoffrey Pinchingdale-Snipe, who had served as second in command of the League of the Purple Gentian, had also received his marching orders from the War Office. A search for Jane's name in the records of the British Library was sure to yield nothing, but what if I looked for Lord Pinchingdale? Ever since reading the papers at Mrs. Selwick-Alderly's flat, I'd been meaning to look into Geoffrey Pinchingdale-Snipe, anyway, if only to add more footnotes to my dissertation chapter on the internal workings of the League of the Purple Gentian.

I hadn't had a chance to pursue that angle because I had gone straight off to Sussex.

With Colin.

The agitated *bleep* of the computer as I accidentally leaned on one of the keys didn't do anything to make me popular with the other researchers, but it did bring me back from the remoter realms of daydream.

Right. I straightened up and purposefully punched in "Pinchingdale-Snipe." Nothing. Ah, déjà vu. Futile archive searches had been my way of life for a very long time before I had the good fortune to stumble across the Selwicks. Clearly, I hadn't lost the knack of it. Getting back into gear, I tried just plain "Pinchingdale." Four hits! Unfortunately, three of them were treatises on botany by an eighteenth-century Pinchingdale with a horticultural bent, and one the correspondence of a Sir Marmaduke Pinchingdale, who was two hundred years too early for me, in addition to being decidedly not a Geoffrey. There was no way anyone could confuse those two names, not even with very bad spelling and even worse handwriting.

The logical thing to do would have been to call Mrs. Selwick-

Alderly, Colin's aunt. Even if the materials I was looking for weren't in her private collection, she would likely have a good notion of where I should start. But to call Mrs. Selwick-Alderly veered dangerously close to calling Colin. Really, could there be anything more pathetic than looking for excuses to call his relations and fish for information about his whereabouts? I refused to be That Girl.

Of course, that begged the question of whether it was any less pathetic to check my phone for messages every five minutes.

Preferring not to pursue that line of thought, I stared blankly at the computer screen. It stared equally blankly back at me. Behind me, I could hear the subtle brush of fabric that meant someone was shuffling his feet against the carpet in a passive-aggressive attempt to communicate that he was waiting to use the terminal. Damn.

On a whim, I tapped out the name "Alsworthy," just to show that I was still doing something and not uselessly frittering away valuable computer time. From what I had read in the Selwick collection, Geoffrey Pinchingdale-Snipe had been ridiculously besotted with a woman named Mary Alsworthy—although none of his friends seemed to think terribly much of her. The words "shallow flirt" had come up more than once. Geoffrey Pinchingdale-Snipe's indiscretion might be my good fortune. In the throes of infatuation, wasn't it only logical that a man might reveal a little more than he ought? Especially over the course of a separation? If the War Office was sending Lord Pinchingdale off to Ireland, it made sense that he would continue to correspond with his beloved. And in the course of that correspondence . . .

Buoyed by my own theory, I scrolled down through a long list of Victorian Alsworthys, World War I Alsworthys, Alsworthys from every conceivable time period. For crying out loud, you'd think their name was Smith. The foot-shuffling man behind me gave up on shuffling and upped the level of unspoken aggression by conspicuously flipping through the ancient volumes of paper catalogs next to me. I was too busy scanning dates to feel guilty. Alsworthys, Alsworthys everywhere, and not a one of any use to me.

Or maybe not. My hand stilled on the scroll button as the dates 1784–1863 flashed by. I quickly scrolled back up, clumsily engaging in mental math. Take 1784 away from 1803 . . . and you got eighteen. Um, I meant nineteen. This is why my checkbook never balances. Either way, it was an eminently appropriate age for an English debutante in London for the Season.

There was only one slight hitch. The name beside the dates wasn't Mary. It was Laetitia.

That, I assured myself rapidly, scribbling down the call number, didn't necessarily mean anything. After all, my friend Pammy's real first name was Alexandra, but she had gone by her middle name, Pamela, ever since we were in kindergarten, largely because her mother was an Alexandra, too, and it created all sorts of confusion. Forget all that rose-by-another-name rubbish. Pammy had been Pammy for so long that it was impossible to imagine her as anything else.

Behind me, the foot-shuffling man claimed my vacant seat with an air of barely restrained triumph. Prolonged exposure to the Manuscript Room does sad, sad things to some people.

I handed in my call slip to the man behind the desk and retreated to my own square of territory, nudging my plastic bag with my foot to make sure everything was still there. Between Mary and Laetitia . . . well, I would have chosen to be called Laetitia, but there was no accounting for taste. Maybe she got sick of dealing with variant spellings.

Except . . . I scowled at my empty manuscript stand. There *was* a Laetitia Alsworthy. Just to make sure, I scooted my computer to a more comfortable angle, and opened up the file into which I had transcribed my notes from Sussex. Sure enough, there it was. One Letty Alsworthy, who appeared to be friends with Lady Henrietta Selwick. Not close friends, I clarified for myself, squinting at my transcription of Lady Henrietta's account of her ballroom activities in the summer of 1803, but the sort of second- or third-tier friend you're always pleased to run into, have good chats with, and keep meaning to get to know better if only you had the time. I had a bunch of those in college. And, in its own way, the London Season wasn't all that different from college, minus the classes. You had a set group of people, all revolving among the same events, with a smattering of culture masking more primal purposes, i.e., men trying to get women into bed, and women trying to get men to commit. Yep, I decided, just like college.

Pleased as I was with my little insight, that didn't solve the problem that Letty was a real, live human being with an independent existence from her sister Mary. Her sister Mary who might have corresponded with Geoffrey Pinchingdale-Snipe.

I should have known that Mary wouldn't be the writing type.

Behind me, the little trolley used to transport books from the bowels of the British Library to the wraiths who haunted the reading room rolled to a stop. Checking the number on the slip against the number on my desk, the library attendant handed me a thick folio volume, bound in fading cardboard, that had seen its heyday sometime before Edward VIII ran off with Mrs. Simpson.

Propping the heavy volume on the foam stand, I listlessly flipped open the cover. I had ordered it, so I might as well look at it. Besides, the computer in the back was now occupied, and I doubted its present occupant would show me any more mercy than I had shown him. A salutary lesson on "do unto others," and one that I was sure I would forget by lunchtime.

The documents at the front of the volume were far too late, Mitfordesque accounts of nightclub peccadilloes during the Roaring Twenties. I'd come across this kind of volume before, letters pasted onto the leaves of the folio with glorious unconcern for chronology, medieval manuscript pages sandwiched between

Edwardian recipes and Stuart sermon literature. Otherwise known as someone cleaning out the family attic and shipping the lot off to the British Library. Checking the number I had scribbled down from the computer, I saw that it had marked the Laetitia Alsworthy material as running from f. 48 to f. 63, and then again from f. 152 on.

After lunch, I was really going to have to give in and call Mrs. Selwick-Alderly.

Turning by rote to page forty-eight, my hand stilled on the crackly paper. The letter pressed into the center of the page was short, only three lines. Despite its having been pasted into the folio quite some time ago, I could still make out the phantom impressions of two deep lines incised into the paper, one vertically, one horizontally, as though it had been folded into a very small square, the better for passing unseen from hand to hand. There was also a series of crinkles that prevented the paper from lying completely flat against the page, as though someone had crumpled it up with great force and then smoothed it out again.

But it was the signature that caught my attention. One word. One name.

Pinchingdale.

As in Geoffrey, Lord Pinchingdale. The signature was unmistakable. It most certainly wasn't Marmaduke. What on earth was he doing writing to Mary's sister? Forgetting about computer hogs and lunch plans and the way the wool of my pants rasped against my waist, I settled the folio more firmly on its stand and hunched over to read Lord Pinchingdale's short and peculiar note.

"All is in readiness. An unmarked carriage will be waiting for you behind the house at midnight. . . ."

Chapter One

L etty Alsworthy awoke to darkness.
Midnight coated the room, blurring the edges of the furniture and thickening the air. Letty's tired eyes attempted to focus, and failed. The armoire in the corner was top-heavy with shadow, like a lopsided muffin spilling out of its pan. On the other wall, the drapes fell flat and opaque against the one window, no grains of light filtering through the cheap material. The fireplace across from the bed was a hollow cavern, bare even of ashes, nothing more than a darker patch in a landscape of shadow. A fire in June would be an extravagance, the sort of extravagance the Alsworthys could ill afford.

All was dark and still.

Rolling her face into her pillow, Letty came to an irrefutable conclusion. It wasn't morning yet.

She let her head slump back into the pillow, accompanied by a satisfying crackle of feathers. If it wasn't morning, there was no reason for her to be awake. She could just snuggle back down into the sagging mattress, pull the sheet back over her shoulders, plump her pillow, and go back to sleep. Her eyelids approved of that assessment. They were already dragging steadily shut.

But something had woken her.

Letty struggled reluctantly up on her elbows; the movement unleashed a nagging ache behind her temples, which agreed with her eyelids that she really was not supposed to be awake yet. Yanking her unraveling braid out from under her left shoulder, she peered blearily around the room. There was little to peer at. The narrow room contained nothing but the armoire, a wobbly night table, and one chair that had previously belonged to the drawing room, but had been banished due to a poorly repaired crack in the frame. When the owner advertised the house as "furnished," he intended the word in its most minimal sense. Between her mother's and sister's excesses among the bonnets and ribbons of Bond Street, and her father's inability to pass a book without buying it, Letty had been in no position to argue. As it was, they were fortunate to be able to eke out another Season in London. Letty had learned to pinch a penny until it screamed for mercy, but there wasn't much more left to pinch.

In the hall, the crooked grandfather clock emitted the high-pitched whine that passed for a ping. Beneath its nasal wheezings, Letty heard a strange rustle and rattle, followed by a click.

Letty froze, suspended awkwardly on her elbows.

That click had not come from the clock. In the stillness that followed the twelfth chime, Letty heard it again, this time accompanied by a scramble and a shuffle, like movement hastily muffled. Someone was scurrying about in the room next door.

Burglars? If they were, they were going to be very disappointed burglars. Her mother's jewels sparkled nicely by candlelight, but they were nothing more than paste. Anything real had long since disappeared into the gaping maw of household expenses. Her sister Mary had one pair of genuine pearl earbobs left, and Letty had a rather pretty pair of enamel bracelets—at least, until the next butcher's bill came due.

On the other hand, burglars might turn vicious if they didn't find what they were looking for. And that was Mary's room they were in. Mary was not likely to submit docilely to the extraction of her last pair of genuine pearls.

Folding the sheet carefully back, Letty lowered herself to the ground. Her toes curled as they touched the cold boards, but luck was with her. There was no telltale squeak.

Letty groped for her candle, and then thought better of it. There was no need to advertise her presence. As a weapon, the candleholder was too short and stubby to be of any use. It was more likely to irritate than stun. Instead, Letty gently eased a poker from the iron stand beside the fireplace. The slight clink as the tip caught on the edge of the stand reverberated like a dozen crypt doors clanging. She froze, both hands on the shaft of the poker. Deadly silence assaulted her ears, a listening sort of silence. And then the scrambling started again. Letty's breath released in a low sigh of relief. Thank goodness.

With her weapon clenched close to her side, Letty crept out into the corridor. Like everything else in the house, the hallway was small and narrow, papered a serviceable brown that trapped the shadows and turned them to mud. A triangle of light, like a large wedge of cheese, extended into the hallway from Mary's half-open door.

"Put that there." A woman crossed the room in a swish of blue skirt. From somewhere behind the door, a rustle of fabric followed, and the chink of the wardrobe door being shut. "No, not that green. The other green."

Letty's grip on the poker relaxed. That wasn't a burglar; that was Mary.

What Mary was doing wearing her best driving dress at midnight was another matter entirely. As Letty watched, Mary turned and deposited a pile of scarves in the arms of her maid, filmy creations of gauze designed more to entice than warm. Their purchase had set Letty's housekeeping accounts back at least two months.

"Pack these," Mary directed. "Leave the wool."

Clutching the pile of scarves, Mary's maid looked anxiously at her mistress. "It's past midnight, miss. His lordship—"

"Will wait. He does it so well." Bending over her dressing table, Mary opened the lid of her jewel box and contemplated the contents. Closing it with a decisive click, she thrust the box out to the maid. "I won't be needing these anymore. See that Miss Letty gets this. With my love, of course."

There was only one possible reason for Mary to bequeath her bagatelles. And it wasn't love.

Taking care not to let the poker scrape against the floor, Letty tiptoed back into her own room, leaning the unwanted weapon carefully against the wall. She wouldn't be needing it. At least, she didn't think she would. In the course of her long career as de facto keeper of the Alsworthy ménage, Letty had confronted all manner of domestic disruption, from exploding Christmas puddings to indignant tradesmen, and even, on one memorable occasion, escaped livestock. Letty had bandaged burns, coaxed her little brother's budgie out of a tree, and stage-managed her family's yearly remove to a rented town house in London.

An attempted elopement was something new.

The whole situation was straight out of the comic stage: the daughter of the house hastily packing in the middle of the night with the help of her trusty (and soon to be unemployed) maid, the faithful lover waiting downstairs with a speedy carriage, ready to whisk them away to Gretna Green. All that was needed was a rope ladder and an irate guardian in hot pursuit.

That role, Letty realized, fell to her. It didn't seem quite fair, but there it was. She had to stop Mary.

But how? Remonstrating with Mary wouldn't be any use. Over the past few years, Mary had made it quite clear that she didn't care to take advice from a sister, and a younger sister, at that. She responded to Letty's well-meaning suggestions with the unblinking disdain perfected by cats in their dealings with their humans. Letty knew just how Mary would react. She would hear

Letty out without saying a word, and then calmly go on to do whatever it was she had intended to do in the first place.

Rousing her parents would be worse than useless. Her father would simply blink at her over his spectacles and comment mildly that if Mary wished to make a spectacle of herself, it would be best to let her get on with it as quickly as possible and with as little trouble to themselves as could be had. As for her mother . . . Letty's face twisted in a terrible grimace that would undoubtedly lead to all sorts of unattractive wrinkles later in life. There was certainly no help to be found from that quarter. Her mother would probably help Mary into his lordship's carriage.

Letty looked longingly at the poker. She couldn't, though. She really couldn't.

That left his lordship. London was crammed with men answering to that title at this time of year, but Letty had no doubt which lordship it was. Mary had never lacked for admirers, but only one man was besotted enough to agree to an elopement.

Letty conjured Lord Pinchingdale in her mind as she had seen him last week, dancing attendance on Mary at the Middlethorpes' ball. Discounting the doting expression that appeared whenever he encountered Mary, Lord Pinchingdale's had always struck her as an uncommonly intelligent face, the sort of face that wouldn't have looked amiss on a Renaissance cardinal or a seventeenth-century academician, quiet and thoughtful with just a hint of something cynical about the mouth. A long, thin nose; a lean, flexible mouth that was quick to quirk with amusement; and a pair of keen gray eyes that seemed to regard the world's foibles for what they were.

Which just went to show that physiognomy was never an exact science.

Take Mary, for example. She had the sort of serene expression generally associated with halos and chubby infants in mangers, but her porcelain calm hid a calculating mind and an indomitable will to make Machiavelli blush.

I should have seen it coming, Letty scolded herself, as she jammed her feet into a pair of inappropriate dancing slippers. The signs had all been there, if only she had been looking for them. They had been there in the reckless glitter in Mary's dark blue eyes, in the increasingly brittle quality of her laugh—and in the way she had pleaded a headache after dinner that night, as an excuse to slip away to her room.

Letty had a fair inkling of what Mary had been thinking. Letty's older sister had passed three Seasons as society's reigning incomparable. Three Seasons of amassing accolades, bouquets, even the odd sonnet, but shockingly few marriage proposals. Of the offers that had come in, three had been from younger sons, four from titles without wealth, and an even larger number from wealth without title. One by one, she had watched her more eligible suitors, the first sons, with coronets on their coaches and country estates to spare, contract matches with the chinless daughters of dukes, or bustling city heiresses. The Alsworthys were an old family—there had been Alsworthys in Hertfordshire when the first bemused Norman had galloped through, demanding to know the way to the nearest vineyard—but by no means a great one. They had never distinguished themselves in battle or ingratiated themselves into a monarch's favor. Instead, they had sat placidly on their estate, overseeing their land and adding extra wings onto the house as fancy and fashion demanded. They were comfortable enough in their own way, but there was no fortune or title to sweeten the marriage settlements or to shield them from the mocking murmurs of the *ton*.

Surely even Mary must realize the disgrace that a runaway marriage would bring, not only on her, but on the entire family. Heaven only knew, thought Letty grimly, their family didn't need any extra help when it came to making themselves ridiculous.

She would have to prevail upon Lord Pinchingdale's better judgment—assuming he had any. Up until tonight, Letty had always thought he had.

Snagging her cloak from the wardrobe, Letty settled it firmly around her shoulders, yanking the hood down over her flushed face and frazzled braid. There was no time to twist her gingery hair up. Instead, she shoved everything back behind her ears and hoped it would stay there. Although she had no personal experience in the matter, from what Letty had heard of eloping lovers, they were a fairly impatient breed, and she had no confidence that Lord Pinchingdale would wait patiently by his carriage until Mary deigned to come traipsing down. Letty grimaced at the image of Lord Pinchingdale attempting to scale the skinny branches of the tree outside Mary's window in time-honored heroic fashion. That was all they needed, a peer with two broken knees sprawled on the pavement outside their house. Letty couldn't even begin to imagine the captions in the scandal sheets. "Viscount Laid Low by Love" would be the least of it.

Would it be too much to hope that the French would do something truly, truly awful in the next few hours so that there would be no room left in the papers for frivolities?

Dealing with a thwarted lover in a dark alleyway wasn't the sort of escapade that lent luster to a debutante's reputation. But, Letty reasoned, as she picked her way carefully down the back stairs, she didn't see what else she was to do. She couldn't let Mary elope with Lord Pinchingdale and bring down scandal and ruin on all of their heads. Once she had sent Lord Pinchingdale packing, Letty promised herself, she was going straight back to bed. She was going to climb beneath the covers and pull the eiderdown up to her neck, and let her head sink into the pillow. . . .

Letty hastily clamped her hand over a mammoth yawn.

Emerging from the service entrance into the dark little area at the back of the house that substituted for a garden, Letty took stock of the situation. If she squinted, she could make out the dark form of a carriage hulking among the shadows at the end of the narrow alley behind the house, black against black. Drat. She had so hoped that it would all turn out to be a false alarm, a moment of midnight misapprehension. But that carriage was far too large and solid to be a figment of anyone's imagination. Letty cast a quick look up at the neighbors' windows. All were dark, swathed in Sunday calm.

Holding her breath against the stench of a recently emptied chamber pot, Letty ventured tentatively down the alley, following the soft snuffle of equine breath in what she hoped must be the direction of the carriage. Whoever thought a midnight elopement was a glamorous thing? wondered Letty sourly. Perhaps she would feel differently if it were her own elopement, but Letty rather doubted it. Love went only so far. Some smells were too strong to be ignored, even by the most ardent of Juliets.

"Lord Pinchingdale?" Letty stumbled her way to the coach. Bumping up against one of the rear wheels, she felt her way forward. "Lord Pinchingdale?"

There was no response from the shadowy interior.

Which meant, Letty admitted, that he probably wasn't there.

She didn't much like the alternatives. Lord Pinchingdale might have gotten bored and decided to scale the ivy—but wouldn't she have heard the thud? A new and terrifying possibility struck Letty. What if he and Mary had already fled, leaving the carriage standing outside as a decoy? They would lose precious time searching while the lovers were already tearing up the miles to Gretna Green in a well-sprung traveling chaise, smaller and lighter than the cumbersome coach.

Letty groped along the door, looking for the latch. "Lord Pinchingdale?" she whispered sharply. The restless scrape of the horses' hooves on the cobbles and the sound of the coachman shifting on the box above blotted out her words. Letty twisted the latch sharply, stumbling backwards as the stiff door unexpectedly gave. Catching her balance by dint of grabbing on to the door frame, she leaned head and shoulders inside the cavernous interior, which stretched before her like one of the bottomless caves of fairy tale, so dark she couldn't make out the difference between seats and floor, window or wall.

"You aren't here, are you?"

She realized it wasn't quite the done thing to talk to inanimate objects—or to people who weren't there—but if she didn't say something, she was quite likely to kick something instead.

If they were already gone, there was nothing she could do. She could send a groom after them, in the hopes of arresting their flight and hauling Mary back—but she couldn't see much point to it. The odds of not being seen, or of the groom not telling a friend who would tell a friend, were so slim as to pose no temptation to even the most hardened and reckless of gamblers. The story would be all over London by the time the maids opened the curtains and brought in the morning chocolate.

Behind her, a new sound interrupted the rustle of leaves and the snuffle of snores from someone's open window. At the crunch of booted feet on gravel, relief coursed through Letty, heady as strong tea. They hadn't left, then! Who else would be tromping about in their backyard? The servants were all asleep, worn out with a day that began before dawn. It had to be Lord Pinchingdale.

Extricating herself from the maw of the carriage, Letty swiveled to face the newcomer, prepared to tell him exactly what she thought of midnight elopements and those idiotic enough to engage in them. The words stilled in her throat as her gloom-adjusted eyes took in the apparition before her. Instead of a gentleman garbed for travel, a hunched, hulking thing shambled toward her. As Letty instinctively shrank back against the carriage, feeling around behind her for a weapon, her panicked eyes sought the creature's face. He didn't have one. Letty's eyes scanned for the usual appendages—mouth, ears, nose. Nothing. There was only darkness where his face should have been. Darkness and a pair of eerily light eyes that glittered disquietingly out of the surrounding emptiness.

The edge of the carriage floor bit into Letty's back.

Letty clutched tight to the sides, preparing to hitch herself up and flee out the opposite side. Not being prone to flights of fancy, Letty didn't think of faceless specters and the other stock characters of popular novels. They weren't out on the moors or on the grounds of a ruined abbey, but in the heart of London. Letty defied any specter, with the possible exception of those in the Tower, to make a go of haunting amid the grimy bustle of the metropolis. It just couldn't be done.

No, it was clearly a man, a rather large man with appalling posture, wearing something wrapped around his face and a hat pulled low over his ears. Letty's pulse thrummed with more mundane terrors—robbers, bandits, highwaymen.

"What do you want?" she asked sharply, readying herself to bolt.

The muffled man threw his arms into the air in a gesture of disgust. "What do I want?" he demanded, in a voice that even through the folds of cloth savored of John Knox and Robert Burns. "What do I want, she asks me?"

Letty hadn't thought it that unreasonable a question.

"Get along inside. Orders are I'm to take ye to the inn."

"Orders from whom?" asked Letty suspiciously, even though she had a fairly good idea.

The coachman muttered something generally uncomplimentary about the mental capacities of the other half of the species. "Who d'ye think? Lord Pinchingdale, that's who. Come along now. Himself'll be waiting for ye, and we dinna have all night."

And before Letty had the chance to explain that she wasn't at all the "ye" in question, a pair of large hands closed around her waist and boosted her high into the air.

"Up ye get."

"Put me down!" she hissed, wriggling in his grasp. "You've made a mistake!"

"No mistake," rasped her captor, grappling with her as

though she were a particularly slippery fish just off the hook. Sounding aggrieved, he demanded, "Would ye hold still? I'm just tryin' to help ye into the carriage."

Since her arms were pinned uncomfortably to her sides, Letty did the only thing she could. She lashed out with one small, slippered foot, catching her captor squarely in the shin. Unfortunately, it was the same foot she had stubbed earlier. Pain shot up her leg, but it was almost worth it for the resulting grunt of pain from the coachman. But he didn't let go.

"What part of 'put me down' don't you understand?" Letty whispered fiercely, dealing him an elbow to the ribs.

"Women!" grunted the coachman in tones of intense disgust.

With no further ado, he tossed her unceremoniously into the carriage. Letty landed on her backside. Hard. Above the sound of the door slamming shut, she heard the coachman declare, in a voice that packed as much "I told you so" as one could muster through a scarf, "Orders are ye're to go to the inn, and it's to the inn you'll go." He didn't say, "So there," but the words were firmly implied.

Scrambling to her knees, Letty crawled toward the door, hindered by her cloak, which twisted around her legs as she went, pulling her back. "For heaven's sake!" she breathed, yanking her cloak out of the way. Something ripped. Letty didn't care. If she could just get out before the coach began moving . . . there were so many things she wanted to do that she didn't know where to begin. Lock Mary in an armoire. Give Lord Pinchingdale a piece of her mind about his staff and his morals.

Propping an elbow up on one of the seats, Letty made a grab for the door handle. With a crack like a gunshot, the coachman snapped his whip. Four horses burst into concerted motion, propelling the coach forward. Letty's hand swiped uselessly through empty air as she lurched sideways, banging into the bench. She couldn't scream. Any loud noise would alert the neighbors, bringing down on her head exactly the sort of attention she hadn't wanted. The coach swerved again, sending Letty jolting sideways—right into the other shoulder.

Clutching her wounded arm, Letty glowered helplessly in the direction of the box as the carriage carried her inexorably away toward her sister's assignation.

She knew she should have stayed in bed.

Chapter Two

G eoffrey, Second Viscount Pinchingdale, Eighth Baron Snipe, and impatient bridegroom-to-be stood in the foyer of his family's London mansion and slapped his gloves against his knee in an uncharacteristic gesture of impatience.

"Is there any reason," he asked, deliberately using short and simple words, "that this cannot wait until tomorrow morning?"

The courier from the War Office looked at him, then at the folded piece of paper he held in his hand, and shrugged. "I don't know. I haven't opened it, have I?"

"Let's try this again, shall we?" suggested Geoff, with a quick sideways glance at the clock that hung between two red-veined marble pillars.

Ten minutes till midnight. If he left immediately, he might still make it to the Alsworthys' rented residence before the clock struck the hour.

"If you leave the note with me, your duty will be discharged. I will peruse it at my leisure and send an answer tomorrow morning. *Early* tomorrow morning."

"Can't," replied the messenger laconically. "Early is as early does, but my orders are I'm to have an answer back quick-like. And that means tonight. My lord," he added belatedly.

"Right," clipped Geoff, as the minute hand on the clock slipped another centimeter closer to midnight. "Tonight."

Why did the War Office have to send for him tonight of all nights? Couldn't they have had whatever crisis they were in the midst of the night before, when he was hunched over the desk in his study, scanning the latest reports from Paris? Even better, they might have timed their intrusion for two nights before, when Geoff was being royally beaten at darts by his old Eton chum Miles Dorrington, who wasn't above crowing over it. And when Miles crowed, he crowed very, very loudly.

Any night, in fact, would have been better than this one.

Losing his temper, he counseled himself, would only waste more precious time. It wasn't the messenger's fault any more than it was the War Office's that civilization itself was being menaced by a megalomanaical Corsican with a taste for conquest. If one were to allocate blame, it lay clearly at Bonaparte's door. Which, Geoff reflected, didn't do him terribly much good at the moment. Even if Bonaparte were available to receive complaints, Geoff rather doubted he could be expected to halt his advance across Europe for an insignificant little thing like a wedding.

Geoff's wedding, to be precise.

Or, as it was increasingly looking, Geoff's somewhat delayed wedding. Geoff filed it away as one more grievance to be taken up against Bonaparte, preferably personally, with a small cannon.

With a sigh, Geoff held out his hand.

" 'Thus conscience does make cowards of us all,' " he muttered.

"My lord?" The courier gave him a hard look.

"Give me the letter and I'll pen a reply," Geoff translated. Signaling to a waiting footman, Geoff instructed in a low voice, "Go to MacTavish and tell him to go on ahead with the carriage as planned. I'll catch him up at the Oxford Arms. Tell him to give the lady my apologies and let her know that I'll be with her as soon as duty permits."

Mary would understand. And if she didn't, he would make it up to her. She had mentioned that Pinchingdale House needed redecorating—he rather liked his study the way it was, but if Mary wanted to drape it in pink silk printed with purple pansies, he wouldn't say a word. Well, maybe not purple pansies. A man had to draw the line somewhere.

Cracking the seal of the paper in his hands, Geoff quickly scanned the contents. They were, as he had suspected, in code, a series of numbers marching alongside Greek letters that had nothing to do with their Roman counterparts. A month ago, a note delivered within London, carried less than a mile by a trusted—if not too intelligent—subordinate of the War Office would never have elicited such elaborate precautions.

Of course, a month ago, England and France had still been observing a precarious peace. That hadn't stopped Bonaparte from flooding the English capital with French spies, but they had grown decidedly bolder since the formal declaration of war. Even Mayfair, heart of England's aristocracy, no longer provided a haven. A mere three weeks ago, one of the Office's more agile agents had been found, a well-placed hole in his back, sprawled on the paving stones outside of Lord Vaughn's London mansion. Whichever way one looked at it, the new precautions made sense.

They were also a bloody nuisance.

A message in code meant that it would have to be decoded. Even knowing the key, decoding the message and coding an answer in return would take at least half an hour.

As if on cue, the minute hand jerked into the upright position, and a pangent ponging noise rousted out the echoes from their shadowy corners.

Refolding the note, Geoff said in a matter-of-fact voice, "This may take some time. If you'd like to take some refreshment in the kitchen . . ."

"I'll wait here, my lord."

Geoff nodded in acknowledgment and turned on his heel, setting off through a succession of unused rooms to his study. He knew the route well enough to make the branch of candles in his hand redundant, as his legs, without conscious direction from his mind, skirted small tables and pedestals bearing classical busts.

His boots clattered unevenly on the shiny parquet floor of a ballroom that hadn't seen a ball since Geoff was in the nursery, across the fading Persian carpets of a drawing room whose drapes had been drawn for two decades, through a state dining room glistening with silver and hung with crystal that had seated its last serving back in the days when men affected red heels and women wore skirts that spanned the width of a stair. The Sabine women, painted in mural along the sides of the room, smirked at Geoff as he passed, but he didn't notice them any more than he noticed the lowering portraits of his ancestors or simpering French shepherdesses that graced the walls of the silent music room.

Shutting the door of his study firmly behind him, Geoff crossed to his desk, removing the ormolu ornament on the left-hand leg with one economical movement. From the tiny cavity, he wiggled out a closely written sheet of paper, screwing the fitting back into place with a practiced flick of the wrist. In contrast to the rest of the house, his study showed signs of recent habitation. A half-empty decanter stood on a round table by the long French windows, estate accounts warred for space on the desk with the latest editions of the weekly newssheets, and the broken bindings on the long wall of books provided silent testimony that they served for use rather than ornament.

From the row of broken bindings, Geoff drew an elderly copy of Virgil's *Aeneid*. That particular work had been chosen on the theory that the French, being a simpleminded sort of people, would never expect a code premised on Greek letters to lead to a Latin poem, and would fritter their time fruitlessly away trolling for hidden meanings in obscure fragments of plays by Sophocles.

It had worked brilliantly so far; Geoff's Paris informant assured him that agents of the Ministry of Police had commandeered all the available copies of Plato's dialogues, and that there was scarcely a volume of Aristophanes to be found in all of Paris.

No more or less battered than any of the other books on the shelf, the poem's margins were filled with what appeared, to the casual eye, to be nothing more than schoolboy scribbles, scraps of translation jostled against fragments of amateur poetry and scrawled notes to a classroom companion complaining about the schoolmaster and contemplating mischief. Although the ink had been carefully faded to give the impression of age, none of them dated back further than the previous year. Geoff was nothing if not thorough.

Shifting impatiently from one foot to the other, he spread Wickham's note and the paper bearing the key side by side. The first number in Wickham's cipher brought him to "souls drifting like leaves through the underworld."

"Leave," wrote Geoff with one hand, flipping to the next indicated page with the other.

As codes went, it wasn't perfect. Virgil had failed to anticipate the existence of Prinny or of Bonaparte, and words like "canon" and "artillery" translated oddly from their archaic counterparts. But it did have the benefit of having baffled Bonaparte's agents since the League of the Purple Gentian had first put it into practice. Before that, it had worked just as effectively as a means to bedevil their tutors at Eton, men considerably better versed in the classics than Bonaparte. Or, at least, so they claimed when parents came visiting. Geoff had always had his doubts.

Within ten minutes, the tattered volume was back on the shelf, and Geoff held a heavily marked-up page that had reduced itself to the message "Leave for Eire soonest. Situation urgent. See early tomorrow for instructions." It would have been only eight minutes if he hadn't wasted two precious minutes puzzling over the word "air," alternately translating it as "ere" and "e'er" before hitting on Eire. Both "early" and "soonest" were unmistakable. Both had been heavily underscored.

Ireland wasn't the place Geoff would have chosen for his honeymoon—he had cherished romantic images of bearing his bride off for a tour of the Lake District, where they could dally among Norman ruins and read poetry by the waterside—but years of managing the affairs of the League of the Purple Gentian had taught Geoff the importance of flexibility. Plans were all very well and good, but homicidal maniacs brandishing swords generally didn't take it kindly when you informed them that they were supposed to be rushing at you from the other side of the room.

Besides, reflected Geoff with a rakish grin, all one really needed for a honeymoon was a bed and a bride. And he was willing to compromise on the former.

Confining himself to essentials, Geoff jabbed his quill into the inkpot and wrote quickly, "Some difficulties. Explain tomorrow."

Wickham, Geoff thought, neatly transcribing his words into a meaningless mess of numbers and symbols that took up far more space than their content deserved, was not going to be overjoyed with the sudden addition of an extra party. But that was something to be hashed out in person, not crunched into code. Rapidly reducing Wickham's note to ash, Geoff dribbled sealing wax on the folded page, stamped it shut with his ring, and looked triumphantly at the clock. Ha! Only a quarter past the hour.

Geoff pushed away from the desk and made purposefully for the door, threading his way back through the empty rooms that wouldn't be empty once he brought Mary home as his bride. If he rode quickly, he might be able to catch the more cumbersome coach before it even reached the Oxford Arms. His blood—and other parts of his anatomy—quickened at the thought of Mary already tucked away into his coach, speeding through the night to be by his side. He still couldn't believe, even with the preparations made, the coach dispatched, the precious special license crackling in his pocket, and the parson summoned, that she had really chosen him.

Geoff remembered her as he had first seen her two years ago at the start of her first Season. Two years, one month, and three days to be precise, since time as Geoff reckoned it had never been quite the same again. There might have been the proverbial clap of thunder, but Geoff couldn't tell for sure; he couldn't hear anything over the sudden roaring in his ears. She had favored him with a dance. It had been a country dance, of the sprightlier sort, but to Geoff, every skip and hop seemed suspended in the air, every turn about the room a journey of a thousand miles. The music, the feet pounding the floorboards, the voices and laughter, had all receded somewhere behind the garden gate created by Mary's smile, and the periodic press of her hand in his.

And that had been all. The dance had ended and Mary's other admirers had closed back around her with all the finality of brambles around a sleeping princess. The following day, Geoff had returned to France to resume his duties in the League of the Purple Gentian. He had tucked the image of Mary away with his volumes of poetry and his collection of Renaissance etchings as something to be taken out and marveled over, something beautiful and pure in a world gone mad. Something worth fighting for. The hazy memory of Mary's face, lit like a Madonna with a hundred dripping candles, buoyed Geoff through his forays into the grim underworlds of Paris.

It seemed nothing short of a miracle that she should, after two years, still be unwed, and even more of a miracle that out of all the men in London she would look favorably upon him.

It wasn't that Geoff didn't know he was accounted a good catch. As society reckoned such things, he was right up there with the heirs to earldoms and considerably above ambitious second sons. He had a title, a respectable fortune, and all his own hair—although the latter fact was immaterial to most of the matchmaking mamas who thronged London's busy ballrooms. He could have been a knock-kneed dwarf with a hook for an arm and still made it to the upper end of the matrimonial lists. Viscounts, after all, weren't exactly thick on the ground, not even in Mayfair.

But he also knew that his wasn't the sort of face and form to set fans fluttering and females swooning when he swaggered into a ballroom. Geoff didn't swagger; he walked. He had never perfected the pose in the ballroom door, never cultivated the slow stare that stripped a lady down to her chemise in one easy arc of the eyes.

On the contrary, much of Geoff's life had been spent in learning how to deflect attention rather than command it. He had learned stillness in the quiet corridors of Pinchingdale House, and his lean form and aquiline features possessed the benefit of being unobjectionable, unremarkable, and entirely unmemorable. Miles, whose attempts to disguise himself generally resembled those of an elephant sticking a lamp shade on its head, had observed disgruntledly that Geoff didn't even need a disguise to slip about unseen.

"My dear boy," replied Sir Percy Blakeney, with a debonair twirl of the quizzing glass, "sink me if our Geoffrey isn't a very prince of shadows."

And so Geoff had gone on his shadowy way, gathering information, thwarting French plots, and building up an impressive repertoire of contacts in cities across the Continent. Richard might live for the dashing escapade, and Miles might garner genuine glee from bashing French operatives over the head, but Geoff was more than content to mastermind from the shadows. He had his friends, his books, his work—and he believed himself happy.

Until he met Mary Alsworthy.

Handing off his message to the courier, Geoff drew on his riding gloves and bounded down the steps at the front of the house. His groom held his horse for him, saddled and ready, not all that happy to have been dragged from the warm stables, and completely unaware that he was about to carry his master to the most momentous event of his life.

If Geoff had had his way, he would have shown up at Mary's door, hat in hand, and endured the requisite interview with her father, the one that began "I assure you, it is my every intention to make your daughter happy," and ended with an announcement in *The Times*. Then he would have ridden out to Gloucestershire to endure a decidedly less businesslike—even if just as predictable—meeting with his mother, who tended to regard her only surviving child with the same sort of proprietary air that Bonaparte felt for most of Europe. He knew his mother would cut up stiff about his engagement, with a gale of recriminations that would make her tantrums upon being told that Geoff was going to France look like a pleasant afternoon's tea party. It was, reflected Geoff, rather like the challenges tossed before heroes in old storybooks. If he could weather a full week of his mother's vapors, he would have more than earned his princess.

But on Friday, just as Geoff's valet had been loading his trunks into his curricle in preparation for a weekend house party in Sussex, Mary had sent him a note with "urgent" underscored four times. Fearing the worst, Geoff told the groom to unhitch the horses, ordered the trunks placed back in his dressing room, and rushed off to meet Mary in the appointed place in the park.

With her well-bribed maid standing a circumspect three trees away, Mary had tearfully informed him that All Was Lost.

"Sweetheart, don't fret," said Geoff, who had never learned to think in capital letters. "Surely it can't be as bad as all that."

Mary hastily averted her eyes, her entire form drooping like a wilted tulip. "No—it's worse!"

After a great deal of coaxing, Geoff had succeeded in persuading Mary to remove her hands from her face and tell him, as

Mary put it, the Terrible Truth. Her parents, she explained, wished to marry her off forthwith.

"That is rather the point of the marriage market," commented Geoff with a hint of amusement. "And if that's your parents' goal, I'm sure we can satisfy them on that score."

"You wish to marry me?"

"Surely you can't be under any doubt," said Geoff fondly, thinking of how lovely she was, and what a miracle it was that she should be so unaware of her own powers.

Mary's dark lashes veiled her eyes. "But what about your mother? I have no family, no fortune. . . . What if she objects?"

There was no "if" about it. Snobbery vied with hypochondria for preeminence as his mother's favorite pastime. She would take noisily to her bed, threatening imminent demise. When that failed, she would set a cry that would be heard all the way from Gloucestershire to London, and probably as far north as Edinburgh. His mother, when she forgot her delicate condition and failing nerves (or was it her failing condition and delicate nerves? Geoff had never been quite clear on that point), revealed the possession of a set of lungs that would be the envy of any Master of the Hounds.

"She can object," replied Geoff practically, "but there's not much else she can do about it."

"Oh, if only we could be married at once!" Mary wrung her gloved hands. "You say you love me now, but there will be talk . . . and your mother . . . How can I be sure that you won't forsake me?"

With a crooked smile, Geoff lightly touched her hand. "Trust me. There's not much danger of that."

Mary paced two rapid steps away from him and came to an abrupt stop, her finely boned back quivering with emotion through the film of blue muslin. "I couldn't bear it! Not after . . ." Her voice failed her.

Geoff's smile faded. Bounding after her, he possessed himself of both her hands, asking earnestly, "What proof of my devotion can I offer? How can I convince you how highly I honor and esteem you?"

Her only answer was a muffled sob and an emphatic shake of her bonneted head. One perfect tear trickled down the sculpted loveliness of her cheek.

Geoff did what any sensible man would do when confronted with a weeping woman. He began promising things. Anything. Just so long as she would smile again. A phoenix feather from the farthest end of the earth, John the Baptist's head on a platter, jewels, furs, rotten boroughs, just so long as she would consent to stop crying.

And so it was that Geoff found himself staggering back to Pinchingdale House through the twilight, having promised a beaming Mary that he would present himself at her door—or, at least, somewhere beneath her bedroom window—in two nights' time, with a speedy traveling coach, a special license, and a set of matched rings. In that same bemused daze, he had canceled his trip to Sussex, postponed all his engagements for the next two weeks, and rousted out a tame parson who was more than willing to conduct a midnight wedding ceremony so Geoff and Mary could set off into the sunrise as man and wife.

He might not like the idea of an elopement, but if the end result meant that his goddess was going to be his wife, Geoff wasn't going to tempt fate by being too persnickety about the means.

As he clattered down Kingsway toward Holborn, passing shuttered shops and the odd drunken dandy straggling away from the pleasures of Covent Garden, Geoff spotted a familiar vehicle lumbering away up ahead. The family coach might not have much to recommend it in the way of speed, but it was outdated enough as to have become easily recognizable. Geoff would have spurred his horse on, but the cobbles were slick with a recent rain and the effluvia from dozens of windows, so he was forced, instead, to keep to a responsible trot as he gradually closed the distance.

He caught the coach up just as it pulled into the forecourt of the Oxford Arms. Flinging his reins to a sleepy ostler, Geoff vaulted off his horse, and, without waiting for the postboy to unfold the steps, or even for MacTavish to bring the carriage to a full stop, he wrenched open the door, every nerve fired by clear, pure joy—stronger than brandy in his blood. Every inch of his skin, every bone in his body, felt intensely alive, thrumming with an imperative that went straight back to the Garden of Eden.

When the door of the coach racketed open beneath his hand and he saw the vague outline of a cloaked figure for him within, Geoff acted on pure instinct.

He grasped her by the shoulders and scooped her eagerly into his embrace.

Chapter Three

The moment was everything Geoff had known it would be.

After an initial startled gasp, his intended bride dissolved into his arms, returning his kiss with more fervor than she had ever shown before. They were on the verge of being married, after all. Amazing what a difference imminent vows could make.

Her hands, originally poised against his chest as though to push him back, slid slowly up to his shoulders and stayed there, as her head tilted back, her lips matched to his. Warm and soft beneath the voluminous folds of her cloak, she fit perfectly into his arms. The dark interior of the carriage closed around them like the velvet lining of a jewel box, blotting out the inn behind them, the unfortunate scents of the courtyard, and the very passage of time.

It was quite some time before it began to dawn on Geoff that she might be just a bit too soft. The arms encircling his neck were a little rounder than he remembered them, and her shoulder blades seemed to have receded. Geoff's hand made another tentative pass up and down her back, without breaking the kiss. Yes, definitely smoother. It might just be the added padding of the cloak, but other discordant details were beginning to intrude upon Geoff's clouded senses. Her fragrance was all wrong, not Mary's treasured French perfume, but something fainter, lighter, that made him think without quite knowing why of the park at Sibley Court in summer. It was a perfectly pleasant scent, but it wasn't Mary's.

He was kissing the wrong woman.

In the sudden rush of clarity, Geoff arrived at another painful realization. The roaring noise he had been hearing, which he had cheerfully ascribed to the pounding of his blood in the heat of the moment, wasn't coming from within at all. Someone was actually roaring, and not far away. The roar had a decidedly jeering quality to it, and it was coming from right behind him. Whoever it might be was clearly having a rousing, roistering good time—at Geoff's expense.

Stiff with horror, Geoff pulled away, breaking the kiss with an audible pop. He could hear the woman in his arms, the woman who wasn't Mary, draw in a ragged breath, as if she were just as shocked as he.

Devil take it, whom had he been kissing?

"Nice work, Pinchingdale!" called a voice behind him, and Geoff swung around, still poised on the brink of the carriage, to see Martin Frobisher saluting him in a gesture of exaggerated approbation. "I give that at least three minutes without coming up for air, don't you, Ponsonby?"

As inebriated as his companion and slower on the uptake under any circumstances, Percy Ponsonby stumbled into the small circle of light cast by the carriage lamps and peered owlishly at the woman behind Geoff. "I say, Pinchingdale, what's all this?"

All this was very clearly not Mary Alsworthy.

The woman so recently entangled with Geoff yanked back with enough force that her hood slipped back, revealing a confusion of ginger-colored hair that glinted like a fuzzy halo where the light struck the individual strands. It could not have been farther from Mary's sleek fall of black hair, which ran silver and blue in the candlelight like a midnight stream. Mary's eyes were delicately tilted at the corners; this woman's were perfect rounds of shock, primrose to Mary's sapphire. The only similarity lay in the lips, full and generous—though some more generous than others. Mary had never responded like that.

"Well, well, well," said Martin Frobisher, rolling the word over his tongue like a fine port. "Well, well, well."

Once he found a syllable he liked, he stuck with it till the bitter end. At least, Geoff was feeling bitter, not to mention decidedly unwell.

He had just been kissing his future sister-in-law. With considerable relish. That undoubtedly counted as incest under an obscure ecclesiastical law dating to the early years of the Reformation, complete with a punishment involving a sack, a beehive, and a large pot of honey.

In his preoccupation with incest, Geoff realized he had completely missed a crucial step. What was Mary's little sister doing in his carriage in the first place? He felt rather as though someone had just whacked him over the head with a very thick plank. Nothing made sense and the world was still spinning.

"If it isn't little Letty Alsworthy," continued Frobisher, looking like the cat who had gotten the canary that had fallen into the cream pot.

Letty Alsworthy very rapidly snatched her hood up over her head. "No, it isn't," she trilled from the depths, in a palpably false fluting soprano. "Can't you see it's Mary, you silly, silly man?"

Percy might be dim, but even he wasn't that dim. He crossed his arms over his chest, peered into the carriage, and said, "No, you're not."

"How can you be so sure? It's dark."

For a moment, Percy wavered, swayed by the obvious truth of that last statement. He shook his head. "You're still Letty. Can't fool me there. They don't look a'tall alike, do they, Pinchingdale?"

"No," said Geoff grimly, "they don't."

One would have thought he might have noticed that before he swept her into his arms. But it had all happened so quickly. . . . One moment he was at the door, the next his arms were around her, and after that, he didn't remember much at all.

At least, he was trying very hard not to remember. If he could, he would scrape his mind clear with sand, obliterate from his memory the way the swell of her chest had felt pressed against his, the curve of her waist beneath his arm, the arch of her neck as his hand had stroked upward into her hair. None of that, he told himself firmly, had ever happened. It wasn't allowed to have happened.

Unfortunately, there were witnesses willing to attest that it had.

"Well, well, well." Geoff could learn to hate that word. Despite being somewhat wobbly on his feet, Frobisher still managed to direct a creditable smirk at Geoff before stumbling into Percy. "Caught by the oldest trick in the book."

"I say, Frobbers, that can't be right." Slinging an arm around his friend, Percy blinked sagely. "What about that trick played by those Greek chappies—something about a horse . . ." Percy subsided into academic reflection.

"Or, in this case," snickered Frobisher, "a carriage."

"No," protested Percy, shaking his head obstinately. "It was quite definitely a horse. Unless it was a rabbit. Maybe that was it. A rabbit."

"Neatly snared, too. Bagged yourself quite a catch, old girl," lauded Martin, in a triumph of mixed metaphors. "Well played."

Framed in the door of the carriage, Letty violently shook her head. Planting both hands on either side of the door frame, she leaned earnestly out. "It's not what you think. It isn't!"

"I know what I'm thinking," muttered Martin, nudging Percy. "Eh, Perce?"

His gaze was directed well below the lines of propriety. Underneath her cloak, Letty wore nothing but a linen night rail.

With its high neck and long sleeves, it might at one point have been perfectly respectable, but frequent washings had reduced it to a whisper. Through the thin fabric, the carriage lamp illuminated the curves of breast and hip in a way far more erotic than mere nudity.

Flushing, Letty snatched the edges of her cloak back together, but not before the image was indelibly imprinted on the eyes of all three gentlemen. Percy, blissfully inebriated, saw not one but three. Percy was a very happy man.

Geoff hastily closed his mouth, which had been hanging open.

Being caught kissing Letty Alsworthy in his carriage was bad enough. Being caught kissing Letty Alsworthy in a night rail . . .

Who ever knew that she could look like that?

Geoff hastily banished such dangerous irrelevancies. Moving to block Letty from the others' view, he said ominously, "If you'll excuse us for a moment, gentlemen?"

"I don't know, Perce," drawled Martin. "Can we trust them alone together?"

Geoff ignored him, which was usually the best way to deal with Martin Frobisher.

"Where is Mary?" he demanded in an urgent undertone, keeping his eyes scrupulously above Letty's neck. It was an unnecessary precaution, since Letty was clutching her cloak closed with enough force to turn her knuckles white.

Letty glanced over her shoulder at Percy and Martin with wide, hunted eyes. "She's not here."

"I realized that."

Letty flushed and pressed her eyes closed, as though for composure. "I mean, she was delayed."

In the course of his work for the League of the Purple Gentian, Geoff had interrogated all sorts of liars. Some adopted a guise of innocence, others feigned indignation, still others a dithery, forgetful manner, as though recalling a story piecemeal might lend to its veracity. But all of them had one thing in common. It wasn't the shifting eyes, because he had seen accomplished liars who held his eyes throughout, and did it with a conviction that could hoodwink the agents of the Inquisition.

It was something in the voice itself, a hollow ring where the kernel of truth ought to have been. Geoff could hear it the way an accomplished singer could pick out the difference between an A flat and a B sharp.

Every instinct he possessed screamed that Letty Alsworthy was lying.

No matter what his instincts told him, the notion of Letty Alsworthy engaging in a deliberate entrapment of her sister's suitor was equally incredible. He didn't know her well, but in the course of his courting her sister, they had said the odd hello, danced the odd dance, all in perfect good humor and goodwill. She had never hung on his arm, pursed her lips in his general direction, or tried to wheedle him out onto a balcony (none of which could be said about Mary's closest friend, Lucy Ponsonby, who had relentlessly attempted all of the above). Letty was a good-natured, straightforward sort, and he had never seen her use the flirtatious flutterings and wiles that made so many of the Season's debutantes a blight on civilization.

But there was something about the way she said "delayed" that sent all his internal alarm bells ringing. It was a prevarication, and a poor one.

And then there was that night rail.

"Did Mary send you?" Geoff asked, deliberately keeping his voice neutral.

A pause, and then Letty shook her head again, this time in negation. "No."

Geoff's face settled into hard lines. "I see."

It was like discovering that the Archbishop of Canterbury had a sideline in smuggling French brandy.

"Sniffing around the carriage, looking for ye, she were, my lord," came the mournful voice of his coachman from the box.

Letty stuck her head out the door in indignation, nearly losing her grip on the edges of her cloak in the process. Percy watched with interest, but he was doomed to disappointment; the fabric held together. "You threw me in! You practically kidnapped me!"

The idea of MacTavish, the most confirmed misogynist since John Knox had his infamous encounter with Mary, Queen of Scots, voluntarily kidnapping any woman would have been laughable had Geoff had any inclination to laugh.

Innocent. Ha. That kiss ought to have alerted him that Letty Alsworthy was anything but innocent. It had been a toe-curling, reputation-compromising, clothing-tightening kiss, the sort of kiss Saint Paul had had in mind when he had said it was better to marry than to burn. A few moments more, and the carriage would have gone up in flames.

Caught by the oldest trick in the book, indeed.

"Doing it a bit brown, aren't you, old girl?" drawled Martin. "Best save your breath for other things, eh, Pinchingdale?"

"What in the devil are you doing here, anyway?" demanded Geoff. He probably ought to have asked earlier, but between the kiss and the night rail, his faculties were not in their best functioning order. In fact, they seemed to have migrated somewhere below his waist.

Percy's face lit up. At last, a question he could answer! "We were just—"

"—protecting the lady's honor," cut in Martin smoothly. "Now that you have been *seen*."

"Hard to see much," contributed Percy, squinting in illustration. "Dark, y'know."

Not nearly dark enough, thought Geoff. Any darker, and Percy and Martin wouldn't have recognized him. Any darker, and none of them would have seen that disastrous night rail. It was the night rail that really did it. The kiss he could lay at his own door—he, after all, had grabbed her—but why go out in a night rail unless it was for the purpose of being compromised? Especially a night rail like that, which combined the specious illusion of innocence with a transparency to make a courtesan blush. And then there was her hair, tumbling down over her shoulders in a wanton mass that suggested dalliance and decadence.

"Still," Percy continued blithely, "you're going to have to marry her, you know. Devil of a shame."

"Thank you, Percy," said Letty acidly.

Percy waved a hand in a gesture of modest denial. "Least I could do. Always glad to be of service."

Geoff didn't bother to ask what sort of service that might be. The night rail, her enthusiastic response to his kiss, MacTavish's grumbling testimony, even the convenient appearance of Percy Ponsonby and Martin Frobisher might all, taken severally, be explained innocently. Put together, they spelled entrapment. His. It had all been quite cleverly done. If Letty grew bored with matrimony, he had no doubt she could have a brilliant career working for the French Ministry of Police.

Turning his back on the two men, Geoff slammed the carriage door closed.

"Let's get you home, shall we?" It was a command, rather than a question.

"I couldn't agree more," said Letty fervently.

Still clutching her cloak, Letty burrowed back into the corner of the seat, out of range of Percy Ponsonby and Martin Frobisher. She hadn't felt this befuddled since the time she fell out of a tree in the orchard in the process of retrieving her brother's pet bird. She had lain there on her back, with a double cast to her vision and a ringing in her ears, dizzy, vaguely ill, and not entirely sure what had just happened.

Falling out of a tree was nothing in comparison to being kissed. At least, with the tree, she had known where she was. For those first few moments, when Lord Pinchingdale's arms closed around her, and his lips merged with hers, she hadn't known and she hadn't cared.

That dreadful moment when he let go had been worse than hitting the ground from ten feet up. With a jarring thump, she had remembered where she was, and, even worse, who she was. That kiss hadn't been hers. All the affection, all the warmth, all the tenderness in his touch had been borrowed under false pretenses, stolen from the store intended for her sister. It had always been meant for Mary. And she—she had just been in the way.

Huddling her cold hands into the warmth of her cloak, Letty forced herself to focus on practicalities. Having gotten in the way, she somehow had to get out of it again, before she found herself stealing more than a kiss from her sister. It was the worst sort of ill luck that Percy Ponsonby and Martin Frobisher should have stumbled across that accidental embrace.

Or was it? Sluggishly, the outlines of a suspicion began to form. If Mary went to the trouble of arranging an elopement, she wouldn't want to leave anything to chance. As much as Lord Pinchingdale professed to adore her, there was always the danger of being compromised and discarded. They had all heard the stories of penniless young ladies being wooed with promises of marriage, then discarded long before they got anywhere near Gretna Green. A few witnesses, on the other hand, could work wonders in getting a wavering groom to the altar. Percy Ponsonby was the brother of Mary's closest friend. . . . Like one of the larger varieties of canine, Percy was as loyal as he was daft. If Mary had asked him to look in at the Oxford Arms at midnight, Percy was quite likely to obey without bothering with whys or wherefores, especially if he could combine it with a few flagons of anything fermented.

Either way, it was nothing short of disaster. Percy was a good-natured ignoramus, and Letty generally didn't mind him, but Martin Frobisher was another kettle of fish entirely. Letty had never liked Martin Frobisher. The feeling was mutual, especially since that incident last month, when Henrietta Selwick had poured ratafia all down Martin Frobisher's new coat and Letty had committed the unpardonable sin of laughing. Heartily. There had also, Letty remembered guiltily, been a certain amount of pointing along with the laughing. At the time, it had seemed a perfectly reasonable reaction.

The ratafia incident was merely the crowning touch. Frobisher had borne her a grudge ever since the prior Season. Like so many men, he had been dangling after Mary, although whether his intentions were marital or merely amorous had been left highly unclear. Being somewhat keener than most (his own assessment, not Letty's), he had come up with the cunning notion of pressing his suit under the auspices of Mary's impressionable little sister. Unfortunately for Frobisher's amorous designs, Letty wasn't nearly so impressionable as she looked. After accepting the lemonade Frobisher had fetched her, and hearing out his tale of unrequited love, she had flatly refused to lure Mary into a secluded alcove for him. Not only would it be improper, but Frobisher wasn't on any of Mary's lists. His fortune was decent enough, but he was at least four heirs away from a title—not very good odds from a marriage mart point of view. Mary could do far better.

It probably hadn't been diplomatic to inform him of that.

No wonder Frobisher had been pushing Lord Pinchingdale to do the honorable thing! It certainly wasn't concern for Letty's well-being. Frobisher probably hoped that if Lord Pinchingdale were forcibly removed, it would leave the field clear for him. Letty grimaced at the ceiling of the carriage. It was a forlorn hope on his part, but it would be nearly impossible to convince him of that. He really ought to have listened more closely to Letty's home truths about his lack of a title.

Even so, there had to be some way to silence him. She couldn't marry Lord Pinchingdale, no matter what Percy had said. Even if Lord Pinchingdale weren't already in love with Mary . . . No, it would never do. Letty shut that thought away in the realm of forbidden daydreams, locked in a box with a triple padlock. The idea that Lord Pinchingdale might, under any circumstances, have welcomed the idea of marriage with a little freckle-faced homebody like herself was nothing short of ridiculous.

Besides, she assured herself, she had simply been trying to prevent the scandal of an elopement. She certainly didn't object to Lord Pinchingdale marrying Mary if they went about it in the normal way. Even if she did have her doubts about Mary's feelings for him . . . that was none of her business.

The whole carriage incident would just have to be squished out of existence.

Her parents wouldn't be a problem; they would still be fast asleep, along with the rest of the household. Her father did have a habit of nocturnal wandering, but those wanderings invariably took him from bedroom to study, never to check on his sleeping offspring. Mary wouldn't tell, of course. Martin Frobisher could be threatened into silence; like so many bullies, he was really a coward at heart. As for Percy Ponsonby . . . One word to his mother, and half of England would know by noon and the other half by tea. On the other hand, if Mary could get to Lucy, and Lucy could get to Percy before Percy spoke to Mrs. Ponsonby . . .

Letty rocked forward as the coach jolted to a halt. Once again, the door was wrenched unceremoniously open. This time Lord Pinchingdale's intentions were clearly anything but amorous.

"Ready?" he demanded.

Letty didn't answer. All her attention was focused elsewhere, on the first floor of her parents' rented town house, where every single candle of their month's allowance was melting cheerfully away.

"Oh, no." Letty would have liked to say something stronger, but the training of a lifetime restrained her. "They can't be awake."

"Can't they?" Lord Pinchingdale said ironically, offering her his arm in a gesture so courtly it couldn't be anything but a mockery. "I'm sure they always sleep with all the candles lit. So much more conducive to rest."

With an effort, Letty refocused, frowning down at her partner in impropriety. Avoiding the outstretched arm, she felt cautiously for the step with one inadequately shod foot. "You don't need to come in with me. In fact, it would be better if you didn't."

"And forgo the pleasure of sharing the happy news with your parents?"

Letty looked up from the all-absorbing task of trying to place her feet on the proper steps without tripping over the hem of her cloak.

"I can manage this much better on my own."

Lord Pinchingdale took her by the elbow and all but lifted her down the last two steps. "I'm sure you can."

Wrenching her arm out of his grasp, Letty started to say something that began with, "If you would only—"

Geoff silenced her by the simple expedient of dropping the knocker. The sound of iron hitting oak drowned out whatever it was she had been about to say.

No sooner had a sleepy maid wrestled open the door than slippered feet padded rapidly down the stairs. Decked out in a ribboned nightcap, Mrs. Alsworthy took one look at her disheveled daughter, let out a shriek, and sagged against her husband, nearly knocking him down the last few steps.

"Is that my daughter? Oh, tell me the worst!"

Staggering under the impact, Mr. Alsworthy retreated a safe few paces away. "If you must faint, my dear, kindly contrive to do it in the other direction."

"Shouldn't you be asleep?" demanded Letty, taking a step inside. Automatically, she blew out the candles in the sconces on either side of the door. Candles were so dear, and the household finances were precarious as it was.

The silent presence of Lord Pinchingdale, looming behind her like a nightmare in the closet, forcibly reminded Letty that their finances weren't the only thing hanging in the balance. She planted herself firmly in front of him, a gesture that had all the effectiveness of a squirrel trying to block a tree.

"Sleep? Sleep!" Mrs. Alsworthy's beribboned head quivered with indignation.

"Yes, sleep, my dear," murmured Mr. Alsworthy. "It is what one generally does at night."

"How could I sleep with my daughter out wandering goodness only knows where, falling into the hands of rogues and seducers and . . . and . . . pirates!"

"What very enterprising pirates they must be," commented Mr. Alsworthy, "to venture so far inland, just to kidnap our daughter. You do see the honor being done to you, don't you, my Letty? If the pirates have come all that way, just for you, it would be a positive discourtesy not to let them kidnap you."

"Speaking of kidnapping," began Letty, "the oddest thing happened tonight. . . ."

"Mr. Alsworthy!" exclaimed Letty's mother. "How can you laugh at such a matter! Although, I must say, I would have thought if a pirate were to kidnap anyone, he would kidnap Mary. She looks quite as I did in my youth, and I'm sure a pirate would have wanted to kidnap me."

"Don't taunt me with lost opportunities, my dear."

"As you can see," interjected Letty firmly, before her parents could be off again, "there were no pirates, and I'm quite safe. There was just a small—"

"But where were you, you impossible child? You cannot possibly imagine the agonies I've suffered! The hours I have paced this floor . . ."

Mrs. Alsworthy illustrated her statement with a representative turn around the room, which ended abruptly when the flowing end of her nightrobe caught on an uneven piece of flooring, ending her progress with an unfortunate rending noise.

"That would all be very affecting," put in Mr. Alsworthy, as his wife clucked over her ruined peignoir, "if you hadn't awakened a mere ten minutes past."

"Ten minutes? Ten minutes!" Mrs. Alsworthy looked up indignantly from her abused hem. "You cannot reckon how time moves within a mother's heart."

"A curious sort of mathematics, to be sure."

"If you would pardon the interruption . . ."

Geoff neatly sidestepped Letty and strode into the room. Being forced to marry the wrong woman was bad enough; being tortured with a Punch and Judy show in the intermission was more than a man could be expected to bear.

Mrs. Alsworthy shrieked and affected to swoon, and even Mr. Alsworthy momentarily abandoned his customary pose of indolence.

"There, my dear," said Mr. Alsworthy, "is your pirate."

"Don't be absurd, Mr. Alsworthy!" exclaimed Mrs. Alsworthy, taking a step forward to attain a closer look, just in case. "That's not a pirate; that's Lord Pinchingdale. Lord Pinchingdale? Whatever are you doing here?"

Lord Pinchingdale was beginning to seriously consider a career on the high seas.

"I should think that much is clear," replied Mr. Alsworthy, before either Geoff or Letty could say anything at all.

"Why must you always be so provoking?" protested his much put-upon wife. "Saying things are clear when they're not the least bit clear at all. Why, they're as muddy as . . . as . . ."

"A pirate's conscience," put in Mr. Alsworthy, enjoying himself hugely.

"Pirates, pirates . . . what have we to do with pirates?"

"You brought them up."

"I most certainly did not!"

"As fascinating as this is, can we return to the matter at hand?" Geoff's voice cracked through the small foyer, lashing both the Alsworthys into silence. "I have come to request your daughter's hand in marriage."

Chapter Four

The idea of their being married was absurd.

Letty would have said so had she been able to get a word in edgewise, but her mother pipped her to the post. Mrs. Alsworthy clapped her plump hands together. "Dearest Mary will be so pleased!"

"Your daughter Laetitia's hand in marriage," Lord Pinchingdale specified tersely.

"This is quite unnecessary!" protested Letty in her loudest voice.

No one else paid the slightest bit of attention to her.

"Ah." Mr. Alsworthy's heavily pouched eyes moved from his bedraggled daughter to the irate viscount. "Not at all what I expected, but an interesting twist. A very interesting twist, indeed."

"I don't understand." Mrs. Alsworthy wrung her hands in her effort at cogitation. "You wish to marry Letty?"

"No, he doesn't," put in Letty.

" 'Wish' might not be exactly the right verb, but it will do for lack of a better. I believe our daughter is compromised, my dear," explained Mr. Alsworthy mildly. "You should be very proud."

Mrs. Alsworthy flung herself at her daughter with a delighted squeal that made the crystals in the chandelier quiver.

"My dearest daughter! My very dearest daughter!"

"Mmmph," said Letty, whose head was buried beneath her mother's ruffles.

"Oh, so many things to do!" Mrs. Alsworthy clutched her new favorite daughter to her beribboned bosom. "The wedding clothes . . . the guest list . . . an announcement in the *Morning Times* . . . Oh, it is too much happiness!"

"Mother . . ." Letty fought her way free of the clinging ruffles.

The movement was a mistake, since it brought her into full view of Lord Pinchingdale's face, stiff with revulsion. It was enough to make her wish herself into indentured servitude in the farthest antipodes. She wasn't quite sure whether they had indentured servants in the farthest antipodes, or even quite where the farthest antipodes were, but she was sure they must need servants.

Letty fought a craven urge to hide in her mother's bosom. It might not be the antipodes, but at least it was there.

Mrs. Alsworthy released Letty long enough to grasp her by both shoulders and hold her at arm's length. "My daughter." She sighed on a wave of maternal pride. "A viscountess!"

With a strength borne of ambition, she wrenched Letty around to face the silent men. "Viscountess Pinchingdale! Doesn't it sound well?"

"My dear"—Mr. Alsworthy's voice filled the uncomfortable silence—"before you exclaim any further, be so kind as to give the rest of us a moment to adjust to our extreme rapture."

"All this rapture," managed Letty, wriggling out of her mother's grasp, "is decidedly premature."

Mrs. Alsworthy, with the word "viscountess" ringing in her ears, was incapable of hearing any others. She brushed off both her daughter's and husband's demurrals with equal inattention.

Both hands extended, she advanced on Geoff. "You must think of me as a mother now, my dear boy."

Geoff backed up several steps.

"I have commitments that demand my attendance abroad within the week," said Geoff rapidly, directing his words at Mr. Alsworthy. "We will be married as soon as I can procure a special license."

"No!" Mrs. Alsworthy's alarmed cry shook the chandelier. "But the lobster patties! Think of the lobster patties! You cannot possibly have a wedding without lobster patties!"

"My dear," interjected Mr. Alsworthy, "I don't believe the world will topple off its axis for lack of lobster patties at our daughter's wedding breakfast."

"Have a wedding without lobster patties! I'd as soon have a turban without feathers!"

"And so you ought," murmured Mr. Alsworthy.

Mrs. Alsworthy plunked both hands on her hips. "Do you mean to imply, Mr. Alsworthy, that you do not approve of my headgear?"

"I merely mean to say, my love, that the birds might approve if you left them a few of their feathers to fly with."

"Ooooh! If you understood the first thing about fashion—"

Letty ended the discussion by dint of marching between her parents.

"This," she said firmly, "is ridiculous."

"I should say so!" exclaimed Mrs. Alsworthy. "My bonnets are exceedingly becoming!"

Letty could feel the last fragile threads of patience beginning to snap. "Can we all just speak reasonably!" she demanded. "For five minutes? Is that too much to ask?"

It was. As Letty plunked her hands on her hips and glowered at her parents and her accidental abductor, a new voice entered the fray. A soft voice, pitched just loud enough to carry, with a plaintive note that whispered around the small foyer like an enchantress's charm.

"Geoffrey?" ventured Mary.

Mary must, thought Letty cynically, have taken the time to change out of her traveling clothes when she heard the hullabaloo downstairs, because she was impeccably garbed for bed, her white linen night rail entirely wrinkle-free and every black lock falling in gleaming perfection along her lace-frilled shoulders.

"Oh, Mary!" exclaimed Mrs. Alsworthy. "Your sister is to be married. Isn't it above all things marvelous?"

"Look and learn," added Mr. Alsworthy. "A bit more practice and you, too, could be compromised, my girl."

Mary's deep blue eyes widened in a way that suggested the concept of being compromised was entirely foreign to her. In a gesture worthy of Mrs. Siddons, one elegantly boned white hand extended toward her former lover, halted, and, as if the retraction caused her extreme pain, dropped again to her side. Mary's eyelids drooped and her lightly parted lips quivered in a way meant to suggest passionate emotion nobly contained.

It was a masterful performance.

Lord Pinchingdale's throat worked in a way that wasn't feigned at all. Turning abruptly on his heel, he addressed Mr. Alsworthy in a rapid monotone. "I will call on you tomorrow to make the arrangements. Your servant, ladies."

And with a brief nod in the direction of the center of the room that never quite made it as far as the white-gowned figure on the railing, he achieved the door and was gone, leaving an unhappy hush behind him.

From her position on the stairs, Mary raked Letty with a long, appraising gaze. "I never knew you had it in you."

Letty stared at her sister. "But I never meant . . . This wasn't any of my doing! Mary . . ."

Letty held out a hand in mute appeal.

Mary narrowed the midnight blue eyes her admirers had compared to sapphires, velvet, and the water off the coast of Cornwall. Currently, they were as hard as agate, and as dark as a scoundrel's heart.

"Who asked you to interfere?"

Flinging her glossy tresses over her shoulder, Mary retreated up the stairs with all the dignity of an exiled queen. In the painful silence, Letty could hear the swish of her hem sweeping across the steps like a train, until a door thudded shut on the story above and even that small sound was blotted out.

Letty's mouth opened and closed but Mary wasn't there to argue with anymore. All the reasons that had seemed excellent two hours ago turned to dust at the back of Letty's throat.

"Wait!"

Lifting the hem of her cloak, Letty scrambled up the stairs after her sister, slipping and skidding on the treads. It was as if twelve years had rolled back, and she was a roly-poly little six-year-old again, scrabbling after her older, more interesting sister, desperately wanting to be allowed to do whatever Mary did, play whatever Mary played.

But no matter how she tried, she was always the one stumbling after, the one with tears in her dress and scrapes across her knees. Always the one running behind.

On the landing, Mary's door was closed. Letty barreled into it, scarcely taking time to turn the knob before tumbling into the room. Inside, all the candles were lit, branches and branches of candles, burning like little stars against the dingy wallpaper. The wallpaper had once been white with blue stripes, but time and indifferent care had faded the whole to a dull pewter. The room bore the signs of hasty action: Mary's traveling dress lay strewn across the unmade bed, and a portmanteau slopping over with scarves slumped next to the window. Letty could see the corner of Mary's silver-backed brush sticking out of one corner, smothered beneath a length of spangled gauze.

Mary stood by her dressing table, which, like the wallpaper, had once been white. Her perfect profile was averted, staring fixedly at nothing in particular, or, rather, nothing that Letty could see. Her stillness terrified Letty more than a dozen screaming rages.

"Mary?" she whispered.

At the sound of Letty's voice, Mary's head slowly lifted, her spine straightening. By the time she turned, moving as deliberately as an actor in a court masque, she was once again entirely in command of herself, her face as composed as a porcelain figurine, and about as warm.

"What would you like me to say?" she asked. "Congratulations?"

"Of course not! Mary, you know I didn't . . . I wouldn't . . ." Letty's protests faltered against her sister's unruffled regard.

"But you did," said Mary.

It was a simple statement of fact.

And there was nothing Letty could say to refute it. In the face of Mary's implacable poise, all her perfectly sensible arguments crumbled on her lips, like so much chipped paint.

It had always been like this.

"You didn't love him," objected Letty. "You can't claim you did."

Mary reached to rearrange a strand of her hair, and turned to examine the effect in the spotted glass of the mirror. "No. I didn't. Did I? You know best, of course. You generally do."

Doubt lacerated Letty's heart with ice.

"If you do really care about him . . ." she began uncertainly.

"I suppose it could be worse." Mary's voice was as finely edged as frost. "At least one of us gets him. We keep it all in the family."

She smiled at Letty, the tight, social smile of the hostess speeding the parting guest.

"If you don't mind, it is quite late. I need my sleep if I'm to set my cap at a new prospect tomorrow. Good night."

Letty found the door neatly closed in her face.

There was very little she could say to a door, especially when she didn't know what she wanted to say in the first place. *Please don't hate me? I'll make it right?* She had been so sure that Mary's feelings for Lord Pinchingdale went no deeper than his title and fortune. Admittedly, there was a good deal there to love, but it wasn't the sort of love that drove susceptible maidens into a decline. If she barged back in, demanding answers, Mary would merely smile her enigmatic smile and reply in stinging commonplaces, turning Letty's questions back against her like a mythical hero's enchanted shield. It was impossible to tell whether Mary was speaking the bald truth and mocking herself for it, or hurt and hiding it. Either way, the acid tone was the same. Either way, she kept Letty on the other side of a door harder to breach than wood.

It had always been that way, too.

Well, nothing was final yet. If Mary wanted him, she could have him. One hand on the banister, Letty hurried back down the stairs in search of her father. There had to be some way around this ridiculous situation. It was ridiculous, as ridiculous as one of the Greek tragedies of which her father was so fond, where the hero inevitably managed to charge straight into whatever doom he was trying to evade. Letty had never had much patience for those heroes. Yet here she was, having tried to thwart an elopement, winding up having accidentally eloped herself.

Accidentally eloped. The very words made Letty wince. One didn't accidentally elope. One accidentally picked up the wrong book at Hatchards, or paired a dress with the wrong-colored shawl. One didn't accidentally find oneself in a carriage at the dead of night with a member of the opposite sex, bound for matrimony.

She supposed Oedipus hadn't exactly intended to kill his father and marry his mother either.

Letty nearly barreled into her father, who was just starting up the stairs, nightcap on his head and candle in hand. "I must speak with you."

"Must you?" Mr. Alsworthy stifled a yawn. "As much as I hate to agree with your mother, the hour is, indeed, unnaturally advanced."

"Papa . . ." Letty said warningly.

Mr. Alsworthy bowed to the inevitable. "If you must."

Letty's breath released in a long rush. "Thank you."

Mr. Alsworthy led the way into his book room, a tiny square of a room filled with the boxes of books he had insisted on bringing down from Hertfordshire, augmented by his purchases since their arrival in London. The volumes filled the shelves and tottered in uneven stacks along the corners of the room. With the ease of long practice, Letty edged between two tottering piles and removed another from the room's only extra chair.

"How did you get yourself into such a pickle, my Letty?" inquired Mr. Alsworthy kindly, as Letty lowered the tower of books to the floor with a decided thump.

"With the best of intentions," began Letty irritably.

Mr. Alsworthy wagged a reproving finger at his favorite child. "That should cure you of those."

"I *thought* we were being robbed."

Mr. Alsworthy grimaced at the dust furring the edge of his desk. "A most undiscriminating burglar, to be sure."

Letty had long ago learned that the only way to conduct a conversation with her father was to ignore his little asides. "Instead," she continued determinedly, "I found Mary packing for a midnight elopement."

"Unsurprising," murmured Mr. Alsworthy. "Unfortunate, but not unexpected."

"I went downstairs to talk some sense into Lord Pinchingdale," Letty hurried on before her father could interrupt again, "and was accidentally carried off. It was all a ridiculous mistake. And now . . ." Letty frowned at a battered copy of Burke's *Reflections on the Revolution in France*.

Mr. Alsworthy steepled his fingers in front of himself. "Shall I begin for you? You," he said, "wish to remove yourself from this hasty arrangement. Oh, yes, it is hasty. There can be no two ways about that."

"And ill advised," replied Letty decidedly.

"I said hasty, not ill advised." Mr. Alsworthy contemplated the tassel on his nightcap. "The two are entirely different things."

"Not in this instance," Letty put in firmly, before her father could go off on a philosophical tangent about the merits of hasty action, as exemplified by the ancients. "This is entirely unnecessary. Don't you see? We'll just put it about that it was Mary in the carriage instead of me. Everyone knows how Lord Pinchingdale feels about her—goodness knows he hasn't exactly been subtle. It's far more believable than his being discovered with me."

"Truth is stranger than invention?" mused Mr. Alsworthy, who had developed the cheerful ability to turn any situation into an aphorism. "Be that as it may, it won't do. I take it you were seen?"

"By Percy Ponsonby," retorted Letty. "But Percy Ponsonby is a positive pea-brain. Everyone *knows* Percy Ponsonby is a positive pea-brain."

"Nonetheless, he was there on the spot, and that counts for more than intellect in such situations as these."

"This is the man who leaped out of a second-story window because he thought it seemed like a good idea!"

"It does make one wonder about the continued survival of the human race, does it not?" When Letty declined to follow him down that particular byway, Mr. Alsworthy recalled himself reluctantly to the situation at hand. "People are willing to believe anything that bears the promise of scandal. And you, my dear, have created rather a nice little scandal for yourself—I know, I know," Mr. Alsworthy said as he raised an admonitory hand, "with the best of intentions."

"Do you think I was in the wrong?" demanded Letty.

"I think," said her father gently, "that you reacted the only way that you could, being no other than yourself."

It wasn't exactly vindication. In fact, it sounded uncomfortably like a kindly worded condemnation.

"What else was I to do?" protested Letty, planting both hands on the desk as she leaned forward. "Let Mary elope? I couldn't."

"My point precisely," said her father. While Letty grappled with that, he added, "Pinchingdale is a good man and will deal with you fairly."

"Fairly! He wants to strangle me!"

"I often feel so about your mother, but, as you see, we've rattled on these twenty-odd years together."

Letty looked mutinous. "There's no reason to ruin three lives over a silly mistake."

Her father leaned forward in his chair, and, placing both hands on the desk, looked at her directly for the first time. The watery eyes, magnified by spectacles, weakened by reading by candlelight, regarded her kindly, and Letty found herself remembering a million other interludes before her father's desk, a million times she had come to him with a household problem or an amusing anecdote or just for the comfort of his gentle, detached voice after her mother's shrieks and Mary's mercurial moods. For all his vagaries and absentness, she knew he loved her, and she believed, with the last desperate hope of the child she had been, that Papa couldn't possibly let anything bad happen.

"Be kind to your brother and sisters when you are a viscountess."

There were times when speaking with her father was quite as maddening as dealing with her mother.

"I am not going to *be* a viscountess."

"I don't see that you have much choice in the matter, my dear. When one marries a viscount, the title tends to follow."

"What about Mary?"

"In as much as bigamy continues to be frowned upon, one assumes that she will not be marrying the viscount."

"Papa!"

"Well, my dear, if you persist in wearying me with inconsequentialities in the wee hours of the night, you must resign yourself to being wearied in turn. Although I must say . . ."

"Yes?" Letty urged hopefully.

"I have frequently wondered why they are commonly called 'wee,' when these nocturnal hours always seem to stretch on longer than all the rest put together. Have you ever considered that, my dear?" Her father beamed innocently at her over his spectacles.

"No, I haven't," Letty said bluntly, shoving back her chair. "If you'll excuse me, I believe it's well past bedtime."

Why had she, after all, thought this occasion would be any different from any other? Her father lived in a dreamworld of books and philosophers, far more real to him than the demands of household and family. Hertfordshire or London, it was all the same to him. And whether it was repairing the roof or a daughter about to be rushed into an imprudent marriage, his reaction never varied: if it required any effort, he wanted nothing to do with it. Not even for his favorite child.

Letty wasn't numb enough that she didn't feel the sting of it.

"If you won't think of me," she said bitterly, "think of yourself. Who will keep you in candles?"

"Ah," said her father. "Think how selfless I am being. I don't know how we'll get on without you. Your mother will spend us into the poorhouse within the year, and your sister will undoubtedly find some new scandal to visit upon herself. As for your younger siblings, I have no doubt that they will contrive to find some way to bring the house down about our ears. Such a pity, but it can't be helped."

For a moment, Letty harbored a host of mad fantasies. She could flee far from London and find employment in a rural inn as a maid of all work. Of course, that fantasy discounted the fact that she hated scrubbing things and her accent would give her away in two seconds as a—what was the slang word for it? A "toff"? A "nob"? Something like that. How could she hope to pass as a serving wench when she couldn't even speak their language? As for running away and joining the gypsies, she wasn't at all sure they would have her. She couldn't play the guitar; her idea of fortune-telling was to say, "If you don't pick that up, you'll trip on it"; and she would look ridiculous in a kerchief and gold bangles.

Recognizing the stubborn set of her chin, her father warned, "Don't think to take matters into your own hands."

"What else am I to do?"

"Marry him," said her father bluntly. "He'll serve very well for you, my Letty, very well, indeed."

"You can't really mean for me to go through with this?"

Her father's only response was to blow out the candle.

Letty exited the study, head held high, determined to prove her father—and Lord Pinchingdale—wrong. All they had to do was make sure that the story didn't get out. How hard could it be?

Chapter Five

B y noon the following day, no fewer than twenty-eight versions of what was popularly being called the Pinchingdale
Peccadillo were making the rounds of the *ton*.

By the time Geoffrey trudged down the hall of the War Office, the number had escalated to fifty-two, complete with several
minor variants. There was even a rollicking ballad that was being sung in the coffeehouses to the tune of "Greensleeves." Not
to be outdone, the printers of broadsheets, loath to miss out on a
lucrative bit of libel, had rushed into action, publishing some of
the more lurid versions of the tale, complete with crudely tinted
illustrations. As he made his way from Doctors Commons to
Crown Street, Geoff had spied no fewer than five cartoons. One,
subtitled "How to Chuse," featured a leering Geoff with an
Alsworthy in either arm, each in a considerable state of disha-
bille. Geoff knew it was meant to be him because the author had
considerately labeled it, just in case there might be any mistakes
as to the intended identity. Another would-be wit had put out a
tinted woodcut, with the heading "All's Worthy in the Dark,"
that left little of what might be considered "worthy" to the imagination.

Geoff's only consolation, if consolation it could be called, was that the pictures in the cartoons looked nothing like any of them. He had been able to slip entirely unnoticed through the gossiping throngs in which his name was being bandied about with unabated gusto.

"You," pronounced Wickham, without looking up from the letter he was signing, "are late."

Geoff refrained from reminding Wickham that his relationship with the War Office was conducted on an entirely voluntary basis. Back in the old days, before Richard had decamped for the pastoral pleasures of life in Sussex with his bride, the League of the Purple Gentian had operated autonomously from their base in Paris. Geoff plotted and planned; Richard undertook the more dashing sorts of escapades, the ones that called for black cloaks and mocking laughter; and Miles served as their contact with the powers that be back home, to ensure that they trod on no official toes. The War Office occasionally nudged them in one direction or another, but, on the whole, the League merrily went its own way, freeing prisoners from the Temple Prison, filching secret documents, and generally doing everything in their power to harry the assistant to the minister of police into a precipitate decline. They had their own web of contacts, their own personnel, and, most important, they were all the way across the Channel, too far for Wickham to snap his fingers and expect them to come running.

It wasn't that Geoff didn't respect William Wickham. He did. The man was doing the best he could in a damnable situation, trying to rope flighty émigrés into line, encourage sedition in France, and discourage the same within England. Geoff didn't envy him the job. He just wished Wickham would leave him to his.

But the situation on the Continent was too dire to quibble about such minor matters as lines of command. Geoff slid into the chair across from Wickham's desk, placing his hat and gloves neatly on one knee. "Circumstances detained me."

"Let us hope they do not continue to do so." Without further preamble, Wickham struck straight at the heart of the matter. "You're aware that Robert Emmet is back in Ireland?"

Geoff dragged his mind away from his own difficulties and onto England's. As far as the safety of the realm was concerned, Robert Emmet spelled trouble.

"So I heard. Along with Russell, Quigley, and Byrne."

"Exactly," said Wickham. "All veterans of the rising in 'ninety-eight. I hardly need tell you what this signifies."

Like many Irish nationalists, Emmet had fled to France in the wake of the abortive rebellion of 1798, leaving behind his country, but not his cause. It was too much to hope that Emmet might have been distracted by the legendary wine and women of France. As far as Emmet was concerned, a tavern was just a convenient place to hold clandestine meetings. Had they been on the same side, Geoff would have found that tendency admirable. As it was, it was merely alarming. Since their arrival in France, Emmet and his fellow United Irishmen had been laboring tirelessly to drum up funds and troops to have another go at what they had been unable to accomplish in '98.

Emmet's reappearance in Ireland could mean just one thing.

"Unless they've suddenly changed their tune?" Geoff propped one leg against the opposite knee. "Rebellion."

"They are moving far faster than we anticipated. We had hoped Emmet would remain in Paris until he could be sure of French aid. It would, at least, have given us more time," Wickham said tiredly. "You know how the situation stands in Ireland."

"Unfortunately," replied Geoff. The reports from his informant in Dublin had grown increasingly bleak over the last few months. The word "desperate" had been liberally scattered through the last. He knew how they felt.

"'Unfortunately' is too mild a word. We've been systematically stripping our garrisons there to swell our defenses at home.

A damnably shortsighted strategy, but there it is. Keeps the people back home happy, makes them feel safe in their beds." Wickham's grimace betrayed what he thought of the shifts of politicians. "We're short of men and we're short of munitions. We've made it ludicrously easy for them. All Bonaparte needs to do is to stir the waters a bit, give the rebels their heads. . . ."

"And the back door to England lies open to him," finished Geoff grimly. "Why do something yourself when you can get someone else to do it for you?"

Wickham rubbed one wrist with the opposite hand in a habitual gesture of fatigue. "Bonaparte will let the rebels do their worst, and then march his men in at as little bother and expense to himself as possible."

"Unless," said Geoff, his keen gray eyes fixing on the map of Ireland above Wickham's head, "the rebellion can be snuffed out before it begins. Bonaparte won't be willing to invest in a full-scale invasion. He doesn't have the money."

"Not snuffed out," corrected Wickham. "Rooted out."

Geoff weighed the distinction, nodding slightly to signify understanding. "That's where I come in."

"Exactly. The Pink Carnation is already in Dublin, working to subvert Emmet's contacts with France. I want you to cover the Irish side." Wickham began ticking off tasks on his fingers. "We'll need the names of the ringleaders, their methods of operation, and their sources of funds. We know they've been manufacturing and storing arms. Those caches will need to be found and confiscated." Wickham paused, frowning abstractedly into space. "Emmet has rented a house in Butterfield Lane in Rathfarnham under the name of Robert Ellis."

"Hardly the most creative of aliases," commented Geoff. "You think he meant to be found out?"

"Precisely. We waste our resources watching the house in Rathfarnham while he wreaks havoc in Dublin. He's a clever man, even if he does write damnably bad poetry."

An unexpected stab of pain caught Geoff somewhere just below the heart. In the study at Pinchingdale House sat a half-finished poem, dedicated to his Mary. He never had succeeded in rhyming "entice" with "delight." It was too late now. Any poems he addressed to Mary at this point would be elegies, rather than love lyrics.

With an effort Geoff pulled his attention back to the matter at hand. "Emmet's verse was bad enough that Richard and I suspected it might be a code, but it didn't prove susceptible to any of the usual tests."

Wickham nodded. "I had Whittlesby in Paris look Emmet's poems over. He arrived at the same conclusion. You'll have to look farther than his poetry to divine his plans."

Geoff nodded and rose to his feet. "I have some ideas."

Wickham held up an admonitory finger. "One more thing. You know that your friend Dorrington has apprehended the Black Tulip?"

"He mentioned something to that effect," replied Geoff. "But he didn't go into details."

As to why Miles hadn't gone into details . . . well, there were some things the War Office just didn't need to know.

In response to a summons from Miles, as urgent as it was incoherent ("Black Tulip has Hen. Help!"), Geoff had gone haring off to Loring House, ready to do his bit for the rescue mission. Instead, he had found the fray already over, and a very battered Miles and Henrietta beaming at each other in a way that didn't bode well for Miles's continued bachelordom. Where there was Miles, one could usually find Henrietta, but one didn't usually find Henrietta with her arm around Miles's waist, gazing up at him as though she were Cortez and he was her newfound land.

Geoff had retreated with a haste that bordered on flight.

He was happy for them. Truly. He couldn't imagine two people more ideally suited than Miles and Henrietta.

He just wasn't awfully keen on the word "marriage" at the moment.

"I assume you know the Marquise de Montval?" Wickham inquired, reaching for a small packet toward the end of his desk.

"Peripherally," replied Geoff. The English-born widow of a guillotined French nobleman, her undeniable beauty had made her hard to miss. Ever since her arrival in London, she had been determinedly pursuing Miles, much to the distress of Henrietta.

Henrietta had had a ridiculous theory that the marquise was working for the French, that she was, indeed . . .

Geoff frowned. "You don't mean to say . . . ?"

"The Black Tulip," confirmed Wickham.

"With all due respect, sir," countered Geoff, "are you certain?"

Geoff couldn't deny that all the details fit. The marquise had been in France at the start of the Terror; she had, according to Geoff's informants in Paris, belonged to a series of revolutionary societies devoted to liberty, equality, and the chopping off of heads. Her revolutionary credentials were impeccable. By all accounts, her marriage to the marquis had been a miserably unhappy one. Whether the last fact was relevant to the former was a matter of pure surmise, but, human nature being what it was, Geoff suspected that a loathing for one aristo in particular might have had something to do with the marquise's sudden spurt of egalitarian fervor.

But, try as he might, Geoff couldn't fit the Marquise de Montval into the frame marked out for the Black Tulip. Her looks were too showy, her pursuit of Miles too heavy-handed. None were what Geoff would have expected of the archrival of the League of the Purple Gentian, the operative who had personally accounted for the deaths of several of their best men. The hallmark of the Black Tulip had always been a shadowy subtlety in keeping with the silhouetted image of the flower he had chosen for his name, not the brazen bustle adopted by the marquise.

Geoff grimaced. He was sure Wickham would be thrilled to entertain a theory that flew in the face of all logic, simply because he, Geoffrey Pinchingdale-Snipe, was having an attack of masculine intuition.

Not to mention that Geoff's intuition didn't seem to be in the best working order these days. He would have been prepared to swear that Mary's little sister was a good-natured, well-meaning sort of girl, and look where that had brought him.

"Quite certain." Wickham yanked on the string that bound the package in front of him. In a nest of brown paper lay a piece of silver shaped like the pawn from a chess set, but smaller; a tiny crystal vial; and a flimsy piece of paper twisted into the shape of a cylinder.

Geoff reached for the pawn first, knowing what he would find before he even turned it over. On the underside, just as he had expected, a series of deeply incised lines marked out the silhouette of a round-bellied flower. A tulip.

"These were discovered on her person," explained Wickham, keeping a proprietary eye on the tiny cache.

Geoff turned the seal over in his hand, feeling the faint residue of wax along the edge, his skin scraping against the nicks in the silver that came from long and careless use. The knob fit neatly into the palm of his hand. Against the tangible reality of the seal, his objections seemed even more illusory.

"You have her in custody?" he asked.

"We did."

"Did?"

Geoff waited for Wickham to elaborate. He didn't. Instead, he tapped a finger against the scarred surface of his desk, and said, "We have reason to believe that the marquise is even now on her way to Ireland."

Geoff set the seal down on the desk with a distinct click. "Won't she wonder at my sudden appearance in Ireland? The Dublin Season doesn't begin until December."

Wickham handed Geoff a folded piece of paper. "You," he instructed, "are in Ireland to purchase a horse you wish to run in the Epsom. Naturally, you would wish to inspect the animal yourself. All of your instructions are on this piece of paper. Read it and then burn it."

Geoff refrained from commenting that it had never occurred to him to carry out those tasks in the opposite order. Wickham would not be amused.

He was also still speaking. "A packet leaves for Dublin by way of Holyhead tomorrow afternoon."

Geoff resisted the craven desire to run for the packet and disappear into Hibernian obscurity where scheming adventuresses in search of a title would fear to follow. But the special license— the new special license—was already in his pocket, the papers drawn up, and the parson engaged.

With a twist of his lips, he shook his head. "I can't leave tomorrow. I have one small annoyance to deal with before I can leave for Ireland."

Wickham frowned. "See that this small annoyance doesn't detain you too long."

"Oh, it won't," said Geoff blandly, drawing on his gloves. "You can be sure of that."

Wickham lowered the Black Tulip's seal to the desk with a fatalistic thump. "Lord Pinchingdale, the one thing I have learned is that it is best never to be sure of anything."

Given last night's events, Geoff was inclined to agree. Until midnight last night, he had been quite sure that the dawn would see him married to Mary Alsworthy. Instead . . . instead he found himself making hurried—and unwanted—preparations to marry her scheming sister.

Replacing his hat, Geoff took his leave of Wickham. He had one last, unpleasant errand to undertake before he could seek out his study and a bottle of brandy, not necessarily in that order.

Sleep would have been an impossibility the night before, even if there had been any night left to sleep in. Instead, upon departing the Alsworthys', Geoff had gone straight to his study. Stacking his working papers to one side, he had pulled out a blank piece of paper and dipped his quill in the ink pot. And got no further. The sound of ink dripping from his pen joined the steady tick of the clock on the mantel.

Crumpling up the first sheet, Geoff had tried again. That time, he got so far as "My very dearest Mary" before the ink splotches took over the page. What, after all, could one say? *I may be marrying your sister, but I will love you always*? That page joined the others on the floor. It would be the worst sort of selfishness to attempt to bind Mary to him with declarations of affection when he had nothing more to offer her. Better by far, resolved Geoff, attacking a fourth page with enough force to crack the nib, for her to go on with her life, and find someone who would be free to offer her the things he could not: a home and a name.

But he couldn't force his pen to shape the words that would free them both.

Geoff stared around the well-worn room, the familiar books on the shelves, the bust of Cicero on its stand in the corner, the decanter on the table by the window. Outside the study door, the empty rooms pressed down upon him, like a vision of his future. No Mary to sweep in sunshine with her, no children waking the echoes with their laughter. Instead, nothing but more sleepless nights in his study, poring over dispatches from France.

And when the war with France was over—as one assumed it must eventually be—what then? A squirrelly half-life of gaming hells and kept women? A place on the fringes of his friends' families? Neither was an attractive prospect.

He supposed he would have to come to some sort of amicable arrangement with his unwanted bride, if only to prevent his cousin Jasper from inheriting. In books, people might die of balked desire, or live celibate lives mourning the loss of their own true love, but Geoff had estates to administer and responsibilities to fulfill, among which was included the production of an heir.

Prior to Mary, he had never expected a love match. He hadn't expected thunder or violins or any of those other overblown sentiments that filled the covers of romantic novels and spilled over into reams of limping verse. He had always thought that someday, in the fullness of time, he would marry a nice, sensible sort of girl, the sort who could be trusted to oversee the house, speak articulately at the dinner table, and bear healthy and reasonably intelligent children. In fact, before Mary had invaded his dreams, his vision of his future wife had been someone not unlike Letty Alsworthy.

Or, he corrected himself darkly, as he climbed the steps of a narrow-fronted house on Brewer Street, what he had supposed Letty Alsworthy to be. His cousin Jasper's lodgings were on the third floor, enough of a climb to discourage Jasper's more faint-hearted creditors, as well as his adoring mother. Geoffrey rapped on the door with the head of his cane.

A brusque "Enter!" sounded from within. Jasper's man of all work was seldom present when there was any work to be done, and Jasper preferred not to lower himself to such menial tasks as opening doors.

Turning the knob with a smart click, Geoff let himself in, removing his hat as he ducked through the low lintel of the door.

Several versions of last night's story, ink smeared from hasty printing, mingled with the other debris on the floor around his cousin's chair, the one on top bearing the legend VARIETY-LOVING VISCOUNT SWITCHES SISTERS! SEE FULL STORY ON PAGE 2.

Jasper indicated the paper with a swipe of the foot. "You can't really mean to go through with this?"

Although it was already evening, Jasper looked as though he had just climbed out of bed. He lounged in an easy chair in his bachelor lodgings, with a dressing gown of heavy brocade negligently tied around his waist, an empty carafe and three stained glasses on a small table next to him bearing testament to last night's activities. A captain in the Horse Guards, Jasper never walked when he could swagger, never smiled when he could leer, and had the art of mentally undressing a lady down to the flick of an eyelash. He and Geoff had cordially hated each other since the time they were old enough to be put in a room together and told to play nicely.

It had seemed oddly appropriate to ask his most reviled—if closest—relative to stand best man to him at a wedding that looked to contain about as much genuine affection as a harlot's kiss.

When Geoff didn't answer immediately, a wide grin spread across Jasper's broad-boned face. He slapped his knee. "You are, aren't you! Devil take it, you're actually going to marry the scheming chit. I say, that *is* rich. I haven't been so entertained this fortnight."

Geoff paced to the pier glass at the other side of the room, kicking an empty bottle out of the way as he went. "I don't see that I have a choice," he said tersely. He regarded the long trail of dust adhering to his otherwise impeccable Hessians with distaste. "Good God, Jasper, does your man ever clean? Or do you just keep him around to ward off your creditors?"

His cousin ignored the slur on his housekeeping and leaned forward avidly. "I've been hearing the most fascinating stories all afternoon. Do tell, is it true that you were discovered in an inn with the little Alsworthy, both of you lacking certain crucial articles of clothing?"

"No," said Geoff curtly.

After all, they hadn't been in the inn, merely in front of it. And he couldn't vouch for her, but all his clothes had been firmly attached at all times.

"Pity. I knew it was too much to hope that our virtuous Geoffrey had been chivied naked out of bed. But it makes such a delightful *on dit*, doesn't it? You've quite replaced Prinny in the gossip mills today."

Jasper kicked his slippered feet up on a threadbare footstool. In contrast to the faded furniture, the slippers, like the robe, were of heavy crimson silk embroidered in gold thread. Jasper, as Geoff knew, had a convenient habit of switching tailors whenever his account came due. He changed lodgings with equal alacrity.

"Deuced unlucky, that's what I call it," Jasper drawled. "It's a sad, sad day when a man can't dally with one sister without getting hauled off to the altar with the other."

"I doubt that it's a universal predicament." Geoff paused in his perambulations to fix his cousin with a forbidding stare. "And I wasn't 'dallying' with Mary Alsworthy, as you so eloquently put it. I intended to marry her."

"More fool you. Marry . . . Mary . . . Unmarried Mary . . ." Jasper waved his pipe languidly through the air. "There's a pun in that, if only I had the wit for it. Ah, well. You know what they say. The wine is in and the wit is out."

"More wine than wit from the look of it," commented Geoff dryly, casting a pointed glance at the drained decanter by Jasper's elbow.

"Not all of us can afford genuine, smuggled French brandy," retorted Jasper. "But I miss my manners. Care for a drink, coz?"

"Not with you."

"Off to moon over your dear lost Mary? Don't look so, coz! One sister will do as well as the other in the dark."

"I'll ascribe that statement to the wine, and leave it at that."

"Or you'd what? Call me out?" Jasper blew out a thick ring of smoke, and ran it through with the stem of his pipe. "Think how it would upset your dear mama. But our family paragon wouldn't do anything so foolish, would he? Unless . . . I have always wondered, how far can our virtuous Geoffrey be pushed before he cracks?"

"Push too far and I'll refuse to pay your bills the next time your creditors get too much for you," amended Geoff calmly. "Think how much that would upset *your* dear mama."

His cousin regarded him coldly. "You do know how to make a man regret his parentage."

"The sentiment is mutual. Do you know, Jasper," remarked Geoff, "I do believe you grow more loathsome every time I see you."

"I aim to please, dear coz."

The two men bared their teeth at each other in complete understanding and mutual loathing.

"You'll stand up with me tomorrow?"

Jasper stretched his long legs out in front of him. "Delighted to. I've always wanted to preside at an execution. Yours, for choice."

"Don't forget your black cap."

"I say, old chap," Jasper called after Geoff. "If this sister were to snuff it, you couldn't marry the other one, could you? Shades of Henry VIII and all that. Deuced hard luck for you."

Geoff left Jasper's lodgings to the sound of his cousin's mocking laughter. Jasper, he thought grimly, had really missed his calling when he went into the army rather than take up his well-deserved place on the boards of Drury Lane. Geoff decidedly regretted the impulse that had driven him to Jasper's lodgings.

It had clearly been a mistake to assume the day couldn't get any worse.

Chapter Six

The groom declined to carry the bride over the threshold.

He could not, however, refuse to offer his arm, not with three hundred wedding guests thronging around them, eagerly awaiting any further tidbit of gossip that might be gleaned from the occasion. To her credit, she didn't grab or cling. She didn't need to. The deed was done. The fatal words had been said. One "I do" apiece, to be precise. As they moved through the crowded rooms of Pinchingdale House toward the ballroom, where the wedding breakfast had been laid out with enough lobster patties to satisfy even the Prince of Wales, Geoff felt the light touch of Letty's fingers burning through his sleeve like a brand.

Mary hadn't attended the wedding. She had been unexpectedly called away to minister to a sick relative, although Geoff suspected it was more an exercise in tact than charity. The identity of the relative had already changed several times in the telling.

Next to him, Letty's hair whispered against the stiff lace ruffle that framed the back of her collar. From the corner of his eye, he caught a quick, frowning glance of the sort she had been sending him all morning. Geoff pretended he hadn't seen.

He would have liked to pretend her away altogether, but she was too corporeal to ignore. The faintly flowery fragrance of her hair mingled with the warm smell of clean skin taunted his nostrils with memory, and the plump shoulders revealed by the cut of her dress were already pink from the heat of the crowded room. A freckle perched right on the edge of her collarbone. The French, who, in the lazy days of the ancien régime had tended to name such things, would probably have given it a silly sort of name, like a "*tatez-y*," or a "touch here." It beckoned the eye as effectively as a well-fluttered fan.

As to where the eye was drawn . . . Given the standards of the Season, her bodice was modest, even prim, but from the angle at which Geoff was looking, it did little to conceal the lush expanse of flesh so faithfully outlined in the carriage two nights before. The same night she had so effectively laid her trap.

Geoff abruptly relocated his gaze. No matter how charmingly her freckles beckoned, it didn't change the fact that she was a scheming little opportunist who had ruined her own sister's happiness in her pursuit of social advancement. Whatever her allure, he despised her for her perfidy. And himself for his.

The object of his unpleasant meditations tugged lightly on his sleeve. Geoff allotted her the most perfunctory of glances. "Yes, my sweet?"

Letty frowned up at him with eyes as wide and blue as the summer sky and as treacherous as the sea.

"Could we please go someplace private?" she whispered.

Geoff smiled and nodded as someone he had never met before proffered insincere good wishes. "Eager to make sure we can't annul?" he asked pleasantly.

It took a moment for the meaning of his words to sink in, and when they did, Letty colored right up to her eyebrows. Her fingers tightened on his arm. "To *talk*."

"We have plenty of time for that." Deftly extracting his arm, Geoff brushed the back of Letty's hand with the merest pretense of a kiss. Pretense it might have been, but it still made Letty uncomfortably warm in a way that had nothing to do with the crush of people in the room. Over her knuckles, his gray eyes bored into hers. "Till death do us part, in fact. So if you will excuse me . . ."

His departure was so neatly done that Letty hardly saw it happen. One moment, his fingers had tightened on hers to the point of pain; the next, he was gone, leaving her standing alone at her own wedding reception in a breach of etiquette the size of Scotland.

Clearly, he was not in the mood to talk.

Snagging a glass of champagne off a tray, Letty tilted it recklessly back, coughing as the bubbles seared the back of her throat. Liquid overflowed her glass and splashed onto the hem of her hastily refurbished best dress as someone jostled into her from behind.

"All right there, my girl?"

With a glass of negus in his hand, his white hair rumpled and his glasses askew on his nose, her father looked to be enjoying himself immensely. Letty had never been quite so delighted to see one of her parents.

"It depends on what you mean by 'all right.'" Letty paused for a moment to consider. Her reputation was in tatters, she was irrevocably married to a man who was assiduously avoiding her, and she had just spilled champagne all over the hem of her best gown. "Actually, no."

"Good, good." Mr. Alsworthy patted her absently on the shoulder. "A splendid illustration of the human comedy, isn't it, my little Letty?"

"More farce than comedy," said Letty, taking refuge in another sip of champagne. Any drama of seduction and discovery that featured her in a leading role had to be farce. All that was needed was a jealous older husband and a comic serving wench hiding in a wardrobe.

"We have all the seven sins displayed before us in fine array," Mr. Alsworthy continued cheerfully, as though Letty hadn't spoken. He waved a hand at the groups of chattering people, the dripping champagne, and the young fop who had collapsed in a corner of the room and was being discreetly hauled by his feet through the double doors by a pair of liveried footmen. "Gluttony, sloth, vainglory, even a spot of lust."

"I think you missed a few," said Letty. "That was only four."

"I did miss out envy, didn't I? Your mother is quite outdone. I saw at least three ensembles sillier than hers in the music room alone." Mr. Alsworthy rubbed his thin hands together in contemplation of it.

As always, Letty marveled at her father's ability to be so easily diverted. Why couldn't she do that? Her predicament would be far easier if she could step back and view the chattering wedding guests from the lofty height of condescension, scorning their petty gossip and pitying their small-mindedness.

Of course, her father wasn't the one being invited by elderly roués to participate in the reproduction of salacious French prints.

"I would find it all more amusing if I weren't the object of it," said Letty bluntly.

Mr. Alsworthy patted her reassuringly on the arm. "Buck up, my girl. There will be a new scandal next week, and you will be all but forgotten."

"But I will still be married," pointed out Letty, lifting her glass again to her lips. The bubbles didn't hurt quite so much, and the sour liquid was beginning to spread a comforting warmth from her cheekbones straight back to her ears.

"Alas, so go we all eventually. It is an unenviable but inevitable part of the human condition." Mr. Alsworthy's eyes lit upon a portly gentleman who was dipping his cup directly into the punch. "Ah, that's where Marchmain got to! His recent letter in the *Thinking Man's Monthly* on the implications of that man Smith's theories was entirely misguided."

"Was it?" muttered Letty.

She should have known better than to seek reassurance from her father. After all, this was the man whose idea of comforting a child afraid of the dark was to explain Plato's allegory of shadows on the wall of the cave. As a strategy, it had worked better than one might have expected. The story had put her straight to sleep, mooting the entire question of monsters in the closet.

Unfortunately, she didn't think a misconceived marriage could be similarly bored away with an explanation of the wealth of nations, not unless she slept for a very long time, indeed.

Some of the strain in Letty's tone must have penetrated her father's philosophical fervor. Mr. Alsworthy paused a moment in his pursuit of greater truths to comfort his daughter in her time of need.

"In navigating the shoals of matrimony, my best advice to you, my dear," he said briskly, "is to invest in a subscription to the circulating library and a stout pair of earplugs."

"Your very best advice is *earplugs*?"

"Yes, earplugs. I favor wax, although a bit of wadded cloth will do, as well." His duty discharged, Mr. Alsworthy beamed at his daughter, set his spectacles more firmly on the bridge of his nose, and said, "Pardon me, my dear. I'm off to set Marchmain straight. The man doesn't know the first thing about the principles of political economy."

With a gleam in his eye not unknown to Roman Caesars and the more bloodthirsty sort of pugilist, Mr. Alsworthy set off for the punchbowl and his prey, leaving his daughter prey to another sort of emotion entirely.

Earplugs. Letty shook her head, a crooked little smile curving her frozen lips. She didn't think they would do very much good in her situation.

Taking a fresh glass from a footman's tray, Letty scanned the crowd for her errant husband. He was standing with one arm braced against the plinth of a statue of Daphne, deep in conversation with Miles Dorrington and his wife, Lady Henrietta. As Letty looked on, he arched an eyebrow and said something to Lady Henrietta that caused her to swat him with her fan, and Dorrington to fold his arms across his chest in a gesture of mock menace. Lord Pinchingdale's lips curved fondly, and he shook his head at Lady Henrietta's retaliatory rejoinder. Watching them, Letty wanted, painfully, to be part of that charmed circle of easy camaraderie. She wanted Lord Pinchingdale to bend his head attentively toward her, as he was toward Lady Henrietta, to lift a dark eyebrow at her, with a hint of a smile lurking about his lips to take the sting from the gesture.

Letty looked dubiously down into the trickle of liquid left in her glass. Goodness, the stuff must be stronger than she had realized, to make her go all mawkish over her husband's inattention.

Husband. How absurd that a flimsy web of words, hastily gabbled by a sleepy cleric, could transform a stranger into the closest sort of relation. Wasn't there supposed to be something more to it? Affection, understanding . . . Letty sighed, wrapping her gloved hands around the coolness of a fresh glass of champagne, wishing she could press it against her burning cheeks instead. At this point, she would have abandoned any hopes of undying devotion and settled for a simple, "Hello, how are you?" Even a friendly smile would do.

She didn't even know if he expected there to be a wedding night. A proper wedding night, that was, involving one bed and two bodies. One wasn't raised in the country without a fairly good notion of what that entailed.

Letty firmly squelched the memory of the interior of a dark carriage, of gloved hands in her hair and warm breath against her lips and a strong arm across her back, pressing her to him as though she could never possibly be close enough. Those moments hadn't been hers. They had been borrowed from Mary under false pretenses.

But that didn't mean they couldn't come to some sort of amiable understanding, did it? Now that they were bound till death did them part, under pain of thunderbolts, the only sensible thing was to accept what couldn't be changed and make the best of it. From what Letty had seen back in Hertfordshire, one didn't need grand passion and undying devotion to make a marriage, just a certain amount of goodwill and forbearance. And earplugs. Perhaps her father was more sagacious than she had given him credit for.

She would just walk up, pause next to them, and say, "Good evening, my lord." Just a simple little *Good evening, my lord*. How difficult could it be?

"Good evening, my lord," Letty muttered under her breath, taking a tentative step forward. She worked at arranging her stiff lips into a suitable sort of smile. Curve the lips, bend the head slightly, try not to break the stem of the champagne glass. "Good evening, my lord."

Still yards away, Lord Pinchingdale turned his head to say something to Lady Henrietta. His eyes caught on Letty's. The genial smile froze on his face. His spine straightened and his shoulders stiffened, leaving a cold stranger in the place of the smiling man who had stood there a moment before. There was more warmth in the marble statue behind him. Letty felt an answering chill settle across her own face, and she hastily looked away, her greeting turned to ashes on her tongue. Turning her back defiantly on the little grouping in the alcove, she pretended to be fascinated by the scrapings of the musicians on their plinth on the far side of the room.

"Poor girl," said Lady Henrietta Dorrington, a small furrow forming between her hazel eyes as she watched the transparent pantomime. "How dreadful for her this all is."

"Dreadful for *her*?" echoed Geoff incredulously. Christian

charity was all very well and good, but that was taking it a bit too far.

Geoff scowled at Henrietta, who was making sympathetic faces at Letty's back. How did Letty get to be "poor girl," while he was cast as the villain of the piece? It wasn't as though he had climbed up through her window and hauled her off to have his wicked way with her. Geoff's conscience prodded him with the memory of that ill-advised kiss in the carriage. But that had been an accident. It wasn't as though he had *meant* to kiss her. Her as her, that was.

The devil with it! Geoff made a face of extreme annoyance. None of it, not the kiss, not this hideous party, not any of it, would have happened had Letty not been where she was decidedly meant not to be: in his carriage. And there was no reason for her to be in his carriage unless she had chosen to be there. In one fell swoop, she had deprived him of the right to marry as he chose, and a very large dollop of pride. She was about as pitiful as Napoleon Bonaparte.

And Henrietta was supposed to be *his* friend. What had happened to loyalty?

"May I point out that this poor, innocent creature happened to find her way into my carriage in the middle of the night? Your sympathy seems somewhat misplaced."

"These things happen to the best of us." Henrietta dismissed the point with a wave of her hand. "Think how terrifying it must be for her, forced into a loveless marriage with a man she barely knows."

Geoff raised an eyebrow at Henrietta. "I'm not sure I appreciate being cast as a fate worse than death."

Undaunted by the eyebrow, Henrietta shot Geoff a repressive glance. "Don't be silly. I didn't mean it literally."

"I'm immeasurably reassured."

"And don't go all supercilious and sarcastic," ordered Henrietta. "For heaven's sake, go talk to her. You can't avoid her forever."

"No, but he can try," contributed her husband cheerfully, leaning comfortably back against the wall. "It was a rum thing she did, you must admit."

"You"—Henrietta wagged a finger at her husband—"are not helping."

"I'm helping Geoff," explained Miles benignly.

"Such touching loyalty," murmured Geoff automatically, his eyes still on the small figure across the room.

"I thought so," agreed Miles.

"Didn't you recently promise something about forsaking all others and cleaving unto me?" demanded Henrietta of her husband.

Miles stretched complacently. "I don't think that was the kind of cleaving they were talking about, Hen."

Henrietta's cheeks pinkened. She hastily turned and gave Geoff a little push. "Shouldn't you be doing some cleaving of your own?"

"Later," Geoff prevaricated, thinking it might be a very good thing if all newlyweds were shunted off to an island somewhere until the initial phase of insufferable gooiness wore off. The fact that he was newly wed and not feeling the least bit gooey just made their cooing that much more annoying.

Sensing the need for masculine solidarity, Miles charged to the aid of his friend. "There's no rush. They do have the rest of their lives, you know."

"You do know how to cheer a fellow up, Dorrington."

"I try," said Miles modestly.

"Well, don't."

"Buck up, old chap. Forced marriages aren't all that bad." Miles gave his wife's waist a squeeze. Henrietta smiled up from under her lashes at Miles in a way that made Geoff's future seem even bleaker than it already did.

"Yes," Geoff agreed dryly, deliberately breaking into the tender moment, "but only when it's someone you *want* to marry."

Miles tugged at his cuffs. "I was hoping you would miss that bit."

"It was hardly likely to escape my notice."

"Give her a chance," urged Henrietta, adding, as though it settled everything, "*I* have always liked her."

"Hen," said Geoff wearily, "I appreciate your attempt to shove me into married bliss. I am happy you are happy. At present, I am not happy. And I am not going to be made any happier by your nagging at me. Can't we just leave it at that?"

The stubborn tilt of Henrietta's chin spoke more clearly than words.

Viewing it easier to deflect than to argue, Geoff turned to Miles. "If you have a moment, I need to discuss something with you."

"Something . . ." Miles indulged in an alarming series of facial contortions designed to imply clandestine activity. He mostly succeeded in looking like the victim of an unfortunate twitch.

"Something along those lines," agreed Geoff with a faint smile, feeling some of the hard knot of bitterness lodged in his chest loosen a bit. Even the best of romances might wither eventually, but friends . . . those lasted. He had his friends and he had his work, and in the grand scheme of things, while his pride still smarted at how easily he had been duped, he was still luckier than most.

Naturally, he couldn't express any of that to Miles, at least not without giving him a thorough drubbing at the same time, so he simply inclined his head toward the ballroom doors, and said, "If you'd like to join us, Hen?"

Henrietta shook her head. "Letty has been accosted by the Ponsonbys. And since someone ought to rescue her . . ." With a reproachful glance at Geoff and a kiss blown to her husband, she was gone, moving purposefully toward the far end of the ballroom.

"Do you think we ought to help Hen rout the vultures?" asked Miles, tilting his head in the direction of his wife.

Geoff's face hardened at the memory of Percy's appearance the other night, the final tug on a trap he had been fool enough not to realize was tightening around him.

"No," he said, steering his friend out of the room. "Under the circumstances, I'd say the Ponsonbys and my wife are most likely happily engaged in an orgy of mutual congratulation. Let's leave them to it, shall we?"

"WELL," SAID MRS. PONSONBY, leaning her powdered cheeks uncomfortably close to Letty's. "You have made a spectacle of yourself, haven't you?"

There was really no justice, reflected Letty, in being accused of being a spectacle by someone who had seen fit to cram no fewer than three peacock feathers into her frazzled coiffure. The stem of the central one had broken, and the unmoored eye bobbed in Letty's direction like the Dowager Duchess of Dovedale's infamous lorgnette.

"I wasn't without help," said Letty, thinking of Percy. The Lord had been clearly having an off day when he created the Ponsonbys. Percy was dim, Lucy insufferable, and Mrs. Ponsonby . . . Letty could only describe her as an unfortunate cross between Grendel's mother and Lady Macbeth.

Mrs. Ponsonby flicked closed her impossibly feathery fan and regarded Letty with extreme displeasure. "You, of all people!"

Letty knew that roughly translated as: *An insignificant little thing like you!*

"How could you?" admonished Mrs. Ponsonby. "Stealing your dear, dear sister's beau like that!"

Translation: *Why you and not Lucy?*

"Poor Mary," sighed Lucy, getting in a bit of a gloat at the expense of her prettier, more popular friend. "How humiliating for her."

Letty and her sister might not always be on the best of terms, but she certainly wasn't going to let Lucy Ponsonby stick her hypocritical little claws into her. "Mary has assured me that her affections are attached elsewhere," lied Letty stoutly.

In fact, what Mary had said was, "Now that you've pinched Pinchingdale I shall have to bring someone else up to scratch within the Season," but Letty didn't see the need to elaborate.

"Putting on a brave face, no doubt." Mrs. Ponsonby's bosom filled with pleased pity. "But for Mary to lose her beau—to you! Who would have ever thought it!"

"Who, indeed?" tittered Lucy.

She directed a telling look at Letty's gingery hair, which was, as usual, escaping its pins. Letty caught herself tucking the stray wisp behind her ear, and forced herself to stop.

Lowering her hand to her side, she leveled a long, hard look at Lucy, with her pretty face and discontented mouth and her dresses as fussy as the dressmaker could be persuaded to make them. Lucy had been on the marriage market for even longer than Mary, never quite seeming to grasp that her titters and flutters drove men away, even as Mary's beauty attracted them. For over a year, Letty had been forced to endure Lucy's jabs about her dress, her hair, her clothes, a million little snubs under the guise of being "helpful" to Mary's younger sister. And since there was nothing she could say without looking a shrew or causing a fuss, Letty had curbed her naturally blunt tongue and let Lucy jab.

Not anymore.

In a voice that sounded strange to her own ears, Letty said, "You're just upset that you didn't think of it yourself."

Lucy's mouth fell open in an entirely unflattering and gratify-ing way, and two round pink spots formed on her cheekbones. "Well, I never!"

"No, you didn't," agreed Letty, deciding that there were advantages to being ruined. "But it wasn't for lack of trying. I saw the way you tried to get Lord Pinchingdale out on the balcony at the Middlethorpes' ball. If you could have stolen him from Mary, you would have in a minute."

"I don't know how you can say such things," fumbled Lucy, tugging at the edges of her gloves in her anxiety. "Mama!"

"Because it's true," said Letty calmly. "You don't think Mary didn't realize? She found it amusing. Because she knew you couldn't possibly be a threat."

Lucy recoiled as though slapped.

Mrs. Ponsonby turned an alarming puce that contrasted unfortunately with her Nile-green frock. "Young lady . . . ," she blustered.

Letty lifted her head high and looked Mrs. Ponsonby levelly in the eye, buoyed by champagne and a year's worth of pent-up indignation. In a voice as quiet as it was deadly, Letty asked, "Don't you mean, 'my lady'?"

Those two simple words proved too much for Mrs. Ponsonby. "Lucy! We are leaving this house of . . . of . . . ill repute!" Mrs. Ponsonby grabbed her daughter, who was still desperately trying to explain to no one in particular just how Lord Pinchingdale had come to be on the balcony at the Middlethorpes' ball, and swung her in a wide circle.

Turning, she fired one last parting salvo at Letty. "You may be a viscountess, but you shall never be received in my house again!"

"I shall look forward to that," said Letty.

Behind her, Letty heard the low, rhythmic sound of someone clapping. Startled, she twisted around to find Lady Henrietta Dorrington, hazel eyes alight with glee, watching the retreating Ponsonby party with no little satisfaction.

"Well done!" applauded Henrietta. "I've been waiting for something like that for years. She looks just like a turtle from the back in all that green, doesn't she?"

Letty returned her smile, clasping her hands around the stem of her glass to stop them shaking. "I don't think I'm going to receive an invitation to Mrs. Ponsonby's next Venetian breakfast."

"Do you think if I stand conspicuously next to you, she'll stop inviting me, too?" asked Henrietta hopefully. "I would so love to be snubbed."

"Don't say that," said Letty soberly, feeling the energy that had buoyed her through her confrontation with Mrs. Ponsonby beginning to ebb away. "It isn't nearly as enjoyable as one might think. Except by the Ponsonbys," she added, with a valiant attempt at a smile.

Henrietta, who had only escaped a similar fate through the felicity of having committed her own indiscretions in another country—and the machinations of a mother whose ability to manipulate public opinion put Bonaparte's agents to shame—made a sympathetic face.

"I'm sorry. If there is anything I can do to help . . ."

Letty felt unaccustomed tears prick her lids, and blinked them quickly away. Aside from her father's advice on earplugs, Henrietta's was the first kindly meant statement she had heard all day. At least, the first kindly meant statement that was truly kindly meant, when one discounted all the double-edged barbs that began with "you poor, dear child," and inevitably ended with cheering comments about ways in which she might possibly atone for her disgrace—at some point in her declining years.

"I hadn't thought you would want to speak to me," Letty admitted. "You were friends with Lord Pinchingdale long before you knew me. And he can barely bear to speak to me after all that happened."

"What did happen?" asked Henrietta. "I certainly can't believe that either you or Geoff would behave in the way the scandal sheets claim."

"You've seen those?"

Henrietta looked a little guilty. "I only read them for the articles."

"Ah, Hen! There you are!" A large form bounded up, slinging an arm around Henrietta with a force that nearly knocked her off her feet. Letty prudently moved a step away. Belatedly noticing Letty, Miles mustered an unenthusiastic, "Oh, hullo."

"Where is Geoff?" demanded Henrietta, as Letty contemplated the best way to quietly fade into the background.

Miles tweaked one of his wife's curls. "You're meddling again, aren't you?"

"And you're trying to change the subject," riposted Henrietta, grabbing Letty by the arm before Letty could slip away. "Don't worry. Geoff will thank me for this later. Where is he?"

"It's a little difficult to say."

Henrietta just looked at him.

"Oh, all right! Geoff is . . . gone."

"You mean he's gone out?" ventured Letty, automatically turning to look at the door of the ballroom.

"I suppose you could say that," mumbled Miles, studying his own reflection in the polished tips of his boots.

"To his club?" Letty prompted. All gentlemen had clubs, even her absentminded father. She doubted theirs was the same club, since the one to which her father belonged featured a membership on the older side of sixty, chiefly known for their ability to hold a paper steady and doze at the same time.

"Er, no," said Miles. He cast a look of wordless entreaty to his wife.

Not having the slightest idea what he was entreating, Henrietta returned the look with interest, and more than a touch of exasperation. "And?"

"He's gone away," elaborated Miles, looking slightly hunted. He gestured helplessly with his hands. "Really away. Away, away."

"Away, away?" repeated Letty.

"What is that supposed to mean?" demanded Henrietta.

Miles contemplated the floor. "It means," said Miles, looking uncomfortably from Letty to his wife and back again, "that Geoff has gone to Ireland."

Chapter Seven

"Ireland." Letty turned the name over on her tongue. "As in the *country*?"

Miles cast a wary look over his shoulder at the remnants of the chattering, jabbering guests, those who hadn't either collapsed beneath the furniture or decorously gone home.

"Perhaps we should all adjourn to Geoff's study," he said with forced cheerfulness. "Hen?"

"Exactly what I was going to suggest," agreed Henrietta, nodding emphatically in approval. She slipped her arm through Letty's, leaving Letty feeling like a very small trout being towed along by a pair of determined fishermen.

Miles led the way unerringly down a series of corridors, away from the madding crowd in the reception rooms. It didn't escape Letty's attention that both Mr. Dorrington and Lady Henrietta appeared to know her new home far better than she did. Or that they referred to Lord Pinchingdale familiarly and fondly as "Geoff."

"After you." Miles wrenched open a door to a small, book-lined room, and set about lighting candles to alleviate the evening gloom, while Henrietta solicitously settled Letty into a large leather chair. The pale gauze overlay of Letty's hastily refurbished dress contrasted incongruously with the dark leather of the chair, a feminine intrusion into a masculine stronghold.

There was something rather unsettling about being in a room so clearly marked by her new husband's presence. His papers and books dominated the desk, all squared into tidy piles with the edges all lined neatly into place. The bindings on the books were as well-worn as her father's, if their placement more orderly, in a staggering array of subjects and languages. Letty made out the ornate, curled letters of the German presses, thin pamphlets in French, heavy treatises in English, and curious, narrow little books with Greek letters incised into the spine, the gilt letters glowing uncannily in the candlelight, like the aftermath of a wizard's spell.

Magic, indeed! Letty squirmed upright against the slick leather of the chair, determined not to fall prey to fancies. There was nothing at all magical about Lord Pinchingdale's departure—just something craven. Had he been planning, all along, to flee as soon as the vows were said? The study showed no signs of disarray; every drawer was neatly closed, every book in its place. Beneath a layer of indignation and champagne, Letty felt another emotion stir, an emotion that felt curiously like disappointment.

She would have thought Lord Pinchingdale many things, but not a coward.

"How long ago did he leave?" asked Letty, more sharply than she had intended.

"Half an hour. Maybe more," said Miles curtly.

Casting a reproachful look at her husband, Henrietta moved to stand protectively behind Letty.

Letty stared at the clasped hands in her lap, and rethought her question. "*Why* did he leave?" she asked.

Over her head, Miles and Henrietta exchanged a long look.

"He didn't even give an excuse, did he?" said Letty disgustedly.

"He doesn't really owe you one, does he?" said Miles, folding his arms across his chest like a Roman gladiator staring down a particularly uppity lion. "Not after the trick you played on him."

Letty grasped the arms of the chair and hauled herself upright. "The trick I played on him?"

"That's right," said Miles, nodding. "He told me all about it."

"What trick?"

"Oh, so you deny it."

"How can I deny it if I don't even know what I'm denying?" Letty paused and frowned, running back over the words in her head. There was something wrong with the sentence, but there was so much wrong in general that syntax and the possible odd double negative were the least of her worries.

"You mean to say that you didn't arrange for Geoff to be—" Miles paused in his role of Grand Inquisitor to cast a quizzical glance in the direction of his wife. "Dash it, Hen, what's the male equivalent of 'compromised'?"

"You think I compromised Lord Pinchingdale?" Letty's champagne-soaked brain boggled at the image.

Miles shrugged uncomfortably. "Something like that. So you can't blame old Geoff for haring off first chance he got."

"Why would I . . . but how would I . . . ?" Letty broke off and tried again. "But I didn't even know about the elopement until five minutes before!"

"I told you so," said Henrietta smugly, coming around to perch on the arm of Letty's chair.

"Told him what?" asked Letty anxiously.

"That you weren't a scheming adventuress," explained Henrietta.

"You all thought . . . think . . . I'm an adventuress? Me?" It was quite as absurd as her being perceived as a fallen woman, so miserably inapt that all Letty could do was gape.

"It did seem a little unlikely," Miles admitted, scuffing one booted foot against the red-figured Oriental rug.

Henrietta sent him a repressive look. "Not that you couldn't be a brilliant adventuress if you wanted to be," she said soothingly.

Miles rolled his eyes to the study ceiling at the vagaries of women, and went to uncork the brandy decanter. Laying the crystal stopper to the side, he poured amber liquid into a round-bottomed glass.

"I thought—" After the past few minutes, it was hard to remember what she had thought, or that she was capable of thought at all. Letty shook her head to clear it, and continued, "I thought Lord Pinchingdale was sulking because I'd gotten in the way of his elopement. Because I had interfered with his plans."

She straightened and squinted a bit as Miles pressed a glass into her hand.

"Brandy," explained Miles. "You look like you need it."

Letty didn't entirely agree, but she took the glass anyway, curving her hand around the rounded bowl to keep it steady. Whether it was her hand or her glass she was attempting to keep from shaking, she couldn't quite say.

"How could he have thought I planned this? It doesn't make any *sense*."

"It made sense when Geoff explained it," muttered Miles, making a second trip to the brandy decanter.

"Men!" declared Lady Henrietta, swinging a slippered foot back and forth as she perched on the edge of Letty's chair. "Incapable of adding two and two, the lot of them."

"I say, Hen, that is harsh."

"It's no more than you deserve for leaping to conclusions," said Henrietta, entirely undermining her stern words by throwing a kiss.

Letty hastily looked away. She took a tentative sip from the glass Miles had handed her. Being of a lamentably healthy disposition, she had never had the opportunity to taste brandy before. Letty made a face as the first drops hit her tongue. It didn't taste nearly as pretty as it looked in the glass. It tasted almost salty.

Letty took another small, diagnostic sip, and decided it wasn't nearly as bad the second time. A third sip rendered it almost pleasant, although she still couldn't understand why gentlemen seemed quite so enamored of it. But then, gentlemen were enamored of the oddest things. Cards, for example, and curricles, and punching one another for recreational purposes.

"Now that we've got all that straightened out," Henrietta continued, although Letty couldn't see that anything was straightened out at all, not even the chair, which persisted in swaying in a most alarming way, "where on earth is Geoff off to?"

Miles propped himself against the edge of Lord Pinchingdale's desk and took a fortifying gulp from his glass before venturing to respond.

"It was something to do with a horse."

Letty lifted the glass in her own hand so that the candlelight struck gold sparks off the pale liquid, and announced, "I don't think I've imbibed enough to believe that."

Miles grinned at her, a grin that both approved the sentiment and tried to make up for earlier mistrust. Letty appreciated the gesture, even if she did still feel as though someone had hit her repeatedly with a very large mallet. "Then you clearly need some more."

"What we all need," said Henrietta, protectively resting a hand on Letty's shoulder as Miles sauntered over with the decanter to top off Letty's glass, "are some explanations. Miles? Or did Geoff not bother to provide those?"

"Oh, he did. You know Geoff, thorough to a fault." Miles surrendered the decanter, stretched out his booted legs in front of him, and said apologetically, "It really was about a horse. A very special horse," he added hastily, as though that might mitigate the blow to Letty's pride. It wasn't very heartening to take second place to a horse, even a very special one. What horse could possibly be that special? It only reinforced Letty's conviction that his real motive had been to avoid her.

"I still don't see why he had to go tonight," mused Henrietta, giving voice to Letty's thoughts. "It could have waited till morning."

"No, I really don't think it could," said Miles, and there was a quelling note in his voice that Letty didn't quite comprehend. "This was a very elusive sort of animal."

"Ah," said Henrietta.

"Ah," agreed Miles.

"I don't understand at all," protested Letty.

"Have some more brandy," said Miles.

"To aid the understanding?" Letty wrinkled her nose in disbelief.

"No, to dull it. Trust me, it works," said Miles.

It wasn't working well enough. Letty's mind insisted on circling back over that awful scene in her parents' foyer—her mother had congratulated her on being compromised! Hugged her and praised her. And she, what had she done? Letty struggled to remember. She thought she had protested. She thought she had made clear that the match wasn't any more to her liking than his. But had she? Or had it all been said later, in private, with her father? That was the problem with memory, thought Letty despairingly. One knew what one had said—or thought, or felt—so one assumed that everyone else knew it, too.

Images, out of order, flashed through Letty's brain. Martin Frobisher, talking about snares. Mary, looking guileless in white at the head of the stairs. Lord Pinchingdale, barely meeting her eyes at the altar that morning, brushing a kiss across the air above her hand as though he could barely stand to be near her. And there was Martin Frobisher again, always there just when one didn't want him, talking about bagging a catch. Of course, Letty had known she hadn't planned any such thing, but to Lord Pinchingdale ... Suddenly, a great many things made a good deal more sense, and Letty rather wished they didn't.

No wonder he had gone to Ireland. It was only amazing he hadn't chosen Australia.

Letty buried her head in her hands and groaned.

"Letty?" Henrietta's hand closed around her shoulder and gave a gentle shake. "Letty, dear?"

"Yes?" croaked Letty, without looking up.

"Your hair is in your brandy."

"Oh!" Sure enough, one long lock had straggled out of her coiffure and found its way into her glass.

Letty peered owlishly at the soggy tress. "How did it do that?"

Henrietta exchanged a long, worried look with her husband. At least, Henrietta looked worried. Miles merely looked intrigued by the absorbent properties of hair.

"Letty, dear." Henrietta hunkered down next to her chair. "Would you like to come to us tonight? Rather than staying here on your own?"

"No." Letty shook her head determinedly. The word sounded good, so she said it again. "No. I'll be . . ." Drat, she knew there was a phrase for such things. Where had it gone? "I'll be all right. I'll be quite all right."

Ha! That was it. Letty felt as though she had accomplished something quite monumental; if only the floor would stay in one place. Funny, she had never noticed before how pretty the pink ribbons on her slippers were. Pretty, pretty pink ribbons. Pretty pink ribbons for a wedding that wasn't a real wedding. Letty felt tears welling up beneath her lower lids and closed her eyes hard, to keep the moisture where it belonged. It seemed to work. When she opened her eyes again, the room had a hazy glow, like peering into a lit room through a frosted window on a winter's afternoon, but the tears had gone.

Over her head, the Dorringtons were speaking softly, so softly that Letty only caught bits and snippets.

". . . nothing to be done now . . ." That from Miles.

". . . can't leave her . . ." said Henrietta.

The large form of Mr. Dorrington, effectively blotting out the candlelight, moved in front of her, and looked down at her with a practiced eye.

"You, Lady Pinchingdale," said Miles, not unkindly, "are going to have a hell of a head in the morning."

Letty latched on to the only relevant part of the sentence.

"I'm not really Lady Pinchingdale," Letty hastened to correct him. "It's all . . ." She meant to say "a mistake," but the words wouldn't come out right, so after three tries she substituted, ". . . wrong. It's all wrong."

Henrietta's hand gently touched her hair. To her husband, she said, "I may have to murder Geoff when he gets back."

"Don't joke, Hen," said Miles, sotto voce, but not quite so sotto that Letty couldn't hear him. "Someone else may do it for you first. You know he didn't have any choice."

"Not in that," Henrietta said, sounding immeasurably frustrated, "but he did in this."

Miles put his arm around his wife's shoulder in a way that made Letty suddenly feel very cold, despite the flames of the tapers in the candelabrum next to her and the brandy inside her. "It's a damnable situation all around, Hen, but it is what it is. I'm sure Geoff will sort it out when he gets back."

"I suppose," sighed Lady Henrietta.

"Please." Letty grabbed Henrietta's hand, struck by a sudden thought. "Could you . . . Could you not tell anyone he's gone?"

Henrietta didn't ask for any explanations. She cocked her head and thought for a moment. "We can tell everyone you've both already gone upstairs and don't want to be disturbed. That should give all the gossips something else to talk about," she concluded triumphantly, looking immensely pleased with herself.

"What about tomorrow," asked Miles, "when they see that she's here but Geoff's not?"

"Blast," said Lady Henrietta, looking less pleased. "Are you sure you wouldn't like to come to us? We could hide you. . . ."

"For two months?" interrupted Miles skeptically.

"Two months?" repeated Letty, wondering why her tongue suddenly felt far too thick for her mouth. "You think Lord Pinchingdale will be gone that long?"

"At least."

"It's only three days to Dublin," argued Henrietta.

"In good weather," countered her husband. "Besides, the, er, horse may take some finding."

"Is the horse missing?" asked Letty confusedly, still not entirely convinced there was a horse. It was very nice of them to try to pretend that Lord Pinchingdale wasn't just avoiding her, but this really was outside of absurd.

"It's a very dark horse," supplied Henrietta, with a very uncharacteristic curl to her lip.

Since it wasn't polite to ask too many questions when people were trying to do one a kindness, Letty removed a floating hair from her brandy, regarded the liquid philosophically, and finished the glass.

"Oh, dear," said Lady Henrietta, belatedly removing the glass from Letty's hand. "You're quite sure you'll be all right?"

Letty nodded, and the room nodded with her.

"I'll call on you tomorrow," said Henrietta, "and we'll think of some story to tell. Just remember, you're not alone in this. Right, Miles?"

"Absolutely!" said all three of Henrietta's husbands in unison.

"Thank you," whispered Letty, but the door was already closing, leaving her alone with the shadows in the recesses between her husband's books. There was a bust in a corner of the room, clearly a Roman, although Letty didn't know her Romans well enough to discern which Roman he might be. An eminent one, no doubt. Were there any noneminent Romans? There must have been, but nobody bothered to carve statues of them.

Taking up a candle, Letty made her way very carefully over to the marble head, holding on to the edge of the bookshelves for balance. Her pink slippers were terribly pretty, but they seemed to have grown harder to walk in. Letty paused in front of the statue, swaying slightly, and shone the light in his big, empty marble eyes.

"Well, what do you think I should do?" she asked, since it seemed a logical thing to do.

The Roman simply regarded her with a supercilious expression that reminded her uncannily of her husband. Funny, there was something familiar about that long, thin-bridged nose, too.

"Can't stay here," muttered Letty, shaking her head at the statue, who very kindly shook his head back. If she did, oh, how the Mrs. Ponsonbys would gloat! Poor Letty Alsworthy only married a day, and her husband already left her. Haven't you heard, my dear, he fled the country—yes, the country—just because he couldn't face the thought of spending a moment longer in her company. And who could blame him, such a mouse, you know? Not such a mouse, the way she tricked him—didn't you hear how she tricked him? My dear, why, everybody knows! No wonder he left!

"But I didn't," Letty protested, pressing her hands against her ears to blot out the whisperings of malicious voices. "I didn't."

She had to find some way to tell him the truth, right away, before all the malicious voices got to him. She had to convince him, convince him beyond a shred of suspicion that it had all just been a hideous accident, and that she was as much a victim of circumstance as he. That was all it had been. A hideous accident. Surely he would believe her if she could only just tell him. . . .

Letty stared at her new friend, the Roman bust, for a long, wide-eyed moment. That was it! The answer to all her problems.

Immeasurably cheered, Letty gave the startled head of Cicero an impulsive hug, not even wincing as his stone nose mashed into her ribs. It was quite the best idea she had had in a long time, an idea as brilliant as the shiny pink ribbons on her slippers.

If she could only manage to find the door . . .

A GOBLIN WITH A SAW was scraping away at Letty's head. She could hear the rhythmic scratch of it, directly against her skull. *Screech, scratch, screech, scratch.* She begged it to stop, but it only laughed and started rocking her back and forth, faster and faster, until Letty knew she was going to be ill, but she couldn't allow the demon the satisfaction of it. Her gorge rose and the room swayed and Letty moaned, burying her face into something that crackled and scratched. Letty paused, frowning in her sleep. A pillow. There was a hard surface beneath her, and a blanket scratching the underside of her chin. Letty's breath went out in a long sigh of pure relief. She was sleeping, of course, dreaming, in her own bed, and any moment now the maid was going to come to tell her she had overslept and hurry her downstairs to breakfast. Only the thought of breakfast made Letty's stomach lurch, and for all that she pressed herself as close as she could to the bed, the room persisted in swaying slowly from side to side, again and again, in a rhythmic rocking motion.

Letty's curiously swollen fingers began an exploratory expedition along the edge of the sheet. The weave was coarse, the edges frayed. Letty ran her fuzzy tongue over her chapped lips, not liking what she was feeling. She couldn't remember having been ill. She didn't remember much of anything at all, and the attempt made her head hurt. With a monumental effort, she pried open her crusted eyes. All she could see was a stretch of wooden wall, unpainted, unpapered, and marred with knots and wormholes.

Letty pressed her eyes shut again, fighting another wave of intense nausea, complicated by a pain that began somewhere behind her temples and marched relentlessly across the breadth of her forehead, like an entire troop of soldiers with a maliciously firm tread, all banging regimental drums.

With a little whimper, Letty pressed one tight fist to her forehead in a futile attempt to make the battalions stop marching.

"You've been sleeping *forever*," announced a cheerful voice, drilling against Letty's head like a hammer against tin.

Letty could only groan.

"You don't suffer from *mal de mer*, do you?" continued the relentless voice. "Because if you do, the voyage is going to be dreadfully dull."

"Voyage?" croaked Letty, wondering if she could still be dreaming, and, if so, how she could feel herself hurt so. Her very skin felt sore.

A weight plopped down next to her, causing the thin mattress to shift and settle. Letty swallowed hard as another wave of nausea surged against the back of her throat. Very slowly and carefully, Letty rolled from her side onto her back.

"You are seasick, aren't you?" demanded the girl, because by now, Letty had managed to crack open her swollen eyelids, and could see that her tormentor was a girl with black hair that bobbed about her face in unfashionably long ringlets. She looked unfortunately corporeal for a figment of Letty's imagination.

"I don't know," said Letty honestly. "I've never been to sea."

The girl laughed and sprang up off the side of Letty's bed, and Letty revised her opinion of her companion's putative age. For all the childishness of her bouncing ringlets, her face lacked the roundness of youth.

"Oh, I do like you! I thought I would, but you went to sleep as soon as you arrived last night, so it was impossible to be sure."

"Last night," Letty repeated fuzzily. Her throat felt raw and strange, and her voice didn't sound like her own. "Please," she asked, around the drums in her head, "is there any water?"

Her companion smiled brightly enough at her to make Letty's

bloodshot eyes ache, flipped her dark curls over her shoulder, and announced, "I imagine there must be. I'll be back in a trice!"

Letty let her head sink painfully back to the pillow, closing her aching eyes, weakly grateful to be left alone. Unfortunately, she was now entirely convinced that she had to be awake. She felt too awful not to be awake. She hadn't felt this awful since . . . well, never. Was there still plague in the world? If there was, Letty had caught it. The room swayed again, and Letty's stomach swayed with it. Whatever she had was clearly the prelude to a lingering and painful death.

Letty touched a tentative hand to her head, marveling that even the muscles in her arm hurt. The skin of her forehead felt cool and dry to the touch. Not ill, then, but . . . An unaccustomed glimmer on her finger caught her attention, a band of gold mounted with a greasy-looking green stone.

Married. Good Lord, she was married.

Letty swallowed hard over another surge of nausea as memories began returning, disjointed memories of the endless walk down the aisle, the groomsman's impudent eyes on her modest bodice, the shuttered look on her husband's face as he had turned away from her in a crowded ballroom. After that, it all grew distinctly fuzzier. Letty passed her furry tongue over her chapped lips and tried to remember. Lady Henrietta had been there, hadn't she? And Mr. Dorrington. Letty remembered the dancing points of candle flames in a dark room—even the image of light remembered made her wince—and Mr. Dorrington pressing a glass into her hand, calling her Lady Pinchingdale, and saying something about a horse. A horse? None of it made any sense. There was something else, something crucial. Pink ribbons . . . it had something to do with pink ribbons.

Pink ribbons and a midnight flight from the house. Oh, goodness. Letty clasped both hands over her mouth. Her trunk had still been packed, and she had ordered a footman to bring it

downstairs, blithely informing him that she and Lord Pinchingdale were going on honeymoon, and urging him to tell his
friends, all his friends, especially if any of those friends happened
to be in service in the Ponsonby household. Letty winced at the
memory. Oh, dear, she hadn't really, had she? But she had, she
really had. Why would she remember something like that if it
hadn't happened? And there was her trunk, lashed to the wall to
keep it from skidding.

Letty let out a little moan that had nothing to do with the pain
in her head.

It would have been less upsetting to have been kidnapped. At
least then she wouldn't feel quite so irredeemably idiotic.

"Oh, you poor dear!" The black-haired girl waltzed back in,
letting the door slam behind her with a reverberating bang that
set off an entire cannonade in Letty's skull. Letty was willing to
forgive her that for the life-giving ewer she held in one hand. A
bucket dangled from the other.

"The nice man suggested I bring this as well," reported the
girl, swinging the bucket so enthusiastically that Letty instinctively flinched. "Just in case." She dropped the bucket, setting off
a new avalanche of cranial pain, and poured from the ewer into a
glass that looked like it had seen better days.

Letty was in no mood to be picky. Taking the glass, she ventured, "Have we . . . met?"

"Oh, what an addlepate I am!" The girl looked like she was
about to bounce on the bed again, but, mercifully, she checked
herself and stuck out a hand instead. "I'm Emily Gilchrist."

"I'm Laetitia Als—" Letty broke off. She wasn't anymore,
though, was she? She was Laetitia Pinchingdale now. But that
wouldn't do, either, to announce to the world that she had run
off without her husband. As if she hadn't caused enough scandal
already! "Laetitia Alsdale. I'm Laetitia Alsdale," she finished, on
a desperate impulse.

"Are you from London, Miss Alsdale?"

"Mrs.," amended Letty, the gears of her mind grinding very slowly, but beginning to grind for all that. "Mrs. Alsdale. I'm . . . a widow."

"But you're not in mourning?"

"It was very recent," prevaricated Letty. "I hadn't the time to get clothes made up."

Emily nodded as though that made sense, setting her determinedly childish curls bobbing. "There'll be plenty of time for that when we get there. I do love shopping, don't you?"

Letty ignored the question at the end of Emily's statement. Running her tongue over her cracked lips, Letty forced herself to utter the fateful question. She thought she might know the answer, but . . .

"Get where?"

Emily regarded her indulgently. "You are bamming me, aren't you, Mrs. Alsdale? Dublin, of course. Where else would one go on a Dublin packet?"

Chapter Eight

By the following Wednesday, it was quite clear that he just wasn't calling. Even allowing for boy-time, a week and a half meant serious time lapse. Three days was normal. A week? Not optimal but still okay. But a week and a half? Lack of interest.

Pushing my computer bag more firmly up on my shoulder, I battled my way through the throngs of tourists on Queensway up toward the Whiteley's shopping center. Depression or not, a girl had to eat, and my little fridge had been remarkably barren of late.

Rather like my love life.

I had spent the past week in that purgatorial state between elation and despair, leaping for the phone every five minutes, drifting off into gold-tinged daydreams on the tube, and generally behaving like a besotted fourteen-year-old. I had replayed every word we'd ever spoken—with improvements—overanalyzed every look, and named all of our children. There were three of them, and they were named Amy, Richard, and Gwendolyn (by then I'd hit the outer realms of slaphappiness). They all had Colin's golden hair and my blue eyes, except for little Gwendolyn, who had red hair like me.

It was the children I really felt sorry for—poor little things, with no chance to ever exist.

To my right, Warehouse beckoned, with large signs boasting up to forty percent off on selected items. Usually, those red signs would have occasioned a fierce struggle with my better nature, an immediate abrupt turn to the right, and the purchase of completely unnecessary articles of clothing that would do nasty things to my credit card statement and live at the back of my closet with the tags still on for the next six months. Today, the sale signs failed to exercise their usual siren call. My feet and mind both continued inexorably on their chosen paths.

Last Monday, still buoyed by memories of the weekend, I had plunged into Letty Alsworthy's letters with nothing but contempt for the blind devotion that led Geoffrey Pinchingdale-Snipe to be bamboozled by her scheming sister. It was, I reflected smugly, just like a man to be so taken in by a lovely face and a vapid smile—and most likely other attri-butes as well. The only thing that confused me was how so intelligent a man as Geoffrey Pinchingdale-Snipe could fool himself so thoroughly. I had two theories, neither the sort one shares with academic journals, one being that the smartest men are often the most at sea when it came to dealing with the opposite sex (witness every computer science major I had known in college, and most of my male colleagues in grad school). Either that, or it was a reaction to the war, like all those men who rushed off to get married before shipping off for the front in World War II. The situation wasn't quite the same, but I would bet if I looked into it, there is literature on the topic about the need to create stability in a sea of troubles, the reestablishing of the fundamental human connection in the face of barbarism, and so on.

I didn't even have a war to blame.

I scowled at my own reflection in the window of Jigsaw as I stalked past, hating the comparison but unable to think of any convincing way to refute it. I knew it was true. A fat lot of right

I had to be psychoanalyzing Geoffrey Pinchingdale-Snipe, when I was doing the exact same thing, pinning all my hopes and desires on someone I barely knew—largely because I barely knew him. There's nothing so attractive as a blank slate. Take one attractive man, slap on a thick coat of daydream, and, voilà, the perfect man. With absolutely no resemblance to reality.

After all, what did I know of Colin, other than that he was a descendant of the Purple Gentian, he had a very nice aunt, and he was appallingly rude to visiting researchers? That last wasn't exactly a plus. I didn't even know where he had gone to school or what he did for a living. Somehow, in our few encounters, it had never come up. For all I knew, he could be the Demon Barber of West Sussex, slicing off people's heads and baking them into pies.

So much for Geoff building a future out of a pair of fine eyes. I had spun a fable out of a handsome face, a cute accent, and a few chance references that happened to resonate with me. Taken apart, bit by bit, my treasured hoard of memories was as tarnished and trumpery as a child's ring fished out of the bottom of a cereal box. So he had mentioned Charles II. Big deal. We were in England; unlike America, one could expect a certain basic familiarity with the country's more notorious monarchs. I had fallen, I realized, into that horrible, early stage of crush where everything becomes a point of commonality. If he compliments a song, your heart takes wing because, yes, you like music, too! Clearly, you are Meant to Be.

As one of my college roommates put it after I had run through a breathless round of perceived similarities that didn't mean much of anything at all, "Ohmigod! He breathes! And you breathe! It must be love!"

I hadn't succumbed to one of those all-consuming crushes since college. I had assumed it was one of those things one suffered through once and then got over—like the chicken pox. Unpleasant, messy, embarrassing, but once you've had it, you're done for life. I should have remembered that there are those rare sufferers who are cursed with recurrence—and it's always worse the second time around.

The weather didn't help. It had rained for four straight days, the sky night-dark when I left my flat in the morning, with no discernible change by the time I returned home at night. I had begun to feel like the little girl in the Ray Bradbury story who lives on a planet where the sun only comes out once in a cycle of years, and then for a brief hour while she's locked in the broom closet. In my case, it was the British Library, not the broom closet, but it came to much the same thing. My raincoat was beginning to attain the dispirited air of an old dog, limp and slightly mangy. We won't even discuss the state of my shoes.

If the research had been going well, perhaps none of this would have mattered. I could forge boldly through the dripping umbrella spokes outside the British Library, sit obliviously in the steamy confines of the tube, and endure with equanimity the ruin of my raincoat. But today I had come to the end of the Letty Alsworthy papers—at least, all the Letty Alsworthy papers the British Library would acknowledge owning—and I was no closer than I had been before to discovering the machinations of the Black Tulip in Ireland. Geoff and Letty's marital difficulties might be interesting reading, but their romantic peccadilloes did not a dissertation chapter make. I could just see the expressions of polite skepticism on the faces of the scholars assembled for the North American Conference on British Studies as I delivered my paper on "The Lives and Loves of the Associates of the Purple Gentian." They'd be dropping off in droves. And, incidentally, so would my grant money.

At that point, I was so low that I couldn't muster more than a feeble flicker of alarm at the thought.

If I were being fair, it wasn't really that bleak. I might have run to the end of the Alsworthy papers, but I did have a hunch as to where to look next—a hunch that didn't involve calling on either Colin or his aunt. Letty had written her parents, claiming to be on a wedding trip with her husband, but another letter, the very last in the collection, told a different story entirely. In the last two of her letters, addressed to her father immediately after her marriage, Letty had confided that she had followed her disappearing husband to Ireland. She urged her father to tell her mother that she had accompanied Lord Pinchingdale on a honeymoon trip, in the hopes that her mother would then blithely spread the misinformation around town. She was traveling, she informed her father, as a widow, under the name of Alsdale, and any urgent matters should be addressed to her in Dublin under that name.

I had to admire her nerve. It was beyond gutsy of her to pick up and go after her errant husband like that. Raw indignation had seethed through every line of that last letter, from her terse account of her husband's departure to the punctures in the paper where she had dotted her I's with piercing precision. Would I have had that sort of nerve in a similar situation? Probably not, when I couldn't even bring myself to call Colin. I would have sat alone at home and called it pride—much as I was doing now.

Tomorrow, I promised myself, dodging around a crowd of teenagers, I would type "Alsdale" into the computers at the British Library and see what came up. With any luck, there might be something from Letty's sojourn in Ireland, something I could use to track the movements of Jane and Geoff without having to resort to the Selwicks. And if my search for the apocryphal Mrs. Alsdale yielded nothing . . . Well, I'd have to think of something else. Maybe even a trip to the archives in Dublin, in the hopes that something might turn up there. But I would not, not, not call Colin. I thought about it and added another "not," just in case the previous three had seemed insufficiently resolute. He had made it quite clear that he didn't want to speak to me, and if he didn't want to speak to me, I didn't want to speak to him. So there.

Ducking around the big Christmas tree that was already up

in the middle of the mall, I skirted the booth selling sheepskin slippers and made straight for the Marks & Spencer at the far end of the mall. Above me, the PA system was already blasting out Christmas music, and the front display of Whittard's tea shop boasted a wide array of winter-themed items, from little mulling packets for wine to tins of cocoa decorated with stylized snowflakes and happy skaters. The front of Marks & Spencer was piled high with tinned plum pudding and dispirited-looking miniature fir trees in gold foil–covered pots. If they looked brown around the edges now, I couldn't imagine how they would survive till December, much less Christmas. It was only mid-November now, hardly late enough in the season to start buying Christmas trees.

At home, it would be nearly Thanksgiving.

Pammy would be having a Thanksgiving dinner for expats and assorted hangers-on at her mother's house in South Kensington next week, but it just wasn't the same. There wouldn't be my little sister dangling bits of Aunt Ally's organic pumpkin bread to the dog under the table, or any of the hundreds of other unspoken traditions that made Thanksgiving more than just another dinner party. Picking up a black plastic shopping basket from the pile in the front of the store, I wandered dispiritedly past the rows of preprepared sandwiches, unable to get excited about the wonders of egg and cress or chicken and stuffing, all in triangular little packages. It wasn't the right kind of stuffing. Stuffing wasn't supposed to be crammed into sandwiches and sold in plastic wedges. Stuffing wasn't stuffing without gobs of turkey fat clinging to the mushrooms and a large, bickering family digging into the gooey mess, scattering bits of corn bread across the tablecloth. Here, they ate stuffing in sandwiches and turkey for Christmas.

I was sick of here.

Everything that had seemed quaint when I first arrived in London had become alien and irritating. Those tiny little bottles of shampoo that cost as much as a full-sized one back home. The way the coffee shops all inexplicably closed by eight. The strange way street names had of changing halfway down a block. The fact that I couldn't get a tub of American peanut butter and no one seemed to sell skirt hangers. I wanted to go home. I missed my little apartment in Cambridge where the sink leaked and the closet door wouldn't close. I missed the rutted brick streets of Harvard Square, where my heels stuck between the stones and my boots slid out from under me in slushy weather. I missed the musty, charred smell of Peet's Coffee that clung to my hair and wouldn't wash out of my sweaters. The thought of the microfilm readers at Widener made me weak with nostalgic sorrow.

With my plastic basket hanging from the crook of my arm, I stared through blurry eyes at the array of preprepared foods. Instead of Lancashire hotpot and chicken tikka masala, I saw the weeks spreading out before me in an endless row of fruitless research and dinners for one. Same old library, same old dinners, same old rainy gray sky. Tomorrow and tomorrow and tomorrow, world without end, amen, with only the occasional outing with Pammy to enliven the gloom, and no chance of home till Christmas.

Only the buzz of the phone in my pocket stopped me from dropping my head into the frozen foods section and bawling.

Resting the edge of my basket on the shelf, I dug into the pocket of my quilted jacket, where I had stuck the phone for easy access during my incessant phone-checking stage. It would probably be Pammy again, I thought listlessly, tugging the phone clear of a fold in the lining. If it was, I'd have to hit ignore and pretend to have left my phone at home. I'd been avoiding Pammy, who tended to regard relations with men as though she were Napoleon and they an opposing army. She mustered her artillery, chose her position, and attacked. Over the past week, we had proceeded from "I don't see why you don't just call him already," to "You could find out where he lives and just buzz and see if he's home," to "If you're not going to call him, I will."

"No, you won't," I informed the buzzing phone.

Only, it wasn't Pammy's number on the screen. In my confusion, my grip loosened, and I had to do a little juggling act with the phone to keep it from plummeting into a pile of prawn sandwiches. It wasn't a London number at all, which ruled out Pammy, nor was it an American number, which ruled out my parents, my siblings, college roommates, and, of course, Grandma.

My withered spirits flamed to life with a surge that sent the blood rushing clear down to the tips of my fingers and up to my hairline. Sussex! I didn't know what the area code for Sussex was, but this was an English area code, and one that decidedly wasn't London.

I jammed down on the receive button so hard that I nearly broke a nail.

"Hello?" I demanded breathlessly.

"Hello, Eloise?" It was a male voice on the other end, but not the male voice I'd been hoping for. It was a nice enough voice, deep and wellmodulated, but it wasn't Colin's. Even across the uncertain cell connection—my cell wasn't terribly fond of the Whiteley's shopping center—his accent was decidedly American.

"Hello?" the voice repeated, as I stood there, disappointment seeping through me along with the chill of the freezer case.

"Oh, hi. Yes, this is Eloise," I replied belatedly, getting a grip on my emotions and my phone. If it was an American calling from somewhere in England, it had to be someone I knew. He certainly seemed to know me, if he was calling and asking for me by my first name. Maybe that Duke grad student I had met at the Institute of Historical Research? "How are you doing?" I gushed, to cover my confusion.

"I'm fine." The voice at the other end of the line sounded mildly perplexed, but game. "How are you?"

"Um, I'm okay. Just on my way home from the library," I provided cheerfully and unnecessarily, playing for time. It was no use. I was still drawing a complete blank in my attempt to determine the caller's identity. I gave up. "Who is this?"

"This is Jay."

"Jay!" I enthused, desperately digging about in my memory for any Jays I might know. There had been one in college, but that had been a very long time ago, and I had heard he preferred to go by James these days, anyway, now that he had become a serious proponent of postmodern literary criticism. "Hi!"

Damn, I'd said that already, hadn't I?

I was about to go for another round of "So, how are you?" or maybe a leading "So, what are you up to these days?" when the unidentified Jay stepped in, his voice turned to gravel by the uncertain reception of my cell phone. "You have no idea who I am, do you?"

"None," I admitted, scooting out of the way of a very large woman with a basket filled entirely with cat food.

There was a pause on the other end, and an exhalation that might have been a sigh, a breath, or simply interference on the line. The voice returned. "Sorry, I should have explained. Your grandmother gave me your number."

"Oh!" I stopped dead in the middle of the aisle. "Of course! She did tell me. I just . . . well, forgot."

Between midnight elopements, rebellion in Ireland, and disappearing Englishmen (by which I meant Colin, although I supposed it applied to Geoffrey Pinchingdale-Snipe, as well), grandparental setups had been low on my list of priorities. Besides, I never thought he would call.

"And you didn't think I'd call," supplied Jay.

"It's not nice to read the mind of someone you haven't even met yet," I said, leaning back against a tower of biscuit tins.

"It wasn't mind-reading," clarified the voice from Birmingham, "just common sense. I probably wouldn't have called—"

Should I be offended by that? I wondered, quickly shifting my weight back onto my own two feet as the biscuit tins started to wobble. Of course, I wouldn't have called someone Grandma was trying to set me up with either, but that was beside the point.

"—but it turns out we have a friend in common."

"Who?" I asked, deciding to abandon righteous indignation in favor of curiosity.

"Alex Coughlin."

"You know Alex?" I exclaimed, pressing myself back against the biscuit tins as a mother holding a small child's hand went by.

Just to be clear, Alex is not an Alexander but an Alexa. She is also my best friend. We had gone to school together from kindergarten until twelfth grade, parted with the utmost reluctance for different colleges, and maintained a voluminous e-mail correspondence ever since. We'd spoken and written less of late, due to a combination of the transcontinental time difference and Alex's grueling schedule as a second-year associate in the litigation department of one of the bigger New York law firms, but it was the sort of friendship that was too deeply rooted to be shaken by absence. Pammy might be on-the-spot, but Alex was a soul mate.

There was the sound of tapping in the background and a pause before Jay answered, in a preoccupied way, "She's dating my college roommate."

"Oh," I said. "Wow, small world."

"Hey," said Jay abruptly. "I'm going to be in London next Tuesday on business. Are you free for dinner?"

"Tuesday . . ." I stalled. "Um . . ."

It would make Grandma way too happy if I went. She might start giving my number out to yet more men. Probably unfortunate ones without all their own hair, into which category Jay might fall, for all I knew. And his mother was named Muffin. Or Mitten. Or something like that. And Alex's Sean was a nice guy, but wasn't there just a little something too incestuous about going out with his roommate?

And what if Colin called?

I looked down into my basket at the lonely little pack of chicken strips, the sparse array of yogurts, and the tiny carton of milk. Tonight, I would sit at the little round table in my subterranean flat, with a book propped up on the plastic flowered tablecloth scarred with the burn marks of a former inhabitant. After my solitary dinner, I would take my solitary plate to the sink, and fix myself an equally solitary cup of cocoa. If I wanted to be truly festive, I might even let myself have a marshmallow in it.

"Dinner would be lovely," I said firmly.

"Cool. Listen, I have to run, but I'll call you Tuesday and we can work out the details."

"Looking forward to it!" I trilled, and then winced at how eager I sounded. Like a pathetic, desperate spinster, delighted at any date. But it was too late to rectify it with a qualifying "Always nice to meet a friend of Sean's," or "It will be good to hear an American accent," or "Too bad my boyfriend is out of town for the week, or you could meet him, too." Jay had already rung off.

It was just dinner, I reminded myself, as I headed for the checkout. A casual, friendly dinner with a friend of a friend. Nothing to get all stressy about. Anything had to be better than another night staying in and watching reruns of *Frasier*. Not that I object to *Frasier,* per se, but there's something deeply depressing about having nothing better to do in a foreign country than watch American television.

And Colin wasn't going to call. Ever.

Alex was getting a phone call within the next day. Alex, I remembered guiltily, had left a "Hey, something just happened—give me a call!" message on my voice mail yesterday, but I'd been too preoccupied to call back. I would wager the entire collection of yogurts in my basket that the message had something to do with her boyfriend informing her that his college roommate was being set up with her best friend. I tried to imagine how that conversation must have gone, in boy-speak.

JAY: "Some crazy old biddy is trying to set me up with her pathetic granddaughter."

SEAN: "Bummer. Pass the chips."

Sean had gone to Stanford, and thus, like many New Englanders who had sojourned briefly on the West Coast, liberally flung around expressions like "bummer" and "dude" that real Californians would blush to employ.

I considered and substituted the sound of crunching chips for passing chips, since Sean was in New York and Jay in England, thus ruling out chip-passing, game-watching, beer-spilling, and those other rituals of male communication. My name would have been offered up, chips would have been spilled on Sean's end, and Alex would have called over to the phone to provide enthusiastic bona fides, along the lines of "She's my best friend in the whole world! You have to call her!"

JAY: "But her grandmother . . ."

ALEX: "No, really, she's fabulous. What a weird coincidence."

Unless, of course, Alex didn't want to encourage him to call me, in which case the hypothetical conversation would have been played in much the same words, minus the "You-have-to-call-her" bit, but in a tone of cagey wariness. Or did I mean wary caginess?

Tuesday with Jay. It sounded like the title of a Neil Simon play. It even rhymed. But at least pumping Alex for information and planning my wardrobe should get my mind off Colin.

I shoved my last yogurt into a plastic bag, firmly resolved. I would have dinner with Jay, delve into the intricacies of the Pink Carnation's escapades without any more help from the Selwicks, and generally forge ahead on an independent, Colin-free course. If the Alsdale lead didn't pan out, I could always try searching under likely aliases for Jane and Miss Gwen, or go at the problem sideways by researching Emmet's rebellion, on which there was a wealth of scholarship, looking for names or facts that just didn't fit the established narrative. Any one of those anomalies might lead me straight to the Pink Carnation—and, while I was at it, the Black Tulip.

I heaved my bag of groceries off the counter and strode boldly out into the mall, buoyed by my new-formed resolutions. And, unbidden, one last little mischievous thought crept across my mind.

Wouldn't it be wonderful if it made Colin jealous?

Chapter Nine

"Didn't I tell you it would be a splendid crush?" demanded Emily.

Letty wasn't quite sure "splendid" was the word she would have applied. Peering into the drawing room of the narrow red brick house on Cuffe Street, she was tempted to turn around and go straight back to her recently acquired lodgings. But going back to her lodgings meant being alone. Being alone meant thinking. As for thinking . . . It had become a very dangerous pastime.

Back in London, her thoughts had run along straightforward lines, organized into compartments such as "servants' wages," "placating parents," and "preventing sister from eloping." Ever since she had woken up on the Dublin packet, an entirely new category had monopolized her thoughts: Lord Pinchingdale. Late at night, long after Emily was fast asleep, Letty lay awake, rehearsing endless scenarios in her head. It hadn't escaped her notice that she grew more eloquent, and Lord Pinchingdale more easily convinced, in each successive daydream. By the time the boat had docked, delayed by a slight squall a mere day out of Dublin, Lord Pinchingdale was brushing a strand of hair off her cheek, gazing meaningfully into her eyes, and declaring soulfully that he had never truly seen her before.

Naturally, that was what would happen. Right after she was crowned Queen of France.

Reluctantly, Letty retrieved the remnants of her common sense. Soulful glances might not be terribly likely, but the more Letty thought about it, the more optimistic she was about her impromptu journey—at least, once the initial headache faded, and her mouth stopped feeling like a well-worn camel path. Thanks to Henrietta's revelations, she at least understood why Lord Pinchingdale had been treating her like the more disgusting sort of leper. Aside from that slight aberration, he had always struck Letty as a kind and reasonable man. Once she convinced him that she hadn't deliberately set out to ruin his life, they could both apologize to each other, and go on from there.

It all made excellent sense. Or, at least, it had while she was still on the boat.

Tomorrow, she promised herself. Tomorrow she would seek out her husband in his Dublin lodgings.

As for tonight . . . well, Emily would have been very disappointed if Letty hadn't accompanied her to Mrs. Lanergan's party, Letty rationalized to herself. Emily had kept up a constant monologue on the boat about all the wonderful things she wanted to do—and darling Mrs. Alsdale to do with her—once they got to Dublin. While shopping figured prominently, Mrs. Lanergan's annual party headed the list. Emily had planned her toilette, fretted over the ship's delay, and chattered about how many beaux she planned to attach.

"How do I look?" Emily demanded, swishing her pale pink skirts.

"Lovely," answered Letty, submitting to being towed into the drawing room, where women in pale gowns mingled with red-coated officers and dandies in gaudily colored frock coats. For such a butterfly creature, Emily had a surprisingly strong grip. "Really."

"Mere physical appearance," announced Emily's guardian, Mr. Throtwottle, repressively, stalking over the threshold behind them, "is a matter of extreme indifference to those who devote their lives to the cultivation of the mind."

Anyone could see that Mr. Throtwottle practiced what he preached in terms of dress. His clothes were a rusty black, his frock coat outmoded, his linen decidedly musty. The buckles on his shoes were so old that whatever paste jewels might have originally resided within the frames had long since fallen out, leaving only empty prongs in their place. Letty couldn't imagine a more inappropriate guardian for the flibbertigibbet Emily. Neither, apparently, could Mr. Throtwottle, who had gratefully handed Emily off to Letty for the duration of the voyage. By the time they had reached Irish shores, Letty's head rang with exclamation marks and swam with superlatives. Next to Emily's determined girlishness, Letty felt about a hundred years old.

Letty reached to straighten one of the pink flowers Emily had twined into a chaplet on top of her curls. "The flowers are a nice touch."

"Oh, thank you!" Emily beamed. "I wore them in honor of the Pink Carnation. He's so dreadfully romantic, don't you think?"

Letty had to confess that she had never given the matter serious thought. She found the whole topic of spies vaguely silly, at least the sort of spies who had their exploits written up in the illustrated papers and were dubbed romantic by empty-headed girls. Really, some of them were no better than highwaymen, constantly attention-seeking. One would think that a good spy would do his best to remain inconspicuous, rather than indulge in needless dramatics with black cloaks and mocking notes.

"I've read everything there is to read about him," said Emily dreamily, illustrating Letty's point admirably. "They say that he's a dispossessed French nobleman, flung out into the world. But I think he must be English, don't you, Mrs. Alsdale?"

"I haven't the slightest notion," said Letty, who was saved from replying further by the appearance of a middle-aged woman wearing a gown far too young for her years. The white contrasted unfortunately with the high color in her cheeks, and the soft muslin clung unforgivingly to her ample form.

Introducing herself as their hostess, she said eagerly, "I do hope you are enjoying my little party."

"It is as the poet says: 'And to Arcadia I go,'" intoned Mr. Throtwottle solemnly.

"Don't you mean *'et in Arcadia ego'*?" Letty asked. Her father had a habit of trotting out Latin aphorisms, largely because it drove her mother, who couldn't understand a word of it, utterly mad.

"Of course." Mr. Throtwottle's arched nostrils quivered briefly in her direction. "Isn't that what I just said? I translate from the Latin, of course," he added, for the benefit of the unenlightened, in which group he generously included Letty.

Mrs. Lanergan clasped her beringed hands to her bosom. "Such a joy it is to have a man of learning by one's side! Mr. Throtwottle, you simply must visit again."

"I certainly shall, my good woman. But now, if I may, I will seek out the solitude of your library."

Mrs. Lanergan's brow furrowed. "There is the colonel's book room. . . ."

"Would it be too much to hope that you possess a copy of the *Consolations* of Eusebius?"

"Boethius," muttered Letty, who had alphabetized her father's library no fewer than three times before finally giving up.

"Bless you," said Mr. Throtwottle, offering her his handkerchief.

Mr. Throtwottle departed for quieter regions, while Mrs.

Lanergan chattered on beside her, pointing out other guests to an enthralled Emily. *Et in Arcadia ego* seemed an inopportune sort of phrase with which to begin an evening of revelry, signifying, as it did, the presence of death and decay even in the midst of life's pleasures, like the snake twining through the apple-laden leaves in the Garden of Eden. Perhaps, thought Letty, Mr. Throtwottle was tonight's snake in the garden, a grim figure in his rusty black as he stalked among the party guests in their gauzy gowns and bright regimentals. Put a scythe in his hand, and he would look just like the picture of avenging Death in an allegorical woodcut.

The frivolous young couple just in front of him rounded out the morality tale beautifully, decided Letty. Aside from their more modern costume, they looked exactly like a Renaissance painter's image of an amorous shepherd and his lass in the classic pose of seducer and seduced, her head tilted up toward him, his hand on the back of her chair as he leaned to whisper in her ear behind the fragile screen of her fan, his dark head bent close to her fair one.

Whatever he whispered must have pressed the bounds of propriety, because the girl with the silver-gilt curls furled her fan and rapped her suitor sternly on the shoulder. Stepping neatly out of range, he captured the hand with the fan—and Letty caught her first full view of his face.

The room felt very close, and the band that fastened beneath her breasts very, very tight. The other guests pressed around her like birds of prey, too loud, too shrill, too near. The room was too hot, the scents too oppressive, and her eyes ached with the smoke of the candles. She wanted, desperately, to be back in London. Anywhere but here. Even tea with Mrs. Ponsonby would be preferable. Anything would be preferable to watching her husband kiss the hand of another woman.

All of Letty's daydreams charred and shriveled, like a posy fallen too near the fire.

If only there were an innocent explanation! Letty toyed with the stock characters of fiction, the unexpected double, the long-departed twin. For a moment, the latter almost seemed believable. The features might be the same, but this man, with his too-knowing eyes and his leering lips, had nothing in common with the contemplative man who had so tenderly paid court to her sister. But Lord Pinchingdale was an only child. She knew that, because she had overheard him telling Mary about it once, what seemed like a very long time ago, in a London ballroom. His father, older brother, and two younger siblings had all been carried away by the same virulent attack of smallpox when he was eight.

The girl couldn't be a long-lost sister or an Irish cousin. One didn't lean that close to whisper into the ear of a cousin, or smile at a long-lost sister in that slumberous, heavy-lidded way. Every movement screamed seduction. He had never looked at her like that, or even at Mary. With Mary, he had always been respectful, almost reverent, never with that challenging sexuality simmering just near the surface. It made Letty squirm with embarrassment, and something else, something that she didn't care to analyze.

Across the breadth of the drawing room, her husband was lifting the blond girl's hand to his lips. He paused in that pose, toying with the circumference of the sapphire bracelet that circled her wrist, running one finger around the jeweled length.

Letty's own hands clenched into fists. She could feel the Pinchingdale betrothal ring, the only concrete proof of her marriage, boring into her palm. On the boat, she had turned it around on her finger, wondering about the man who had given it to her, and what it would mean to make a true marriage with him. She had been naively, blindly optimistic, taking the ugly ring as a tangible token of things to come. Of promises given and meant. Oh, she knew that he didn't want to be married to her—it was hard to miss—but she had thought him an honorable man, not the sort to dishonor his vows a week after the wedding. Vows were vows, after all.

How could she have been such a fool? Spinning pretty daydreams while her husband of less than a week chased after the first skirt that caught his fancy.

Letty writhed in an agony of wounded pride. She remembered the endless conversations she had rehearsed in her head on the voyage over, the apologies she had made to him, the way his handsome face turned from condemnation to respect as she explained what had really happened that fateful night. Shaking his head with self-reproach, he would apologize for having misjudged her, and apologize again for having run off (in Letty's daydreams, he did a great deal of apologizing), pressing her hand between his and declaring that if he had known what she really was, he would have stayed. Sometimes, when Emily was fast asleep in the next bunk, and the ship rocked gently on the tide, and anything seemed possible, he would even lift her hand to his lips for a gentle kiss.

As Letty watched, Lord Pinchingdale kissed, not the woman's hand, but one gloved finger, turning the simple gesture into an act of homage so erotically charged that Letty blushed just to witness it, and more than one woman in the vicinity resorted to her fan. The blonde wagged her head and simpered in a way that was more invitation than discouragement.

Letty felt ill in a way that had nothing to do with the overspiced mutton she had eaten for dinner.

"Who is that?" she asked Mrs. Lanergan, doing her best to imbue her voice with nothing more than polite interest. "The girl with the blond hair."

Always delighted to assist where gossip might be had, Mrs. Lanergan leaned forward, her bosom straining precariously against her décolletage as she peered past Letty.

"Oh, that's Miss Gilly Fairley. Quite an heiress, they say—and a beauty, too! The woman with her is her aunt, Mrs. Ernestine Grimstone." Mrs. Lanergan indicated a dark-garbed woman who sported a ferocious scowl. The scowl, Letty was pleased to see, was trained directly on Lord Pinchingdale. At least someone in the room showed some sense. Lowering her voice slightly, Mrs. Lanergan added, "Between the three of us, she's a cold fish, that one. Or do I mean a sour grape?"

"Don't tease, Mrs. Lanergan!" protested Emily, sweeping aside Mrs. Lanergan's culinary metaphors with a shake of her dark curls. "Who is the gentleman?"

Under the circumstances, Letty found the use of the word "gentleman" decidedly inapt.

"That," said Mrs. Lanergan importantly, "is Lord Pinchingdale, newly come from London. And to my little soiree!"

"I take it that Lord Pinchingdale is, as yet, unwed?" The words cracked off Letty's tongue like buckshot. She wondered fleetingly what the penalties for bigamy might be. Mrs. Grimstone didn't seem the sort to let her charge settle for anything less than matrimony.

Unsuited to nuance, Mrs. Lanergan answered the question but ignored the tone. "Oh, quite! And a most eligible gentleman, too. I hear he has a splendid estate in Gloucestershire, and an income of no less than forty thousand a year. Although, from the looks of it, he'll not remain a bachelor long," she added, with a smiling nod at Miss Fairley, who was fluttering her unfairly long lashes with enough determination to set up a squall in the Irish Sea.

Letty set her chin and tried to convince herself that her husband's blatant defection didn't matter to her in the slightest. How could it, when he had never been hers to lose? The only hold she had on him was words spoken under duress. From what she had witnessed, she didn't want any hold on him, under duress or otherwise. Miss Fairley was welcome to him, infidelities, betrothal ring, and all. A pity there wasn't some way Letty could just sign Lord Pinchingdale over to her, as one might any other kind of property for which one no longer had any use, like a piece of barren land, or a horse with a tendency to buck.

"Don't despair, my dear," said Mrs. Lanergan, patting Emily reassuringly on the arm. "We have another unmarried peer present. He came over on his own private yacht. Just fancy! He's a bit older than Lord Pinchingdale, but still a very handsome man for all that."

Letty resolutely turned her attention back to her companions, away from Lord Pinchingdale's "handsome" face. He was a rake, a scoundrel, a cad, a bounder—there weren't enough words in the English language to plumb the depths of his vileness. And she didn't care. Not one bit.

But no matter how hard she tried not to look, all she could see was her husband, breathing amorous accolades into another woman's ear.

"THEY HAVE FIVE HUNDRED MUSKETS being stored at the depot on Marshal Lane," the notorious Lord Pinchingdale murmured seductively to the beauty simpering beside him. "And they've ordered one hundred pairs of pocket pistols and three hundred blunderbusses."

Miss Gilly Fairley plied her fan so that her silver-gilt curls wafted in the resulting breeze, the shining strands glittering like a web of diamonds in the candlelight. Beneath the cunningly contrived blond wig, not a strand of Miss Jane Wooliston's own stick-straight brown hair slipped out. In the flighty creature arrayed on a low settee next to Geoff, no trace remained of the chilly beauty who had excited the admiration of the dandies at Mme. Bonaparte's salons little more than a week before. Diana, they had called her, paying tribute to her reserve and her classical features alike, as the poets among them composed odes to the symmetry of her face and the gravity in her gray eyes.

There was nothing the least bit antique about Miss Gilly Fairley, whose cheeks were pink with the excitement of a party, and whose eyes were rounded in perpetual circles of naive wonder. Through the magic of her paint pots, Jane had somehow contrived to make her face appear rounder, her fine-bridged nose broader. The ribbons fluttering about her face and a careful application of shadow along her lids convincingly tinted her eyes with blue, and rendered her entirely unrecognizable, even to those who had known her before. It had taken Geoff several moments before he realized that the gushing creature who descended on him in a welter of ruffles was, in fact, the poised young lady with whom he had plotted to release his best friend from the clutches of the French Ministry of Police a mere two months before.

It was, thought Geoff in sincere admiration, a masterful transformation, all the more impressive for being so understated. Over the past two days, his admiration had only grown. Jane and her chaperone had arrived a week before, and they had already amassed an impressive dossier of treasonous activities.

The previous night, they had all attended the theater, intercepting a basket of oranges with messages stuck beneath the skins. Smelling faintly of citrus, Geoff had followed that up with a clandestine trip of his own down to the rebel depot on Marshall Lane, where he had lurked behind the windows in the guise of a beggar, eavesdropping on a rather uninspiring session of drink and folksong.

What was it about rebel movements that always seemed to demand expression in song? The French had gone for the same, coming up with catchy numbers about the liberty of the common man. Geoff had had that interminable "*Ça ira*" song stuck in his head for months after infiltrating a group of Jacobins in 1799. It still popped back into his head at inconvenient moments. Geoff caught himself humming "*Quand l'aristocrate protestera, le bon citoyen au nez lui rira*" under his breath and made himself stop. Wrong country, wrong mission, and it didn't even scan.

"Have you discovered the manufacturer of the weapons?" Jane asked in a breathy voice that managed to convey forbidden trysts and wavering virtue.

Geoff deftly stole her fan, holding it just out of reach as she squealed and made a deliberately abortive grab for it, causing her décolletage to swell perilously above her bodice.

"Daniel Muley. He lives at 28 Parliament Street," he whispered into her ear, as her hand joined his on the ivory handle of the fan. "It's unclear whether he's one of them, or just in it for his fee."

"The liaison?" Jane tilted her head back as though brought to the verge of a swoon by his improper suggestions.

"Miles Byrne. He works in a timber yard on New Street. I mean to examine it more closely tomorrow."

"Excellent," murmured Jane. She snatched the fan back from him, exclaiming, in a voice pitched to carry, "La, sir! How you do tease!"

"La?" inquired Geoff under his breath. "La?"

Jane permitted herself a tiny grimace behind the shield of her fan. "Needs must," she murmured.

"There can be no doubt that the devil is driving," acknowledged Geoff, remembering some of the scenes he had witnessed in Paris. The streets hadn't quite run with blood, at least not by the time Geoff and Richard had made it out of there, but severed heads weren't something a man forgot in a hurry.

Miss Gwendolyn Meadows, garbed in the widow's weeds of Mrs. Ernestine Grimstone, devoted and overprotective aunt, scowled disapprovingly at her fellow agent. "Refer to that Corsican upstart as the Prince of Darkness and you'll give him ideas above his station."

"Don't you mean below his station?" inquired Jane delicately, making sure to simper guilelessly at Geoff as she said it.

"Lord of the Underworld is too good for some people," objected Miss Gwen with a sniff.

Geoff and Jane exchanged a look of shared amusement that owed nothing to their theatrical talents.

"At least if he were in Hades he would be less trouble to those of us up here," pointed out Geoff.

Miss Gwen's parasol thumped against the ground dangerously close to Geoff's foot. "Occasionally you make sense, Pinchingdale. But tonight is not one of those occasions."

"I can only strive to improve myself under your tutelage," replied Geoff mildly.

"Hmph," said Miss Gwen, casting a suspicious glance at Geoff from beneath her veils. "Save the compliments for those gullible enough to enjoy them. I know a gammon when I see one."

Geoff prudently removed himself behind Jane before Miss Gwen's parasol could swing once again into action. They had tried to part Miss Gwen from her parasol, as too recognizable an element of her original persona, but Miss Gwen clung stubbornly to her sunshade, insisting that its utility as a weapon outweighed the possible threat of recognition. Geoff suspected she simply couldn't bear to give up poking people. Nonetheless, he and Jane had been forced to accede. It was either that or wrestle the implement from Miss Gwen's bony grasp.

Geoff managed quite a credible leer in the direction of Jane's bodice, patterned on his cousin Jasper at Jasper's most objectionable, as he leaned down and whispered, "Still no sign of Emmet?"

Jane lowered her eyelashes becomingly. "It is early yet. The note didn't assign a time."

"Pity, that." Geoff straightened slightly, using his new vantage point behind Jane to scan the occupants of the room, looking for any sign of Emmet.

The worst part of any mission was always the waiting. Waiting for their quarry to appear. Waiting for the quarry to say something useful. Hoping like the devil that the quarry wouldn't feel the need to sing.

The orange they had intercepted at the opera last night had

been entirely clear on one point at least; Emmet was to meet with his French contact at Mrs. Lanergan's annual soiree. It made, Geoff had to admit, perfect sense from the conspirators' point of view. Mrs. Lanergan's party was always a crush, crammed with the soldiers from her husband's regiment and those of the Anglo-Irish community who could be found in town during the summer months. As long as one sounded and looked like a gentleman, nearly anyone could achieve admittance, blending in with the crowd. From where he stood, Geoff could barely hear the pianoforte in the far corner of the room, where a young lady was singing a plaintive air, surrounded by three admiring second lieutenants and one none too sober captain.

There was something particularly cheeky about staging a treasonous assignation right under the noses of a quarter of the Crown's Dublin garrison. Not that any of the garrison would recognize treason if it stomped on their toes and ran back and forth, waggling its ears and singing, "Death to the tyrannous usurpers!"

In the guise of a foppish aristocrat fearing for his own safety, Geoff had broached the topic of rebellion with Colonel Lanergan earlier that evening. "Nothing to worry about," snorted the colonel, his broad, red fingers stretched comfortably across his waistcoat. "Demmed nonsense! Safer than Bond Street, Dublin is. The Irishers wouldn't think of rising, not after what happened in the 'ninety-eight. They've learned their lesson."

If they had learned any lesson, it was that it was damnably easy to conduct a full-blown conspiracy straight under the noses of the meager British force headquartered in the castle. It was quite exceptionally well-chosen timing. Most of the great Anglo-Irish nobles who might have sniffed out the whiff of treason among their tenants were off in London for the Season, their mansions shuttered and manned by skeleton staffs. The officials at the castle, missing the gaiety of home, were either doing their damnedest to reconstruct it in the bottom of a cask of claret, or had hared off for a spot of sport elsewhere, leaving Dublin for the rebels to bustle in. Even General Fox, commander in chief of His Majesty's forces in Ireland, was talking of leaving Dublin for a jaunt to the west.

Not far from him, Geoff could hear the shrill voice of Lanergan's wife, elevating his income by ten thousand pounds a year for the benefit of her audience. It made him feel a bit like one of the animals in the Tower menagerie. *This sceptr'd isle*, Geoff reminded himself. Cry God for Harry, England, and Saint George—or, in this case, King George. If his ancestors could shed their blood on the field of Agincourt, he could bloody well endure being eyed like a pig at market by a willowy miss and a comfortable-looking sort of widow in a gown that showed the signs of recent dyeing.

There was something familiar about that particular widow, something about the set of her shoulders and the tilt of her head that plucked at his memory. The lighting in the room was too dim to discern her hair color, and her face was entirely hidden from view. But there it was again, that twinge of recognition. Could she be Emmet's French contact? Geoff began to mentally run down his list of female spies he had known. Absent recent amputation, she was too petite to be the Marquise de Montval. She certainly wasn't that harridan who had gone for his eyes at the Sign of the Scratching Cat in Le Havre; she would have to have lost four stone, at the least. Fat Mimi, they had called her, none too imaginatively. The woman next to Mrs. Lanergan was pleasantly rounded, but Fat Mimi would have made four of her.

As Geoff's eyes narrowed on the little group, the woman tilted her head back to say something to the black-haired girl next to her, unwittingly positioning herself full in the glow of the sconce on the wall behind her. The candlelight struck amber glints in her exuberant mass of marmalade-colored hair, outlining with faithful precision a pair of wide blue eyes, a tip-tilted nose, and a mouth too generous for fashion. As he watched, she lifted her left hand to tuck a strand of hair behind her ear, and the ring on her third finger caught the light, the dark stone in the middle shining greasily in its heavy, almost barbaric, setting.

Geoff's stomach hit the gaily patterned carpet and kept on going.

"Oh, no," said Geoff, shaking his head. "It can't be."

"I assure you it can," replied Miss Gwen, looking affronted. "I decoded the message myself."

Geoff ignored her.

There might be hundreds of girls who might, at a distance, in an unevenly lit room, be taken for Letty Alsworthy, but there was only one Pinchingdale betrothal ring. The thing was so hideously ugly that no one would ever bother to fashion another. His grandmother, a pithy woman who delighted in scandalizing her vaporish daughter-in-law, had described it as a carbuncle masquerading as a jewel. It was a cabochon-cut monstrosity dating back to a medieval ancestor, a thrifty Norman warrior, who, rather than invest in unnecessary feminine baubles, had simply pried the jewel out of his sword to present to his bride— reportedly over the body of several of her recently slain relatives, who had just fallen prey to that selfsame sword. The last was just the sort of story his grandmother liked to tell, and was probably untrue, but it was too vivid an image to entirely banish.

And he, Geoff realized in disgust, was rambling. He was rambling to himself, which made it even worse. At least, in the context of a conversation, one could excuse rambling as part of a social exercise. But to ramble to oneself surely had to be a first step on the perilous path to madness.

"Lord Pinchingdale!" Miss Gwen's sharp voice called him to account, along with a nudge in the ribs.

Geoff blinked a few times to clear his vision. Perhaps he was mad already. How could one of sane mind possibly explain the appearance of his unwanted bride—and the Pinchingdale betrothal ring—both of which he had last seen five days before in the ballroom of his London town house? True, the passage from London to Dublin sometimes took as little as two days, but how would she even know he was going to Ireland? He had only told . . .

Miles.

Geoff's mind lurched back into place, and the world righted itself again. He wasn't mad; he wasn't hallucinating; he was just the victim of a critical error of judgment. Madness might have been preferable.

At the time, informing Miles of his travel plans had seemed a perfectly logical thing to do. He needed information about the Black Tulip, of which Miles possessed more than anyone else in London, having recently had a close and personal run-in with the woman. Miles, being an agent of the War Office himself, wasn't likely to go blabbing about Geoff's whereabouts, not unless he wanted to be one friend short.

He had failed to take into account the Henrietta factor.

Damn.

He should have foreseen that anything that he told Miles would be automatically passed along to Henrietta. And with Henrietta intent upon bridging what she perceived as a senseless rift between Geoff and his new bride . . . It was enough to make Paris during the Terror look like an interlude of halcyon peace. Aside from the small matter of the guillotine, of course.

"Oh, dear!" Jane's voice, deliberately shrill, sliced into Geoff's reverie as something thumped onto the floor just in front of Geoff's booted feet. "Lord Pinchingdale, I seem to have dropped my fan. Would you be so good as to retrieve it for me?"

Automatically, Geoff swept down to his knees, extending the fallen fan to Jane with a courtly gesture meant to recall Sir Walter Raleigh.

"We have a problem. A very large problem," he said.

"We?" cackled Miss Gwen, bestowing her gimlet eye on Geoff.

"We," affirmed Geoff, trying not to flinch as Jane batted him playfully about the head with her fan. A concussion was the least of his worries.

"Don't try to go foisting off your problems on us, young man." Jane waved her to silence. "What sort of problem, Geoffrey?"

"Not what," replied Geoff hoarsely, grabbing the edge of Jane's chair for balance as he wove unsteadily to his feet. He felt a bit as he had the first time he had drunk too much brandy, from a flask smuggled between him and Richard and Miles, hiding from their housemaster in an unheated back corridor at Eton. There had been that same sickening lurch in the pit of his stomach, and the vague feeling of something very wrong with the world. "Who."

"Isn't that what she just asked?" Miss Gwen tapped her parasol impatiently. "Don't waste time shilly-shallying over semantics. Who is it, Pinchingdale?"

"My . . ." Geoff choked on the relevant word. How could he admit to the presence of a hitherto undisclosed wife, when the integrity of their mission depended upon the continued pretense of his bachelorhood?

"Spit it out! We haven't all night."

Geoff made sure his back was turned to the room, grateful that they had chosen a corner that abutted a wall, not a window. "My wife."

That silenced even Miss Gwen.

Unfortunately, it didn't silence her for long.

"How could you be so irresponsible as to acquire a wife at this critical juncture?" demanded Miss Gwen.

"It was not a considered course of action," replied Geoff tightly.

"Clearly," sniffed Miss Gwen. "Was she a youthful indiscretion? A childhood betrothal?"

"There's no need to go into the details now," said Jane, effectively forestalling Miss Gwen. "Necessities first. Is she going to make a scene?"

Geoff glanced back at the small group next to a crude reproduction of a red-lacquer Chinese cabinet. His wife was frowning
at the carpet in a way that suggested that she had spotted him—
or, more precisely, that she had spotted him with Jane. But she
hadn't said anything. At least, not yet.

"I don't know. I don't think so."

It was infuriating not to be able to give a more definite answer, but what, after all, did he know of her? Nothing. Other
than that she had a damnable habit of turning up where she
wasn't wanted.

Jane nodded, content in that answer. "If she does, we'll deal
with it then."

"I'll think of something to tell her," said Geoff grimly. He
could think of several things. Most of them involved putting her
right back on the next ship bound for England.

Jane's keen eyes narrowed on Letty's deceptively guileless profile. "You don't trust her with the truth?"

Geoff's answer was succinct and heartfelt. "No."

"Hmm," said Jane.

Geoff didn't notice. His attention was arrested by something
else entirely. Or, rather, someone else entirely. A newcomer had
joined the little party around his wife, bowing in a way better fitted to Versailles than Cuffe Street.

"This was just what tonight needed," muttered Geoff.

"She seems to be occupied for the moment," commented Jane.

Geoff looked abruptly down at her, only belatedly remembering to leer. "I forgot. You haven't been in London for some
time, have you?"

"We," sniffed Miss Gwen, "have been rather occupied elsewhere." Her tone managed to imply that everyone else's time had
been lamentably misspent.

"Last month," Geoff explained tersely, one eye still on the little group around his wife, "Miles asked me to look into the background of one Lord Vaughn, who had recently returned to

London after ten years on the Continent. Miles thought he might be the Black Tulip."

"Which he wasn't," interjected Miss Gwen, with a superior look that conveyed exactly what she thought of Miles's deductive abilities.

"Which he wasn't," confirmed Geoff. "However, his behavior was still deuced odd. According to Miles, in the course of events, Vaughn admitted to an earlier association with the marquise. An association," he quickly added, before the gleam in Miss Gwen's eye could translate into speech, "of a romantic nature."

"And?" Miss Gwen flicked at the tassels on Geoff's boots with the point of her parasol.

"Miles and Henrietta entrusted the marquise into the custody of Lord Vaughn." Geoff met Jane's eyes, still and watchful behind the fringe of her fan. "Within the hour, she had escaped."

"With Lord Vaughn's connivance?" inquired Jane.

"That remains unclear." Geoff's lips twisted into a wry smile. "He, of course, claims not."

"Is there a point to this recitation?" demanded Miss Gwen. "Or are you merely trying to enliven a dull hour?"

"That," said Geoff grimly, indicating the man bending solicitously over his unpredictable little wife, "is Lord Vaughn."

Chapter Ten

"Lord Vaughn!"

Mrs. Lanergan flapped the fringes of her shawl in the direction of a man who stood a few yards away. Unmoved by Mrs. Lanergan's cry, he carried on his aloof perusal of the assemblage, contriving to project disdain without uttering a single word.

With a complete want of propriety that put even Letty's mother to shame, Mrs. Lanergan caroled, "Lord Vau-aughn!"

Looking distinctly pained, the man slowly pivoted on one silver-buckled shoe, and trained his quizzing glass in the direction of the unseemly hullabaloo. A study in shadow, the strict adherence to dark evening garb that looked distinguished on Brummell bestowed upon Lord Vaughn an otherworldly air, like an enchanter newly descended from his tower. Subtle silver threads lent luster to the otherwise drab fabric of his frock coat and edged the lace at throat and cuffs, mirroring the shading of silver along the sides of his dark hair. The only color to enliven his ensemble was a single ruby, set precisely into the center of his elaborately tied cravat, that smoldered like the fire at the heart of a dragon's cave.

"Ah," he drawled, allowing the quizzing glass to dangle from fine-boned fingers. "Our estimable hostess."

Lord Vaughn made a courtly leg, his silver rings flashing in the light as his hands gracefully inscribed the air in an obeisance that smacked of mockery.

Mrs. Lanergan preened. "Why, Lord Vaughn, how gallant you are!"

"How could I be otherwise to the one who has gathered together such an . . . entertaining company?" Lord Vaughn trailed his quizzing glass in a lazy circle that began with the shrill girl at the pianoforte, passed over two inebriated soldiers arguing about whose horse was faster, and landed upon the floral tribute perched haphazardly on top of Emily's black curls.

Letty would have winced for her hostess, but she was preoccupied with worries of her own. Concentrating on being inconspicuous, she sidled away from the betraying glare of the candles. Hopefully, Letty thought, Lord Vaughn wouldn't equate Mrs. Alsdale, widow, with Miss Laetitia Alsworthy, reluctant debutante.

She didn't think he would recognize her—most men were in too much of a rush to get to Mary's side to take much notice of her little sister—but something about Lord Vaughn's quizzing glass made Letty distinctly uneasy. His attentions had been fixed on Lady Henrietta Selwick, but that hadn't prevented him from dancing some five or six times with Letty's sister, nor had it prevented Mary from doing her best to inveigle Lord Vaughn into a declaration more solid than dancing. An earl trumped a viscount, especially when the earl was rumored to have some of the finest family jewels in England, and a country estate larger than Chatsworth.

Either Mrs. Lanergan knew about the country estate as well, or the yacht had been enough to convince her. With a matchmaking gleam in her eye, she laced her plump arm through

Emily's. "My lord, this is Miss Emily Gilchrist, newly come from school in England."

"How very edifying."

"And this," said Mrs. Lanergan, chivying Letty forward like a sheepdog with a particularly recalcitrant ewe, "is Mrs. Alsdale."

Lord Vaughn's heavy-lidded eyes conducted a knowing sweep of Letty's face, until she was quite sure he could have recited the location of every one of her freckles with unerring accuracy.

"Mrs. Als*dale*, is it?" he inquired delicately, with an emphasis on the last syllable that made Letty want to climb inside the Chinese cabinet and stay there.

Letty knew she should have quietly slipped off while Mrs. Lanergan was introducing Emily. But where? It wouldn't do for her cad of a husband to see her wandering alone through the party. The thought was enough to make Letty toss her ginger hair and smile archly up at Lord Vaughn.

"Indeed, my lord."

"Quite amazing, isn't it, how many familiar faces one may encounter in a Dublin drawing room."

"Really?" inquired Letty brightly, wondering if it would look suspicious if she suddenly ducked behind Emily. Emily, unfortunately, had already drifted away in search of greener gentlemen. Letty was on her own. "I haven't found it so."

"I could have sworn that we two have met before, and not so very long ago. In London."

"Have we?" Letty modeled her simper on Miss Fairley. "I'm afraid I don't recall."

"Ah, but I do." Lord Vaughn's polished smile allowed for no denials. He flicked his wrist in the direction of Letty's mourning dress. "You were not so somber then."

"My circumstances have changed."

"So it would seem. Married and widowed in . . . three weeks? How very expeditious of you, Mrs. Alsdale."

"It was all quite sudden," replied Letty helplessly.

"There are many ladies in society who would be glad to learn that trick of you."

"Tell them to use hemlock," suggested Letty. "It's faster than arsenic."

Lord Vaughn's eyebrows lifted. "Remind me never to offer you the protection of my name."

"Never fear, my lord, you are too corporeal for my taste." Better for Lord Vaughn to think her husband imaginary, rather than merely misplaced.

He accepted the misdirection with an appreciative inclination of his silvered head. "You are, I believe, a very resourceful young lady."

"One does what one has to."

A whisper of a smile played about Lord Vaughn's thin lips. "Just as I said."

"There is nothing heroic about necessity," demurred Letty.

"There is," riposted Lord Vaughn, wagging his quizzing glass at her, "in retrospect."

"That doesn't help one much at the time, though, does it?"

"You, my dear Miss . . . pardon me, *Mrs.* Alsdale, are too much the pragmatist. You have the resourcefulness, but you lack the heroic mentality."

"I don't see anything heroic in gilding base actions with the passage of time."

"Base is it?" said Lord Vaughn. "What of Odysseus? Trickster, liar, philanderer . . . hero."

The list of attributes all too forcefully brought to mind a more modern man, who could not be conveniently closed away within the pages of a book, his sins lightly debated as an antidote to a dull party. It was impossible to distinguish his voice among the general chatter, but Letty could feel his presence behind her like a large burr in her back. A particularly prickly one.

"A hero conceived by a man," retorted Letty.

"My dear girl," drawled Lord Vaughn. "I find that highly unlikely."

"You don't think Homer was . . . Oh." Letty's cheeks rivaled Homer's wine-dark sea.

Having achieved his desired effect, Lord Vaughn quirked an inquisitive eyebrow. "You, I take it, would prefer the prudent Penelope?"

Letty pictured Penelope steadily stitching away as Odysseus cavorted with Circe, a Circe with silver-gilt curls and a come-hither way with a fan. Odysseus was a rotter who wasn't worth the waiting. At that rate, Penelope should have turned out the suitors, taken over the kingdom, and ruled Ithaca alone.

"That doesn't leave me much to choose from, does it?" said Letty with a grimace. "Either the philanderer or the woman foolish enough to wait for him."

"I suppose you don't approve of Patient Griselda either."

Letty had always thought Patient Griselda the worst sort of ninny. "Patience," she said in her best governess voice, "is only a virtue when there is something worth waiting for."

Lord Pinchingdale most decidedly wasn't, any more than Odysseus had been, with his sirens in every port. What was she to do now? She could go back to London, to the spiteful conjectures of the *ton*. She could slink back to Hertfordshire, to her narrow childhood bed and quiet orchard. Neither option was terribly appealing.

Maybe that was why Penelope and Patient Griselda had persevered, not out of love, but from lack of alternatives.

Lord Vaughn spoke, uncannily echoing Letty's thoughts. "I have found that very few things are worth waiting for, Mrs. Alsdale." His face had settled into cynical lines, and Letty noticed, for the first time, the deep hollows beneath his cheekbones, and the lines on either side of his mouth. "That is why the prudent man takes and the fool merely anticipates."

"But then you simply have something not worth having a little earlier," said Letty, wondering where she had lost the skein of thought. "How is that any better?"

"Isn't the having better than not having? Asceticism is decidedly out of fashion these days." Vaughn's languid gesture took in the overly ornate room and equally overdressed guests.

His hand stilled with uncharacteristic abruptness just in front of a sallow youth, who was shambling over to them, scuffing his boots along the rug as he walked. In contrast to Lord Vaughn's elegant attire, the newcomer was positively unkempt, his mop of brown hair not so much fashionably windblown as simply unbrushed. Rather than attempt the intricate creases fashion demanded for the cravat, he had tied the cloth worker-style around his neck, tucking the edges under his limp shirt points.

No matter how unpleasant the newcomer, Letty couldn't help but be relieved to have been rescued from the tête-à-tête with Lord Vaughn. Her head ached with the effort of keeping away from the sharp side of his tongue.

"Ah, Mrs. Alsdale, I have a new pleasure in store for you." The way Vaughn drawled the word "pleasure" made it clear that it was anything but such a thing, and Letty felt a twinge of sympathy for the disheveled young man, who flushed and scowled at the design of vines on the carpet.

Lord Vaughn, reflected Letty, did seem to have that effect upon people.

Vaughn left only enough time for the sting to be felt, before continuing smoothly, "May I present to you my cousin, Augustus Ormond. But we like to call him Octavian. He is," commented Vaughn, with a sly, sidelong look at his cousin, "too early for empire."

"It is very hard being the youngest," said Letty warmly, trying to catch the boy's eye. Shamed out of all countenance, he continued to stare resolutely at the floor, his lips puffed out in an unattractive pout.

"I'm afraid your sympathies are wasted in that quarter, Mrs. Alsdale. Augustus may be young in looks, but he is old in sin."

"Looks are seldom any indication of character," responded Letty, her mind on her husband's ascetic features, the features of a poet or a philosopher, not a base philanderer who couldn't wait even a week after his wedding to pursue his amours.

Vaughn trained his quizzing glass on her abstracted face. "Do you truly think so, Mrs. Alsdale? I beg to differ. Unless, of course," he added, a slight smile playing about his lips, "a deliberate deception is employed."

"A deception upon others, or ourselves?" asked Letty bitterly.

"An intriguing point. The dandy, who seeks to convince himself that he is better than he is. The beauty, who is none. The widow . . ." Letty stiffened beneath her false mourning as Lord Vaughn's voice dwelled meditatively on the word. Lord Vaughn smiled pleasantly, inclining his head in the direction of Letty's dark dress. "But far be it from me to impugn another's honest grief."

Hamlet had used the word "honest" with Ophelia in just such a double-edged way. Right before he drove her mad. How apt, thought Letty irritably.

"You aren't going to advise me to get myself to a nunnery, are you?"

Vaughn acknowledged the point with a mild arch of the eyebrows. "How can I, when I am but indifferent honest myself?"

"And mad north by northwest, too, no doubt," muttered Letty.

"Tut-tut, Mrs. Alsdale. It's against the rules to borrow from a different speech."

"I wasn't aware there were rules," said Letty in frustration.

Vaughn's eyes glinted silver. "There are always rules, Mrs. Alsdale. It is simply more amusing to break them."

"Except for those who are left to pick up the pieces," drawled a new voice, from somewhere just behind Letty's left shoulder.

Letty started, unintentionally bumping against the man who had moved silently behind her. His sleeve brushed against the bare skin between her glove and sleeve. It was an inadvertent touch, but Letty felt the shock of it all the way down to her slippers. The faint hint of bay rum cologne clung to the fabric, redolent with memory.

Letty looked down at her gloved hands, not willing to give him the satisfaction of acknowledging his presence. The Pinchingdale betrothal ring glowered back at her, the dark surface of the cabochon-cut emerald seeming to swallow rather than reflect the light, an ill-omened ring for an ill-omened marriage.

"Ah, Pinchingdale!" Vaughn greeted the new arrival. "What an unmitigated . . . surprise."

"Vaughn." Lord Pinchingdale acknowledged the greeting with an almost imperceptible inclination of his dark head, moving forward slightly, so that he stood between Letty and Vaughn. "What brings you from London this time of year?"

Vaughn lazily raised his quizzing glass. "I might have asked you the same, my Lord Pinchingdale. Such an unfashionable time of the year to be in Dublin. One might have almost thought you were running away from something. Or someone."

Lord Pinchingdale shot Letty a hard look. Safely out of range of Vaughn's quizzing glass, Letty softly shook her head in a silent denial.

Vaughn missed the movement, but caught the direction of Lord Pinchingdale's gaze. "But I forget my manners! Have you made the acquaintance of the charming Mrs. Alsdale?"

Lord Pinchingdale bowed over Letty's hand. Under the guise of the seemingly impersonal touch, she could feel his fingers dig hard into hers through the kid of her gloves in a quick, warning squeeze.

As if she needed to be reminded!

"Mrs. . . . . Alsdale and I are some little bit acquainted," said Lord Pinchingdale, which was, as Letty reflected, true as far as it went. Aside from the tenuous formality of the marriage vow, they might as well be strangers.

"We have mutual friends," elaborated Letty, smiling innocently up at Lord Vaughn. "Percy Ponsonby, for one . . . Ouch!" Lord Pinchingdale's fingers had clamped in a viselike grip around the bare skin just above Letty's glove.

"Mrs. Alsdale," he drawled, "may I interest you in some lemonade?"

Letty shook her head sadly. "I find there is very little to excite the attention in a glass of lemonade. It is so uniformly yellow."

Lord Pinchingdale's lips smiled, but his eyes didn't. "If you object to yellow, perhaps we can find you a beverage of a different color."

"And if I don't want a beverage?"

Lord Pinchingdale's grip tightened in a way that convinced Letty that acquiescence was decidedly the better part of valor.

"I find I am suddenly seized with an intense longing for a beverage."

"I had thought you might be," murmured Lord Vaughn. "Enjoy your refreshments, Miss . . . pardon me, *Mrs.* Alsdale."

"You look overheated, Mrs. Alsdale," said her husband blandly, steering her forcibly across the room. "Let me escort you toward the window."

"What of my lemonade?" inquired Letty, just to be difficult.

"I'm sure you will find the fresh air far more bracing," replied her husband in a tone even nippier than the climate.

Letty pulled back against the iron grip on her arm, all but digging her heels into the carpet as he dragged her inexorably toward the darkest corner of the room. "The night air is reputed to be very bad for your health."

"That," muttered her husband, yanking her into the relative privacy of the window embrasure, "isn't all that's bad for your health."

"Was that a threat?" demanded Letty.

Geoff smiled charmingly. "Given the company you keep, consider it more of a prediction."

"At the moment, that would be you." Letty bared her teeth right back at him, using the opportunity to deliver a sharp jab in the rib with her elbow. "Would you kindly loosen your grip? I lost all feeling in my arm about five minutes ago."

"We've only been speaking for three."

"Funny, it feels like much longer."

Hidden beneath the crimson swags of Mrs. Lanergan's draperies, the two glowered at each other in untrammeled enmity. Geoff found himself grimly amused. Well, they were agreed in this, at least; neither of them wanted to be anywhere near the other. Which was more than he could say for his shameless wife's tête-à-tête with the highly suspect Lord Vaughn. A few inches closer, and the old roué would have been crawling in her bosom, like the asp to Cleopatra.

Leaning an elbow against the windowsill, Geoff demanded abruptly, "What were you discussing with Vaughn?"

"Certainly nothing of the nature you were discussing with Miss Fairley," Letty shot back.

"That," replied Geoff sharply, "is none of your affair."

"No, it's your affair, isn't it?"

"Coming over the jealous wife, my dear?" enquired Geoff, in a tone that could have corroded the iron railings around the door. "Don't you think that's a bit unconvincing under the circumstances? You're playing it a bit too brown."

"I'm not playing it, as you so eloquently put it, any way at all. Which is more than I can say for you! '*We're some little bit acquainted,*'" Letty mimicked in a passable imitation of her husband's urbane drawl.

"While you were being entirely aboveboard, *Mrs. Alsdale?*"

Letty flushed, and Geoff felt a childish pleasure at having scored a hit.

Taking a corner of her black-dyed sleeve between his fingers, he rubbed the fabric. "What are you in mourning for, Mrs. Alsdale? Your lost freedom? Or were you planning to kill me off, and merely donned the black as an anticipatory measure?"

"For that sort of joyous occasion, I would have worn crimson." Letty jerked her sleeve out of his grasp, inexplicably angered by the intimate gesture. She glared mutinously up at him. "You should be thanking me for traveling under another name. Or you might have some explaining to do to your Miss Fairley. A wife would certainly get in the way of your courtship, now, wouldn't she?"

That wasn't all that a wife was likely to get in the way of. Any residual pleasure he might have derived from baiting Letty abruptly dissipated as the true consequences of her appearance struck him. All it would take was one injudicious word from Letty—to Lord Vaughn, perhaps—and the entire underpinning of the mission would come unmoored. Oh, there were undoubtedly ways around it; Geoff frowned as he tried to think of one. After their display of amorous intentions, it was too late to pass Jane off as a relative. Having her play his mistress would deny her and her chaperone entrée into the drawing rooms of Dublin, effectively cutting off one of their most reliable sources of information. Miss Gilly Fairley and her aunt could conveniently disappear, to be replaced by some other combination of persons, but it was too late in the game for such a transformation. Her abrupt disappearance would raise questions, and a new persona would take time to develop, time they didn't have.

All of Geoff's frustration crackled through his voice as he rounded on his inconvenient little wife and demanded, "What in the devil possessed you to come out here?"

"I had something to tell you." She looked up at him, lips pressed together into a mask of self-mockery that made her look much older than her nineteen years. "It doesn't matter anymore. None of it does."

Geoff crossed his arms across his chest. "You're with child, aren't you?"

"What!"

Geoff's eyes lingered insultingly on Letty's lush bosom, which needed no help from ruffles to fill out the bodice of her dress. "Why else would you be so eager to seek the protection of my name? You needed a husband in a hurry, and I was there."

The words came out with much less conviction than Geoff had originally intended. It might have had something to do with the way Letty was staring at him, as though he were newly escaped from Bedlam.

"You think I'm with child?"

"That was the theory, yes," said Geoff, beginning to wonder how he had lost control of the conversation. This wasn't at all how he had envisioned her reacting. Tearful denials had been more the thing.

Letty shook her head disjointedly, looking anywhere but at Geoff. "This can't be happening," she muttered. "This just can't be happening. This isn't real life. It's . . . it's a Drury Lane melodrama!"

"So was your maneuvering me into marriage at the expense of your sister. Which play did you steal that from?"

"I most certainly did not. . . . May I point out that your coachman was the one who kidnapped me?"

"He couldn't have kidnapped you if you hadn't been there."

"An irrefutable piece of logic if ever there was," scoffed Letty.

"Fine," clipped Geoff. "Then you tell me what you were doing next to my carriage in the middle of the night."

"I was trying to protect my family's good name, which some people were doing their best to sully!"

"Oh, that makes sense. Save your family's good name by loitering about half-clothed in the wee hours of the morning."

It didn't help Letty's temper that the same objection had occurred to her. Several times. But what else was she supposed to have done under the circumstances? Roll over, go back to bed, and let Mary ruin herself? Blast it all, if he hadn't had the hare-brained notion of eloping with her sister, she wouldn't have been in that predicament in the first place.

"I—oh, why am I even bothering? What do I care for the good opinion of a philandering reprobate?"

Geoff itched to refute the charge, but when it came to a choice between the moral high ground and England, self-justification would have to wait. It galled him to be tarred with her brush, philanderer to her schemer, but there was nothing he could bloody well do about it.

That realization did nothing to improve his temper.

"An excellent point," he drawled, experiencing an entirely un-just satisfaction as Letty bristled at the insouciant response.

"Tell me," Letty demanded, "did you ever intend to marry my sister? Or were you going to carry her off and discard her when you tired of her?"

England was all very well and good, but some things were too much to be borne.

Geoff's hands closed into fists at his sides. He took a step closer, so close that the frill that edged her bodice brushed the folds of his cravat, and said, in the sort of implacable tone that preceded thrown gauntlets and swords at dawn, "I loved your sister."

"It didn't take you long to forget her."

"I—" Geoff broke off, hating the look of triumph on Letty's face at the telltale pause.

He hadn't forgotten Mary. He just hadn't thought about her much over the past week. The two were not the same thing. And whose fault was it that Mary had been driven from his mind? Not Miss Gilly Fairley's, certainly. Not even Napoleon Bona-parte's. It was all the fault of a stubborn woman with reddish hair, who persisted in turning up at the most inconvenient times and places and driving him utterly, bloody mad. Fine for her to twit him for forgetting Mary, when she was the one who had torn them apart. Geoff could feel his self-control beginning to fray, like a rope in the hands of a malicious child with a knife.

"At least I didn't steal my sister's betrothed," he snapped.

"You don't have a sister," flung back Letty.

"That," replied Geoff, a muscle beginning to tic dangerously in his cheek, "is not the point. The point is—" Geoff froze, arrested by a sound from outside the window.

"Ha!" retorted Letty triumphantly. "You don't even have a point, do you?"

"Shh!" Geoff flung up one hand to quiet her.

There it was again, a regular rhythmic tapping. With a muffled curse, Geoff whirled toward the window. Sure enough, there, just outside the glow cast onto the street by Mrs. Lanergan's brightly lit windows, a man with close-cropped dark hair was tapping his cane against the cobbles, deep in thought. And he was walking away.

"Don't you dare shush me!" Letty planted her hands on her hips. "I haven't even begun to tell you what I think of you."

"You'll have to begin again tomorrow," said Geoff, moving her rapidly aside. "We can finish our discussion then. Your servant, madam."

And with a bow so brief it was barely a nod, he was gone.

"What do you think you're—"

Letty bit off the angry words, partly because Lord Pinchingdale was already halfway across the room, but mostly because it was clear to the most intellectually challenged village idiot exactly what he was doing. He was leaving. Again.

How dared he run away just when she was winning the argument!

This time, she had had enough. She wasn't going to allow it. They were going to have it out here and now, or her name wasn't Letty Alsworthy . . . Alsdale . . . well, Letty.

Without pausing to grapple with the difficulties of identity, Letty wiggled and shoved her way through the crowd with a great deal less finesse than her perfidious husband. Mumbling, "Pardon me," and "I'm sorry," in a continuous monotone, she fought free of the crush, grabbing on to the handles of the drawing room doors with a huge gasp of relief.

Ha! She would show Geoffrey bloody Pinchingdale that he couldn't run away from her!

With a deep breath, she flung the portal wide and plunged into the hall—straight into a blue-and-scarlet mountain that grabbed her by the arms and wouldn't let her go.

Chapter Eleven

Why was it that whenever Letty Alsworthy turned up, everything went wrong?

Geoff swung himself down the front steps of Mrs. Lanergan's town house, landing lightly on the balls of his feet. Pausing, he peered down either side of the street. There was no sign of Emmet.

Geoff wished he could conclude that Emmet had just slipped around the back of the house, the better to conduct a clandestine meeting. Unfortunately, that theory was marred by the fact that when he had spotted him, Emmet had been heading away from the house. Unless it was merely a clever ploy to mislead pursuers, that could mean only one thing. The rendezvous was over. They'd come, they'd plotted, they'd left. And Geoff had missed it all. Every last syllable.

When he should have been scanning the room, he had been staring at his wife with Vaughn; when he should have been circulating through the crowd, he had been dragging his wife across the room; and when he should have been following Emmet to his rendezvous, he had been so busy slinging insults that Emmet and his contact could have had a revolutionary sing-along in the front hall and Geoff wouldn't have noticed. If it hadn't been for that rapping noise knocking him to his senses . . .

Over the throbbing of his thoughts, Geoff could still hear it, marking a measured rhythm against the cobblestone. Geoff stilled, willing it to be more than the pounding of his pulse or an aural illusion produced by his imagination. Holding his breath, he strained to listen. There it was again, a faint clicking in the distance. Emmet was still nearby.

Without wasting any more time, Geoff slipped off after the phantom thread of sound. It was coming not from the east, where Clanwilliam House and the Whaley mansion lorded it smugly over St. Stephen's Green, but from the west, the streets that led to the workers' districts just outside the bounds of the city proper. As he increased his pace, Geoff could just make out the dark form of Emmet ahead of him, taking the bend that led from Lower to Upper Kevin Street. Geoff didn't have high hopes that his pursuit of Emmet would lead to anything interesting— at least, anything more interesting than several new verses to "Lord Edward's Lament" and other fine examples of rebel song.

Geoff had followed Emmet along a similar route two nights before, down Thomas Street, through the White Bull Inn, and out a back door at that establishment, into a tiny yard that gave onto a nondescript house on Marshal Lane. Between dusk and dawn, Geoff had quietly searched the premises, taking note of the sacks of saltpeter in the cellar, ready to be mixed into gunpowder, the shrouded piles of muskets shoved beneath tables, the baskets of grenades hidden behind a false wall in the attic. And then there had been the pikes, thousands and thousands of pikes, stacked one on top of another in the loft, ready to be placed in the eager hands of volunteers.

There had been more pikes than guns. Geoff couldn't tell whether the profusion of pikes was a sign of lack of funds, since pikes could be manufactured easily and cheaply on the premises, with lumber provided by Miles Byrne from his brother's timber yard, or merely an indication that the more sophisticated weaponry was being hidden at another depot. Geoff knew there were others—he had searched two more the night before, one on South King Street, the other in the Double Inn on Winetavern Street, just opposite the majestic bulk of Christ Church. Both had been empty, only a trail of saltpeter and a lone grenade giving any indication of their prior purpose.

The weapons had to have gone somewhere. Into the hands of supporters? Geoff didn't think so, not without a firm date for a French landing. The United Irishmen weren't going to make the same mistake they had made back in '98, when a French force had landed a full month after the local population had already risen and been defeated. At least, they weren't going to make that same mistake without some help from him and Jane.

No, Emmet would want to make sure that his men didn't rise prematurely. If he had any sense—and he did—he would keep the armory concentrated in his own hands, to prevent an overeager follower from sparking an abortive uprising. But where?

Moving as softly as his stiff boots would permit, Geoff slipped down Lower Kevin Street after Emmet, taking care to keep his pace slow and his stance relaxed, merely a gentleman out for an evening constitutional after a too crowded party. Someone who slunk along the sides of buildings, making a point of keeping to the shadows, was far more conspicuous than someone who blithely occupied the center of the street. Emmet either subscribed to the same theory or had no thoughts of pursuit. He moved easily and openly, his boots clicking firmly against the cobbles of the street. His half-shuttered lantern cast an uneven glow around him, swaying from side to side as he walked.

And why should he worry about being pursued? Geoff wondered bitterly. If his own performance at Mrs. Lanergan's was anything to go by, Emmet and the United Irishmen had nothing to worry about. He could only hope that Jane and Miss Gwen had been more alert and might have garnered some clue as to Emmet's mysterious contact. Even so, it galled him to have to rely upon others for a task he ought to have completed himself.

It was bloody lucky that Emmet was in the habit of tapping his cane against the ground when overtaken by thought, otherwise Geoff would probably still be standing in that thrice-damned window embrasure, pointlessly quarreling with his wife.

And losing, which only served to add insult to injury.

Geoff was almost relieved when a sharp turn from Emmet distracted his attention from an increasingly uncomfortable line of thought. One minute Emmet was in front of him, the next he had disappeared sideways, taking a sharp left down New Street. That was not the route to the Marshall Lane house. Geoff felt a familiar anticipation beginning to build. He strolled casually through the juncture of New Street and Patrick Street, straight through to Dean Street, ascertaining with a quick sideways flick of his eyes that Emmet was still there. Emmet was hurrying down New Street as though proximity to his goal gave new urgency to his steps.

The street was all the clue Geoff needed. Emmet had to be headed for a rendezvous with Miles Byrne, at Byrne's brother's timber yard. And if Emmet intended to inform Byrne of the latest word from the French . . . A triumphant smile spread across Geoff's face. Despite Letty's interference, the evening wasn't lost yet.

Clanking down heavily on his heels to make his footsteps echo, Geoff kept on going just far enough down Dean Street to allay any potential suspicions. Switching to the balls of his feet, he doubled back to New Street, keeping to the shadows cast by the narrow houses that crowded close together in this poorer section of town.

Emmet glanced nervously behind him before slipping into the garden of the house that neighbored the timber yard, pursing his lips in a low whistle. An answering signal must have been given, because Emmet abandoned his shadowed niche in the lee of the garden gate, hurrying into the timber yard.

Geoff ducked into a small alley, not even so much a proper alley as a glorified gutter, against the side of a high-gabled house as a man hurried out to meet Emmet, bounding over piles of lumber with the enthusiasm of the very young. Geoff settled himself more firmly into his niche, trying to breathe as little as possible. His alleyway was clearly more used to housing sewage than spies.

It was too dark to be sure, but Geoff thought he could guess who the second man was. Miles Byrne, only twenty-three, and already in treason up to his neck. His curling, light brown hair was less elegantly dressed than Emmet's, and his small mustache twitched with excitement as he called out something in a low tone. A third man, an unknown, scuttled through the shadows to join the group, moving more soberly than Byrne. He was older than Byrne, his hair streaked with white in the pale light cast by Emmet's lantern, and wore the distinctive dress of a car-man.

It was a well-chosen disguise, reflected Geoff, making a mental note to assign someone to infiltrate the ranks of Dublin's hackney drivers. What better guise could there be for a revolutionary than posing as the driver of a cab? One had an excuse for being at strange places at odd hours, not to mention the chance of overhearing key tidbits from passengers who tended to treat a driver as little more than an extension of his horse. It certainly trumped standing in a pile of sewage, thought Geoff ruefully, regarding the muck clinging to the sides of his boots.

Instead of dragging his confederates inside, as Geoff had expected, Byrne gestured to a pile of timber hard by the garden gate. Emmet asked something and Byrne nodded, bouncing a bit on the balls of his feet. The third man shrugged, in a way that could have indicated doubt, impatience, or simply a stiff back. It was too far away, and Emmet's lantern emitted too little light to tell for sure. If only they would go into the office of the timber yard to carry on their discussion, Geoff thought wistfully. That would make his task far easier.

Going down on one knee, Emmet settled one of the large

beams over his shoulder and struggled to his feet, while the other two followed suit. Emmet, unaccustomed to such work, staggered a bit under the weight, while Byrne walked with a jaunty step and the third man, the car-man, followed steadily behind. They paraded past his hiding place, long slats of wood protruding behind them like cats' tails. Geoff pulled back to avoid being whapped in the face by the bobbing end of Byrne's plank, squared off at one end, and splattered with mud.

Geoff exited his smelly hiding place and followed them back up New Street, grateful for the labored breathing and heavy footsteps that filled their ears and masked any sounds of his own quiet pursuit. Any time they paused, he froze, ducking into doorways or between buildings. When they resumed, he resumed, like a child's game of statues. They passed the turnoff to Dean Street without stopping, and Geoff's pulse quickened with anticipation. Wherever they were going with their awkward burden, it wasn't the Marshall Lane depot.

Partway down Patrick Street, the odd cavalcade came to an abrupt halt, right in front of number twenty-six. As Geoff crouched behind a bush one house down, his chest swelled with silent satisfaction, despite the mud seeping through the knees of his pantaloons and the unfortunate smell wafting from his ruined boots. He had found the missing depot.

Of course, he still wasn't any closer to discovering the identity of their French contact, or what his business had been with Emmet.

Byrne turned his head to ask Emmet something, the plank on his shoulder swinging dangerously with the movement of his body, causing the third man to duck, stumble, and curse loudly as his own burden went crashing down to the ground. It made an odd noise as it connected with the cobbles, not a solid thunk, but an ominous cracking sound, as the entire piece of timber split down the middle. Something else hit the ground with a metallic clang, rolling dangerously close to Geoff's hiding place.

It wasn't a gun, or even a pike. It was a long cylinder of iron, and before the third man snatched the object back up, cursing beneath his breath all the while, Geoff saw that it had a pointed head, like an arrow.

Geoff had never seen one himself before, but he thought he knew what it was.

Where in the devil had the rebels acquired rockets? And, more important, how were they planning to use them?

SPARKS OF RED, GOLD, AND BLUE exploded in front of Letty's eyes.

Blinking did nothing to dispel them. They were, she realized after a confused moment, not the results of the blow to her head, but the component colors of the gaudily decorated tunic that currently filled her entire line of vision.

"Dear lady," exclaimed a rich masculine voice just above Letty's head, "this is well met, indeed."

"I can't quite agree," Letty gasped, struggling for breath. The stranger was holding her very hard, and the gold buttons on his tunic were digging into her ribs. She tried to turn her face away from the overwhelming smell of his cologne, scratching her cheek on the wool of his tunic. "Do you think you could let me go, please?"

"When you are the very woman I've come all this way to find?" he murmured somewhere in the vicinity of her hair. Letty could feel his hot breath all the way down to her scalp.

Letty's irritation turned to genuine alarm. Either she was the victim of a case of mistaken identity or she was being held captive by a madman who made a practice of wandering into parties to kidnap the first unescorted female who happened to barrel into him.

"I think you must be mistaken, sir," she objected, beginning to struggle in earnest. "Now, if you'll just release me . . ."

To her surprise, the crushing grip loosened, sending her staggering back several steps, fetching up against a small marble-topped table that tottered ominously on its spindly, gilded legs.

"My dear madam!" The madman flung himself at her feet. "Are you hurt?"

He reached for her hand. Letty scuttled sideways until the pressure of marble in her midriff arrested her progress. "No, no," she said rapidly. "I'm really quite all right. Please don't let me stand in the way of your going along into the party."

Much to her relief, the madman rocked back on his heels away from her and straightened. Maybe not so much to her relief, Letty amended, as the madman rose to his full height, the impression of size amplified by the breadth of the red and blue facings that made up his uniform. He probably wasn't any taller than her husband, but given her own lack of inches, it didn't take much to dwarf her.

Fortunately, he didn't seem to be preparing for another assault. Instead, he took his red-plumed hat from his head, revealing a thatch of carefully combed curly brown hair that tapered into long sideburns on either side of his face.

Sweeping a neat bow, he said, "Perhaps I ought to reintroduce myself. We met at your wedding, Lady—"

"Mrs.," gabbled Letty hastily, before he could utter the fateful name. Drat. She ought to have known this would happen sooner or later. What had she been thinking? She had been thinking, she realized grimly, that she would be reconciled with her husband, and there would be no further need for subterfuge. More fool her.

"Mrs.," she repeated. "Mrs. Alsdale."

Instead of arguing, the man regarded her with dawning understanding, and something underneath it that Letty didn't like at all. He looked oddly smug, although just what there might be about her marital difficulties to make anyone smug—other than Mrs. Ponsonby—she couldn't comprehend.

Before she could stop him, the officer took her hand and

raised it. With his lips hovering just above her knuckles, he stared meaningfully into her eyes.

"My cousin is a fool."

Letty removed her hand with more force than was strictly necessary. "Your cousin?" she asked warily.

Fortunately, the stranger showed no further inclination to seize any part of her person. He merely tucked his plumed hat beneath his arm, and smiled carefully down at her. "I am Jasper Pinchingdale. I stood groomsman to your husband at his wedding. Perhaps you remember me?"

Letty did. More precisely, she remembered the way he had managed to cut through several layers of cloth with one neat flick of his eyelids—and then yawned, as if the exercise hadn't been worth the effort. She didn't like him one bit better for the recollection. At present, his eyes were focused firmly above the neck, gazing at her as guilelessly as the most persnickety dowager could demand. All he needed was a white smock over his uniform and a candle in his hands to provide a credible imitation of a choirboy at evensong.

He took a very tiny step forward, saying, with studied humility, "Forgive me for prying, but I couldn't help but notice that you and my cousin seem to be at odds."

"Oh, we just travel under separate names for our own amusement," replied Letty pithily. "It's a little game we play."

"So beautiful," murmured Jasper, reaching out to place two fingers beneath Letty's chin, "and so brave."

"You're too kind." Letty slid neatly out of the way, leaving him crooking two fingers into empty air.

Jasper rallied rapidly. "I was desolated to hear that you had left town."

"Your spirits must be easily depressed."

Jasper threw his head back and laughed, revealing very large, even teeth.

"How could my cousin not appreciate such a wit?" Letty

could have told him that snippiness and wittiness weren't quite the same thing, but Jasper had learned his lesson. Without pausing for her response, he said expansively, "On the contrary, my lady—"

"Mrs.," corrected Letty.

Eyes narrowing slightly in irritation, Jasper soldiered gamely on. "On the contrary, Mrs. . . . er. On the contrary, I was simply disappointed by your departure. I had hoped to get to know you . . . better."

Letty only just refrained from rolling her eyes. That was all she needed, another rake. Another Pinchingdale rake, at that. The family appeared to breed them in excessive supply. Drat! Letty threw a quick glance in the direction of the front door, which was now firmly closed, the sound of her husband's boots no longer audible through the thick panels. While she had been detained by the suspiciously complimentary Jasper, the primary rake, the one to whom she was actually bound in matrimony, had managed to make good his escape.

There hadn't been awfully much time for Lord Pinchingdale to have arranged with his cousin to detain her, but it wouldn't take very much arranging, would it? Just a quick "Stop that woman!" tossed over his shoulder as he fled down the stairs, one rake to the other.

Letty pushed away from the wall. "Your duty to your family does you credit, Mr. Pinchingdale," she said acidly. "Now if you will excuse me . . ."

"I can excuse anything"—Jasper moved to intercept her—"except your absence."

It was a line straight out of *The Rake's Guide to Seducing Gullible Women*. It was an insult to her intelligence and to all of womankind.

"Why, Mrs. Alsdale!" trilled Gilly Fairley, emerging from the drawing room on a wave of perfume that rivaled Cousin Jasper's cologne. "Are you leaving already?"

Maybe not all of womankind.

"I was attempting to," replied Letty tightly, trying to think of one reason why she shouldn't dislike the woman, and failing miserably. One was supposed to be kind to poor dumb creatures, but that didn't mean one had to like them, especially not when they possessed graceful necks and willowy arms—or did she mean willowy necks and graceful arms? Either way, Miss Fairley had them and she didn't.

"But you can't go!" wailed Miss Fairley, lovely even in distress.

"Exactly what I was telling her," seconded Cousin Jasper, with a forceful nod.

With one impatient flick of her dainty wrist, Miss Fairley dismissed Cousin Jasper as if she were shooing away a fly. She looked appealingly at Letty. "Mrs. Lanergan said the most lovely things about you. I was so hoping to make your acquaintance!"

"Some other time, perhaps."

"What a brilliant idea! Oh, Mrs. Lanergan wasn't exaggerating in the least when she said you were a clever-clocks."

Letty was still reeling under being called a clever-clocks—*clever-clocks?*—as Miss Fairley carried impetuously on. "You will come to me for tea tomorrow, won't you? Oh, say you will, dear Mrs. Alsdale! We're at number ten Henrietta Street, the dearest little house. I just know we'll have the loveliest chat, and you can tell me all sorts of clever things."

Letty attempted to answer in a language Miss Fairley would understand. "Not to be a silly-socks, but—"

"Splendid!" Miss Fairley clapped her elegant hands in delight. "Two o'clock, then?"

"Unfortunately"—Cousin Jasper wiggled his way between Miss Fairley and Letty, no small feat for such a large man—"Mrs. Alsdale is already promised to me for tomorrow afternoon."

"I promised no such thing," protested Letty.

"In that case"—Miss Fairley beamed disingenuously at Letty—"there can be no obstacle to our having a lovely little coze."

Other than one inconvenient husband, that was. Letty looked from Cousin Jasper, who was stroking the plume on his hat with the complacent air of one who knew himself irresistible to women, to Miss Fairley, guilelessly beaming at Letty from her frothy nest of curls. It wasn't much of a choice. Even if Jasper's smugness weren't repellent in itself, her conscience pricked her on. Someone was going to have to warn Miss Fairley about Lord Pinchingdale. The girl clearly didn't have the sense that God gave a goose, and even if Letty didn't particularly care for her, she couldn't just stand by and let her be ruined. It vaguely occurred to Letty that this sort of reasoning had gotten her into trouble in the past.

But what more could possibly happen? She was already married to the man. It couldn't get any worse than that.

"No," Letty said glumly. "No obstacle, at all."

Chapter Twelve

It was sheer coincidence that Jay chose a restaurant in South Kensington.

As a dweller in the less posh segments of the city, I seldom had cause to come out to South Ken. The last time I had trudged up those tube steps, past the Kodak store and a vendor improbably hawking Persian carpets, I had been on my way to Onslow Square to visit Mrs. Selwick-Alderly, descendant of the Purple Gentian, and aunt to Colin.

At the time, the former had seemed far more important than the latter.

As I scurried across the street to the Brompton Road, I peered over my shoulder to the left, half expecting to see a phantom figure in a green Barbour jacket strolling into the aureole of the streetlamps, like Sherlock Holmes emerging from a Victorian fog. On the tube on the way over, I had run through half a dozen versions of the imaginary encounter. I would express surprise at seeing him, of course. He would remind me that we were just around the block from his aunt's flat (which I would pretend to have forgotten). He would ask what I was doing in South Ken, and I would let drop, ever so casually, that I just happened to be on my way to a date. Yes, a date. With a man. Leaving out little details like the fact that it was a grandparental setup and the guy lived in another city. Around that point, a cab would zoom too close to the curb. Stumbling back, out of the way, I would bump into Colin. He would put an arm out to steady me, but once there, he would find he couldn't look away. . . .

You get the idea.

And then I would hop back up, thank him for catching me, and exclaim that I really had to run, or I'd be late for my date.

There was another version, spun out in quite satisfying detail in the British Library cafeteria that afternoon, where I didn't pull back right away. "I meant to call you," he would say, as I swooned glamorously over his arm, defying gravity in the best of all possible ways. "But I was [hit by a cab; gored by a wild bull; in hospital with cholera]. Come to dinner with me, and I'll make it up to you."

Three bottles of imaginary wine, two drip-free candles, and one classical CD later . . .

I'd gone through the story so many times in my head, down to the worried lines on either side of Colin's eyes when I said "date," that it came as a shock when no tall, blond figure strolled up to me out of the mist. I caught myself craning my head backward, searching the rapidly moving pedestrians for a telltale glint of light on a blond head. Where was he? Didn't he know he was supposed to be here?

Clearly not. All I got was the screech of tires and a phrase of indecipherable abuse in a thick cockney accent as a cab narrowly missed clipping me in the knees.

It didn't seem quite fair for the cab to show up, but not Colin.

That, I reflected, shoving my gloveless hands into my pockets and concentrating my gaze grimly ahead, was the danger of day-dreams. Go down that route frequently enough, and they attained their own sort of reality. Maybe it all came of being in a profession where one lived within one's own head most of the time, consorting with the shadowy reconstructions of long-buried individuals.

Hunching my shoulders against the wind, I concentrated on not bumping into anyone. In the premature dark of November, with an overlay of rainy-day mist, the people hurrying past on either side of me might have been something out of a Magritte exhibition, nothing but walking raincoats and the occasional hat. They all seemed to know exactly where they were going.

I tried to remember where I was supposed to be going. I had spent so much time planning the imagined encounter with Colin that I hadn't devoted very much to the actual date. I knew it was an Indian restaurant, and I had a vague notion that it should be on the right-hand side. Jay had caught me on the mobile just before I'd gone into the Manuscript Room that morning. I hunched in the far corner of the third-floor balcony, speaking in a low mutter and trying to look as though I weren't on the phone. In about three minutes, he had efficiently conveyed all the salient information. Indian restaurant. Brompton Road. Seven thirty. I verified that I would be there, and he rang off.

It was a bit like making a doctor's appointment.

Unfortunately, I hadn't had the good sense to actually look up the restaurant on the computer before charging out to South Ken. After all, it was on Brompton Road, and even I knew where that was. How hard could it be to find? I had forgotten that Brompton Road goes on quite a ways. And I can get lost in my own room. I shoved my hands deeper into my pockets in a futile attempt to bring the two sides of my raincoat together, wishing the short, belted coat covered more of my knees. The clammy wind bit through my tights in the crucial gap between boots and skirt, making inroads up my thighs.

I knew I should have worn pants.

But the Colin daydream had demanded a skirt. So, like the deluded creature I was, I told myself it was all about being a good granddaughter and looking nice so that when Jay reported to Muffin or Mitten—or whatever her name was—Grandma wouldn't have to blush for her progeny's progeny. I hared off home early from the British Library, trading my sensible brown wool pants for a herringbone skirt and a clingy cashmere sweater. My last pair of tights had a run in them just above the knee, but I figured if I turned them the wrong way around, so the run was in the back, Colin—er, I meant Jay—would never notice.

Taking stock of the final effect, I'd been pleased—it looked like the sort of outfit I could have worn to the library, or at least the sort of outfit a nonacademic might imagine someone wearing to the library. Brown suede boots, only slightly mangy-looking from the incessant rain; herringbone skirt with leather piping that matched the boots and made my legs look longer than they actually were; and soft, cream-colored cashmere sweater that clung in all the right places, and darkened my hair from red to russet. The overall effect was quite pleasing. It was also cold.

Fortunately, just as I began to fantasize about woolly pajamas, the smell of curries arrested my attention. I made a sharp left, cutting off two people heading in the opposite direction, and stumbled gratefully through the doorway, almost colliding with a coat-tree. It was definitely a South Kensington restaurant. The Indian restaurants near me in Bayswater looked more like Chinese restaurants back home, with small, linoleum-topped tables crowded close together in low-ceilinged rooms. Here, both the decor and the clientele had a determinedly trendy look about them. The tables were all in bright primary colors, set with equally bold plates, shaped like a child's attempt to draw a square, all the lines just slightly off-kilter. Ahead of me, a long, glass bar, backlit with blue bulbs and red fittings, dominated the front of the room, dotted by tall stools topped in red, green, blue, yellow, and purple, like an uneven row of very ugly flowers.

I spotted Jay right away, standing by the bar, but not at it, just to the right of a bright red stool.

I would have known him even if he hadn't been scanning the

room in that blind-date sort of way, more apprehension than hope. There was something indefinably American about him. My father always says you can tell by the shoes, but I thought it had more to do with the way his brown hair was a little too neatly brushed, and his features a little too clean-cut, as if everything had been pressed out of a plaster mold, from the top of his neatly parted hair to the leather tassels on his loafers. Like a Ken doll.

I wondered if he bent at the waist. My Ken didn't, which was a source of great annoyance to his harem of Barbie dolls, who could never get him to sit down for dinner in the Barbie dream house. Maybe that's why he was standing instead of sitting at the bar.

Pushing such irrelevancies out of my mind, I gave a little smile and wave—just enough to indicate greeting, but not enthusiastic enough to be misconstrued as "take me now!"—and made my way toward the bar.

"Eloise?"

His voice in person was better than on the phone, less gravelly. Which made sense, given that it was coming from right there, rather than through strange, wireless contraptions.

"Hi!" I said, sticking out a hand. "And you're Jay?"

Rather than shake my hand, he did a clasp and pull. Taken off balance, I stumbled slightly as his lips brushed my cheek, landing heavily against the bar, and trying to look as though I'd meant it all along.

"Are you hungry?" he asked, signaling to a waiter.

I wondered what he would say if I said no.

"Starved," I replied.

As witty repartee went, so far we were scoring a zero. Next we'd be talking about the weather. No wonder I hadn't been on a date in over a year; it was about as lively as a trip to the dentist. The waiter stuck two menus under his arm and marched off among the brightly colored tables with their mismatched plates. We followed.

"Did you have a nice trip from Birmingham?" I asked, in the interest of keeping the conversational ball rolling.

"Not bad," he said, draping his too neatly folded raincoat over the back of his chair. And there was silence. I concentrated on shaking the deep blue napkin out over my skirt. Jay rearranged his coat. The waiter hovered solicitously.

"Would you care for a drink to start?" the waiter asked.

Would I ever.

I ordered white wine. Jay ordered beer.

As the waiter retreated, I observed Jay covertly from behind my menu. At least he wasn't a wine snob. That was a point in his favor.

But beer ... it was so deliberately unpretentious that it smacked of pretension, like a plaid shirt. It screamed, I'm just one of the guys. Wouldn't a man who was comfortable with his own masculinity be able to order a glass of wine? What was he trying to prove?

I realized I was staring, and scuttled back behind the neatly printed rows of saags and naan, feeling like an idiot.

I was going to stop it *now*. Ordering beer didn't mean anything other than that he felt like beer. And I wasn't allowed to read into his entrée order, either, or the fact that he'd chosen to wear a jacket but not a tie. A jacket without a tie was a bit like a designer beer, too dressy to be really casual. I'd be willing to bet his apartment was filled with furniture hewed off at odd angles, expensive electronic devices from Sharper Image, and dishes that had been deliberately treated with a lumpy glaze designed to make them look like the painstaking product of Guatemalan peasants (only twenty bucks per plate at Bloomies).

Staring unseeingly at a neat column of entrees, I remembered something Alex had said to me ages ago. Okay, fine, three months ago, but it felt like ages. I'd been moaning about my single state, and griping about the dearth of datable prospects in London. After I'd explained why every single person at Pammy's latest dinner party—even the single ones of the right age who didn't live with their parents and had no obvious deformities—was ineligible for some reason or other, there had been a long pause.

"Nobody wants me," I moaned. "I'm going to be alone forevvvvvvver."

In one of those very measured voices that people use when they know they're saying something that their hearer is not going to like, Alex had said, "Have you ever thought, Eloise, that it's not that they write you off—it's that you write them off?"

No, I hadn't. Me write them off? Who was kidding whom here? I couldn't help it if men were scared away by the fact that my degrees were better than theirs.

"Uh-huh," said Alex.

She just didn't understand. How could she, when she'd been with Sean since college? Dating had changed. After about twenty-six or so, it got gruesome, all those defensive men out there who were just looking for sweet young things to bolster their egos. Look at the way Grant had ditched me for that twenty-two-year-old art historian, the one who thought all his articles were brilliant, giggled at even the lamest of his puns (and a pun is, by definition, lame), and would never have pointed out that his argument in footnote forty-three made no sense. I had little lines next to my eyes when I smiled, and sometimes even when I didn't smile. I was too old, too prickly, too opinionated.

Maybe Alex had been right.

After all, here was a perfectly presentable specimen of American manhood sitting in front of me, whose only flaws thus far were excessive grooming and dubious beverage choice, and I was already racking up the reasons why we would never work and preparing a mental report to Grandma on same, to be presented in bullet points, in triplicate.

It wasn't his fault he wasn't a snippy Englishman.

In fact, that ought to be to his credit. That, I thought, scowling at the menu, was my problem. My stomach always went into flutters for the wrong sort of man. I chose the showy, the flashy, the obvious. I gravitated to those men who exuded brash confidence, the sort who could usually be found dominating a podium or monopolizing the conversation at a cocktail party. Underneath the garrulous exterior, they were inevitably melting marshmallows of insecurity. But by the time I discovered the gooey center, it was always too late. I was stuck.

Take Grant as case in point. Brilliant at a podium, needy as hell in private.

"Would you like to share some naan?" I asked Jay, as part of my genuine, good-faith effort to give the date a chance.

We solemnly discussed the merits of onion as opposed to garlic naan. Countries have been ceded and boundaries redrawn with less deliberation. The waiter hovered a bit, left to bring our drinks, and then hovered again. I could practically see him thinking, "Sod it all, just order them both and get it over with."

We finally settled on onion and placed our order. I ought to have felt a sense of great accomplishment. Instead, I just felt tired. And hungry.

I settled back in my chair, which had a curious egg-shaped back, and wrapped my fingers around the stem of my wineglass.

He really was perfectly good-looking. No warts. No visible deformities. He didn't have a squeaky voice, or a lisp, or an embarrassing overbite.

It shouldn't matter that the sight of him didn't set little butterflies fluttering in my chest. I'd had flutters for Grant in the beginning, and, far more recently, for Colin. Flutters didn't last. Shared background and experience did. As he handed his menu back to the waiter, I totted up all the reasons why Jay was a good idea. Nice boy. No warts. Friend of the family. Steady job. I didn't even know if Colin *had* a job.

Jay, I reminded myself. I was supposed to be focusing on Jay. Not Colin.

"What are you doing in England?" I asked, beginning the obligatory first-date inquisition. "Grandma didn't say."

"I help technological service providers actualize their human resource objectives," Jay said.

I could have sworn the individual words were all in English, but they didn't seem to fit together in any comprehensible way. I broke it down into its component parts and attempted a translation. "You work with computers?"

Jay smiled tolerantly. "Close. I work with people who work with computers."

"Ah," I said intelligently. "So what's your role, then?"

I won't attempt to reproduce the answer—I couldn't do it justice. Essentially, his role seemed to have something to do with herding temperamental computer scientists into line and making them work harder and more efficiently. This was followed by a long explanation of something called "interfacing," which boiled down to being a middleman between clients and the computer scientists. The computer scientists apparently spoke Java, with a side of Klingon, and the businesspeople communicated in various dialects designed to maximize the number of syllables, while minimizing actual content.

"How interesting!" I exclaimed. It sounded deathly dull. "How did you get into that?"

It turned out that when he graduated from college, with a degree in econ, he knew a guy who knew another guy. Three guys later, we had made it past the first joyous euphoria of the Internet bubble, politely mourned the wreckage of his first two Internet start-up companies, and gone backpacking in the Himalayas. At least, I think he said the Himalayas. Wherever it was, they had mountain peaks and no hair-dryers.

"Birmingham must be pretty dull after that," I said.

"I'm not there most weekends. My mother said you're in school here?" Jay asked, politely turning the conversation to me. He added, "I have some friends at the LSE."

I'd been through this before. Independent researchers, not affiliated with an English university, tended to occupy a somewhat
anomalous position, for all that there were a lot of us in London.

"I'm actually doing my doctorate at Harvard, but I'm here on
my research year," I explained. "So I'm still affiliated with Harvard, even though I'm over here. Almost everyone in the history
department goes abroad in their fourth or fifth year to do their
dissertation research."

"And you're in . . ."

"My fifth year," I supplied.

He didn't say "And you're not done yet?" although I could tell
he was thinking it. I gave him points for that. I'd never forget
Grandma's reaction when I told her my degree would take an av-
erage of seven years, possibly more. Panic on the other end of the
phone, followed by, "You can leave if you get married, can't you?"

"That's a lot of time," he said instead, which I supposed was a
more neutral way of expressing the same sentiment.

"It's a long program," I agreed. "We used to have fourteenth-
years floating around the department, but they just passed a ten-
years-and-you're-out rule."

"Ten years?" Jay choked on foam. "My MBA was only two.
And that was one year too long."

"Well, people get sucked into teaching," I explained. "You're
only funded for your first two years, so after that, you have to
teach to support yourself while you write the dissertation. But
teaching tends to expand to fill all available time, so it just becomes a vicious cycle: You teach so you can write, but you're so
busy teaching that you have no time to write. It just goes on and
on, and suddenly people wake up, and they've been there for ten
years. Like Rip Van Winkle," I added helpfully.

"What's your dissertation on?"

"Spies during the Napoleonic Wars. You know, like the Scarlet Pimpernel."

"The who?" Jay squinted at me over his beer.

"The Scarlet Pimpernel. There was a book about him, by Baroness Orczy. It's pretty well-known."

I tried to tell myself that it didn't matter that he didn't know who the Scarlet Pimpernel was; after all, most Americans have only a nodding acquaintance with English history and literature, and I'd already shown I know nothing at all about either computers or business. If he was willing to overlook that, I could overlook historical illiteracy.

Alex would be so proud of me.

Jay was clearly making an effort, too. "What was it called?" he asked.

"*The Scarlet Pimpernel*," I said apologetically.

"Oh," said Jay.

Since that was proving to be a conversation killer, I hurried on. "But he's only one of the spies I'm researching. Right now, I'm looking into the role of English spies in quashing the Irish rebellion of 1803."

It belatedly occurred to me that if Jay didn't know who the Scarlet Pimpernel was, he certainly wasn't going to know about the Irish rebellion of 1803. Oh, well. The name was fairly self-explanatory—like the color of George Washington's white horse. The boy had gone to Stanford; he should be able to figure it out. At least, I hoped he could.

"An Irish rebellion." Jay mulled it over. Well, he'd gotten the salient bits right, even if he seemed to have forgotten the year already. "It doesn't upset you?"

Many things upset me. The computer in the Manuscript Room. Miss Gwen's handwriting. The fact that the BL cafeteria had been serving watery potato soup for lunch, and had been all out of croutons, to boot. But I couldn't say the Irish rebellion was on that list.

I took a sip of my wine. "Why should it?"

"Come on," said Jay, grinning at me. "Red hair. Kelly. You have to feel some loyalty to the Irish side."

I shrugged. "It was two hundred years ago. It's hard to maintain a grudge for that long."

"Lots of people do. Look at the Balkans."

"I'd rather not," I said honestly. Genocide depresses me.

"Don't you feel like you're betraying your ancestors?"

"I would hope my ancestors would have more sense than that."

Actually, I had my doubts about that. My ancestors may have been many things, but sensible wasn't high on the list. I switched tactics.

"The English behaved horribly in Ireland, but they had their reasons for what they were doing at the time, even if they weren't what we would consider good reasons. It's like reading *Gone With the Wind*," I tried to explain. "You know that slavery is morally wrong, but while you're reading it, you can't help empathizing with the South anyway."

It belatedly occurred to me that a man who hadn't read *The Scarlet Pimpernel* most likely hadn't read *Gone With the Wind*, either.

Jay leaned back in his chair and folded his arms across his chest. "So you're a moral relativist, then."

I hate people who act like they have you all figured out.

"I didn't say that," I said quickly.

Jay had clearly been a debater in college. His eyes gleamed with the thrill of argument—or maybe just the beer. Dammit, where was the waiter with our food?

"Then what would you call it?"

I planted my elbows on the table. "Look, you have to evaluate events in context. To the English, Ireland was a dangerous security threat. They were fighting a losing war against the French; their continental allies were entirely unreliable; and they were in constant danger of being invaded."

"And that justifies their behavior?"

"It's not a question of justification." I could hear my voice rising with annoyance, and quickly resorted to my wineglass. Adopting a gentler tone, I tried again. "My job as a historian isn't to justify or to judge. My job is to try to get inside their heads, to understand their world on their own terms."

"Sounds like a cop-out to me."

"It isn't a cop-out; it's responsible scholarship. Otherwise, what you have isn't a scholarly work. It's an op-ed piece."

"I like op-ed pieces," opined Jay.

"So do I," I gritted out. "In context. Oooh, look! There's our food."

It wasn't, actually. It was the next table's food. But it provided an excellent distraction. Jay immediately turned around to look. As he did, the door to the street burst open, and three guys barreled through in a blast of cold air and masculine banter, the steam from their breath adding to the haze on the glass door. One pointed to the bar, while another shoved out of his coat. And the third . . .

Those traitorous flutters, those flutters that hadn't so much as quivered when I saw Jay at the bar, woke up from their nap and started dancing a Highland fling, complete with tartan and bagpipes.

Colin was back in London.

Chapter Thirteen

The following afternoon, Letty stood on the stoop of a pleasant redbrick house on Henrietta Street, itemizing all the things she would rather be doing than taking tea with Miss Gilly Fairley. Tooth extractions ranged high on the list, along with being dragged by wild horses, kidnapped by bandits, and forced to listen to recitations of epic poetry in the original Greek. Actually, the last wasn't all that alarming, but Letty was beginning to run out of ideas, and the brass knocker loomed large before her shadowed eyes.

Letty's face, hideously reflected in the polished brass of the knocker, looked indecisively back at her, all immense nose and strange, squinty little eyes. How did one tell a woman that her suitor's intentions were dishonorable? She couldn't very well walk in, take a biscuit, and say, "Do forgive me for interfering, Miss Fairley, but Lord Pinchingdale happens to be married to me. Just thought you ought to know, and thanks so much for the tea."

Perhaps she should just shove an anonymous note under the door and run in the other direction.

Feeling like Joan of Arc mounting a pile of kindling, Letty reached for the knocker and rapped smartly at the door, as if she could compensate for the weakness of her purpose with the firmness of her knock.

Inside, a scurry of footsteps signaled an immediate response, cutting off her last hope of retreat. A maid opened the door, bobbing a curtsy, and ushered Letty inside. Letty might have been small, but she was very effective. Letty was in the hall, and the door closed behind her before Letty had a chance to flee.

Letty caught a glimpse of herself in the mirror in the hall as she loosened her bonnet strings. She looked like a Mrs. Alsdale in her black walking dress, like a respectable widow of reasonable but not excessive means. Even her rebellious hair had been tamed into a semblance of order for the occasion, smoothed with water, and twisted into a braided knot before it could escape again. There was something very unsettling about seeing herself so convincingly tricked out as someone else, as though the real Letty, the Letty of figured muslin dresses that had been turned one too many times, the Letty whose hair was always falling down and who was generally too impatient to hunt for her gloves or bonnet, had been entirely subsumed within the quiet, modest figure of Mrs. Alsdale, whose gloves were perfectly tidy and whose hair stayed where she had put it.

Letty caught herself wishing she had worn something more flattering, and made herself stop. It wasn't a competition. And if it were, she thought ruefully, as she followed the maid up a narrow flight of stairs to the first floor, she would lose.

"Right through here, miss," said the maid, turning the knob on one of the two doors that opened off the narrow landing, stepping out of the way to let Letty pass.

After the dark hall, it was an unexpectedly pleasant parlor, if somewhat old-fashioned, decorated with a pale paper patterned with green lozenges. A heavy wooden dresser stood against one wall, boasting a few precious pieces of French porcelain, surrounded by examples of more homely stoneware, with scenes of local interest painted in blue on a white background. From her vantage point in the doorway, Letty could see Miss Fairley, seated at a small round table facing the door, addressing a remark to someone just out of Letty's line of vision. It couldn't be Mrs. Grimstone, because that lady was sitting to Miss Fairley's left, haughtily inspecting the contents of her cup as if the beverage displeased her. Due to the angle of the door, Letty couldn't make out anything of the third person, not so much as a hand on the table or a corner of a flounce; the only evidence of her presence was a third cup, sitting slightly askew on its blue-and-white saucer, a dark ring of coffee staining the sides.

If Miss Fairley had other guests, Letty couldn't very well apprise her of Lord Pinchingdale's dishonorable intentions, could she? Letty knew she shouldn't feel relieved, but she couldn't help it.

"Ah, Mrs. Alsdale!" Miss Fairley broke off, and half rose from her place at the table to beckon Letty in, ribbons and curls bobbing. "You are wonderfully prompt. Do come in."

The brisk words were entirely at odds with the gushing Miss Fairley of the night before, but Letty only barely noticed. All her attention was fixed upon the mysterious third party, whose cup rattled on its saucer as he pushed his chair abruptly back from the table.

"Lord Pinchingdale?" stammered Letty.

Her husband appeared incapable of speech.

Not so Miss Fairley. "I believe you are already acquainted," said Miss Fairley pleasantly, looking calmly from one to the other.

Lord Pinchingdale's gaze narrowed on Miss Fairley.

"I did not agree to this," he said levelly.

"No," Miss Fairley acknowledged, in a voice that wasn't like Miss Fairley's at all. "But if you weren't going to be reasonable, you had to be made to be reasonable. Hence this afternoon's arrangement."

"Perhaps I should go," suggested Letty, inching her way backward. She stumbled as her heel came into painful contact with the lintel of the door, catching at the doorframe for balance. "I wasn't aware you had other guests. . . . Some other time, perhaps . . ."

"Not at all." Miss Fairley's voice was still pleasant, but there was a note of command in it that arrested Letty midflight. "Do sit down, Mrs. Alsdale."

Letty moved away from the door, but refused to take the chair her hostess indicated. She felt safer standing. There were strange currents making themselves felt across the table; Mrs. Grimstone was looking superior, Miss Fairley determined, and Lord Pinchingdale displeased. And all of them knew something Letty didn't.

That alone was enough to make Letty refuse the chair.

"I am quite comfortable as I am," Letty declared, ruining the effect by shifting her weight off her throbbing heel.

"As you will," Miss Fairley said equably, pausing to take a sip from her almost-full cup. "I suppose you won't take any coffee either?"

Letty shook her head in negation, anxious to hasten the strange interview to its close. The whole scene made her oddly uneasy. Miss Fairley's sudden, unexpected poise. The malicious gleam in Mrs. Grimstone's black eyes. Lord Pinchingdale's air of watchful expectation, as he leaned back in his chair, lips pressed tightly together, and arms folded across his chest. He looked as though he were waiting for something. . . . They were all waiting for something. But for what?

Half a dozen scenarios straight out of the annals of sensational fiction presented themselves to Letty's rapidly whirring mind, as she stood impaled in the center of the circle of eyes, like a hart in a medieval tapestry. There were ways of getting rid of an unwanted wife, weren't there? A drug in the coffee, a quick trip to a mental asylum to have her declared incompetent. Not long before she left London, Charlotte Lansdowne had pressed one of Richardson's novels on her, in which a virtuous young lady was tricked into residence in a brothel under false pretenses, driven to degradation and eventually death by the vindictive madam. Mrs. Grimstone, with her cold eyes and grasping hands, would make an excellent bawd.

But such things didn't happen outside of fiction; it was too strange, too sensational—wasn't it?

Despite the sun slanting through the long windows, Letty shivered. She knew no one in Dublin, no one except Emily Gilchrist and Mrs. Lanergan, and they didn't even know her under her proper name. As far as her family was concerned, she was on an extended honeymoon trip. What better time for Lord Pinchingdale to divest himself of an inconvenience? He could return home, the grieving widower, and pick up just where he had left off, philandering his way through London's ballrooms. And no one would ever suspect . . .

Letty's hands closed around the curved wooden chair back. "Why did you ask me here? Not for coffee, I take it."

"No," agreed Miss Fairley, "not for coffee. For this."

With one graceful movement, she reached up and swept the entire mass of silver-blond curls off her head.

Letty didn't know what she had been expecting, but it wasn't that. Where Miss Gilly Fairley's foaming locks had been a moment before, shining pale brown hair had been coiled into a graceful knot that accentuated the classical planes of the woman's face. Without the elfin curls and gaily colored ribbons, her entire appearance was transformed. Instead of a flighty wood nymph, she reminded Letty of a marble statue of Minerva, intelligent and slightly alien.

"It does feel good to get that off," murmured Miss Fairley, dropping the wig with obvious distaste on the table next to the coffeepot. "The ringlets itch terribly."

The transformation made Letty's disguise seem decidedly amateur.

There were altogether too many people in disguise. Her own

had been donned out of desperation, on a moment's impulse, but what about Miss Fairley? What excuse could she have? Suspicion trickled through Letty, as unpleasant as cold coffee, as she looked at Miss Fairley's serene countenance, all the more beautiful for being unadorned. She didn't look much like Mary—her hair was fair where Mary's was dark, her eyes almond-shaped where Mary's were round, her lips thinner and the bridge of her nose narrower—but there was a similarity that transcended the differences in coloring, a certain inherent stateliness and an underlying beauty of bone structure.

Letty rounded on her husband, who was watching Miss Fairley with an expression that she could only term grim resignation. Grim resignation, but not the slightest drop of surprise. If Lord Pinchingdale could come to Dublin and pay court to a young lady without revealing his prior marriage in London, couldn't it also work the other way around?

"Is there something I ought to know?" Letty asked sharply.

"The less you know," said Lord Pinchingdale, and although the words were ostensibly addressed to her, Letty knew they were really intended as a warning for the alien beauty sitting at the head of the table, incongruously attired in Gilly Fairley's frills and flounces, "the better."

"The better for whom?" demanded Letty. "For you?"

Lord Pinchingdale's lazy posture didn't change, but something in his face hardened. "Of course. Whom else?"

With the unforgiving light from the windows picking out the rich brocade of his waistcoat, glinting off the sapphire in his cravat, she saw him for what he really was, a pampered aristocrat who thought nothing of running amok through the lives of others in the pursuit of his own pleasure.

Loathing, pure and painful, rose through Letty like lava, bubbling up at the back of her throat, nearly choking her.

"You might try thinking of someone other than yourself for a change. Just for variety."

Lord Pinchingdale raised an indolent eyebrow. "As you do? I'm sure your appearance here last night was arranged entirely for my convenience."

"Why should I think of your convenience when you are so adept at doing so for yourself? How many other women do you have tucked away in far-flung bits of the world? One in Scotland, perhaps, to go with the grouse shooting? A harem in Paris?"

Lord Pinchingdale's lips twisted with amusement at a joke that eluded Letty. "Not of the sort you're imagining."

"I have no interest in hearing the sordid details."

"I do," interrupted Mrs. Grimstone, who had been listening avidly. "A harem would be just the thing."

"Mrs. Grimstone is engaged in writing a sensational novel," explained Lord Pinchingdale in a tone drier than the kindling in the hearth. Turning to Mrs. Grimstone, he added, "Do make sure to change the names. My reputation appears to be black enough already."

"Certainly I shall," sniffed Mrs. Grimstone. "Pinchingdale is an absurd name for a hero."

"I'm sure Mrs. Alsdale will vouch that it works excellently well for a villain."

"You do yourself too much honor," said Letty scathingly. "Villains, at least, have a certain grandeur to them. Reprobates have nothing to recommend them."

"How quickly the pot turns on the kettle."

"If you weren't so entirely debased yourself, you wouldn't be so quick to judge others by your own standards!"

"If you find yourself running short of terms of abuse, I suggest 'degenerate cad' for your next go. Or you can just slap me and get it over with."

"Only if I had a gauntlet to do it with!"

"Are you challenging me to a duel? I'm afraid that's not done, my dear."

"I forgot." Letty drew herself up to her full five feet, enjoying the sensation of being able to look down on Lord Pinchingdale. "You have no honor to defend."

"Well delivered!" exclaimed Mrs. Grimstone. "I couldn't have done it better myself."

"Before we descend any further into absurdity," Miss Fairley broke in calmly, sounding as unruffled as though she were supervising a philosophical discussion at the Bluestocking Society, "someone really ought to provide an explanation to our guest."

"What sort of explanation did you have in mind?" inquired Lord Pinchingdale. His voice was perfectly calm, but there was a bite to it that suggested he wasn't quite so blasé about slights to his honor as he might pretend.

"The truth."

"Fiction is so much more entertaining," mused Mrs. Grimstone. "Especially my fiction."

"But not necessarily conducive to domestic peace," countered Miss Fairley.

Lord Pinchingdale looked rather tight about the lips, in a way that suggested that he found the possibility of domestic peace just as unlikely a goal as Letty did. Not, thought Letty mutinously, that he had any right to look grim. After all, he was the one keeping a harem.

He folded his arms across his chest and nodded toward Miss Fairley. "Since this was your idea, Jane, why don't you do the honors?"

"Who," demanded Letty, rather shrilly, "is Jane?"

Miss Fairley flicked the wig fastidiously aside, and looked Letty straight in the eye. "My name is Jane."

"Not Gilly?" Letty knew there were other things she probably ought to be asking, but that was the first that rose to her lips.

Miss Fairley—Jane—smiled at her kindly. Too kindly. Letty hadn't seen an expression like that since the time the cook had been delegated to tell her that her favorite dog had died. "No, not Gilly."

"And you may address me as Miss Gwen," announced Mrs. Grimstone, whose Christian name was supposed to be Ernestine, which, as far as Letty could tell, bore no discernible relation to Gwen, by any stretch of linguistic acrobatics. "However, you may do so only in private, when there is no danger of anyone overhearing, or you will jeopardize the entire mission. Do you understand?"

"Mission?"

"We are all," Jane said gently, "agents of the Pink Carnation."

Chapter Fourteen

"Oh, for heaven's sake," said Letty. "You can't expect me to believe that."

It wasn't precisely polite, but, then, neither was taking off one's hair at the tea table.

Did they really think she was that naive?

Letty saw her husband throw Jane a quick, shuttered look, and felt her temper rise.

"Next you'll tell me you're all really missionaries, here to convert the heathen, or a troupe of traveling players, or—" Letty's imagination failed her. "Spies! It's unthinkable!"

"Well, start thinking it, missy," snapped Miss Gwen, or Mrs. Grimstone, or whatever her name might be. Letty didn't particularly care.

With her usual graceful efficiency, Jane unfastened the ribbon she wore around her neck and passed the bauble across the table to Letty.

"Will this serve to convince you?" she asked.

Acting automatically, Letty reached out to take the locket, wondering, even as she did so, how on earth a piece of jewelry could be expected to make her believe the most absurd sort of absurdity. Letters, perhaps. A signed statement from His Majesty's undersecretary of something or other, vouching for his agents. But a locket?

The metal was still warm from the other woman's skin. It was a commonplace enough trinket, a simple golden oval with a flower inset in enamel on the front. On the back . . . Instead of encountering smooth gold, Letty's fingertips caught on a series of deeply incised lines.

Her breath catching in her throat, Letty flipped the small disk over. On the obverse, where it would be hidden in the hollow of the wearer's throat, was engraved the complex form of a many-petaled flower.

Even Letty, who had no use for spies, recognized it. She had seen it reproduced in half a dozen broadsheets, on fans, on hand-kerchiefs, even embroidered on gentlemen's stockings.

It was the seal of the Pink Carnation.

"I thought it made a nice change from the traditional ring," commented Jane with a smile.

Letty stared down at the locket, running one finger over the thin line where the two halves joined. On one side, a slight bump identified the presence of a catch. . . .

Miss Gwen reached over and snatched the locket out of Letty's grasp, handing it back to Jane, who tied the ribbon neatly around her neck.

Once again, it was only a young girl's ornament, a pretty bauble to set off the neckline of a dress.

Only, it wasn't.

"It could merely be an ornament," argued Letty, as much for herself as for the three sets of eyes regarding her from around the table.

"It could," agreed Jane mildly, giving the knot a final twist. She seemed entirely unperturbed.

"You might simply like flowers."

"Many people do."

Letty looked from the locket to the wig and back to Jane, calm and businesslike at the head of the table. She couldn't bring herself to look at her husband. But she did notice—it was impossible not to notice—the complete lack of tender attentions to the woman now known as Jane. Where last night, he had hovered over her as though distance would be the death of him, today, he sat calmly apart. It wasn't the sort of distance that betokened a lovers' quarrel. It was the distance of complete indifference. And if they weren't lovers . . .

Letty could still feel the imprint of the deeply incised lines on the pads of her fingers.

"Oh my goodness," muttered Letty.

"It took you long enough," complained Miss Gwen.

"One doesn't encounter such situations every day," countered Jane. "I'd say she's bearing up quite well."

Feeling a bit unsteady, Letty grappled with the implications of this new information. "Then . . . last night . . ."

"Was all part of a cunning ruse to confound the French," announced Miss Gwen, looking cunning.

"So, what you're telling me," said Letty hesitantly, looking from Miss Gwen to Jane, and anywhere but at her husband, whose long fingers were drumming softly against the tabletop, "is that Dublin is full of French spies."

"Not quite full," said Jane, "but enough to create a good deal of bother."

"I think I'm going to sit down now," said Letty, and she did, more heavily than she had intended. "But if this is true, then you shouldn't have told me any of it."

"For once, we agree," murmured her husband.

Letty addressed herself to Jane. "Not that it wasn't very kind of you, but how do you know I won't go babbling about it to half of Dublin?"

"Kind!" Miss Gwen looked appalled.

"It isn't kind," said Jane briskly. "It's just good sense. You could cause us far more bother bumbling about under false impressions."

None of them said "like last night," but Letty could feel the words hanging over them all. Her color deepened as she remembered the way she had made Lord Pinchingdale all but drag her across the room, into the quiet of the window embrasure.

"As for your propensity to babble," Jane's cool voice intruded on Letty's fevered recollections, "you had half a dozen opportunities last night to identify Geoffrey as your husband. And yet you chose not to. Not the actions of a woman who can't hold her tongue. Coffee?"

Jane elevated the fluted china pot with the air of a woman who considers she has proved her point beyond dispute. Letty could think of half a dozen objections to that logic. And if she could, she was sure Lord Pinchingdale could, too.

"Yes, please," said Letty, extending her cup so that Jane could pour the dark liquid into it.

"Geoffrey?" Jane tilted the pot, and Letty's eyes followed, creeping like a thief in his direction, but never making it as far as his face.

Mechanically, Letty lifted her cup to her lips. The coffee tasted flat and slightly acidic on her tongue, tepid from too long in the pot. If everything Jane said was true, it meant her husband wasn't a philandering cad, or even the weak-willed sort of man who would run off on his wedding night for no better reason than disinclination. Those men, she could have dealt with.

This new Lord Pinchingdale was something else entirely. In the space of the removal of a wig, he had gone from reprobate to hero, and she had gone from wronged wife to . . . what did that make her? Letty grimaced into her coffee. Not the heroine, that much was sure.

"I'll book passage back to London tomorrow," said Letty abruptly, placing her cup firmly back into its saucer. "It will be easiest that way."

Across the table, Jane had donned her most enigmatic expression. "Perhaps not."

Unused to Jane's peculiar rhetorical habits, Letty shook her head. "I shouldn't have any trouble finding passage."

"What Jane means," put in Geoff, deciding to end the exercise before it turned into a full-blown Platonic dialogue, "is that your departure at this juncture might arouse conjecture."

Miss Gwen wagged a bony finger. "I say we use this to our advantage. If Mrs. Alsdale disappears, the French will be convinced she's involved in something havey-cavey. They go looking for her, while we deal with them."

"And if they catch her?" inquired Geoff.

As Geoff knew from long experience, the Black Tulip had a nasty way with a stiletto. Not content with sealing wax, she had amused herself, in the early days of the war, by carving her symbol into the flesh of captured English agents. It had been some time, but that didn't mean the Black Tulip had grown any more merciful, merely more subtle in her means of torture. If she got her hands on Letty . . .

He might have his own reasons for wanting to throttle her, but she didn't deserve that.

"Tempting," said Geoff, "but no."

"I'm sorry," Letty said, a furrow forming between her brows. "If I had known . . ."

"You weren't supposed to know," replied Geoff, looking pointedly at Jane.

Jane gazed guilelessly back at him over her coffee cup.

Geoff raised his eyebrows just enough to show her that he knew exactly what she was doing. After last night's shenanigans—and that missed rendezvous between Emmet and his French contact—it was clear that Jane had arrived at the conclusion that the best possible way to neutralize the problem posed by Letty was to bring her into the conspiracy. Not fully, of course. Just enough to make Letty feel committed to the cause. With Letty in their corner, rather than outraged wife at large, they could keep to their original pose as a courting couple.

Jane, thought Geoff irritably, was altogether too sure of herself sometimes.

Not to mention that she didn't know Letty Alsworthy. Not like he did. She didn't know that Letty's wide blue eyes hid a mind as cunning as Bonaparte's, that her self-effacing air masked a will stronger than Caesar's, and that her modest black dress cloaked a bust that would put Cleopatra's to shame. Geoff realized that his gaze was most improperly fastened on that last-mentioned attribute and hastily rearranged his features into their accustomed blandness. The larger the bosom, he reminded himself, the more room for asps to nest there. Or something along those lines. At worst, the addition of Letty Alsworthy spelled trouble. At best . . . Geoff was having a great deal of difficulty thinking of a best.

Jane smiled apologetically at Letty. "I am afraid you will have to be Mrs. Alsdale for some little bit longer."

"I don't mind," said Letty.

"I do," muttered Geoff.

"In fact," said Jane to Letty, "you might even be of some use to us."

"I would be glad to," said Letty, just as Geoff demanded, "What sort of use?"

Miss Gwen, watching both of them, emitted the harsh chuckle that served her for a laugh. Geoff saw nothing at all humorous about the situation. But, then, he had always suspected that Miss Gwen's sense of humor ran to watching matadors gored by bulls.

"Nothing like that," said Jane soothingly.

Geoff remained unconvinced. He wouldn't have put it past Jane to hand Letty an armful of explosives if she thought it would best serve her purposes at the time. As for Letty . . . he didn't like to think what she might do with an armful of explosives. She was dangerous enough armed with adjectives.

"This isn't a game," he said flatly.

"Of course not!" harrumphed Miss Gwen. "Games are for amateurs."

"Nor," added Geoff, with a quelling look at Letty, "is this a church fete."

"I didn't think it was," said Letty.

"What I mean"—Geoff drummed his fingers against the polished tabletop, wishing the War Office provided guidelines for situations such as this, with handy subheadings like "Unwanted wives, for the removal of"—"is that you can't just pitch in and help. It's not as though you're lending a hand with flower arrangements. The situation is deadly serious. Do you know anything of what is happening in Ireland?"

Letty looked like she wanted to claim that she did. Her head tilted, her mouth opened—and then closed again.

"No," she admitted.

"My point exactly." Geoff turned to Jane. "The idea is ridiculous."

"How much does she need to know?" demanded Miss Gwen, whom Geoff was quite sure was championing Letty's cause merely to be contrary. It was, she had informed Geoff in an unusually mellow moment after their successful raid on the opera house, one of her great pleasures in life.

As for her other great pleasure, Geoff could only be glad her parasol was safely tucked away in a corner of the room, well out of reach.

Miss Gwen turned to Letty. "The Irish are revolting and the French are invading. We're here to stop them. There," she said triumphantly to Geoff. "She knows all she needs to know."

Geoff didn't groan out loud. But he wanted to.

Working alone, that was the way to do it. There was a reason that Beowulf had gone into Grendel's cave alone. Otherwise, you wound up with too many cooks throwing unwanted impediments who happened to be married to you into the broth.

"That's only the very tip of it," he told Letty, whose eyes had gone round at the mention of revolt, and even rounder at invasion. Her eyes were a paler blue than her sister's, with a peculiar depth to them, like the sky after a rain, or the endless expanse of a sunlit sea.

"Rebellion?" Letty swallowed hard. "Here?"

Her gesture encompassed the peaceful parlor, the square patches of sunshine on the carpet, the leaves of a tree brushing against the windowpanes.

"Here," Geoff confirmed. "The United Irishmen have been planning rebellion ever since their last attempt failed in 'ninety-eight. They've had five years to figure out what went wrong last time and to try to fix it. Last time, they mustered fifty thousand men—no small number—and their French friends arrived with eleven hundred troops. We were lucky that they arrived late. It gave us time to mop up the local rebellion first. That was last time."

"And this time?"

"This time"—Geoff didn't need to exaggerate; the facts alone were grim enough—"our garrison has been reduced from seventy-five thousand to thirty thousand. Less than half."

"We are all acquainted with basic mathematics," interrupted Miss Gwen.

"This time," Geoff raised his voice, "Bonaparte is in a more generous frame of mind. We know his minister of war recently met with the United Irishmen's agent in Paris. They are talking of a full-scale invasion before the end of the summer. We don't have the men to fight them off. We don't even have enough men to counter a well-organized local rebellion. Within weeks, Ireland could blow up like a powder keg."

"Oh," said Letty. It was, she realized, an inadequate response, but she didn't know what else to say. Given where her tongue had led her before, it was probably safer not to say much of anything at all. For a very long time.

"If Ireland goes"—Lord Pinchingdale's tone was calm, almost conversational, but something about its very stillness made the hairs stand up on Letty's arms—"the way to England lies open."

"You mean . . ."

"Invasion."

"What can I do?" she asked, feeling more ineffectual than she had ever felt in her life. Guns and rebels and French troops . . . they weren't the sort of problem one could order to their room, or organize out of existence by rearranging a few numbers in a ledger.

"You can keep out of the way." Letty bristled at the brusque words, and, in a slightly gentler tone, Lord Pinchingdale went on, "Do whatever you would ordinarily do. Take tea with friends. Go shopping. Leave us to our work, and I'll take you back to London at the end of it."

Letty wondered if that was meant as a bribe. If she didn't leave him to his work, what then? Internment in an Irish cloister? Or, she realized with a sudden chill, death at the hands of a rebel mob? Letty had never seen a mob herself—farmers celebrating the harvest didn't count, even after a few too many kegs of ale—but she was old enough to remember the reports from France ten years before. Mobs ravaging the countryside, heads paraded on pikes . . . It was a strong argument for good behavior.

"I think we can muster something more interesting than that," said Jane. "Nothing dangerous, of course."

"What did you have in mind?" asked Lord Pinchingdale.

"You can't possibly object to a little jaunt to a historic site, can you?"

"That depends on which historic site."

"What could be more benign—or beneficial to the soul—than a house of worship?"

"It might even put you in mind of your vows," cackled Miss Gwen. "Till death, aren't they?"

Lord Pinchingdale ignored her. "You refer to St. Werburgh's," he said to Jane.

"The very one," replied Jane.

"Saint who?" enquired Letty, leaning forward.

"She's a very minor sort of saint," said Miss Gwen dismissively, giving the impression that she wouldn't stoop to dealings with any but the more major martyrs.

"It is the parish church of Dublin Castle," Geoff supplied, before Miss Gwen could say more. "More important, Saint Werburgh's houses the grave of Lord Edward Fitzgerald."

"Who, I take it," said Letty, trying to sound brighter than she felt, "is not a saint, minor or otherwise."

"It depends on whom you ask," said Geoff. "To the United Irishmen, he's the next thing to it."

"Lord Edward died of wounds he sustained during the rising in 'ninety-eight," explained Jane from the head of the table.

"A martyr to the cause." Letty turned the phrase over on her tongue, her head spinning with spies and rebels and minor sorts of saints.

They were all as far out of her ken as the figures of athletes on a Grecian urn or the intrigues of a Turkish harem, the sort of characters one read about from the safety of one's study, but never expected to encounter. And yet she had somehow, improbably, landed among them, like Cortez washed up upon the shores of the new world.

"But what," asked Letty, feeling as though she were wading very slowly through a South American swamp, "has a grave—even the grave of a martyr—to do with whatever the rebels are doing now?" A gruesome thought struck her, accompanied by images of medieval monks carrying saints' bodies in solemn procession. "They aren't planning to use his bones as a rallying point, are they?"

"I knew I liked her," pronounced Miss Gwen, to no one in particular.

"Nothing so macabre as that," said Geoff, with a quirk of his lip that might have been a smile if allowed to grow up. Letty found herself hoping it would, and oddly pleased that she had put it there. "But it does provide a convenient meeting place. One with symbolic weight."

"Surely, they wouldn't meet there during the day, would they?" asked Letty, whose impressions of spies had a good deal to do with cloaks, masks, and shuttered lanterns. It did strike her as more logical to meet in daylight, under the guise of ordinary activities, rather than skulking about at night, but spies—at least from the accounts in the illustrated papers—didn't seem to be a particularly logical group of people.

"More likely during the day than at night," replied Geoff. "But we're not hoping to surprise a meeting. We have reason to believe that devout pilgrims have been leaving an unusual sort of offering at Lord Edward's grave."

"Paper offerings," put in Jane. "Of more use to the living than the dead."

"You believe his grave is being used as . . ." Letty struggled for the right words. "As a sort of rebel post office."

"A very apt way of putting it. Auntie Ernestine and I"—Jane's voice went up half an octave and she tipped her head towards Miss Gwen with a simper that sat ill on her classical features—"were just discussing a lovely little trip to Saint Werburgh's. Auntie Ernie has some very pressing questions she wants to put to the vicar, haven't you, Auntie Ernie?"

Miss Gwen's spine stiffened until it was sharper than the ribs of her parasol. "I refuse to answer to that detestable nickname."

Jane fluttered her lashes at Letty. "Isn't she the very darlingest of Auntie Ernies?"

"The voice works better when you have your wig on," commented Geoff mildly.

"So it does," replied Jane without rancor, shaking out the blonde curls with a practiced hand. "I'll just go and transform myself back into Gilly, shall I? Auntie Ernie?"

The words were as much summons as question. Like a cat rousted from its cushion, Miss Gwen rose from her chair with an air of majesty that implied she had been planning to do just that anyway.

Letty rose, too.

"Oh, no!" exclaimed Jane. "Don't disturb yourself. We'll only be a moment."

"But—"

"Geoffrey will entertain you, I'm sure. Won't you, Geoffrey?"

Chapter Fifteen

"Far be it from me to disappoint such charming ladies."
Miss Gwen snorted and stalked from the room, looking anything but charming.

"I thought you would see it my way," Jane said cheerfully, and then she too was gone, in a froth of lace-edged flounces.

Folding his arms across his chest, Lord Pinchingdale watched the last frill whisper around the door frame. "I believe that this is Jane's none too subtle attempt to urge us to cry truce."

Letty found she still couldn't think of him by his first name—perhaps because he had never extended her that right. She could still hear Jane's pleasant contralto forming the word, turning it like a potter with a piece of clay until it came out perfectly smooth and rounded. Geoffrey.

Lord Pinchingdale raised an inquisitive eyebrow. "I believe this is where you're supposed to say something."

Letty blurted out the first thing that came into her head. "You don't have a black mask, do you?"

"No." He gave her an odd look. "Nor would I advise you to acquire one. They tend to invite more attention than they deflect."

"I didn't think you would," said Letty ruefully. He would have to be sensible as well as honorable, wouldn't he? A few flaws would make her own ambiguous position more palatable.

"Are you disappointed?"

"No. I've always thought them very silly things."

Letty was aware she was speaking nonsense, and didn't blame Lord Pinchingdale for looking at her as though she might be carted off at any moment. But she was still having a great deal of trouble coming to terms with the notion of having tumbled into a den of spies—and such an unlikely den. With the afternoon sun slanting through the windows, picking out the golden patina of the wood on the table and the quaint scenes painted on the china, espionage seemed as unlikely as a royal visit. The little green-and-white room was made for cheerful family breakfasts, for talk of ribbons and shopping rather than martyrs and crypts.

If it hadn't been for that locket . . .

Letty caught Lord Pinchingdale's eye, and flushed, for no particular reason.

"I've caused you a great deal of trouble by appearing like this, haven't I?"

"That," Lord Pinchingdale replied evenly, "depends on you."

"I'm sorry," she said simply, and she was. Sorry she had come to Ireland, sorry she had tried to prevent Mary's elopement, sorry she had ever left Hertfordshire. Sorry, sorry, sorry.

Not that being sorry did either of them any good.

"I never meant any of this to happen," she added.

"I'm sure you didn't."

Letty winced at the implied barb. "I didn't . . . ," she began, and then stopped.

Geoff strove to conceal signs of impatience as he waited for the inevitable unconvincing protestations of innocence. Where in the devil had Jane got to? The hallway dozed placidly in the afternoon sunshine, unhelpfully empty. There was no avoiding another recitation of the whole tedious package of lies.

For the sake of the mission, whose safety now rested in Letty's capricious little hands, he would have to feign belief. Or, at least, refrain from active disbelief. His Majesty could only ask so much of even his most loyal subjects.

"You didn't . . . ?" Geoff prompted, as Letty scowled at the carpet as though the vines had entangled her tongue.

He thought he had kept his tone carefully neutral, but Letty tilted her head back and looked him straight in the eye.

"You're not going to believe a word I say, are you?"

Taken off guard, Geoff raised an eyebrow in lieu of an answer.

"I thought as much. Do you know what the worst of it is?"

"No," Geoff said honestly. There were too many potential worsts to choose from.

"I wouldn't have believed you, either," finished Letty with grim relish. "It's as absurd as a Greek tragedy."

Which made matters about as clear as mud.

"Have you had a lovely little chat?" Jane bustled in in full "Gilly" mode, every curl bobbing, every inch of fabric frilled and shirred within an inch of its life. "I do so hate when people are unpleasant and cross."

"You are enjoying this role a good deal too much," commented Geoff to Jane by rote, but his eyes followed Letty, still trying to make sense of that Greek-tragedy comment. He devoutly hoped she didn't have any notions about putting out eyes, either his or her own.

"You"—Jane waggled her beaded reticule at him—"are just being an old crossy-kins, like dear Auntie Ernie."

Miss Gwen looked as though she couldn't decide which to be more annoyed by, being called a "crossy-kins" or "Auntie Ernie."

"Time," she proclaimed dourly, jabbing at the mantel clock with her ever-present parasol, "is wasting."

"And we couldn't have that, now, could we?" agreed Jane, sweeping the entire party out to the waiting carriage.

Geoff made a feint in Letty's direction, but was neatly cut off by Miss Gwen, who skewered Geoff with a dampening glare as she swept regally in front of him down the narrow stairs, the tips of her black-dyed ostrich plumes tickling the tip of his nose. Geoff sneezed three times between landings, thinking decidedly ungentlemanly thoughts about Miss Gwen, her taste in millinery, and people who entered rooms in the middle of conversations.

"Once we get there," Letty asked, as Geoff settled into the facing seat of the carriage, "what should I do?"

"Your role is really quite simple. And harmless," Jane added, with a sidelong glance at Geoff. "Miss Gwen has kindly agreed to occupy the rector while Geoffrey and I search the premises." Given the avid gleam in Miss Gwen's eye, Geoff couldn't help but feel sorry for the rector. "However, we cannot discount the possibility that there might be other persons present."

"I'm simply to talk to them?" said Letty.

"Only if you see them showing an inordinate interest in our activities," put in Geoff, watching Letty closely.

Letty earnestly processed the information, looking very young and entirely guileless. Young, Geoff would grant her. As for guileless . . .

"It sounds simple enough."

"That's what you think," retorted Miss Gwen. "It takes talent to distract someone subtly. Talent and practice."

"Mrs. Alsdale is no stranger to deception."

It took Letty a moment to remember that she was supposed to be Mrs. Alsdale. When she did, a slow flush stained her cheekbones. "I've certainly never had this much practice before."

"Not nearly enough, from the looks of it," pronounced Miss Gwen disparagingly. "Any spy who cannot remember her own alias deserves to be caught."

Letty squared her shoulders and looked full at Geoff. "That would solve a problem for both of us, wouldn't it?"

"Don't worry." Jane touched one finger reassuringly to Letty's arm. "It will all soon become second nature. Don't you agree, Geoffrey?"

"It all depends on one's temperament."

"In which case," replied Jane meaningfully, "I believe our Mrs. Alsdale will suit very well."

"Hmph," said Miss Gwen, in a way that amply echoed Geoff's own feelings on the matter.

From the expression on Letty's face, in this, at least, they were in complete accord.

For someone who had managed to dupe her way into matrimony, she seemed to have remarkably little facility for masking her emotions. Then again, Geoff reminded himself, her stunt in stealing her sister's place hadn't required subtlety, merely audacity. And that Letty Alsworthy clearly possessed in spades.

And yet . . . Geoff's eyes narrowed on Letty's face, as if he might be able to glean the truth from the tilt of her chin or the pattern of freckles across her nose. She had seemed entirely confident in her own defense at Mrs. Lanergan's the previous night. He could still remember, with painful clarity, her evasions when he had asked her where Mary was, complete with all the transparent signs of guilt. Last night, there had been no telltale pause, no stutter, no flush, none of the classic signs of dishonesty, nothing but pure, undiluted indignation, as though she had been the one wronged, rather than he.

That was an idea too silly to even entertain.

As if she felt his scrutiny, Letty developed a deep interest in the seams of her gloves.

Jane, meanwhile, looked from one to the other with an enigmatic smile reminiscent of the Sphinx at its most annoyingly smug.

Miss Gwen, mercifully, was not watching anyone at all. She was too busy staring out the window, maintaining a running commentary on the inadequacies of their driver. He was driving too quickly. He was driving too slowly. Had he *deliberately* driven over that pothole?

By the time the carriage drew to a halt before the classical facade of St. Werburgh's, it was unclear who was most grateful to be free of the coach: Letty, Geoff, or the coachman. Geoff swung down first, handing out Miss Gwen, who descended as regally as a dowager duchess on her way to the Court of St. James's, then Jane, who fluttered to the ground in an animated pile of flounces.

Letty peered tentatively through the door like a turtle considering an outing from its shell, clearly looking for a way to descend without requesting his aid.

Geoff impatiently held out a hand. There was no reason for her to treat him like a leper. She was the one who had been so unnaturally eager for a closer union, after all.

"We can at least observe the usual courtesies, if nothing else."

Framed in the doorway of the coach, Letty regarded him warily. "Are you quite sure?"

"I believe I control my baser urges."

Letty flushed, a red stain spreading from the bodice of her muslin dress straight up to her hairline. "Those weren't the ones I was worried about."

Nor had Geoff, until she mentioned it. But their situation was eerily reminiscent of another night, another coach. A moonless midnight in High Holborn with a well-rounded figure in his arms and a pair of lips warm and eager against his. If he propped a foot on the bottom step; if she leaned forward just a little bit more . . .

They would both be better placed to scratch each other's eyes out.

Geoff offered his hand, palm up. "You can take my arm, or you can stay in the carriage. The choice is yours."

"Choice?" To Letty, it seemed about as much of a genuine choice as the others she had been presented with lately. Marriage or ruin. Silence or the fall of the British Empire. For a moment, she was tempted to elect to stay in the carriage, just to see the look on his face—but she didn't particularly want to twiddle her thumbs alone in a musty carriage.

"Oh, fine," capitulated Letty, none too graciously, and took the offered hand.

Once she was on the ground, the hand didn't let go. Letty gave a slight tug. When that had no effect, she tugged harder. Looking up, primed for acerbic commentary, she found her husband regarding her with a furrow between his dark brows.

"We can't go on like this," he said.

"That," replied Letty, freeing her hand, "is the most sensible thing I have heard all day."

"All this bickering does neither of us any good."

Letty nobly refrained from pointing out that he had started it. She, after all, had been perfectly pleasant—*perfectly*—until he had made that crack about her skill at deception in that supercilious, drawling way he had. "What are you proposing?"

Lord Pinchingdale's lip curled, as though at a private and particularly unpleasant joke. "Marriage would be redundant."

Supercilious didn't cover the half of it.

"An annulment might be more to the point."

"But difficult to obtain. For now, I suggest a truce."

Letty wasn't quite sure which to regard with more suspicion, the ominous qualification "for now," or the offer of a truce.

"If you won't do it for my sake," continued Geoff, with a fine edge of sarcasm, "do it for England."

"Far be it from me to resist a patriotic appeal," replied Letty, matching the edge in his voice with her own. "So we let bygones be from this point on? No recriminations, no ill will?"

"Something like that."

It wasn't exactly a wholehearted endorsement.

"Oh, Mrs. Alsdale! Mrs. Alllllsdale!" Jane descended on them like a whole horde of banshees, everything that could flutter fluttering.

This time, Letty just managed not to look over her shoulder before responding, "Yes?"

Jane grabbed Letty's arm and dragged her away from Lord Pinchingdale, toward the steps of the church and a towheaded man in the sober, dark suit of a clergyman.

"You must come and meet the ever-so-charming curate of this ever-so-lovely church!"

As Jane propelled her ever so rapidly forward, Letty thought that she saw Jane's head jerk infinitesimally to the left. Given the constant motion of her curls, it was impossible to tell, but she was sure of it when, behind them, Lord Pinchingdale moved softly to the left, up the stairs to the sanctuary. If Letty hadn't been so preternaturally aware of his presence, she would never have noticed.

The curate clearly didn't. He was a very young clergyman, with a round, open face, his white stock slightly wrinkled, as though he were accustomed to tugging on it; Jane's hand on his arm caused his Adam's apple to bob up and down in an ecstasy of incoherent admiration.

Letty glanced sideways at Jane suspiciously, wondering if her tales of rebel correspondence in the crypt had been just that— fairy stories, designed to distract an unwanted third party while the real activity went on above. Letty reconsidered Jane's request for aid in the coach. There was something quite clever in the notion of distracting an inconvenient observer by enlisting her to distract someone else.

"Lovely Mr. Haverford is going to show us the crypt!" Jane's rapturous exclamation, combined with a sharp pinch, drew Letty's attention back to the blushing curate.

"It's really no place for ladies," said the curate hesitantly, looking at the elaborate flounces at the hem of Jane's dress, and the ribbons fluttering from the brim of her bonnet. His voice was a soft tenor, more Oxbridge than Ireland. "It's very damp."

Just over the cleric's shoulder, the blue-painted panels of the church door settled silently shut.

Releasing Letty, Jane clapped her gloved hands together in girlish glee.

"Oh, how splendid! Just like *The Castle of Otranto*! Or was it *The Children of the Abbey*? Oh, never mind, whichever it was, the crypt was positively drippy. Oh, please, do tell me that there are bones scattered about the floor!"

The curate cleared his throat uncomfortably, and tugged at his clerical collar as Jane fluttered her lashes at him. "I'm afraid all our bones are properly put away in their, er, respective coffers."

"Oh, well." Jane did a marvelous impression of someone nobly striving to overcome a grave disappointment. "We will contrive to manage, I suppose, as long as it is very, very damp and gloomy."

"Oh, very damp and gloomy!" replied the curate, his head bobbing up and down, grateful to be able to please in something.

"Excellent!" Miss Gwen took command of the curate's arm. "You shall escort us. Now, where is this crypt of yours?"

"It's not mine, precisely. . . ."

"Sirrah!" A sharp rap of the parasol indicated that Miss Gwen would brook no shilly-shallying, even from a man of the cloth.

Suitably chastened, the curate said meekly, "It's around the south side of the church. If you will come this way . . ."

With Miss Gwen's arm so firmly latched onto his that it was hard to discern whether he was leading or being dragged, the curate led the way around the sanctuary, leaving Letty and Jane to follow in his wake. The curate did attempt to glance longingly back at Jane, but a sharp poke from Miss Gwen's parasol reclaimed his attention, and made a deep reddish stain spread between his collar and the downy fringe of hair on the back of his neck.

As they rounded the side of the church, picking their way along the uneven passage, Miss Gwen's imperious voice floated back. "You, I take it, are a student of scripture. How do you reconcile 'Blessed are the meek' with 'God helps those who help themselves'?"

"I'm afraid the latter isn't actually in the scriptures, Mrs. Grimstone," said the curate very apologetically.

"Nonsense! You must not have been looking hard enough." Miss Gwen glanced impatiently around her as the party drew to a halt beneath two arched windows covered with grilles. "Why are we stopping?"

"This is the vault, Mrs. Grimstone."

"Where?" demanded Miss Gwen, craning her neck as though a mausoleum might magically materialize for her convenience.

"I believe he means this," said Letty, pointing down. The entrance was little more than a hole in the ground, covered by a sturdy wooden trapdoor with an iron ring set in one end.

Inserting the point of her parasol through the ring, Miss Gwen tugged. The trapdoor opened easily; either, thought Letty, the wood was much lighter or Miss Gwen much stronger than she had thought. Letty suspected the latter. In the resulting gap, Letty could just make out the top of a flight of stone stairs.

Miss Gwen peered disdainfully into the depths. "*That* is your crypt?"

"I did say it was no place for ladies," hedged the curate, falling back a step beneath the force of Miss Gwen's formidable glower, and even more formidable parasol.

Jane fluttered into action. "How romantic!" she breathed, with a warning look at her chaperone. "Why, it's just like the subterranean passageway in *The Horrors of Alfonso!*"

"I'm afraid I haven't read that work," admitted the curate.

"Nor the Bible, either, apparently," sniffed Miss Gwen.

Letty wondered what Lord Pinchingdale was doing back in the sanctuary, and whether her companions would notice if she abandoned them to slip back inside. She glanced briefly back over her shoulder at the narrow alleyway they had just walked down, little tufts of grass sprouting along the sides of trodden dirt. The stone of the sanctuary walls blotted any sound from within.

"Darling Mrs. Alsdale!" Letty was learning to loathe her assumed name. Jane propelled Letty forward with a light push. "Would you do the honors?"

"All right." Yielding to the inevitable, Letty gathered her skirts up. She placed one booted foot on the top step, worn at the middle from generations of feet carrying their funereal burdens. A slight flicker of light lurked in the depths. Picking her way down, Letty was grateful to whomever had thought to keep a torch burning below. There was no rail to cling to, just the uneven stone wall, as slick and damp as any distressed heroine might wish for. Atmospheric, perhaps, but it was wreaking havoc with the palms of Letty's gloves.

Behind her, Letty could hear the slight brush of a slipper against the step, the whisper of fabric on stone, as Jane started down after her, effectively cutting off any retreat.

As the illumination below grew more conspicuous, she asked the curate, "Do you always keep a light lit?"

"A light?" The curate was, from the sound of it, lumbered with Miss Gwen. "I'm afraid the, er, inhabitants have little need for one."

"Unless," pronounced Miss Gwen in sepulchral tones, "they choose to walk."

"I don't believe they have terribly much choice in the matter," said the confused curate. "They're quite stationary."

"Some people have no imagination," snapped Miss Gwen.

Letty was beginning to think she had too much imagination. But that was quite definitely a light ahead of her, no matter what the curate said, and not just reflected light from the opening above. Stepping gratefully down from the last stair onto packed earth, Letty withdrew her stained gloves from the wall and peered forward, into the crypt.

The curate hadn't been dissembling; the vault was just as gloomy as any aficionado of horror novels might have desired. Despite the warm July day, the space beneath the vaulted stone arches was as chill as October, with a curious scent to it, a combination of damp earth, mold, and wet stone that repulsed any whiff of the outside world. Rows of columns supported the heavy stone arches like trees in a strange, subterranean forest.

It was impossible to believe that just above their heads were the clean classical lines of the church. Somewhere directly above them, Lord Pinchingdale was in the sanctuary . . . doing what? Letty doubted he was indulging in a spot of sacral meditation, unless he was praying for release from their unfortunate marriage—and it was a bit late for that. From her post at the base of the stairs, Letty could just make out the shapes of the promised sepulchers, and she wondered whether one of them did belong to a Lord Edward Fitzgerald, or if Lord Edward, like the rest of the story, had been merely a fabrication to keep her occupied.

Even if it had, there was no getting out of the expedition now—or challenging Jane about it in the presence of the bemused curate.

Reluctantly, Letty moved forward, into the interior of the crypt. The light from the trapdoor, balked by the bodies of Letty's companions, made it no farther than the base of the steps. Letty would have been feeling her way by touch from column to column if not for the torch that someone had stuck through a ring on the wall. For all its size, the massive torchiere provided only a reluctant, smoky light in the heavy atmosphere of the crypt, a small, orange ball of flame, like a demon in an alchemist's furnace, trailing a long tail of black soot behind it. A shadow on the wall, darker than the stone itself, attested to the presence of previous visitors and previous torches.

This torch had a companion. A man stood brooding over a

dim slab that could be nothing but a grave, his back to the sullen glow. His dark clothes absorbed the flames, extinguished them, creating a vibrant sphere of dark in the midst of light, as he stood poised over the coffin with a stillness more active than movement. Only the silver head of his cane blazed with reflected fire, held aloft above the grave like a medieval necromancer summoning spirits from the vasty deep.

Chapter Sixteen

⁓

The effect, Letty was sure, was quite deliberate.

"Good day," she said tartly, all the more tartly for her momentary descent into superstition. For a moment, she had half expected the lid of the coffin to clank open, and a shrouded form to rise—and do what? she demanded of herself irritably. Recite poetry? Dance a sailor's hornpipe? Surely the dead had better things to do than entertain the living.

If he noticed the asperity of her tone, it had no effect on the cane's owner. Lord Vaughn turned in Letty's direction with an unhurried movement that was nearly an incantation in itself.

"My dear Mrs. Alsdale, you do appear in the most unlikely places."

"I could say the same of you, my lord," replied Letty, deliberately moving forward to block Jane from Lord Vaughn's view. Since Lord Vaughn was nearly six feet tall and Letty just over five, it didn't work quite as effectively as she had intended. "Unless you make a practice of inhabiting crypts."

"Delightful places, aren't they?" Lord Vaughn's gesture encompassed the looming stones of the roof, the smoky shadow on the wall, the dark bulk of the coffin in front of him. "So restful."

Letty looked at the coffin and shuddered with a distaste that was entirely unfeigned. "Not precisely the sort of rest I aspire to."

The torchlight lent a demonic aspect to the silver streaks in Lord Vaughn's hair, limning them with infernal fire. "It comes to us all in the end, whether we seek it or no."

No ... no ... no ... echoed the stone arches mournfully.

Letty's voice drowned out the echoes. "There's no need to hasten the process."

"You wouldn't fling yourself into the grave like Juliet?"

"Certainly not for Romeo."

Eo ... eo ... eo ... caroled the echoes in funereal descant.

"For someone else, then," said Lord Vaughn softly.

Letty bristled. "Dying for love is a ridiculous notion. Only a poet would think of it."

" 'The lunatic, the lover, and the poet, of imagination all compact,' " quoted Vaughn lazily. "You would prefer to die for something else, perhaps? A cause? An ideal?" He paused, holding up his cane so that the silver serpent at its head blazed in the light. "A country?"

"You left out old age," replied Letty.

"How very unambitious of you, Mrs. Alsdale."

"Alexander the Great died in his bed."

"Not so Caesar," countered Lord Vaughn, adding, with peculiar emphasis, "or Brutus."

Rather than bandy Romans, with whom her acquaintance was strictly limited, Letty resorted to changing the subject. "You never told me what brought you down here. Was it merely a philosophical endeavor?"

"Meditations on the meaning of mortality? No." Lord Vaughn's elegant hand rested briefly on the lid of the coffin in a gesture that was almost a caress. "You might call this more of a social call."

Lord Vaughn's rings glinted incongruously against the dark casket, a reminder of earthy vanities against the grim inevitability of the grave.

"You've put it off a bit long, haven't you?" said Letty, regarding the coffin with distaste. There was no plate on the coffin, no insignia, no name, merely a series of lightly incised lines scratched into the surface. Letty could barely make out the marks.

"Five years too long," said Vaughn.

His gloved fingers traced the scratches. One long stroke, followed by three short ones. An E. Followed by another long stroke. Then . . .

"Alas, poor Edward. I knew him well."

Letty's throat felt very tight as she watched Lord Vaughn trace the final two prongs of the second initial. Edward was a common enough name. But for the last name to begin with an F . . .

"Edward?" she repeated.

Vaughn gazed meditatively at the coffin, like Hamlet surveying the skull of Yorick. "Lord Edward Fitzgerald."

So that much, at least, of Jane's story had been true.

"This is the coffin of *Lord Edward Fitzgerald*?" she announced as loudly as she dared, wondering if Jane already knew, or cared.

"Poor Edward. He cared so deeply for his causes," said Lord Vaughn, in the tone of one marveling at a fascinating incomprehensibility.

"Who was he?" asked Letty, trying to angle herself in such a way that Lord Vaughn would have to move away to speak to her, and leave the field clear for Jane. Perhaps if she moved a little to the left . . . Lord Vaughn remained stubbornly where he was, squarely in front of Lord Edward's coffin.

"My cousin." Lord Vaughn's lips curled in amusement at Letty's involuntary expression of surprise. "You really don't know your Debrett's, do you, Mrs. Alsdale? A lamentable oversight in any debutante."

"I was never terribly good at being a debutante," admitted Letty. "I'm much better at balancing accounts."

Lord Vaughn held up one long-fingered hand. "I shan't ask. For your edification, my ignorant young lady, Edward was the son of Lady Emily Lennox. Lady Emily Lennox married James Fitzgerald, the Earl of Kildare. Lady Emily's father was the Duke of Richmond, who was, in turn, first cousin to my grandmother."

"Which makes you . . . ?" inquired Letty, trying desperately to untangle the mesh of titles.

"Exactly as I am," replied Vaughn, extending an arm. "Shall we rejoin your party? They seem to have strayed."

"Unless," retorted Letty, anxious to divert attention from Jane, who was poking into the foundations of the vault with more antiquarian fervor than one might expect from Miss Gilly Fairley, "we are the ones who have strayed."

"An estimable young lady like yourself?" replied Vaughn, turning her words into something else entirely as he drew her inexorably in the direction of Jane, Miss Gwen, and the beleaguered curate. "Never."

"I was wondering where you had got to!" exclaimed Jane. "Oh, do come look, Mrs. Alsdale, darling, at these wonderful pillars! Can't you just imagine hideous Count Alfonso walling lovely Dulcibelle into just such a crypt as this? I know I shall have nightmares for a week!"

"How lovely," said Letty weakly.

"And a sepulchre!" Jane darted past Lord Vaughn, and stretched out both hands to Lord Edward's humble casket in a gesture of exaggerated rapture.

Within the space of a moment, she had run her hands over the top, peered beneath the base, and come up beaming. Beaming, Letty noticed, and empty-handed. Lord Vaughn's presence precluded a more thorough investigation, but, even to Letty's untrained eyes, the inspection appeared perfunctory. Reflexively,

Letty's head tilted back, up to the vaulted roof, above which Lord Pinchingdale was . . . doing what?

"How gloriously gruesome!" Jane enthused, patting the top of Lord Edward's coffin like a much-beloved pet. "I do prefer the word 'sepulchre' to 'coffin,' don't you? It's just so much more . . ."

"Dramatic?" supplied Lord Vaughn.

". . . horrid!" finished Jane triumphantly, brushing dirt off her gloves.

"Or horridly dramatic," murmured Vaughn.

"My dramatics are never horrid!" protested Jane, batting her eyelashes at Lord Vaughn. She put a finger to her cheek in exaggerated perplexity. "Or do I mean that my horrors are never dramatic?"

"I find it horrifying that we haven't yet been introduced." Lord Vaughn looked to Letty.

"Lord Vaughn," said Letty, since there was little else she could do, "allow me to present you to Miss Gilly Fairley."

"Gilly." Lord Vaughn rolled the silver head of his cane meditatively between his fingers. "An unusual name."

"Short for Evangeline, but I do think that's so dreadfully dull and stuffy, don't you agree, my lord?" Jane simpered up at Lord Vaughn from under the brim of her bonnet. "My mother called me her little Gillyflower. Isn't that ever so sweet?"

"A sweet name for a sweet lady." Lord Vaughn offered Jane his arm, pointing her toward the stairs. "Where I grew up, gillyflowers went by another name. We called them 'pinks.'"

"How charming!" Jane scooped up her long skirt to navigate the narrow steps, which Letty took to mean that Jane was quite finished with the crypt. Letty fell in behind the two of them, relieved to be heading back to daylight. "Pink always has looked very well on me."

"Or sometimes," Lord Vaughn said as he took Jane's elbow to guide her up the stairs, "carnations."

"Are they pink?" Jane asked vacantly. "I must confess, my lord, I'm not the least bit botanical."

"Isn't a carnation supposed to be red rather than pink?" Letty barged in, hurrying up the steps behind them. "I seem to remember some line or other about blood turning the seas incarnadine."

"I've never been to Carnadine," fluttered Jane, pausing at the top of the stairs to look back at Letty. "Is it in Scotland?"

"Near enough," said Lord Vaughn dryly, reaching down a hand to help Letty up the final steps. "I believe the line in question comes from the Scottish play—*Macbeth*," he specified for Gilly's benefit. "Yet another case of treason and skullduggery immortalized in verse. Have you noticed, my dear Miss Fairley, that the villains get all the good lines?"

"I'm not very fond of the theater," replied Jane, blinking her eyes woefully beneath her bonnet. Letty's own eyes smarted in the unaccustomed sunlight, but Jane's expression was more design than nature. "All that prating and running about with toy swords. It's quite fatiguing. I much prefer a dance."

"I am sure many men would be delighted to dance to your tune, my dear Miss Fairley."

"Oh, no," averred Jane, falling into pace with Lord Vaughn as they processed around the side of the church. "I play only indifferently."

Lord Vaughn's head bent attentively toward Gilly's. "I would imagine that that depends upon the game."

"I am told," said Jane demurely, "that I play wonderfully well at charades."

"Lord Vaughn!" intervened Letty. The pair turned back to look at her with identical expressions of inquiry. Letty would have loved to ask Jane what she was playing at, but Jane wore Gilly's slightly daft mask, all wide eyes and parted lips.

"How does your cousin?" Letty finished lamely.

Lord Vaughn's eyebrows lifted. "I don't believe his condition has changed."

Flustered, Letty scurried to catch up with them. "I meant the other cousin. Mr. Ormond."

"Augustus occupies himself," Lord Vaughn said blandly. He smiled down at Jane. Since Jane was only a few inches shorter than he, he didn't have far to look. "He, too, enjoys charades."

Letty decided that she didn't enjoy charades. Not one bit. Letty had never liked playing games she couldn't win. Whatever game Jane was playing, it wasn't one to which Letty knew the rules.

As if to complete Letty's discomfiture, Lord Pinchingdale chose that moment to stride down the steps of the church, looking more self-assured than anyone had a right to be. Every fold of his cravat was neatly in place; his cane swung from his hand at an angle Letty was sure was as geometrically correct as the latest mathematics could make it; and his hat sat just so on his brow, casting just enough of his face into shadow to eliminate any hope of reading his expression.

There wasn't so much as a look exchanged between Miss Gwen and Jane, but, within seconds, Miss Gwen had Lord Vaughn by the arm, while Jane moved smoothly toward Lord Pinchingdale, waving and trilling his name.

"You must help us settle this dispute, my lord," Miss Gwen said imperiously. She jerked her head in the direction of the curate, who was looking mournfully after Jane. Catching the curate by the arm, she dragged him ruthlessly into the discussion, leaving Jane and Lord Pinchingdale to their privacy, like any good matchmaking chaperone. "*He* claims the Lord chose to smite the Ammonites with fire and sword. Sheer nonsense. Why would our Lord wield a sword when there were plagues to be had?"

Letty didn't wait to hear Lord Vaughn's opinions on the proper procedure for obliterating one's enemies. Instead, she drifted as insouciantly as she could after Jane, pretending to be absorbed by the impressive facade of the church.

As she let her eyes roam unseeingly up the massive Ionic pilasters toward the tower, she heard Jane ask, with the merest breath of sound, "And?"

Lord Pinchingdale's eyes flicked to Letty before he answered, equally softly, "Yes."

And that was all.

It was enough to make Letty wonder why they bothered to lower their voices at all. What did they think she was going to discern from a simple, muttered "yes"? *Yes, it's a lovely day? Yes, please pass the mutton? Yes, we still don't trust that Letty creature?*

Jane leaned closer, murmuring something meant for Lord Pinchingdale's ears alone. Both pairs of eyes flicked to Letty, and she knew, with hideous surety, that they were talking about her. Whatever Jane was saying to Lord Pinchingdale, he didn't like it. Letty looked miserably away, feigning an interest in the emblems carved above the door. She would have been willing to hazard a guess as to the nature of the conversation. Jane, in her sensible Jane voice, would be urging Lord Pinchingdale to swallow his personal revulsion for the good of the country.

As for Lord Pinchingdale . . . well, his feelings were clear enough. There was no need to humiliate herself further by putting them into words.

Oh, she wanted to be home! Not her hired lodgings in Dublin, not the stuffy ballrooms of London, but real home, where she belonged, where she was useful and needed and always knew exactly what she was meant to be doing. Letty would have given anything to run howling back to Hertfordshire like a homesick child.

But she didn't belong there anymore, either. Married women didn't return to their parents' homes and pick up where they had left off. It just wasn't done. And even if she did go home, in defiance of all the conventions, it wouldn't be the same. Miss Letty could sit in a tenant's kitchen, with butter dripping off a fresh crumpet, and discuss crops and cows; Viscountess Pinchingdale couldn't. She would be curtsied straight back to the manor house, condemned to a sterile life of genteel uselessness.

Letty swallowed hard, fighting back a sudden wave of tears. Images of her future, without a real home, without a real purpose, eternally on the fringes, danced about her like goblins, jabbing and jeering at her. She could remain in Dublin, on the fringes of a conspiracy she didn't understand, with people who didn't want her there anyway. Or she could return to London, to hover on the edges of her family's existence. Whichever way she chose, she would be a superfluity, like an extra woman at a dinner party where there weren't enough men to make up the numbers.

"Italianate classicism at its best," said Lord Pinchingdale's voice, just above her shoulder.

Letty started. "I beg your pardon?"

"The facade," he clarified.

"Um, yes," agreed Letty, who had received nothing more than a blurry impression of stone. Her voice sounded suspiciously coarse to her ears, thickened with the residue of unshed tears. Taking care to pronounce each word clearly, she added, "It's quite lovely. Not as grand as St. Paul's, but very, um, symmetrical."

"It certainly is that."

Letty waited for the sting, but Lord Pinchingdale's countenance revealed nothing more damning than pleasant interest. Letty wondered if this meant their truce had begun. Weren't they supposed to shake hands, or sign terms, or some such thing?

"Did you see anything interesting inside?" she asked awkwardly, doubting she would ever get the knack of holding an ordinary conversation with a double meaning. He and Jane did it so easily. As for Lord Vaughn, he had elevated the practice to a positive art. But the double-weighted words felt uncomfortable and clumsy on Letty's tongue. "Anything of note, I mean?"

She suspected she had leaned too heavily on the words "of note," and she was sure of it when Lord Pinchingdale's expression became, if anything, blander than ever.

Without looking away from his leisurely contemplation of the skull and crossbones carved above the door, Lord Pinchingdale said reflectively, "The Eucharistic emblems over the reredos are quite fine. And some of the carvings on the pulpit were extremely . . . interesting."

Just when Letty was quite sure that she had imagined the peculiar emphasis on the last word, Lord Pinchingdale looked down at her with a slow, sideways glance that ran through her more potently than brandy.

Letty's formerly depressed spirits did a crazy zigzag into joy, like a tipsy angel winging back to heaven. Whatever Jane had said to him . . . oh, Letty didn't even care. No matter what persuasion it had taken, this sudden amity offered a reprieve from her nightmare vision of perennial exile. Letty could have jumped up and down and hugged him. But she didn't. She might not be fluent in double meanings, but she did understand that much about discretion.

Besides, she still hadn't quite forgiven him for that nasty remark in the carriage.

"The pulpit," Lord Pinchingdale added casually, as if in answer to an unasked question, "is located directly above the crypt."

"Ah," Letty said breathlessly, the pieces falling into place. If the pulpit was above the crypt, it was above Lord Edward's coffin. And if a group of patriotic rebels wanted to use their fallen leader as a posting point, they would find the pulpit far easier to access than the torturous route through the trapdoor into the crypt. "I do so love an interesting pulpit!"

That hadn't come out quite the way she had intended.

Clearly, Lord Pinchingdale didn't think so, either. He fixed her with a long, considering look that made Letty want to fiddle with her hair, preferably in a way that would cover most of her face.

"You really haven't any talent for dissembling, have you?" he said, at last.

"No," admitted Letty dispiritedly, absently drawing the string on her reticule open and closed. It pained her to admit incompetence at anything, especially with their truce so new and raw. "I never really had any need for it. Before."

"Letty." Her name sounded absurdly intimate coming from Lord Pinchingdale's lips. But, of course, what else was he to call her? He couldn't call her Miss Alsworthy anymore, and she had already shown that she was incapable of remembering to respond to her alias.

"Letty," he repeated insistently, "what happened that night?" He didn't have to explain which night he was referring to.

Dry-mouthed, Letty asked, "What happened to our truce? No recriminations, letting bygones be?"

"I'm not trying to attack you." Lord Pinchingdale leaned a hand against the wall above Letty's head, his gray eyes intent on her face in a way that did funny things to Letty's ability to breathe properly. He was so close that tendrils of her hair caught on the dark fabric of his sleeve, so close that Letty could see the tired circles under his eyes, and the shadows left on his cheeks by the fine lines of his cheekbones. He needed feeding up, and a few good nights of sleep. "I just need to know. What happened?"

He seemed sincere—but he had seemed sincere before. And, after witnessing his performance with Jane, Letty didn't place much trust in seeming. The stone of the wall biting into her back, Letty eyed him warily.

"Why now?" she asked. "Why not before?"

"Because—"

"Halloooo!" a voice hailed them.

With the utmost reluctance, Geoff let his hand fall from the wall behind Letty's head. He knew that voice. All too well.

Moving very slowly, in the hopes of warding off the inevitable, he turned in the direction of the voice. There, on Werburgh Street, a tall figure in bright regimentals was swinging down from one of the low-slung carts that served those who preferred not to waste their coin on a hackney. The bright blue tunic and scarlet facings of the Horse Guards uniform made an almost comical contrast with the weathered wood of the noddy, just one step removed from a farm cart.

At least, it might have been comical if it had been anyone else. Miles. Wickham. Bonaparte, even. Anyone but this.

"I see I've come just in time," Jasper Pinchingdale said heartily.

Geoff had learned long ago that the easiest way to be rid of Jasper was to give him money. The more money one gave him, the faster he went.

Geoff reached into his waistcoat. "How much do you need this time, Jasper?"

Jasper shouldered past him, making directly for Letty.

"You wrong me, cousin. I'm not here for lack of funds, but for the charming company of a beautiful lady."

Just in case anyone might be in any doubt as to that beautiful lady's identity, he bowed deeply toward Letty, ending with a little flourish just by her feet. Letty automatically stepped back, closer to Geoff. She looked, Geoff noted, no more pleased to see him than Geoff did.

"I had hoped to persuade you to reconsider our drive," Jasper murmured in an intimate tone that sent Geoff's right eyebrow straight up to his hairline, and made Letty long to fling something, preferably at Jasper.

"I never agreed to go driving with you," Letty said sharply. Turning to Geoff, she added forcefully, "I didn't."

Neither man paid the slightest bit of attention to her.

"In that?" Lord Pinchingdale inquired, gesturing to the ramshackle conveyance Jasper had left waiting on Werburgh Street. Letty had seen several of them in the streets since her arrival, two-wheeled carts drawn by a single horse. The driver smiled and nodded, drawing placidly on a villainous-looking pipe.

Jasper's brows drew together until they met over his nose. The cousins didn't look much alike—Jasper was fairer and broader, Geoffrey darker and taller—but Letty perceived a faint family resemblance in the similarity of their scowls.

"We can't all of us afford a high-perch phaeton, *cousin*," clipped Jasper.

"I don't own a high-perch phaeton." Lord Pinchingdale's eyebrow had climbed so high that Letty was afraid he might do himself permanent damage.

"You could if you chose to."

Lord Pinchingdale looked distinctly unimpressed with Jasper's tale of pecuniary woe.

"So could you, if you hadn't gambled away your inheritance. That was a nice little estate in Wiltshire you came into, Jasper. Would you like to explain what became of it?"

Jasper favored his cousin with such a look of undiluted hatred that Letty took an instinctive step back, closer to Lord Pinchingdale.

Turning to Letty, Jasper bared his teeth in an unconvincing attempt at a smile. "Pay no mind to him, fair lady. He is simply trying to blacken me in your sight."

"Generally," said Lord Pinchingdale, "you do that all by yourself."

Jasper continued to smile determinedly at her, as though his cousin had not spoken, but Letty had never seen anything quite so cold as his eyes. "If not a drive, perhaps an outing? The countryside is very beautiful this time of year."

"Flowers make me sneeze," Letty lied shamelessly. "Someone sent me a bouquet once and I had to take to my bed for a week."

"Indoor pursuits, then," Jasper persevered.

"Not under your roof," replied Lord Pinchingdale pleasantly.

"What of the theater?" Jasper continued doggedly. "Dublin is known for its theater."

"A new opera opened at the Crow Street Theatre this week," put in Lord Vaughn helpfully, strolling up to their little group with Jane on his arm and Miss Gwen stalking behind. He waved a languid hand. "Ramah-something-or-other."

"What a charming idea!" exclaimed Jane, who seemed to

have forgotten that she disliked the theater. "We shall make a party of it! This next week is so frightfully busy but I believe we have Friday free, haven't we, Auntie Ernie?"

"Perhaps Mrs. Alsdale would prefer to attend sooner." Jasper made one last attempt.

"I wouldn't think of going without Miss Fairley," said Letty firmly.

"Oh, aren't you too sweet!" exclaimed Jane. "I just knew we were going to be the best of friends the moment I saw you, didn't I, Lord Pinchingdale?" Without waiting for him to respond, she tilted her head to one side, in deep thought. "If Lord Pinchingdale escorts me, and Captain Pinchingdale escorts Mrs. Alsdale . . . then, Lord Vaughn, you shall escort darling Auntie Ernie!"

Jasper was the only one who looked pleased with the arrangements.

He sent a look of smirking triumph at Lord Pinchingdale, like a child awarded sole use of a disputed toy. Lord Pinchingdale didn't return the compliment; he smiled and bowed to Jane as though he had no other desire in the world but to make a part of her party at the theater—but his attention was on Lord Vaughn as he did so. Letty wondered where Lord Vaughn fit into the equation. Friend, foe, innocent bystander? The latter seemed the least likely, if the tenor of his conversation with Jane in the crypt was anything to go by. On the other hand, he had contrived to sound just as obscurely portentous with Letty last night at Mrs. Lanergan's, turning simple sentences into a maze of hidden meanings. He might be exactly as he seemed: a bored gentleman with a habit of attaching more significance to his words than they deserved. But why was Jane so eager to attach him to their party?

There was Vaughn, and then there was Jasper. Letty would have been willing to stake her dowry (what was left of it, at any rate) that the antipathy between the two cousins was genuine. But . . . he had asked Jasper to be his groomsman. And, last night, she would have been equally eager to wager that Lord Pinchingdale had amorous designs of the worst sort on Miss Gilly Fairley. Could the animosity between the two cousins be as much of a blind as Jane's silver-gilt curls?

Trying to sort out who was pretending what—and to whom—was beginning to give Letty a headache.

Lord Vaughn looked equally pained, but for different reasons. Faced with the prospect of an evening with Miss Gwen, Lord Vaughn chose flight over valor.

"Although it plunges me into the deepest agonies of regret to refuse such an honor as the company of Mrs. Grimstone, I promised young Augustus I would make one of his party next Friday."

Miss Gwen emitted a noise that sounded suspiciously like, "Coward."

Unmoved, Vaughn eyed her dispassionately through the lens of his quizzing glass. "My dear Mrs. Grimstone, sometimes cowardice is merely another word for common sense."

Miss Gwen considered for a moment. "Pithy," she said at last. "I'll give you that."

"I am, as ever, humbly grateful for any gift at your disposal," replied Lord Vaughn, with an elegant mockery of a bow.

"Ha!" said Miss Gwen. "You were never humble in your life."

"We were all young once."

"And probably the worse for it, too." Confident in having achieved the last word, Miss Gwen smirked at the company at large.

Jane quickly intervened, moving to mollify Lord Vaughn with a speed that confirmed all of Letty's suspicions—or, at least, some of them. "My Lord Vaughn, you simply must come, or I shan't ever forgive you."

"How could I refuse anything to such a fair flower?"

As Jane turned to smile at him, a chance shaft of sunlight struck the gold locket at Jane's throat, lighting it like a beacon.

Letty sneezed.

Chapter Seventeen

"I don't think that's ours," said Jay, turning back around.

"Huh?" My eyes were still fixed somewhere just over his shoulder.

"The food," said Jay. "It's the wrong order."

He didn't seem to realize that the universe had just flipped onto its head and started jumping about like a Romanian gymnast in the last leg of the Olympics.

I mustered a weak smile. "Oops," I said. "Sorry."

In an alternative universe, I continued to look and sound like a perfectly normal human being. One leg was crossed over the other, my right hand was loosely clasped around the stem of my wineglass, and my hair fell in a becoming arc just beneath my jaw. Inside, I was a blubbering mess.

I smiled at Jay and made some sort of inane comment about the food. I have no idea what it was, but it must have been perfectly acceptable, because he didn't stare at me as though I'd sprouted three heads or bolt for the door. Meanwhile, my internal monologue was stuck on a repeating loop of *My God, my God, my God*, enlivened with a chorus of *What do I do, what do I do, what do I do*, in stereo sound.

Over Jay's shoulder, Colin didn't seem to have noticed me yet. He and his friends had trooped in a noisy herd over to the bar, Ungh and friends seeking water hole after a long day of mammoth hunting.

At least he wasn't there with a woman.

Oh, no, you don't, I told myself. That didn't change the basic fact that he was back in London and hadn't called. He hadn't even *tried* to call. At least, as far as I knew. I didn't have an answering machine back in the flat . . . but that was because no one ever called me on my landline, anyway, except my parents, and occasionally Alex. Everyone else used the mobile. And the mobile registered missed calls.

Which effectively ruled out the charming picture of Colin nobly hitting redial while the phone rang and rang in an empty flat.

"How long are you in London for?" I asked Jay, in the hopes that if I got him talking again, he might not notice that I found the area just over his left shoulder much more interesting than I found him.

"Just for tonight." Jay flipped open his phone with the air of a habitual cell phone checker. I wondered if it was programmed into him never to be able to discuss time without first looking at his phone. "I fly back to New York tomorrow."

"Oh, are you going home for Thanksgiving?"

The three guys were clustered at the bar in that weird way men have, as though in a football huddle or a Canada goose flight formation, two at the actual bar, the one in the middle slightly behind. The other two were, in a word, unremarkable. The one in back had a shock of red hair and a healthily browned complexion. The other was shorter, darker, and more heavily built, with closely cut curly hair. Just guys. Or, as they would undoubtedly call themselves, blokes.

Colin hadn't seen me yet—at least, I didn't think he had. I

concentrated on arranging my smile at its most becoming angle, just in case he should glance over.

"You're not going back?"

What was he talking about? Oh, Thanksgiving. I forced myself to focus for just as long as it took to reply. "I can't really justify it. I'll be heading home for Christmas in just another month, anyway."

The bartender plonked three large pints on the trendy counter, pale gold and dripping with foam. My eyes strayed to the half-finished glass in front of Jay. Why was it that when Jay ordered beer it seemed pretentious, but when Colin did, it just seemed normal?

Maybe it was because Colin wasn't wearing a jacket without a tie. Or maybe it was because I was a little bit biased.

Just a little bit.

On the other hand, Jay returned calls, and Colin didn't. Returning calls was a big plus.

"—homesick?" Jay was finishing.

I'd missed most of it, but it wasn't hard to guess. I could probably tune out for half the conversation, and come back in half an hour later knowing exactly what had been said.

That, I reminded myself, wasn't fair either. No one said anything particularly interesting on a first date. There was practically a rule against it.

"Not really," I responded to his unheard question, as though I hadn't been on the verge of sobbing into the Marks & Spencer sandwich case a few days before. "An old friend of mine always does a huge Thanksgiving dinner for expats and assorted hangers-on, so I'll get my turkey and stuffing fix for the year."

"It's not the same as going home," said Jay, in a smug way that annoyed me enough to drag my attention away from Colin.

"No, really, you think?"

At least, that was what I wanted to say.

Since that might get back to Grandma, I just shrugged, and said, "You take what you can get. And I've known Pammy and her family since I was five, so it's almost as good as going home. Lots of reminiscing about old times, that sort of thing."

"Pammy is . . . ?"

"The friend who's doing Thanksgiving dinner. We went to Chapin together."

"Right." Jay processed that information as solemnly as though it were a bullet point on a spreadsheet. Did spreadsheets have bullet points? I didn't know. More important, I didn't want to know. I had a feeling Jay would try to tell me if I gave him the chance. Complete with PowerPoint presentation and graphs.

"Does your family make a big deal out of Thanksgiving?" I asked, assuming an expression of great earnestness. My motives were purely ignoble. The more open-ended the question, the longer Jay would keep talking. And the less likely he would be to notice that my attention was largely elsewhere.

His mouth began moving. I nodded and smiled, all the while tracking Colin's movements like high-tech army radar with an enemy warship in range.

I knew exactly how I was going to play it. I wasn't going to smile. I wasn't going to jump up and down and wave like a maniac. I winced at the memory of standing in a ruined cloister in Sussex, with my eyes closed, my head tipped back, and my lips puckered up.

I'd already indicated more than enough interest.

For once, I was going to play it cool. If he came up to me, I knew he was interested; if he stayed on the other side of the room, he wasn't. It was a test of the Emergency Boy Interest System.

There was just a slight hitch to the plan. Colin's back was to me, which meant that, unless he suddenly grew eyes in the back of his head (which would be a distinct turnoff in the dating department), he had no idea I was there.

Details, details.

And, lo, the great dating gods did cast the glow of their countenances down upon me. At the bar, Colin suddenly twitched and plunked his glass back down on the counter. No, it wasn't a sudden epileptic fit or an attack by a killer snake only he could see. It was his mobile, buzzing away in his left pocket. He dove sideways, like John Travolta on the downswing of "Staying Alive," and yanked the phone out of his pocket, swiveling away from his companions as he did so, that marginal move by which cell phone users maintain the illusion of privacy with the minimum actual movement.

Which put him facing directly toward me.

My little sister calls it the Evil "I-Know-You" Look. The Evil "I-Know-You" Look begins with surprised recognition (generally represented by Jillian widening her eyes, dropping her jaw, and poking one finger in the air in a sort of "Eureka!" motion). Recognition is followed by doubt—the finger droops as the viewer leans in closer to get a better look. The final stage is alarm. The outstretched hand is hastily retrieved as the viewer seeks a way to hide before being forced to acknowledge the acquaintance. Hence the "evil" in the Evil "I-Know-You" Look, otherwise, one assumes, it would simply be an "I-Know-You" Look.

Don't ask me, ask Jillian. She made it up.

Stage One: Colin froze with one hand on the mobile. Stage Two: Eyes narrowing, Colin leaned forward, face arranged in just the right blend of curiosity and confusion. Stage Three: . . .

I didn't wait to see Colin go through Stage Three. I hastily wrenched my gaze back to Jay.

"Tofu turkey? Really?" I said breathlessly.

I put an extra few watts into my smile at Jay, just because. It was a sickening display. Grandma would have been so proud.

"Only that one year," said Jay, clearly anxious lest I think them impossibly passé on the Thanksgiving menu front. "And it was just because my brother's girlfriend doesn't eat meat." He made it sound like a personal failing.

"What did it taste like?"

"Turkey," said Jay.

On that scintillating note, a shadow fell across our table.

"Hi," Colin said.

He smelled of the outdoors, of cold, clean air, and falling leaves, and long, open stretches of parkland, a world away from the muggy heat of the Indian restaurant. His pale green shirt was open slightly at the collar, lending a greenish cast to his hazel eyes. His skin looked tanner than the last time I had seen him, the healthy brown of the dedicated outdoorsman, although that might only have been in contrast to Jay's office-park pallor.

There's a Christina Rosetti poem that begins, "The birthday of my life is come / My love is come to me." Well, I couldn't claim—at least not with a straight face—that my heart was like the singing bird that perched upon the watered shoot. And I think Rosetti was talking about Christ, or something equally allegorical and noncarnal. But my spirits did float up like leaves eddying in playful circles in an autumn breeze.

Up—and down. All those ridiculous conflicting emotions one experiences and would like to pretend one didn't. Ecstatic joy that he had gotten up and walked all the way across the room—to see me! Staggering resentment that he hadn't called. Desperate yearning for some sort of sign, some sort of signal, that he would have liked to have called.

And, topping it all off, extreme personal annoyance for all of the aforementioned emotions. What was I, thirteen?

"Hi," I said.

We stared at each other like idiots.

At least, I was staring like an idiot, desperately trying to think of something neutral to say. "Where have you been?" and "Why the hell haven't you called me?" didn't seem to come under that category. Nor did "Colin, take me away!" Besides, that was supposed to be "Calgon," not "Colin."

"Hi," Jay said loudly, completing the conversational circle. He stuck out a hand. "Jay Watkins."

Colin's hand met his with an audible thump, like two gorillas bumping chests in the forest. "Colin Selwick."

"Oh, right, sorry," I said incoherently, shoving the hair back out of my face. It promptly flopped back again. Chin-length hair and a side part do not a convenient combination make. "Colin, Jay. Jay, Colin."

The introductions having been completed—twice—I belatedly remembered my manners.

"How is your aunt?" For Jay's benefit, I added, "Colin's aunt was kind enough to help me out with my research."

"Wreaking her usual havoc," Colin said fondly. "You should ring her. I'm sure she'll want to hear how you're getting on."

"I'll do that." All the excited flutters leached out of me, like air from a burst balloon. Of course, that was why Colin had come over. As a courtesy on behalf of his aunt. A duty visit. That was what the whole thing had been, from the very beginning, and I was an idiot to have ever thought otherwise.

What sort of pathetic creature was I, that I had mistaken plain good manners for romantic interest?

That, by the way, was a rhetorical question. The answer was too grim to contemplate.

I took a bracing sip of my wine. "It's very kind of her to take an interest."

Colin braced both hands against the tabletop, the corners of his eyes crinkling as he leaned forward. "How *are* you getting on?"

"Very well, actually." I couldn't have him thinking that I was entirely dependent on his family's good graces. "I followed a hunch and came across some great stuff in the BL."

"I didn't realize the BL had anything on the Carnation."

"I don't think they realized either." Flipping back my hair, I grinned up at him. "It's all under 'Alsdale'—whoever entered it into the computer clearly just took the name off the bottom of the letters."

"Alsdale? That doesn't sound familiar."

He seemed so genuinely interested that I couldn't resist. Besides, I'd been dying to tell someone. Alex was busy, Pammy couldn't care less, and my adviser responded to e-mails about once every three months. If I was lucky.

"Remember Mary Alsworthy?"

"Vaguely," said Colin cautiously. "It's been years since I read through those papers."

"Her sister Letty married Geoffrey Pinchingdale-Snipe. He went off to Ireland in 1803—"

"That much I did know."

"—and she followed after him, under the name Alsdale."

"So you followed 'Alsworthy' to 'Alsdale'?"

"Mm-hmm," I said smugly. "And it gets even better. Guess who else was there?"

Jay wanted to play, too. "The Scarlet Pumpernickel?"

Colin fell pray to a sudden coughing fit.

"Close," I said, bracing one elbow against the table and leaning encouragingly toward Jay. Even aside from Colin's coughing fit, I did feel a little bad about Jay. After all, it must be very tedious for him to be stuck listening to a detailed discussion on an esoteric topic he knew nothing about—much like I had felt when he had been going on about his three previous companies.

Besides, being on a date with Jay was clear proof that I had never, ever cherished tender notions regarding Colin. And I certainly hadn't checked my phone every five minutes for the past ten days waiting for him to call.

Guilt—and less laudable motives—inspired me to bestow a warm smile in Jay's direction. "It wasn't the Pimpernel, but it was another spy with a flowery name."

Jay shook his head, struggling for words.

"I can't believe you're spending seven years of your life on spies named after flowers."

I abruptly ceased feeling bad about Jay.

"If all of this has been sitting at the BL all this time," said Colin, crossing his arms across his chest, "why hasn't anyone come across it before?"

I shook my head. "I'm not explaining it well, am I? First, it's in one of those jumble folios. Someone just tossed the contents of their attic into a notebook and sent it off to the BL. I don't think anyone's opened it since it got there in 1902. On top of that, Letty doesn't use proper names anywhere. I mean, from time to time she'll throw in a reference to the Carnation or the Tulip, but most of the time you have to work by inference. Everyone—and I do mean everyone—seems to be traveling under an assumed name. The only reason I was able to figure out who was who was because I was looking for it. I knew Letty's relationship to Geoffrey Pinchingdale-Snipe, and I knew that if there was a Jane operating in concert with a Geoffrey, it was probably *the* Jane."

"So you followed Geoffrey to Letty, and Letty to Jane." The words were simple enough, but the admiring look that accompanied them made me want to wriggle and thump my tail like a happy puppy dog.

"Basically. To anyone reading the letters cold, it would all just sound like pointless gossip—he-said, she-said sort of stuff about a bunch of historically unimportant people. You have to read pretty far along before you even get to the first Pink Carnation mention." I tried to look modest and missed by about a mile. "Guess what Jane's alias was?"

"The Scarlet Pumpernickel?"

I bit my lip on a grin and cast him a mock reproachful look. My restraint was entirely wasted on Jay, who was surreptitiously checking his BlackBerry, entirely unaware that he was being mocked. "Not even close. She traveled as a Miss Gilly Fairley."

"Gilly . . . for gillyflower?"

The lad was quick.

"Exactly." I beamed.

Jay slid his BlackBerry back under the table. "Gillyflower?"

"It's another name for a carnation," I explained.

"As in pink," added Colin.

"Oh, right." Jay took a long pull of his beer.

"Are you a historian?" asked Colin politely. A little too politely.

With the conversation directed back where it belonged—him—Jay perked up. "No. I help technological service providers actualize their human resource needs."

I took a peek at Colin, but he had his poker face down pat. "A necessary cog in the great wheel of social progress," he said solemnly.

Damn. Jay was rapidly losing value as a face-saving device. Something had to be done, and quickly.

"Jay made some great suggestions about my dissertation earlier!" I chimed in, like a one-woman cheerleading squad.

Across the table, Jay preened.

"Really?" Colin looked expectantly at Jay.

"Yes! I mean, yes. Jay, um, reminded me that it's all too easy to assume an Anglocentric viewpoint while working with a source base composed primarily of the epistolary product of a privileged segment of English society. He suggested that it might be a useful corrective to factor in the social, economic, and political grievances of the oppressed Irish underclass." I took a healthy swig of my wine. "In the interest of scholarly accuracy, of course."

Jay looked much as I must have when he started going on about actualizing technological potentialities. Ha! I could speak gibberish, too, when I wanted to. No field is without its own useful circumlocutions—which roughly translates as "important-sounding babble."

"Of course," Colin agreed. He seemed to be having trouble controlling the corners of his lips again. He glanced sideways from me to Jay and back again. "How do you two, er, know each other?"

At that point, I would have preferred to claim we didn't. But I was stuck. Stuck, stuck, stuck. Hoist by my own petard.

"Our grandmothers are friends."

"Actually," interrupted Jay sententiously, "it's my mother who knows your grandmother."

"Right!" I said brightly. "Mitten."

"Muffin," Jay corrected.

At least I was close.

"Mm-hmm," managed Colin, in a way that suggested he knew just what was going on. I could tell he was dying to make a scone joke. I hoped he choked on it.

"But that's not all!" continued my big mouth, working overtime to correct the horrible assumption that I might, just might, be on a grandparent-assisted blind date. "My absolute best friend has been dating Jay's college roommate for absolutely ever!"

Two "absolutes" in one sentence. Next thing I knew, I was going to start spouting "like," probably coupled with "totally" and "ohmigod!"

"How convenient," said Colin. Before I could think of anything clever to say to that, he bestowed an avuncular smile on both of us in turn. "Well, I'll leave you to it, then."

"Nice meeting you." Jay reached into his jacket pocket and produced a business card. "If you ever need technical support services . . ."

Colin gingerly accepted the card. It boasted blue and orange lettering and was cut on a slight diagonal, in a way that was probably supposed to look edgy, but more likely just made it difficult to fit into the proper wallet compartment.

"Cheers," he said, tilting the card in ironic salute. "Good to see you, Eloise."

Going, going, going . . . Gone. My shoulders slumped as Colin turned and strolled back through the multicolored obstacle course of tables to his comfortable perch at the bar, his duty to his aunt's protégé discharged. His friends greeted him with raised glasses and pointed glances. Colin shrugged and said something that produced a laugh all around.

I felt my cheeks grow pink before I remembered that, wait, I was the one on a date. He was just there with a bunch of blokes.

My pride was salvaged. I had won the upper hand—so why did I feel so miserable?

A silver basket filled with warm bread materialized just below my nose, the long-awaited naan.

Jay began methodically dividing the naan, half for me, half for him, along precise, geometrical lines.

"Wait." I finished the wine in my glass in one long swallow and thrust it over to the waiter before he could escape. "I'll take a refill, please." If I could have, I would have made it a double.

It was going to be a long night.

Chapter Eighteen

They were late for the theater.

By the time their small party filtered into the box, a gentleman dressed as an Oriental potentate was already on the stage, belting out a complaint whose words were lost between the burr of rolled Rs and the chatter of conversation in neighboring boxes. It was already clear, however, that the main entertainment of the evening was not to be on the stage.

As Geoff struggled to untangle the ribbon of Gilly's opera glass, Jasper stole up behind Letty, cupping her shoulders. Letty could feel the imprint of his fingers through the fabric of her cloak, bearing down on her like a yoke.

"Allow me to help you with your cloak." Jasper's right hand slid from her shoulder to the front of her cloak, bypassed the clasp entirely, and veered straight toward Letty's bosom.

"I'm quite capable of managing," replied Letty, twitching out of his grasp. She would have slapped the roving hand, but that would have entailed touching Jasper voluntarily. Knowing Jasper, he would probably take it as encouragement.

"Surely you wouldn't deny your devoted cavalier such a small service?" Jasper's profession of devotion was only slightly marred by the fact that his eyes were fixed on his cousin as he uttered it.

"Enough, Jasper." Dropping Jane's opera glass unceremoniously in her lap, Geoff crossed the box in two long strides. Miss Gwen snatched the opera glass from Jane and promptly trained it on her companions in the back of the box.

Geoff plucked the cloak from Letty's shoulders.

"There," he said tersely, draping the wrap over his arm. "Shall we sit?"

Jasper grabbed the cloak back from Geoff.

"Confoundedly silly creatures," muttered Miss Gwen.

She was not referring to the actors.

Letty heartily seconded the sentiment. The ride to Crow Street had been an utter misery, with Jasper and Geoff exchanging barbed comments over her head. In a carriage meant for four and crammed with five, a little enmity went a long way. Letty could only be grateful that the use of swords as accessories had gone out of fashion or someone would have been skewered. As she was sitting in the middle, that person would probably have been her.

As far as Letty was concerned, being fought over had little to recommend it, especially when it was blindingly apparent that their bickering had nothing to do with her charms, and everything to do with thirty thousand pounds a year and an estate in Gloucestershire. Jasper Pinchingdale cherished for his cousin an antipathy that made England's Hundred Years War with France look like a minor squabble between friends. The only reason Jasper was laying clumsy siege to her was because she belonged to Geoff—at least, in the eyes of the law and their three hundred wedding guests. What Geoff had, Jasper strove to take. And what Jasper strove to take, Geoff moved to protect. It was as simple as that. She was the equivalent of a dilapidated border fortress that nobody wanted until another monarch tried to grab it.

If it had been Mary . . .

Letty trampled on that thought before it could spread its poisonous blooms. What was the use of comparing herself to Mary? She wasn't Mary. Growing up with Mary, Letty had always felt a bit like a sturdy daisy incongruously planted in the same tub as an orchid. It wasn't just the perfect cheekbones or the willowy waist that so perfectly suited the same high-waisted gowns that turned Letty into a dumpling. No, it was the indefinable art of fascination that Mary had honed to a point more deadly than Cupid's arrows. Mary knew how to tilt the head to convey admiration, and when a smile would serve better than speech. Letty had never mastered the knack of gazing charmingly up from under her lashes; when she walked, her feet quite definitely touched the ground; and, while she could certainly hold her tongue if she had to, she had never seen the point of mimicking a mute to win a man's admiration.

That, Letty told herself firmly, was entirely beside the point. Deeper emotions had never been part of the bargain—any bargain.

Over the past week, she and Lord Pinchingdale had achieved an entente that, if it wasn't quite friendship, might at least be termed camaraderie. True to his promise of truce, Lord Pinchingdale—Geoff, as he had given her leave to call him— had made no reference to botched elopements or forced marriages. There had been no veiled slights, no barbed double entendres, not even a resentful glower when he thought she was looking the other way. Every now and again, she would catch him eyeing her the way she imagined a naturalist would a particularly baffling specimen, like a caterpillar missing a leg. And once, as he handed her down from the carriage, he had paused as though he might say something—but Jane had called out to them, and the moment had fled.

Ever since that moment on the steps of St. Werburgh, when Jasper had interrupted them, Geoff had gone back to treating her as he had a million years ago in the ballrooms of London. Kind. Patient. Detached.

Until Jasper joined them.

"Fine," Geoff was saying, his lips a tight line. "You take the cloak, and I will take the lady."

"I have no objections to that," put in Letty, feeling that, as one of the objects under discussion, she ought to have some sort of say in her ultimate disposition. Her husband acknowledged the point with a wry, sideways glance that didn't do much to mollify Letty.

Jasper jostled his cousin aside. "Miss Fairley might object. You don't want her to doubt your affections, do you, coz?"

"I take responsibility for all the members of my party," said Geoff repressively, placing a hand on the small of Letty's back in a gesture as possessive as it was meaningless.

"Oh, is that what they're calling it now?" enquired Jasper.

"Don't we have an opera to watch?" asked Letty pointedly, squirming away from Geoff's hand, irritated by the intimacy of a gesture where no real intimacy existed. "Unless," she added, folding her arms across her chest and glowering at each man in turn, "you would rather go on squabbling. Don't let me interrupt you if you're enjoying yourselves."

Jasper let his eyes drop to her bosom, pushed into prominence by her crossed arms. "I'm sure we can find more lively entertainment."

Geoff moved to block Jasper's access to Letty. "Don't even think of it."

"Why shouldn't I?" asked Jasper, a dangerous glint in his cobalt eyes as he locked gazes with his cousin. "If you have any claim on Mrs. Alsdale, I'm sure Miss Fairley would like to know."

It was blackmail, pure and simple. Next to her, Letty felt Geoff tense, Jasper's bolt hitting home more effectively than he knew. If Jasper revealed their marriage to "Miss Fairley," Jane would have no choice but to effect a public break with Geoff— what innocent young lady would do otherwise? And if Jane broke with Geoff . . . not being privy to all of their plans, Letty couldn't say just how much havoc it would wreak, but she knew enough to be quite sure that it would be a Bad Thing.

"Shall we sit?" blurted out Letty, a little too loudly. She grabbed Geoff's arm and tugged; beneath the tightly tailored fabric of his coat, his arm muscles were as taut as the gilded iron railings that fronted the box. "Look! We're missing the first act!"

"Well, *cousin?*" drawled Jasper, drinking in his cousin's discomfiture with vicious satisfaction.

"The opera?" demanded Letty, placing herself determinedly in between the two men. Since they were of a height, which put each of them a good head above Letty, the maneuver did little to further her cause.

"Stay away," said Geoff, very softly, "from Mrs. Alsdale."

"Why?" taunted Jasper, lips spreading over teeth that suddenly looked too large for his mouth. "She doesn't bear your name."

Geoff took a step forward. Not much, but just enough to convey a potent physical warning. Not to be outdone, Jasper mirrored the gesture. Sandwiched between them, a black waistcoat on one side, sea-blue brocade with burgundy flowers on the other, Letty had heard enough.

"Oh, for heaven's sake! Why don't you simply hit each other and have done with it?" she suggested irately, squirming out from between them. "I'll just get out of the way and let you have at it."

Geoff almost took her up on it, right there in the middle of the Theatre Royal, with the actors cavorting onstage below, and a dozen opera glasses sure to light on their box at the first sign of fisticuffs.

After a lifetime of Jasper, Geoff had thought he was immune to provocation—and that included the memorable incident where Jasper had "borrowed" Geoff's identity for a particularly sordid evening in a gaming hell. The men who had showed up in

Geoff's bedroom the following morning to collect on their IOUs had been no more amused than Geoff. He had been months untangling that little escapade.

But something about the way Jasper had been slavering over Letty's more noticeable attributes acted on Geoff's acquired tolerance like vinegar on varnish. At that moment, nothing would have given him greater satisfaction than to knock the leer right off Jasper's face with a few well-placed right hooks.

Letty muttered something that Geoff couldn't quite make out, but by the tone, it wasn't complimentary. Geoff glanced down. Glancing down was a mistake. If Jasper hadn't been holding Letty's wrap, Geoff would have wrapped it firmly around her and tied it in a double knot.

"Don't mind us!" Jane bustled up in a frill of flounces, jarring Geoff's attention away from Letty's décolletage. Jane's was considerably lower, but it didn't have the same unsettling effect.

"Auntie Ernie and I are just off to pay some calls," Jane announced, just as a hand crept along Letty's waist.

It did not belong to her husband.

Letty took a hasty step forward. "I'll come with you."

"Oh, no!" protested Jane, with a mischievous smile that didn't seem entirely owing to her role. "I couldn't think of making you miss the rest of the first act."

"The entertainment leaves much to be desired," said Letty darkly.

"Speak for yourself!" smirked Miss Gwen, who had also noticed the roving hand. "I, for one, am excessively diverted."

"Hmm," said Letty noncommittally, because she didn't trust herself to say anything else.

Jane fluttered her handkerchief. It was embroidered about the edges with small, pink flowers—roses, Letty was relieved to note, not carnations.

"Have you seen how many of our lovely friends are here tonight?"

The comment was ostensibly addressed to Letty, but there was an underlying edge to it that was not. Jane gestured out at the tiers of boxes that lined three sides of the theater, and began rattling off names, mostly of young women. Letty suspected that Jane had made half of them up.

Letty wondered just which lovely friends Jane and Geoff were pursuing tonight. She couldn't blame them for not telling her— her first impulse, when anyone's name was mentioned, was to turn and stare. Her companions had learned that the hard way at a masked ball at the Rotunda two nights before. Geoff had been very good about including Letty in the more minor sorts of missions, although the major ones Letty could only guess at from the deepening circles under her companions' eyes and the occasional enigmatic comment across the coffee table.

She had never seen anyone think or act quite so efficiently as Geoff. He tackled mental puzzles with the same economy with which he moved, proceeding from problem to solution in a clear line. And then, just as he had reduced a complicated code to plain English, he would say something wry and funny—and Letty would find herself swamped with an overwhelming sense of hopelessness.

It made no sense at all.

Seeing that Jasper was safely occupied by Miss Gwen, Letty left Jane and Geoff to their faux flirtation and drifted toward the front of the box. Sliding into a seat covered in crimson moreen, she flipped indifferently through her program. The night's entertainment was *Ramah Droog: Or Wine Does Wonders*, which, the managers informed her, was a comic opera written by James Cobb, and produced "with a splendor and brilliancy that reflect additional credit on the Irish stage."

Letty yawned and set the program aside. Splendid and brilliant it might be, but Letty could scarcely hear the singers over the conversation in the neighboring boxes. Below, an orange seller was giggling shrilly as she beat off the attentions of a bunch of amorous journeymen, her voice carrying far better than that of the soprano onstage. At the far end of the third tier, a pair of tipsy gentlemen were amusing themselves by casting gingerbread crumbs and bits of orange peel at a group of apprentices in the pit, unleashing a spate of profane commentary. Someone below cursed loudly as he stepped on a rotten apple, the sour juices blending with the debris of crumbs and orange pips already littering the floor. The theater had only been refurbished a few years before, but the painting of Apollo and the Muses on the ceiling was grimed with the effects of nightly candle smoke, and the king's arms above the stage had begun to flake at the edges.

Letting her eyes drift downward along the tiers, Letty spotted Lord Vaughn and his cousin—the living cousin—in a box not far from the stage. Augustus Ormond looked even more untidy than usual, his cravat tied in an uneven knot and his shirt points wilting at the edges. Next to him, as though in reproach, Lord Vaughn was making a great show of shaking out the lace over his cuffs, his elegant hands adorned with three large rings that caught the light as he moved. He was dressed in full rig, with silver lace at his throat and cuffs and the glimmer of a sword hilt at his side, more in the manner of the past century than the present.

Given the nature of the crowd in the pit, Letty couldn't blame him for coming prepared to fight his way down through the lobby.

From the box next to Vaughn's, Emily Gilchrist, decked out in pink gauze, caught Letty's eye and waved frantically. Light scintillated off the beaded reticule dangling from her wrist as it swung back and forth. Letty smiled and nodded, but Emily's guardian, the soberly garbed Mr. Throtwottle, pulled his headstrong ward back behind the gilded railing before she could respond—or take a tumble into the pit.

Tiring of the Throtwottle domestic drama, Letty shifted her attention to Lord Vaughn's box.

It was empty.

Lord Vaughn, Mr. Ormond—both had gone. Unless they were lurking in the back . . . Letty picked up Jane's discarded opera glass from the seat beside her. Vaughn and his cousin were definitely not in the box. Letty swung the glasses sideways. Nor did they seem to be paying calls on any of the neighboring boxes.

It seemed an odd time to go for refreshments.

Geoff would want to know, Letty decided. It wasn't that she was bored and looking for attention. Of course not. She was just being helpful.

No one had ever told her right out that Lord Vaughn was somehow implicated in the rebellion, but whatever suspicions his appearance by Lord Edward's grave had piqued had been confirmed by her companions' behavior over the past week. When Lord Vaughn left the room, either Geoff or Jane tended to follow. It did make sense; if one cousin had espoused the Irish cause, why not the other? Lord Vaughn's idle disclaimers by his cousin's grave didn't fool Letty for a moment.

Lord Vaughn's dark clothes blended easily with the crowd in the pit, but his ubiquitous accoutrements did not. As Letty scanned the theater, looking for Vaughn, a flash of light caught her eye. It was the head of Vaughn's cane, a silver serpent whose head reared over the ebony body of the cane, poised to strike. In the glare of the footlights, the serpent's fangs glowed an ominous red.

"My lord!" Letty called softly, wafting one hand behind her as she kept her eyes fixed on that telltale silver serpent. "Lord Pinchingdale!"

Behind her, Geoff broke off his conversation with Jane. "Yes?"

"I need your help"—seized with inspiration, Letty fluttered her program in the air—"translating the lyrics."

"I am, of course, always delighted to be of assistance. But the opera *is* in English."

"Such a pity I never learned it properly," gabbled Letty nonsensically. Tugging on his sleeve to bring him down to her level, she hissed, "Look! Lord Vaughn!"

Geoff looked straight toward Vaughn's box without having to ask which it was. Ha, thought Letty. She had been right. It was nice to be right about something after a week of uncharacteristic incompetence.

Seeing the empty row of seats, Geoff cursed beneath his breath. "Did you see where he went?"

Letty trained Jane's abandoned opera glass on the masses below. After a moment's scrutiny, she spotted the striking serpent at the very edge of the pit, just behind a group of rowdy journeymen milking every enjoyment they could out of their six-shilling tickets.

"There." Letty pointed, handing the opera glass off to Geoff.

His eyes still focused on the pit, Geoff blindly reached for the glass, his fingers closing over Letty's.

Letty snatched her hand away.

"Look!" she whispered hastily. "Vaughn's gone backstage."

Even without the glass, she could see the brightly painted door at the side of the stage inch open and then closed again, so swiftly that she wouldn't have noticed if she hadn't been following Vaughn's movements.

"So he has," murmured Geoff.

Letty glanced back over her shoulder, where Miss Gwen and Jane were taking leave of Cousin Jasper—prolonged by the fact that Miss Gwen's parasol had become tangled with Jasper's sleeve, to the irritation of both parties.

"No," Geoff said, as though in answer to an unasked question. "Their plans have nothing to do with Lord Vaughn."

"How did you know what I was thinking?" demanded Letty.

Geoff just looked at her.

"Never mind," said Letty.

Behind them, Miss Gwen and Jasper had finally become disentangled. At any moment, Jasper would be free. Free to pester Letty, that was.

"Will you be all right if I leave you here with Jasper?"

Letty would have liked to say no, but that would have been untrue. Seized with a sudden inspiration, Letty tilted her head toward the row of boxes on the opposite side of the theater. "I'll make him take me to visit Emily Gilchrist."

Geoff looked over his shoulder at Jasper and frowned.

"I'll be fine, really. Go!"

"Good girl."

With a quick, approving smile, Geoff pressed her hand and departed. He disappeared so rapidly that if it hadn't been for the residue of his touch, Letty would have wondered if he had ever been there.

Gathering up the opera glass and her program, Letty stood, feeling oddly dispirited. She knew she shouldn't be. She had done her bit for the war effort. She had even gotten credit for it. Good girl. Like a pet dog.

Letty let out an irritated breath, glancing out over the edge of the box. Time to make good on her word, like the reliable creature she was, and seek out Emily Gilchrist and Mr. Throtwottle. An evening with Emily would be penance for her sins—although what sins those were, Letty was having a hard time putting into words. Silliness, she concluded. That was her fault. Engaging in extreme silliness without the slightest provocation.

Aside from that moment with the opera glass . . .

Oh, for heaven's sake! Behind her, she could hear Jasper's heavy tread, and while she suspected that Jasper would be less likely to press his attentions on her without an audience, it wasn't a chance Letty wanted to take. She didn't doubt her ability to fend him off, just the limits of her temper. If she was very lucky, maybe Emily would flirt with Jasper, and Letty wouldn't have to talk to either of them.

There was just one problem: Emily Gilchrist wasn't there. And neither was her guardian. Their box was as empty as Lord Vaughn's.

As she frowned at Emily's empty box, the heavy crimson velvet curtains came sweeping down, wreathing her world in red. Letty stumbled backward, coughing at the dust as the fabric unfurled, cutting off their box from the rest of the theater as effectively as a wall.

"Alone at last," said Jasper.

Chapter Nineteen

By the time Geoff reached the pit, Lord Vaughn had long since disappeared backstage. Trusting that the audience was more interested in the ingenue's legs than in a stray gentleman on the prowl, Geoff put a hand to the painted panels that masked the stage door and slid around the edge, allowing the door to fall gently shut behind him.

On the other side of the door, the bright paint and proud gilding of the public parts of the theater gave way to unrelieved gloom. In contrast to the glitter of the galleries, the narrow corridor was dimly lit, cluttered with shrouded shapes and bits and pieces of scenery propped against the wall, waiting their turn onstage. Ducking under a rope that dangled from the beams overhead, Geoff moved cautiously down the dingy corridor. Above, exposed beams webbed the ceiling, hung with ropes, sandbags, and the other effluvia of the theater. Breaks in the wall gave onto the stage on one side and onto yet more narrow and torturous passages on the other, like the catacombs below a cathedral. To Geoff's left, a flat painted with the image of a gazebo gave an illusion of pastoral pleasures, while the flames of hell waited for the unwary Don Giovanni farther down the passageway.

There was no sign of Vaughn near either scene, no conveniently dropped handkerchief or lost shoe buckle to give Geoff a hint of his direction. It was no use listening for a stealthy footstep or a whispered conversation; the wings bustled with stagehands hauling flats and furniture, while actors darted on- and offstage, neatly navigating around the spare scenery and one another. Geoff ducked behind the gazebo as a group of ballet dancers, dressed in a costumer's fantasy of Turkish dress, padded flat-footed to the wings, chatting in low voices as they waited for their cue to enter.

Vaughn kept in good trim, but no man's legs were that good.

Slipping past the unwitting dancers, Geoff took a left onto one of the side corridors, away from the stage, hoping that the feint backstage hadn't been merely a blind to draw attention while his quarry slipped through a back door and out to a waiting carriage bound elsewhere. It was a ploy that Geoff himself had used on more than one occasion.

Being led on a fool's errand was one thing, but being tangled backstage while his reprobate of a cousin pressed his heavy-handed attentions on his wife was another matter entirely.

Geoff looked back, a useless gesture since the stage door stood between him and the galleries that fronted the stage. Damn Jasper, a thousand times over. Why couldn't he have stayed in London and gambled away what remained of his inheritance?

Thank God Letty was too sensible to be taken in by him.

Geoff was conscious of a guilty sense of relief that it was Letty in the box instead of Mary. Well, naturally. He had been in love with Mary. How could a man in love stand to see someone else press his attentions upon his beloved? It was the stuff of jousts and duels and ruined kingdoms. It was a perfectly sensible explanation—except that it wasn't true. When it came right down to it, he just didn't trust Mary to have defended herself—or to have had the common sense to see Jasper's attentions for what they were. Whereas Letty did.

Geoff stepped over a coil of rope, ducked beneath a sandbag, and made a neat turn into one of the side corridors, automatically slinking back against the wall as he went, without the slightest awareness of where he was going.

Geoff tried to conjure up Mary's image, but it was as one-dimensional as the scenery propped against the walls. When he tried to remember just what it was he had loved about her—*did* love about her—all he could come up with was the graceful tilt of her head, the serene beauty of her smile. Storybook images, all of them, like the maiden waiting in the tower at the end of a quest, never half so important as the adventure itself. He had plotted and schemed for her dances, spent hours gazing long-ingly at her across a multitude of unmemorable ballrooms, and scraped the limits of the lexicon for words to describe her beauty in verse—but he couldn't remember one memorable word she had uttered, or have said with any certainty whether her favorite color was green or blue.

Ballrooms and musicales were no way to get to know someone; a few words of conversation, and then the patterns of the dance pulled you apart again. With Mary, there had always been a dozen eager swains clamoring to drag her away again. It was nothing like the artificial intimacy of a mission, the long hours spent por-ing over a map or a code, the thrill of a shared adventure.

Except that there was nothing artificial about Letty. Geoff had never, in all his perambulations through high society and low, ever met anyone quite so entirely herself, so completely immune from pretense. She couldn't dissemble if she tried. And she had tried. Watching her attempt to bandy double meanings with Lord Vaughn would have been enough to make Geoff laugh, if he hadn't been so blazingly angry with her at the time. And to-night . . . Despite himself, Geoff grinned at the memory of Letty disclaiming any familiarity with the English language. She would never make a spy.

It wasn't that she didn't try. She did. But every single thought that crossed her mind blazoned itself on her face, like a medieval clock with all the workings out in the open. Her preferred method of solving a problem was not to tiptoe around the edges of it, but to barge right through. Effective, for the most part, but about as subtle as a rampaging bull. After a decade of dwelling among people who changed their aliases more frequently than they changed their linen, Geoff found it oddly refreshing.

But it made his original conclusions regarding her role in their elopement harder and harder to justify.

And if he had been wrong . . . that meant he had wronged her. Rather badly.

Voices—English voices—caught Geoff's attention. With reflexes honed by hundreds of midnight missions, he slid seamlessly up against the wall, a shadow against shadows. A few steps more and he would have gone too far, bypassing the half-open door of a darkened dressing room, no different from a dozen other unused dressing rooms. Except that this one, despite the lack of lamps, was currently in use.

It might have been an assignation, but the sounds involved were not those of pleasure.

As Geoff positioned himself to the side of the doorframe, he heard the first voice say, "She is becoming a distinct liability."

The speaker wasn't Vaughn.

It was a woman's voice, low-pitched, grating in its tonelessness. From his vantage point next to the doorframe, Geoff couldn't make out the speaker. The door opened in, not out, and she was somewhere to his left, behind that inconvenient slab of wood. But he could picture her features, their classical perfection at variance with the flat tones of her voice. High cheekbones, skin as white as any poet could desire, sultry black eyes, and a come-hither smile.

The Marquise de Montval. The Black Tulip herself.

Her companion detached himself from his seat at the vanity and strolled dangerously close to Geoff's hiding place. The cane swinging from his right hand was as unmistakable as the marquise's voice.

"A bit of an exaggeration, surely," replied Lord Vaughn, in tones of intense boredom. "My dear, you must control these tendencies toward hyperbole. They don't become you."

The marquise ignored him. "She never had the skill for it."

"Not everyone has your . . . talents."

"My talents have been hard-won."

"Believe me," said Lord Vaughn wearily, "no one knows that better than I."

"I don't know why I tolerate you, Sebastian."

"Because"—Lord Vaughn smiled sardonically over the head of his cane—"without me, you would still be rotting in London."

"I didn't need your help. I would have gotten out of that myself."

"Not nearly so expeditiously. Nor with so little trouble to yourself. Bribing the guards with your body isn't much in your line, my dear. Unless your fervor for the cause has changed you in more ways than one."

"It might have been more pleasant to have remained in prison. Certainly the company would have been more genteel."

"As you will. You always did have low tastes, Teresa. Robespierre, Danton, Marat . . . not a gentleman amongst them."

"If all gentlemen are of your ilk, I'll take the rabble."

"But only if they come clothed in silk. Much as it enlivens my existence to be insulted by you, did you have a purpose for this little tête-à-tête? Or could you merely not resist an opportunity to get me alone in the dark? For old times' sake, as it were."

"Don't flatter yourself, Sebastian."

"If I don't, who will?" Vaughn's tone changed, and from his vantage point behind the door, Geoff could see his posture change, the lazy line of his back go taut, as he asked, "Do you really mean to eliminate the girl?"

"Unless you can suggest another way."

" 'If it were done when 'tis done, then it were well it were done quickly,' " quoted Vaughn meditatively. It was unclear whether the words were question or command.

"Tonight," said the Black Tulip softly.

The word reverberated through the quiet room.

Unfortunately, a reverberation of an entirely different kind filled the corridor. The quiet hallway rumbled under the weight of a large piece of scenery, being rolled by a full complement of burly stagehands.

"He would have to have an elephant," one of them grumbled, as Geoff flattened himself against the wall rather than be run down by a remarkably one-dimensional pachyderm on wheels.

His companion's answer was indecipherable over the clatter of the rough trolley.

Geoff used the confusion to slip sideways into the dressing room. It was too late. The birds had flown, leaving nothing behind but the smell of greasepaint and a dozen unanswered questions. Who, Geoff wondered grimly, were they planning to eliminate? The first name that came to mind was Jane's. Or, as they knew her, Miss Gilly Fairley. Wherever Jane and Miss Gwen had gone, he hoped they were watching their backs.

But the marquise had indicated that whoever the unnamed nuisance was didn't have much talent for the game. Which led, unerringly, to Letty.

Vaughn had recognized Letty from London, of that much Geoff was sure. Her clumsy charade as Mrs. Alsdale wouldn't fool a child—but it might spark the suspicions of a pair of paranoid French spies. The marquise's pride must be smarting at having been caught by an amateur like Henrietta; she wouldn't want it to happen again. To be caught once by an amateur might be accounted carelessness, but to do so twice meant a quick trip to the inner reaches of the Temple Prison.

Geoff started down the corridor at something close to a run.

Although she didn't know it yet, Jasper was the least of Letty's worries.

"PUT THOSE CURTAINS BACK AT ONCE!" Letty snapped at Jasper, sounding uncannily like Miss Gwen. Letty tugged on the heavy crimson drapes, but once down, the fabric showed no desire to be pushed back again.

"In a moment," Jasper said soothingly.

Letty didn't feel soothed. Jasper was advancing on her in a way that made Letty long for Miss Gwen's parasol, or any other object with a sharp point. Her reticule was too flimsy to do any damage.

Edging away from the curtains, which veiled a direct drop into the pit below, Letty moved carefully around the first row of seats, her back to the wall. She kept her voice calm and low. "I was just going to visit my friend, Miss Gilchrist. You can accompany me if you like."

"You can't mean to run off so soon." Jasper swung neatly over the first row of seats, pinning Letty against the wall. "Not when we're finally alone."

"That," replied Letty sternly, sounding like every governess she had ever had rolled into one, "is exactly why I'm running off."

If she had hoped that would deter Jasper, she was mistaken. He ran one white-gloved finger down her cheek. "Your modesty does you credit."

Letty jerked away, ducking under his arm. "I'm not modest. I'm married. To your cousin. Remember? Geoffrey? The man who just walked out that way?"

"Ah, yes. Geoffrey."

"Yes, Geoffrey," repeated Letty with some asperity. "I realize that you two aren't exactly the best of friends, but I would appreciate it if you could find some other toy to fight over. May I go now?"

Jasper made no move to release her. "He doesn't appreciate you. Not like I do."

"Mmph," said Letty, partly because she couldn't think of any answer to that which wouldn't be hopelessly impolitic, and partly because Jasper's buttons were digging into her chest.

Jasper leaned closer, his breath stroking her cheek. "Why do you cling to your sham of a marriage?"

Letty twisted her head to the side before his mouth could complete its path to her lips. "It has to do with a little thing called vows."

Jasper smiled at her as the serpent must have at Eve. "If he doesn't honor them, why should you?"

"Just because all your friends drove their carriages off a bridge, would you drive off a bridge, too?"

"He doesn't love you, you know."

Letty scowled. It wasn't exactly news, but it still wasn't pleasant to hear it, especially not in that pitying way, and not from Jasper. Most marriages weren't contracted for love; it wasn't as though their situation were strange or unusual . . . at least, not in the lack of a love component. She would admit that botched elopements and spy rings weren't all that commonplace, even among the more eccentric reaches of the *ton*.

"Look at the way he makes up to Miss Fairley, right in front of you. Look at the way he kisses her hand, the way he whispers in her ear—" Jasper suited action to words.

Letty wriggled as far away as she could with the wall behind her and a beefy arm on either side of her.

"I don't want to discuss this."

"Don't be angry," Jasper wheedled. "I yearn only to worship you."

Letty put both hands against his chest and shoved. "All the best worship is done from afar. You might want to try it."

Jasper chuckled, but it sounded a bit forced. "Your cleverness is one of the attributes I admire most in you."

Letty crossed her arms protectively across her chest before he could make a show of admiring any other attributes. "What do you want, Captain Pinchingdale?"

"Why, for us to be together." Jasper favored her with a leer for form's sake, but it lacked conviction. "What a pair we would make, you and I. If only there were no impediment. . . ."

Jasper looked significantly at Letty from under his long, thick lashes.

"What do you mean?"

Jasper shrugged, muscles moving under his regimentals in a way that had undoubtedly been the downfall of many an undiscerning young lady. "Accidents do happen. Hunting accidents, carriage accidents, the wrong sort of mushroom . . ."

Jasper's attentions took on a new and sinister cast as Letty pictured a carriage listing to the side on a heavily traveled road; Geoff stricken with convulsions at the dinner table; a freak fire in his bedroom, while the new heir shook his head mournfully, and mouthed platitudes about the tragedy of it all.

An attempt to seduce his cousin's wife was one thing, murder quite another.

"I can see you have given this a great deal of thought."

"Anything for you, my sweet."

"And once this . . . accident"—Letty had trouble choking out the word—"has happened, what then?"

"Why, then," Jasper said, and ran his tongue along his lips, "then we take our rightful places at Sibley Court. I as viscount"—he held out a hand to her—"you as my viscountess."

Letty regarded the proffered hand with undisguised revulsion.

"Is this before or after the bailiffs cart me away for murder?"

"How droll you are, my love!" Jasper chucked her under the chin just hard enough to be more punitive than affectionate. "No one would ever suspect the viscount's devoted wife. Not on their honeymoon."

"No, of course not," murmured Letty, wondering which part

of his anatomy she should kick first. Did the great oaf actually believe that she was so overcome by his manly charms that she would go along with this?

Jasper pressed his advantage. "Wouldn't you like to have revenge for all the ways he's wronged you? All the times he's slighted you? Think of it: a young, adoring husband. All the jewels you like. Parties, balls . . ."

"Eternal damnation."

"A minor concern, surely, with all you stand to gain. I'm offering you . . . me."

"Let me get this straight," Letty said slowly. "Just to make sure I haven't missed anything. I get to do away with my husband—"

"You can pick any means you like," Jasper offered generously.

"—while you stand safely out of the way, keeping your hands clean."

"Safer for both of us that way," Jasper assured her.

"And then"—Letty clasped her hands together and favored Jasper with a look of wide-eyed adoration—"you get to run through Geoffrey's inheritance, while I'm strung up for murder."

Listening to tone rather than words, Jasper started to nod before he realized that he really shouldn't.

"How could I refuse such a generous offer?"

"You don't understand," urged Jasper, showing a distressing tendency to grovel. "You've gotten it all wrong. I'll adore you. I'll cherish you."

"You mean you'll cherish your new income. Especially once I've been dragged off to the gallows."

Jasper opened his mouth to protest, but Letty cut him off.

"What on earth made you think I would go along with this? Did you really think I was that stupid? Never mind," Letty added hastily. "I don't want to know the answer to that."

Jasper's confident expression wavered. "Does this mean you're not going to cooperate with me?"

"Can I make myself any clearer? I find you repulsive. Your morals are beneath contempt. Your selfishness sickens me. Your conversation is tedious. And," Letty finished viciously, "your side-burns are unbecoming!"

Selfishness didn't bother Jasper, but his hair was sacrosanct. Jasper's expression turned ugly, all attempts at charm abandoned. "You don't understand."

Letty made no effort to hide her loathing. "I understand all too well."

"Why should he have everything when I have nothing? It's not fair. It's never been fair."

"Don't talk to me about not fair," retorted Letty. If he wanted unfair, she could give him enough unfair to make his perfectly tended hair stand on end.

Jasper wasn't listening. His face was contorted with three de-cades of resentment. "He doesn't deserve any of it. Not like I do. Mother always said . . ."

Letty took a step away from him, tainted just by proximity. "What have you ever done to deserve anything? Have you cared for the land? Have you made sure the fences are in repair and the agent isn't cheating the tenants? Have you stayed up all night with a sick cow?" Letty hadn't, and she was fairly sure her hus-band hadn't either, but she was running out of examples. She de-cided to quit before the agrarian imagery got out of hand. "Have you ever, in your life, thought about anything other than gratify-ing your own needs?"

"Oh, so that's what this is about. Saint Geoffrey, always above reproach. Not so saintly, is he? At least, not when it comes to . . . women."

Letty itched to fling his words back in his face, but there was no way she could do it without jeopardizing the mission—and how perfectly ironic that would be, to convince her husband of her unreliability by being too quick to defend him!

Letty bristled. "That's none of your concern! He's still worth ten of you—twenty of you! And if you had any sense, you'd go home to London and crawl back into your hole like the miserable little serpent you are before someone takes a machete to you."

Jasper looked her up and down from head to toe and back again, all five feet of her. Letty resisted the urge to stand on her tiptoes.

"You?" he asked, with palpable disbelief.

"Don't tempt me," spat Letty, feeling rather as though she could gleefully grab up a machete and swing it, if one were at hand. "Stay away from me. And stay away from my husband. Or, by God, I will do everything in my power to make your life more of a misery than it already is."

Whatever spirit had moved her Saxon ancestors back in the days when horned helmets were still au courant had hold of Letty. Little she might be, but Jasper slunk back a step under the force of her glare.

Letty lifted her chin, exuding disdain like the Dowager Duchess of Dovedale. "I believe we've said all that needs to be said. Good-bye, Captain Pinchingdale."

Letty swept grandly out of the box, every inch of her body quivering with indignation.

How dared he! That miserable, crawling, miserable . . . Letty was too angry to think of adjectives. How dared he!

It wasn't nearly as satisfying the second time.

Heels clicking angrily against the Portland stone of the corridor, she stomped toward the stairs, still seething. She wasn't sure what made her angrier, the threat to Lord Pinchingdale or the fact that that miserable, crawling . . . *thing* had actually assumed she would go along with his disgusting designs. Would fling herself into his arms, no less!

" 'I'm offering you . . . me,' " Letty mumbled in savage imitation of Jasper's self-satisfied tones. "Revolting!"

Did he think she would be that pathetically grateful for any attentions shown her that she would just rush out and bump off her husband?

"I should have kicked him," muttered Letty. "No, too easy. I should have shoved him off the balcony and called it an *accident*."

Just thinking of his hideous, rubbery lips shaping the word "accident" made her feel as though she had rolled in pig slop. Letty rubbed her hands up and down her arms as though she could wipe off the taint of his touch.

"Abominable!" she fumed.

"Well, really," she heard someone say, as a pair of ladies passed her on the stairs, "I didn't think the first act was all that bad."

As far as Jasper was concerned, there wasn't going to be a second act; Letty would see to that.

Without conscious thought, she took a sharp right turn, toward the stage door. Goodness only knew what Jasper might do now that his plans were discovered. He must, Letty thought disgustedly, have been awfully sure of himself to have taken the risk of telling her. Either that, or awfully stupid. Or both. Letty supposed she could see his reasoning—the unwanted marriage, the flaunted courtship of a much prettier woman—but it still rankled.

Following the route she had seen Lord Vaughn take before, Letty pushed through the stage door, looking for Geoff. Someone had to warn him before Jasper decided the safest route was to bump him off at once.

Finding her husband wasn't quite so easy as Letty had anticipated. She wasn't sure what she had expected the backstage area to be like, but it hadn't been anything so dark, or so crowded. She darted out of the way as a group of stagehands came through carrying scenery, picking a side corridor at random to duck into. Farther away from the stage, the passageways grew even darker. Letty tripped over a footstool—who left a footstool in the middle of a corridor?—and went limping on her way. At least, she thought, rubbing her aching shin, if she couldn't find Geoff, presumably Jasper couldn't either.

Weren't there laws against planning your cousin's murder? Geoff was the head of Jasper's family; there had to be some suitably draconian edict against threatening one's liege lord. Not to mention attempting to seduce the liege lord's wife. Wasn't that still accounted treason in some contexts? That sort of thing must have come up all the time in the Middle Ages, Letty was quite sure, with punishments to match. Whatever the punishment was, she hoped it was suitably gruesome, involving lots of rusty thumbscrews and maybe a few barrels filled with tacks.

A gasping cry jarred Letty out of her gruesome reverie.

"Hello?" Letty called.

The sound was followed by a thudding noise, like a sack of flour hitting the kitchen floor.

"Blast." Letty picked up her skirts and set off down the corridor at a run, hoping whomever it was hadn't hurt herself too badly. Certainly, it was dark enough in the corridor for someone to have tripped and lost their footing, and there were more than enough obstacles to trip over.

"Are you all right?" Letty's question ended in a gasp of her own as someone charged past her from the opposite direction, banging into her with so much force that they both staggered. Letty caught at the wall to steady herself, just as something tumbled onto Letty's left foot, landing with unerring accuracy on her little toe.

"Ouch," muttered Letty. Clearly, whoever it was couldn't have been hurt that badly if they had the strength to bang into her like that, and then go racing off again without so much as an apology.

Moving very carefully—who knew how many other sprinting lunatics there might be lurking backstage?—Letty bent over to pick up the fallen object. Her toes were quite convinced that it was a brick, but as Letty groped along the ground, her fingers closed around the familiar, rounded shape of a reticule.

"Hello!" Letty called, beginning to straighten. "You've dropped your—"

The beading on the bag bit into Letty's palm as something else caught her eye, pale against the dark wood of the floor. Still half hunched over, Letty froze, her fingers convulsively tightening around the little round bag.

There, on the floor, only a pace away from Letty's slipper, was a small, white hand. It lay pointing toward Letty's shoe, the palm facing up as though in supplication.

Chapter Twenty

The hand was attached to an arm, flung out to the side, like a young child sleeping. And the arm . . .

It was the dress that Letty recognized, pink gauze over white muslin. It had been embroidered around the edges with silver thread, like the brightly beaded pink-and-silver reticule she had been carrying earlier that evening. Her skirts were rumpled where she had fallen, the pale fabric streaked with grime. Veiled by her tumbled mass of black curls, her head was twisted to the side, away from Letty.

"Miss Gilchrist?" Letty exclaimed. "Emily? What are you doing back here?"

Emily Gilchrist didn't respond.

She must have been knocked over by the same rude person who had shoved past Letty. With the corridors so narrow and so crowded, it was no wonder she had banged her head on something as she fell. That, realized Letty, must have been the noise she had heard, that sickening crunch. Not that any of that particularly mattered at the moment. The important thing was to determine how badly Emily was hurt and get her back to her guardian.

Letty sank to her knees beside Emily, murmuring soothing and pointless platitudes. "It's going to be all right. You've just hit your head. Don't worry."

She started to smooth back Emily's tangled hair, grimacing as sticky moisture seeped through the netting of her gloves. A metallic tang underlay the heavy floral scent of Emily's perfume, as sickly sweet as dead flowers.

"Drat," muttered Letty, rubbing her fingers together.

Emily must have hit her head harder than she had realized. Bandages, thought Letty briskly. She had left her shawl in the box, so her petticoat would have to do. It wasn't a particularly sturdy fabric, but it would serve to stop the bleeding until she could find something better. Letty had dealt with head wounds before; her little brother was constantly falling off horses, tumbling out of trees, and jumping off walls to see if he could fly. He hadn't been able to yet, but that never seemed to discourage him.

"Nothing to worry about," she said soothingly, as much for herself as the unconscious Emily, placing one hand on Emily's temple and the other behind her head. If she could turn her head, she might have some idea of how bad a cut it was. A very small cut on the head, Letty had learned from her brother, could yield quite a bit of blood, more disgusting than it was dangerous. "You'll be right as rain as soon as we get you home and bandaged up."

Moving very slowly, trying not to jar Emily more than she had to, Letty eased her head sideways. Her long locks of hair, matted and sticky with blood, fell to the side, leaving long, dark streaks on Letty's skirt and the backs of her hands.

Stains were the least of Letty's concerns.

Scuttling backward, Letty let Emily's head fall from her lap. It hit the ground with an unpleasant thud, but Letty didn't think Emily would notice. Emily wasn't going to notice anything, ever again.

Shaking, Letty staggered to her feet, bracing herself with one hand against the wall. She wasn't going to be ill, she told herself. She would not be ill. Her stomach begged to differ. Letty pressed both hands against her abdomen, fighting for control, and wishing she hadn't eaten quite so much for supper. She was still clutching the reticule. As she pressed her clenched hands against her stomach, Letty could feel each individual bead biting into her palm. She welcomed the sting. Anything to take her mind away from the revolution in her stomach, and the horror that had been Emily's face.

Or what was left of it.

Letty didn't hear the footsteps until they were almost upon her. Whoever it was moved with the subtlety of someone accustomed to silence, his slow steps scarcely audible in the dusty corridor. Acting on instinct alone, Letty whirled, striking out with the reticule. A large hand grabbed hers by the wrist, forcing it down.

Mindlessly, she struggled, hearing only the hoarse rasp of her own breath. She didn't want to die. Not now. Not like Emily.

"Letty! For heaven's sake!"

The harsh whisper didn't sound at all like his normal voice, but Letty would have known that tone of annoyance anywhere.

Going limp with relief, Letty ceased her resistance so abruptly that they both staggered. Her husband grabbed her shoulders to steady her—or restrain her. Letty didn't care. She was just glad he was there.

"Geoff?"

There was a series of reddening scratches on his cheek, courtesy of the reticule that she'd swung with more force than she realized. She lifted a hand to them, drawing it away again just before her fingers would have brushed his skin.

"Sorry," she said, inadequately.

"You might have confined yourself to a simple hello." Geoff had regained his usual urbane tone, but his breathing was still slightly ragged. "What was that all about?"

"I thought . . . Oh, Geoff." Letty lifted a balled fist to her mouth.

Geoff froze, his expression changing in an instant from irritation to concern. Catching Letty's hand, he raised it to examine the dark smears of blood that stained the fabric. "What happened? Did Jasper—"

Letty shook her head, drawing in breath on a choked laugh. Somehow, the notion of Jasper struck her as comical. Jasper had ceased to matter, cast into the abyss of the insignificant. "Not Jasper. I wish—no. Over there."

Letty lifted one hand and jabbed unsteadily to the left. She hoped she was pointing in the right direction, because she didn't want to look to make sure. Once had been enough.

"Good God." Geoff pressed Letty's head into his chest. "Don't look."

From the region of his waistcoat, he heard a shaky voice say, "I already did."

Geoff amended his advice. "Pretend you didn't."

Letty vented her feelings in an incredulous puff of hot air, but she stayed where she was.

Ignoble though it was, Geoff's first reaction was relief that it wasn't Letty lying there. Her hair smelled faintly of chamomile, clean and wholesome as summer. Geoff would have liked to bury his nose in it, and drown out the stench of death.

His second was a great deal more professional. Keeping Letty's head firmly lodged in his waistcoat, Geoff sidled closer, examining what he could see of the corpse. The skirts were rucked up, revealing a webbing on the calf that might have been a particularly outré form of garter, but was more likely a sheath of some sort. It would have to have been a very small knife, one small enough not to make a bump under the fine muslin currently in fashion for evening wear. Something thin and deadly, like a stiletto.

The face was nearly unrecognizable, so covered with blood that Geoff, even with eyes well used to the gloom of the backstage area, could scarcely make out the nature of the wound. One staring eye regarded him through a screen of dark hair. The other . . . There wasn't much left of it. Something sharp, broader than the Black Tulip's preferred stiletto, had entered the woman's left eye, cutting deep. The knife's trajectory had continued downward, on an angle, slicing through the soft tissue of the woman's cheek, and ending somewhere in the region of her upper lip. At a guess, she had been kneeling when the blow struck. There were no signs of a struggle; at least, none that he could make out. None of the scenery leaning against the walls had been overturned, and the dust had only been disarranged by the impact of the woman's body, not by a scuffle.

Geoff frowned, trying to reconstruct the scene. Two confederates, walking in apparent amity. A disagreement occurred—a disagreement, or a prearranged double-cross. Geoff tended to lean toward the latter. The abandoned corridor made an excellent venue for an unofficial execution, if one were so inclined. The woman would have bent down to sweep her knife out of its sheath. As she did so, her intended victim grabbed his own knife, stabbing down. She must have looked up just as he struck, hence the injury to the eye. The force of such a blow would have impelled her body backward, leaving her sprawled on the floor where Letty had found her.

Geoff had a fairly good idea of just who the two actors in that little drama had been. The woman's features might be too marred for a positive identification, but the long black hair and the painfully white skin, made even paler in death, were unmistakable.

Whatever alias the Marquise de Montval had been hiding under, she wouldn't be using it any longer.

Against his waistcoat, Letty began to squirm. "You can let me go now," she said, her voice only slightly muffled. "I'm all right."

"Are you sure?" One's first dead body—at least, he assumed it was Letty's first dead body—was never a pleasant sight, and the marquise's demise had been messier than most. Geoff loosened his hold, but didn't release her.

There was a crease in Letty's cheek where she had pressed against a seam of his coat, and her hair was rumpled, but there was a determined cast to her expression that struck Geoff as surprisingly gallant, like a very small knight steeling herself to enter the ogre's den.

Letty's eyes drifted sideways in the direction of the slumped shape on the floor.

"She was so pretty . . . so young."

"Not as young as you think," Geoff said quietly.

"When I saw her lying there . . . I thought she was alive. I thought she had just fallen and hurt herself. I thought—" Letty broke off, looking up at him with dazed blue eyes. "Geoff, why would anyone do this? To Emily?"

"Emily?" Geoff asked sharply.

"Yes. Emily Gilchrist."

"You knew her." Geoff's expression turned intent, his eyes fixed on Letty's face.

Wrapped in her own recollections, Letty scarcely noticed. "We were on the boat from London together. And now . . ." Letty shivered. "What a hideous way to die."

"There are worse."

Looking back on the Black Tulip's history, Geoff found it difficult to muster much sympathy for her. One of his friends had been a victim of the Tulip, back in the early days of the war, when revolutionary fervor still ran high across the Channel, and the League of the Scarlet Pimpernel still specialized in ushering distressed noblemen to safety in England. Tony had been sent on just such a rescue mission.

The Black Tulip hadn't allowed him nearly so speedy an end as she had been granted.

For Letty's sake, Geoff added, "She died quickly. She wouldn't have felt much."

Letty rubbed her hands along her upper arms as though cold. "I heard it happen. She just . . . gasped, and then fell. I thought someone had tripped. If I had been here a few moments earlier—"

"Let's not go down that byway, shall we?" Geoff tilted Letty's head back with a finger under her chin. "Did either of them see you?"

"I don't know. I heard a crash, and ran forward to help. Someone pushed past me—it didn't seem important then. I just thought he was being rude."

"Damn," muttered Geoff. Vaughn might have been in too much of a hurry to take note of Letty, but he doubted it. Vaughn knew Letty and, more important, Letty knew Vaughn. Vaughn hadn't evaded detection thus far by leaving simple precautions to chance. He would be back. "Let's get you out of here."

"You don't think—?"

Geoff began steering her down the corridor, moving with the sureness of a cat in the dark. "I'm not thinking anything until we're a good ten yards away."

Letty's legs moved numbly, by rote, as he hustled her out a back exit and into a hackney. Somewhere, far, far away, she could hear her husband's voice giving directions, but she couldn't have said with any certainty where he had instructed the driver to go. Instead, she kept replaying the scene in the corridor, hearing that sickening thud—Letty swallowed hard—feeling the jolt as the murderer pushed past her, sending her stumbling into the wall.

And then, something else. Something heavy falling on her toe.

Lifting her wrist, Letty gazed dumbly at the reticule dangling from its silver strap. Used to the weight of a reticule on her wrist, Letty had forgotten she was holding it. It wasn't hers. Hers was black and sensible—and, Letty remembered, with a twinge of annoyance, back in their abandoned box in the theater. There hadn't been much in it, anyway, only a handkerchief and a few coins, in case she was separated from her party. This reticule glittered with silver beading over a pink silk base, a stiffened spray of beads forming an upside-down fan at the bottom. Letty recognized it instantly. She had last seen it dangling from Emily Gilchrist's wrist.

She had been warned that pickpockets operated in the theater, but not that they might turn violent. Still, in a dark corner, if Emily had protested . . . What a horrible, senseless waste. And all for—what? A handful of coins? An embroidered handkerchief? There wasn't awfully much one could fit in a reticule.

Wrenching the strap off her wrist, Letty held it up by two fingers. The reticule dangled in the air between them, its sparkle dimmed with dark smears.

"Geoff, I've figured it out. He killed her for this." Letty regarded the small, pink bag with undisguised loathing. "The murderer dropped it when he bumped into me. It's Emily's. I would recognize it anywhere."

Geoff reached out for the little bag, with its silver clasp and loop of beads fanning out from the bottom. "May I?"

As Letty nodded, Geoff forced open the clasp. It was stiff enough to take considerable pressure. A handkerchief sat on the top, embroidered and scented. Beneath it, Geoff found a small comb and a twist of coins tied into another handkerchief, stuffed into the bottom. There was nothing incriminating about it at all.

Geoff had heard of one case where an agent had used embroidery as a means of communication, so many French knots to the words, but to his inexperienced fingers, the satin-stitched flowers embroidered around the corners felt just as they were supposed to. Well, they would, wouldn't they? He would have to show the handkerchief to Jane later; embroidery was more in her line than his.

"All for a purse," said Letty disgustedly.

Upending the innocuous contents into his lap, Geoff rolled

the empty bag between his fingers, searching for irregularities. His groping fingers located something at the very bottom, in between the lining and the beaded exterior.

"Not just any purse," Geoff said, with great satisfaction. He ripped the lining free with one neat wrench.

"What are you doing?" exclaimed Letty, reaching for the bag.

"This."

Geoff's fingers closed triumphantly around a pawn-shaped object, nestled at the bottom of the bag between lining and beading. The sparkle of the beads would have distracted the eye from any telltale bulge; as for the bag being bottom-heavy, that was cleverly concealed by the spray of beading on the bottom.

He knew what it was even before the pads of his fingers brushed against the lines incised on the bottom.

He dropped the tiny silver trinket into Letty's hand. "Your friend Emily wasn't quite what she seemed."

Letty regarded the silver pawn in her hand uncomprehendingly. "She liked chess? I don't see—"

"Turn it over," suggested Geoff, continuing to root around in the shredded lining.

Letty turned it over. At first, she wasn't sure what she was supposed to be looking for, but after a moment of squinting blankly at the silver disk, the irregularities on the surface resolved themselves into a form of sorts. It was a seal. Like the one hanging around Jane's neck.

And it had been wedged into Emily Gilchrist's reticule.

"Oh," said Letty flatly, adding two and two and coming up with five hundred and sixty-four.

"Exactly." Geoff was still rooting about in the lining, seeking the source of the other bump he had felt. It might be a lumpy seam, or . . . Doing his best not to make loud crowing noises, Geoff withdrew a small cylinder of paper.

"You think Emily was involved in . . . all this?"

Geoff tucked the paper back into the abused reticule, to be

examined later. Even if it weren't too dark to read, it would undoubtedly need decoding.

"What did you know of her?"

"Only what she told me." Which, Letty realized, for all of Emily's incessant jabbering, hadn't been much. Emily talked and talked and talked, but never about herself. It had all been ribbons and shoes and the wonders that awaited them in Dublin. Most of the time, Letty hadn't listened very closely.

"She had just come from a seminary for young ladies outside of London," Letty said slowly. "At least, that's what she claimed. I don't believe she ever mentioned the name of the school."

"If she had," said Geoff, "I think you would find it didn't exist."

"And I didn't ask. I didn't want to know." Letty grimaced at the memory, her voice thick with self-reproach. "I found her tedious."

In the dark of the carriage, Geoff's hand closed reassuringly over hers. "You were supposed to find her tedious. It was all part of her role."

"I suppose."

"I know," said Geoff firmly. "She wasn't worth your sympathy."

Something in Geoff's tone caught Letty's attention. "You know who she is." Wincing, Letty corrected herself. "Was."

"Have you heard of the Black Tulip?"

Letty shook her head. "I've never followed the espionage reports."

Her apologetic tone wrenched a reluctant chuckle from Geoff. "It's probably for the best. At least it means you aren't harboring any absurd misconceptions."

"Like spies wearing black masks all the time?"

"Something like that." Reluctantly, Geoff got down to business. "The Black Tulip appeared right after the Scarlet Pimpernel, in the early days of the Revolution. Wherever the Pimpernel was, there was the Tulip, leaving a trail of dead agents in her wake."

"Charming," said Letty, finding it hard to picture flighty Emily Gilchrist as a flinty-hearted French agent. But that was the point of a disguise, wasn't it?

"When Bonaparte seized power with the Coup of Brumaire in 1799, the Black Tulip all but disappeared. There were any number of theories at the time. Selwick—" Geoff broke off, glancing quizzically at Letty.

"The Purple Gentian. I would have had to have been immured in a tower not to know that much. His unmasking was all over the papers last month."

Letty's reaction to the plethora of Purple Gentian headlines had been something along the lines of "Oh, for heaven's sake, not another spy!" and "Why can't the papers report anything useful for a change?" but she didn't feel the need to confide those details to the spy sitting next to her.

"Right. Richard claimed to have shut the Black Tulip into an Egyptian pyramid during the 1798 expedition. It made an excellent story, but it was hard to verify, especially when neither of us had the slightest idea of who the Black Tulip was. We do now."

"Emily Gilchrist?"

"That was merely an alias. Her real name was Teresa Ballinger, but she was better known by her married name: the Marquise de Montval."

Ballinger wasn't a French name, any more than Gilchrist had been. "She was English? Really English?" Letty asked incredulously. Emily's accent had been impeccable, but for an Englishwoman born and bred to go over to the French . . . it strained credulity.

"And married to a French nobleman. Two of the reasons no one ever suspected her. We all assumed the Black Tulip was French. And a man," Geoff added, as an afterthought.

"Then how did you discover her identity?"

"I didn't." Chagrin softened the ascetic angles of Geoff's features, lending him an unexpectedly boyish aspect. "All the best minds in the War Office searched for the Black Tulip for ten years . . . and Henrietta figured it out."

Letty couldn't quite hide her grin.

"Henrietta felt much the same way," said Geoff dryly. "She gloats very effectively."

"Good for Henrietta," Letty said stoutly. Her grin faded as a less pleasing image floated to the fore. "Although it doesn't make much difference now, does it?"

Her memory conjured up Emily's body, bloodied and lifeless in a forgotten corner of the Crow Street Theatre. It was a chilling reminder of the futility of human endeavor, more effective than any number of tombstones. Whatever she had done in the past, the Black Tulip's plotting days were over.

"I'm sorry you had to see that."

"So am I," said Letty feelingly.

Geoff turned to face her, propping an elbow on the battered back of the seat. "What were you doing backstage?"

It was a sign of her distraction that it took Letty a moment to remember what had driven her backstage. "It was Captain Pinchingdale."

Next to her, Geoff stiffened. "What did he do?"

"He wanted me to murder you!"

"Oh, if that's all . . ." Geoff relaxed against the cushions, remarkably unconcerned by the homicidal designs of his kin.

"All? The loathsome cad actually thought I would be so bowled over by his dubious charms that I would murder you and run off with him."

"Tempted?" Letty could hear the smile in his voice.

"By a hangman's noose? No, thank you."

"It is nice to know that your common sense stands between me and the grave."

"There was another consideration."

"Really?" Draping an arm along the back of the seat, Geoff leaned forward inquisitively. "What might that be?"

"Captain Pinchingdale's sideburns offend me."

"How disappointing for Jasper," Geoff managed to choke out.

"And his teeth are too big," Letty added with relish.

"Poor Jasper." Geoff tried to raise an eyebrow, but found it hard to do while shaking with repressed laughter. "Damned by his dentition!"

That set them both off. Letty tried to contain her giggles, but they kept emerging in a series of explosive snorts that made them both laugh even harder, rolling against the back of the seat in their mirth.

Letty's stomach hurt, her ribs hurt, and her eyes were starting to tear.

"I don't know what's wrong with me," she panted, clutching her aching abdomen. "It's not that f-funny."

Even saying the word "funny" made her break up again.

"Jasper's teeth, or his sideburns?"

"No—" Letty clutched at Geoff's sleeve in supplication. "Don't. Don't make me laugh more. It hurts too much."

Hiccupping, Letty started to swipe at her eyes with the back of her hand, before remembering that her hands were all bloody. Not fancying red streaks all over her face, she made an attempt to dry her cheeks with her elbow, but the attempt left something to be desired.

"Allow me," said Geoff solemnly, although his voice was still slightly shaky with laughter.

Withdrawing a clean handkerchief from his sleeve, he applied it to the area beneath her eyes with the same sort of focused concentration she had seen him devote to decoding a letter or following a suspect. He drew his handkerchief in a gentle semicircle under her left eye, stroking gently up along the curve of her cheekbone until all the tears were gone. Lifting the handkerchief, he moved on to the right eye, repeating the motion.

Letty lost all inclination to laugh. She drew a shaky breath, suddenly very aware that his other arm was curled around her back, holding her steady as he attended to her cheeks with elaborate care. She could feel the warmth of him through the fine wool of his coat, seeping through her dress and rising to her cheeks. She hoped he couldn't feel the sudden heat beneath his fingers, or guess its cause.

Geoff inspected his handiwork. He ran his thumb along the curve of her cheekbone, smoothing her hair back from her face. It must have been tangled, littered with unmoored pins, but his touch was as soft as the brush of an angel's wing.

"Better?" Geoff asked.

She was fascinated with the way his lips shaped the word, molding themselves around the syllables.

Letty could only nod.

"Good," Geoff said, a hint of a hidden smile in his voice.

The handkerchief drifted forgotten to the floor.

Chapter Twenty-one

Letty forgot that her hands were streaked with dried blood. She forgot that they might have homicidal French agents or equally homicidal English relations in hot pursuit. She forgot that Geoff had meant to marry her sister. With his arm warm around her and his breath mingling with hers, none of that mattered. Nothing mattered but the smell of his cologne, the warmth of his skin, the caress of his hand in her hair.

He remained poised a whisper away, not moving, not saying anything, just being. There. With her. It couldn't have been more than a moment, certainly no more time than it took for the carriage wheels to complete a full revolution, but time had taken on curious properties, and it seemed to Letty that they lingered for a lifetime like that, with no sound between them but the rumble of the wheels and the hum of his breath. Letty was holding hers. The world hung suspended in perfect counterpoise, and even a breath might shatter it. A breath, and he might pull away, or say something, or remember that she wasn't the one he had wanted, and then it would all be spoiled.

With infinite care, as though he, too, were afraid of jarring their fragile peace, Geoff threaded his fingers deeper into her hair, tilting her head toward his. Letty's eyes drifted closed.

The expected kiss didn't appear. Instead, Geoff's lips feathered across her temples in a movement as soft as twilight. Working a trail of fire where his handkerchief had been, he brushed a kiss against the tender skin next to her eye, then her cheekbone. His lips grazed the very corner of her mouth, teasing, tantalizing.

Patience had never been Letty's strong suit. She didn't wait to see what he was going to do next. All it took was a slight tug on his ears to direct his head firmly in the right direction. Letty had thought she remembered what it was to be kissed. Over and over, she had replayed the hazy recollections of that night in High Holborn, the smell, the taste, the touch.

Memory was nothing to reality.

Their lips met like two armies clashing—an exercise in organized mayhem. Letty's ears rang as though with fusillades; her heart pounded the tattoo; and her closed eyes dazzled with sparks in a smoky haze. The minute their lips touched, the arms around her tightened. Letty's tightened back, until she was sitting more on him than next to him, and she didn't know and she didn't care. Her hair came down on one side, flopping against her cheek. Murmuring with distress, Letty batted it ineffectually aside.

With a low chuckle, Geoff brushed it aside for her, touching his lips to the exposed corner of her jaw. Letty hadn't been aware that such a portion of her body existed; it was just there as part of the apparatus that supported her head and made it possible for her to speak. She wasn't likely to forget it in the future. Geoff's lips tingled down her neck, awakening unknown nerves. Letty arched her neck to grant him better access, gasping as he kissed the sensitive skin above her collarbone.

His lips moved lower, past the modest pendant that hung around her neck, past the plain lace rim that edged her bodice— and the carriage rocked to a jolting halt.

The abrupt cessation of movement took them both off guard. As the elderly hackney lurched to a stop, Letty and Geoff rocked painfully against the back of the seat. Letty landed on her elbow. Her elbow landed on Geoff's ribs.

"Ouch," said Letty inadequately, rubbing her elbow.

"Indeed," replied Geoff, equally inadequately.

If his voice was muffled, it had as much to do with pure stupefaction as the blow to his ribs. What in the hell had just happened in there?

Certain parts of his anatomy were only too happy to provide the answer to that. Geoff told them to be quiet. They had gotten him in enough trouble already. And they would undoubtedly have gotten him into a good deal more trouble if the carriage hadn't stopped when it had.

Geoff unlatched the door and kicked down the folding steps without waiting for the driver to come around. It would have been better if he could have blamed his behavior on a chance impulse, if the motion of the carriage had flung them unexpectedly together, and finding her suddenly in his arms (the suddenness being the key factor), he had acted on an instinct as old as Adam.

But he had known exactly what he was doing, thought Geoff grimly, swinging down from the carriage without the aid of the steps. There had been any number of moments he could have drawn away, stuck the handkerchief in his pocket, and said something chummy and unromantic, along the lines of, "All right, then?" At least, that was what he ought to have done. No gentleman should take advantage of such a situation. He was sure there had to be a rule about it, sandwiched somewhere between not swearing in the presence of a lady and not coveting one's neighbor's goat. What those proscriptions all had in common was that they were "nots." Such as "not" kissing a woman whose critical faculties had been weakened by the sight of a dead body.

And "not" lusting after one's former fiancée's sister.

That was what lay at the heart of it. Not the pure fact of his having kissed her, not the circumstances of having kissed her, dead body and all, but the wanting to kiss her. Even worse, he had enjoyed it. And certain parts of his anatomy were quite eager to enjoy it again.

He was, Geoff realized with painful clarity, in the anomalous situation of despising himself for betraying his former love by lusting after his wife.

He had become an exercise in illogic.

Handing Letty down from the carriage, Geoff made a concerted effort to regain his usual air of urbane detachment. "We seem to be making a habit of this," he said.

"Of . . . ?" Letty blinked at him, her lips swollen and her hair rumpled.

She looked, in short, alarmingly kissable. Enough so to make any man knock aside his scruples about neighbors' goats and former fiancées, and take up Luther's advice to sin boldly.

"The carriage," Geoff clipped out, moving so rapidly up the front steps that Letty had to run to keep up.

"Oh." Letty's voice went flat as she realized what he meant, another kiss in another carriage, and the unhappy consequences. "Right. That."

"Yes," agreed Geoff, wishing he had never brought up the topic. He brought the knocker down against the door with more force than necessary. "That."

Much to Geoff's relief, a maid opened the door almost immediately. Recognizing Letty and Geoff, she admitted them without question.

"We'll want a pot of coffee in the parlor." Geoff glanced at Letty's bloodstained hands and dress, incongruously grisly in the tidy entryway. "And a basin of water and some towels."

The maid curtsied and took herself off, not betraying any surprise at the gruesome state of Letty's garments. She had clearly seen worse.

Wrapping her offensive hands in her skirt, Letty preceded

Geoff up the stairs, feeling her temper rise with each additional step. It wasn't that Letty objected to the water—she knew she needed it—but the fact that Geoff had ordered it made her feel even more of a horrible hag than she did already. And that comment about the carriage! How could he? What happened to their so-called truce? Clearly, it had disappeared back there in the carriage, along with his handkerchief—and her pride. She had been so pathetically pleased with his attentions, so happy to think that he might care just a little bit about her. That he might want to kiss her. Not Mary.

So much for that hope.

She knew she wasn't Mary, and that he hadn't wanted to marry her, but that gave him no right to kiss her and then throw that back in her face.

Who had kissed whom?

On second thought, Letty would have preferred not to answer that question. If she went back and thought, really thought, about what had just happened in the carriage, it was rather unclear who had kissed whom. Those little kisses along her cheek had, at the time, seemed like the inevitable prelude to a grand romantic encounter. But they might have been intended as nothing more than a calming caress.

Calming. Ha! There had been nothing calming about them. And he certainly hadn't shied away when she kissed him back.

Letty stomped up the last few steps with more vigor than grace. If he regretted the kiss, he should just say so, plainly, not go about making snide remarks about carriages. She hadn't expected words of love, but to bring up their prior interlude in a carriage—where he believed her to be her sister—was a bit much. It made her feel cheap. Interchangeable. Unwanted.

It made it all the worse that all of those were true.

On the landing, Geoff reached for the parlor door. He was as unruffled as ever, his expression as smooth as the impeccably tailored lines of his coat. Letty could feel her hair hanging drunkenly to one side, moored by three remaining hairpins. Her dress was streaked with dried blood like a tricoteuse who had sat too near the guillotine, and her lips felt about three times their normal size.

Letty marched up in front of her husband. "We need to get a few things straight."

"Do we?" Geoff opened the parlor door and gestured for her to precede him.

"Yes, we do." The words lost some of their force when she had to twist her head to deliver them. That just made Letty angrier, especially as she was quite sure he had done it deliberately.

Letty whirled to face him, nearly banging into his waistcoat. No man had a right to move that swiftly or that silently. Letty added that to her growing list of grievances.

"That carriage comment was completely unconscionable."

"I shouldn't have said it," Geoff agreed, with every appearance of sincerity.

"And you shouldn't have—oh." Letty refused to be mollified. Wearing a track on the little green-and-white carpet, she gesticulated helplessly. "You may say that now, but it's going to come up again. And again, and again . . ."

"I believe I have the idea." Geoff sounded amused.

Letty stopped abruptly in her perambulations. It might be amusing to him, but it wasn't to her.

"No, you don't. I know we agreed not to talk about—about what happened that night, but we can't go on like this, just poking around the subject. We might as well have it out now. And you're going to listen this time." Letty folded her arms across her chest and stared defiantly at her husband. "I didn't try to trick you. It was all a nasty accident."

"I know."

Prepared to forcibly present her evidence, Letty stopped short, all the wind knocked out of her sails. "You know?"

Geoff favored her with a wry smile. "Credit me with some sense."

Letty wasn't sure she was willing to go that far.

"When did you come to that conclusion?" Letty asked suspiciously.

"Some time ago."

"I've only been here a week."

"I've always been a quick study."

"Modest, too," said Letty, but her voice was less hostile.

"And—ever so occasionally—wrong. Not frequently, but it does happen."

"Was that an apology?"

"Was it that poorly delivered? I'll have to try again later. I appear to be singularly maladroit tonight."

"Not in everything," said Letty, before she had time to think better of it. Her cheeks turned an uncomfortable pink. "I mean . . . er."

"Thank you," said Geoff, with a smile that sent tingles straight down to Letty's toes, "for sparing my ego."

"Don't let us interrupt," cackled Miss Gwen, pounding her parasol against the floor for emphasis.

Letty and Geoff sprang apart like a pair of scalded cats as Jane and Miss Gwen appeared in the doorway, still wearing their respective costumes.

"No, that's all right. We were just—" More flummoxed than Letty had ever seen him, Geoff looked helplessly around as though the answer might be hidden somewhere among the delftware on the dresser.

"—sitting down," Letty finished. She had just pulled out a chair, and was about to suit action to words, when a sudden movement from Jane stopped her.

"Your hands," said Jane.

Letty automatically looked down, staring idiotically at the streaks of dried blood that marred her gloves.

"Oh, yes," gabbled Letty. Fumbling with the buttons, she stripped off the offending gloves, but the liquid had seeped through the rough mesh, leaving a macabre checkerboard of dark stains. Letty scrubbed ineffectually at one hand with the other. "I forgot about that."

"A lady," pronounced Miss Gwen, eyeing Letty with some disfavor, "never goes out in public with blood on her hands."

Having satisfied herself that Letty wasn't hurt, Jane looked to Geoff, her curls and ruffles sitting ill with her alert expression. "What happened?"

Geoff didn't waste time in trivialities. "The Black Tulip is dead."

For once, even Miss Gwen was struck silent.

As they stood there, frozen in tableau, the maid entered with a basin, a length of toweling draped over her arm.

Jane waited until the maid had departed before she spoke. "Did you—?"

"No," said Geoff, as Letty plunged her hands gratefully into the warm water, scrubbing at the stains with more vigor than science. "We found her backstage in the Crow Street Theatre. Someone had driven a knife through her eye."

The maid, returning with the coffee tray, did not so much as rattle the cups at the mention of murder.

Unblinking, she placed the tray on the table before Jane. Jane nodded her thanks, and the maid departed as noiselessly as she had come. The staff, Letty knew, were all involved in some way with the League, but Letty had never asked, and Jane had never volunteered.

Jane looked closely at Geoff, a fine line between her brows. "Exactly whom did you find backstage?"

"Emily Gilchrist," said Letty, just as Geoff said, "The Marquise de Montval."

Jane's forehead smoothed out again.

"What," she asked carefully, tilting the coffeepot over one

white-and-blue cup, "led you to believe that Emily Gilchrist was the Marquise de Montval?"

"Her murder had something to do with it," Geoff said mildly. "But there was also this."

Upending the reticule, he shook its contents out onto the table.

The silver pawn hit the table with a metallic ping. Four sets of eyes followed its rotations as it rolled on an elliptical path before finally settling to a stop just in front of Miss Gwen's cup.

Jane's hand stilled, and she returned the coffeepot to its place on the tray with unnecessary care. "Now, that is interesting."

She scooped up the little silver die, examining the markings on the bottom with a practiced eye.

"I heard Lord Vaughn in discussion with the marquise," said Geoff, as Jane inspected the seal, "a few minutes before I came upon Letty—and the body."

Remembering that unpleasant scene, Geoff took a quick look at Letty. Across the table, Letty was stirring sugar into her coffee with every appearance of composure. She might have carried off the pose if she hadn't put in eight lumps and stirred with more vigor than was strictly necessary.

Reaching across the table, Geoff snagged the sugar bowl before she could go for a ninth. Looking up, Letty flushed slightly and managed a sheepish smile.

Geoff felt an unpleasant constriction in his chest, like a very bad cold.

Letty's hands were red from scrubbing; her bloodied gloves were wadded into a little ball next to her cup; and her hair was still up on one side, but down on the other. Over the past few hours, she had been propositioned by his cousin, confronted with the corpse of an acquaintance, then assaulted and insulted—by him.

And her only concession to weakness was to put too much sugar in her coffee.

He didn't know whether to take off his hat to her or get down on his knees and apologize.

It wasn't just tonight. Looking at her, resolutely stirring her eight lumps of sugar into a brown sludge, it struck him, for the first time, just how trying the events of the past few weeks must have been for her. When she was the villainess, it hadn't mattered that her likeness was plastered across a thousand broadsheets, her good name dragged through the mud. Leaving for Ireland without her had seemed like an excellent way of thumbing his nose at the woman who had deliberately destroyed his only hope of happiness—and serving England while he was at it. The quintessential case of two birds with one stone.

All of that, of course, was only justifiable in the context of her culpability. Someday, he would find out exactly how she had come to be in his carriage. It didn't really matter anymore. However it had come about, he was sure of one thing: It had been an accident.

And it had hurt her far more than it had hurt him.

Jane returned the seal to the center of the table and reached for the coffeepot, resuming her abandoned duties as hostess. "You heard Lord Vaughn with the marquise?"

Geoff propped one leg against the opposite knee, forcing himself to look away from Letty. Apologies would have to come later. Apologies and . . . Geoff remembered that he was supposed to be carrying on a sensible discussion about Vaughn and the marquise. Anything else would also have to wait for later. "They did not appear to be on the best of terms."

"No," said Jane slowly, passing a cup down the table to Geoff. "They haven't been. Not for some time, if Vaughn is to be believed."

"I wouldn't believe that man if he told me the sky was blue," Geoff said bluntly, remembering Vaughn's artful flirtation with Letty at Mrs. Lanergan's party. No honest man spun such a polished line of patter. "But, given the outcome, Vaughn seems to have been telling the truth in this. Unfortunately, a group of stagehands carrying scenery chose that moment to pass by. I lost track of Vaughn and the marquise. Until Letty found her body."

"You believe," Jane summarized, "that while you were trapped on the other side of the scenery, Vaughn killed the marquise."

Miss Gwen made a derisive noise.

Jane silenced her with a glance. "Tell me, while you were listening, were you able to see the marquise?"

"How did I know it was she, do you mean?" He could understand Jane's question. His interactions with the Marquise de Montval in London had been few, and her most notable characteristic, her unusual coloring, was easily masked by a wig and cosmetics—masked or counterfeited. Some traits, however, were harder to hide than others. "The marquise's voice is unmistakable."

"Oh, I won't argue with you on that," said Jane. She looked oddly relaxed, as though she had come up against a difficult problem and solved it to her own satisfaction. It made Geoff decidedly uneasy. "But you didn't see her, did you? You didn't see what she was wearing?"

Geoff looked grim about the mouth. "No. The angle of the door blocked my view."

"There you have it, then." Jane indulged in a sip of coffee.

"Have what?" asked Letty, looking from Geoff to Jane. She had, Geoff noticed, smartly pushed her sugar-laden cup aside.

"The answer," said Jane. "Your theory would be very sensible—"

"Would?" Geoff raised an eyebrow. Aside from the confusion that assaulted him when confronted with the fatal combination of his wife and wheeled conveyances, all his logical faculties were in proper working order.

"If," Jane continued, "Miss Emily Gilchrist were the Marquise de Montval."

Geoff raised a restraining hand. "Just because I didn't see the marquise wearing Emily Gilchrist's clothes doesn't invalidate the theory. Consider the evidence. First"—Geoff held up a finger—"we can place Vaughn and the marquise backstage at the crucial moment. Second, you have their remarkable similarity in coloring. There aren't many women—in our circle, at least—with hair that dark and skin that white. Finally, we have the seal of the Black Tulip concealed in Emily Gilchrist's reticule. It all points the same way."

"But, you see," said Jane gently, "Emily Gilchrist can't be the Marquise de Montval."

"Why not?" asked Letty, saving Geoff the trouble of doing so. Miss Gwen just smirked.

Jane paused a moment before dropping her bombshell.

"Because the Marquise de Montval is Augustus Ormond."

Geoff's face was a study in skepticism. "*Ormond* is the Black Tulip?"

"Surprised you, didn't it?" gloated Miss Gwen. "A bit of humble pie does any man good. Eat up, sirrah!"

Geoff ignored her. He looked directly at Jane. "Why Ormond?"

Jane lifted her cup, the very image of innocence.

"Because Lord Vaughn is working for me."

If Letty hadn't already been sitting down, she would have. From the smug expression on Miss Gwen's face, she had already known for some time. Geoff, on the other hand, looked as though he would have dearly liked to say something unfit for female ears, and was only restraining himself through an extreme exercise of will.

"*For* you, or *with* you?" Geoff finally clipped out.

Jane smiled to herself over her cup. "He would say 'with.'"

Letty stared down into her cup of sludge, watching the pieces form up like tea leaves.

It was all embarrassingly clear—in retrospect. Jane's banter with Vaughn in the crypt. All that rubbish about charades. At the time, the topic had struck Letty as decidedly unwise. But it hadn't been. Not when Vaughn already knew. As for the meeting in the crypt, that hadn't been by chance either, had it? Jane had always intended for Geoff to examine the pulpit, while she went below for a prearranged meeting with Lord Vaughn. Letty had been a last-minute addition to that party; neither Jane nor Vaughn had made allowances for an extra party. Not that she had posed any problem for them. Letty winced at the memory of being induced to perform the introductions—even worse, the ways she had tried to intervene to protect Jane's identity. How they must have laughed!

Letty could have happily joined her husband in a few choice words.

"Was Lord Edward Fitzgerald really Lord Vaughn's cousin?" Letty asked in a strangled voice.

"Yes." Jane regarded her sympathetically, as though she knew what Letty was thinking. "They didn't get on, though."

Geoff leaned back in his chair with an air of deceptive casualness. "How long has this been going on?"

"Lord Vaughn released the Marquise de Montval from custody on my behalf," Jane explained calmly. "Due to their prior relationship—and certain other factors, which are no one's business but Lord Vaughn's—I believed she would be less likely to question his motives."

It didn't escape Letty's attention that Jane had sidestepped Geoff's question.

Geoff tried again, with no more success.

"How did you happen to make Vaughn's acquaintance?"

"We met in Paris," said Jane.

She did not volunteer any further information.

"Do you mean to say," Letty broke in, "that Lord Vaughn has been minding the Black Tulip for you all this time?"

"Absent the echoes of the nursery, yes. I provided Vaughn with reports to be fed to the marquise, and Lord Vaughn relayed information about the marquise's movements to me." Jane arranged her hands demurely in her lap. "It was a most profitable arrangement."

"I can see your reasoning," said Geoff, with great difficulty, "but you might have saved us all a great deal of bother by informing the War Office of your little arrangement."

Jane looked prim. "I prefer not to confide everything to the War Office. They have a regrettable tendency to lose dispatches to the French."

"Let me rephrase that," said Geoff pleasantly. "You might have seen fit to inform me. Or did you not trust me to hold my tongue?"

"The shoe is not so pleasant on the other foot, is it, eh?" inquired Miss Gwen.

"A necessary subterfuge. Lord Vaughn and I agreed—"

"You mean that you decided," interjected Geoff.

"—that it would be safer for all if we kept our little arrangement a secret."

"Not from me," put in Miss Gwen smugly.

"How could I possibly have any secrets from my dearest Auntie Ernie?"

"But why would someone murder Emily Gilchrist, then?" broke in Letty, deeming it wise to change the subject.

"And how do we explain these?" Geoff gestured to the seal and paper occupying pride of place in the center of the table.

"You said Miss Gilchrist's assailant dropped them?"

"That is a losing argument," countered Geoff, leaning back in his chair. "The marquise would never have carried a pink reticule with a man's costume. She's too careful for that."

"Running about in breeches." Miss Gwen sniffed as though she smelled something unpleasant. "Disgraceful."

"As have I on occasion." Jane cast her chaperone a sideways glance ripe with amusement. "With your connivance."

"That," declared Miss Gwen, with equal parts dignity and illogic, "was different."

"The reticule?" said Geoff.

"It was quite definitely Miss Gilchrist's," said Letty. "I remember seeing it on her wrist earlier in the evening. . . ."

"Gilchrist must have stolen the seal and letter," declared Miss Gwen. "Used them for a spot of blackmail."

"How would she know the value of them if she wasn't involved?"

"Hmph," said Miss Gwen.

"I have an idea," put in Letty, cupping her coffee cup in both hands. "What if there wasn't one Black Tulip, but two? That would explain why they both have seals."

"Why only two?" declared Miss Gwen sarcastically. "Why not three or four?"

"Why not, indeed?" echoed Jane.

Miss Gwen looked at her charge as though she suspected her of having run mad. "Absurd!"

"It might be a syndicate," argued Letty. "Like a merchant trading company."

"More like pirates," said Miss Gwen austerely, "with no respect for their betters."

Jane gazed thoughtfully at the green-and-white pattern on the wall. "Neither analogy is entirely inapt."

Letty struggled to put her idea into words. "It isn't really that shocking when you think about it. After all, you have a league. Why shouldn't they?"

"Something more than a league, I think," said Jane softly. "There was a reason that Geoffrey mistook Miss Gilchrist for the Marquise de Montval."

"To be fair"—Letty rose to her husband's defense before they could rehash that whole argument again—"there wasn't much of her face left to recognize. I only knew her by her dress."

"And by something else," prompted Jane.

Geoff drained his cup. "You can't base a theory on a chance similarity of physiognomy."

"You really believe it was chance?"

"What are you suggesting?"

"I think you know," said Jane.

"I don't," put in Letty.

"Petals," said Jane, her lips curving into a slight smile. "Petals of the Tulip."

Chapter Twenty-two

"Petals, indeed!" declared Miss Gwen. "You have been among the French too long."

"All the better to know how they think."

Miss Gwen's sentiments regarding the French mind were best expressed in a vehement snort.

"There might be something to it," said Geoff, only partly because he enjoyed contradicting Miss Gwen. "It would appeal to a certain sort of humor to employ a series of agents with the same coloring and general physical type."

"Are you saying," demanded Miss Gwen, "that if our adversary's pseudonym were 'the Rose,' we would find ourselves chasing a series of red-haired persons?"

"Possibly," said Geoff. It did sound rather foolish when put that way. But there was something to it, something he couldn't quite put his finger on. "I never liked the idea of the marquise as the Black Tulip. She was never quite clever enough."

"If all these agents are merely petals," broke in Letty, "wouldn't you need . . ." Letty's horticultural knowledge failed her.

"A stem?" provided Geoff, with a smile that turned Letty's

cheekbones a faint pink more becoming than anything found in the botanical kingdom.

"An evil mastermind," mused Miss Gwen, happily oblivious of any undercurrents that failed to involve espionage, treachery, or torture, with a preference for the last. "I like it."

"I'm so glad our deductions meet with your approval," murmured Geoff.

"Not as a theory, young man." Miss Gwen regarded Geoff haughtily over the top of the coffeepot. "For my novel."

"But who is he?" demanded Letty, before Miss Gwen could expatiate further on her literary endeavors.

Miss Gwen cleared her throat ominously.

"Or she," Letty corrected herself. "The real Black Tulip, I mean."

Something about the phrase *the real Black Tulip* caught at Letty's memory, but she couldn't quite place it. Not when Geoff was watching her from the other side of the table in a way that brought back memories not best suited to the drawing room.

Letty took a hasty gulp of her coffee before remembering that it was three-quarters sugar.

"Perhaps this might be of some help," suggested Jane, reaching for the small twist of paper that had fallen out of Emily's reticule. "Have you read it yet, Geoffrey?"

"There wasn't an opportunity."

"Wasting good time in dalliance, no doubt," sniffed Miss Gwen.

Avoiding Geoff's eyes, Letty said hastily, "Have you considered Mr. Throtwottle?"

"Mr. Who?" demanded Miss Gwen.

"Throtwottle," Letty repeated. "Emily Gilchrist's guardian. Or, at least, that is what she claimed. If she was an agent, it seems likely that he was one, too."

"No self-respecting agent would adopt so ridiculous a name

as Throtwottle," declared the faux Mrs. Grimstone. "It's absurd."

"All the more reason why he might be," Jane said briskly, frowning over the paper. Either the code was proving intractable, or she didn't like what she was reading. "How better to hide your devious purposes than picking a name so outlandish no spy would use it?"

While Miss Gwen considered this new angle, Geoff took up the line of questioning. "What do you know of Mr. Throtwottle?"

"Not terribly much," admitted Letty. "We were all on the packet from London together, but I saw far more of Miss Gilchrist than I did of her guardian. When he did appear, it was usually to misquote bits of Latin." She cast a rueful glance at Geoff. "He was exceedingly tedious."

Geoff's lips turned up at the reference to their earlier conversation, a private link between the two of them. "You were meant to find him tedious," he said.

"It worked," said Letty. "Both of them."

"Yes, and?" broke in Miss Gwen. "Do get on. We don't have all night."

"We do, actually," said Geoff. He glanced at the clock on the mantel. It was only just past one. "Unless you have other plans for the evening."

"I don't know about you, but I intend to spend the rest of the night as the good Lord intended. In slumber," she added pointedly.

"Probably hanging upside down like a bat," Geoff whispered to Letty, who bit down on a shocked giggle, her large blue eyes glowing in a way that reminded him rather forcibly that the good Lord had intended the night for things other than slumber.

They were married, after all.

"All right," Geoff said briskly, suddenly eager to have the meeting over and done with. "Let's get on. Is there anything else you can recall?"

"Ye-es," said Letty. "Tonight, at the theater, Emily leaned over the box and waved at me. I thought she was just—"

"Exhibiting her usual lack of propriety?" put in Miss Gwen.

"Something like that. But she seemed too eager. Desperate, even. Her guardian pulled her back into the box. I thought he was just scolding her for leaning out like that. But when I looked back, they were gone."

"Interesting," pronounced Miss Gwen, forgetting to be snide.

"Do you think she was trying to communicate something to you?" asked Geoff.

"Possibly," said Letty. She stared down at her reddened knuckles, reassembling shards of memory. "I think she had before, too, only I was too thick to see it. She brought up the Pink Carnation and the Purple Gentian a good deal. At the time, I simply put it down as another example of her frivolity."

"She thought you were a spy," said Geoff soberly.

"You were traveling under an alias," pointed out Miss Gwen, looking superior. "Albeit a clumsy one."

"Ironic, isn't it?" Letty said, shaking her head.

"Ironic" wasn't the word Geoff would have used. Bloody terrifying was more like it.

"She must have been trying to sound you out," Geoff said grimly. "Either to elicit information from you, or . . ."

"Or?" demanded Miss Gwen.

Geoff frowned. "When I overheard the marquise and Lord Vaughn, they were discussing eliminating an unnamed party who had become a liability. I assumed," he added, nodding to the others at the table, "that they were referring to one of you."

"They won't be rid of me that easily," declared Miss Gwen.

Letty caught her husband's eye. "You think they were talking about Emily Gilchrist."

"It does follow," said Geoff, tactfully refraining from rehashing the details. Letty was grateful for that. Even if Emily

Gilchrist had been a hardened spy, it wasn't pleasant to picture her lying in the hallway of the Crow Street Theatre. "My money is on Vaughn."

"Why Vaughn?" asked Letty.

"The sort of wound we saw isn't in the marquise's usual style. She prefers the stiletto."

"But in her current costume," put in Jane, without looking up from the scrap of paper in front of her, "a knife might be more apt."

Letty preferred not to think too deeply about the nature of Emily's wound; it had been bad enough seeing it once. Instead, she devoted herself to chasing down that elusive sliver of memory. Something about a tulip . . .

"He might be double-crossing you, you know," Geoff was saying.

"There is no real Black Tulip!" exclaimed Letty.

Three sets of eyes fastened on Letty. Even Jane glanced momentarily up from her labors.

"I beg your pardon," said Miss Gwen, in a way that suggested that Letty ought to be begging hers.

"The flower, I mean." Letty had pegged down the elusive scrap of memory that had eluded her before. Triumphantly, she looked around the table. "There is no such flower as a black tulip."

"You are mistaken," declared Miss Gwen. "I'm sure I've seen one."

Letty shook her head. "They don't exist. The only reason I know is that M—my sister"—she couldn't quite bring herself to voice Mary's name in Geoff's presence—"tried to acquire some to set off a white dress."

It was their father who had pointed out that the flower didn't exist—although, in his usual way, he had let them endure several footsore days of searching every flower shop in London before he brought out Jean Paul de Rome d'Ardene's authoritative botanical treatise. They had gone through all fifty listed varieties of tulip before Mary had been ready to admit defeat.

"What if," asked Letty, "they chose a flower that doesn't exist for an agent who doesn't exist? No stem, only petals."

"Wouldn't that make a grand joke on us," mused Geoff. "Fool the English into wasting time and resources hunting down an agent who doesn't exist."

"We don't know that," said Miss Gwen forbiddingly. "Where there are subordinates, there must be a leader to coordinate their actions. Otherwise, all is chaos."

"If they answered directly to the Ministry of Police . . ." Geoff suggested.

"Fouche's mind doesn't run along those lines. It's a clever idea, though," Jane said regretfully. "I wish I had thought of it."

"A bit late for that," pointed out Miss Gwen.

"Thank you, Auntie Ernie. You are, as ever, a source of comfort to me."

"Bonaparte?" suggested Letty. "As the mastermind?"

Geoff shook his head. "Too straightforward. He prefers artillery to horticulture."

"His wife *is* a great gardener, according to the papers," argued Letty.

"But not anyone's definition of a mastermind," said Geoff, who had met Josephine Bonaparte several times in the course of his duties for the League of the Purple Gentian. "Talleyrand might pull a scheme like this off—he's clever enough, and tricky enough—but I've never been sure how firmly he sits in Bonaparte's camp."

"No," Jane said. "I don't think we are dealing with a practical joke on a grand scale. These lieutenants may act in his name, but, somewhere, there is a Black Tulip. And it's not Talleyrand. Or Bonaparte."

"How can you be so sure?" asked Geoff.

"I've spent a good deal of time studying the Black Tulip's past movements. There is a certain similarity to them that bears the stamp of one driving intelligence."

"Or a very good mimic," countered Geoff.

"As long as it's not a mime," muttered Letty.

"Mimes are very distressing," Geoff agreed.

They grinned at each other in a moment of mutual silliness.

Miss Gwen bridled in preparation for a crushing put-down, but Jane spoke first, in a voice devoid of either amusement or scorn.

"Not as distressing as this."

Jane held up the little scrap of paper, covered with a series of numbers and letters. It made no sense to Letty, but it obviously did to Jane. And whatever it was, Jane didn't like it.

"The French are coming."

"That's not news," said Geoff, relaxing against his chair.

"But the timing is. Bonaparte has promised troops for the first of August." Jane looked away, her usually serene face twisted with frustration. "I thought I had put them off."

"How many?"

"There are six French warships already stationed in Brest, with the promise of more to come."

"And our garrison," said Geoff, "is down to just over thirty thousand."

Jane regarded the coded report with extreme disfavor. "They should not have warships ready to put to sea. For the past two weeks, I've been replacing the marquise's dispatches with false reports, minimizing the extent of local preparations and discouraging any immediate action."

" 'Local rebellion not ready yet; don't send troops till further word'?" Geoff supplied.

"It seemed to be working. The Ministry of War naturally discounted more optimistic reports that Emmet sent to his brother in Paris and believed those of their agent. Unfortunately, someone—someone senior to the marquise—appears to have gotten the correct information through."

"The Black Tulip," groaned Letty, who was beginning to loathe the very name.

"What matters now," said Geoff, "is not so much who summoned the troops as how we stop them."

"If," said Jane grimly, "we could ferret out our flowery foe, we might be able to reverse what he set in motion."

The expression on Jane's face did not bode well for the Black Tulip. She looked like the illustration of Athena in one of Letty's childhood books, just before the goddess turned an impertinent mortal into a spider. Letty had the impression that Jane was no more accustomed to being thwarted than Athena had been.

"The time has come," said Jane, "to have a little chat with the Marquise de Montval."

Geoff pushed back his chair and paced to the window, staring unseeingly at their reflections in the glass.

"I have another idea. We don't try to delay, but precipitate. Think of it," he said, before Miss Gwen could muster her counterarguments. "In 'ninety-eight, the local rebellion went off prematurely. By the time the French got here, we had already mopped up the native insurgency."

"And were able to turn every resource to rounding up the French," Jane said thoughtfully. "I see. A species of 'divide and conquer.' "

Geoff prowled back toward the table, formulating his plan as he paced. "Emmet has caches of arms scattered all over the city, but his biggest depot is on Patrick Street."

"Gunpowder?" asked Jane, a comprehending gleam lighting her eye.

"Better. Emmet has been stockpiling rockets."

All three women looked blank.

With the boundless enthusiasm of the male for any sort of explosive device, Geoff went on, "They haven't made much head-way with them here or on the Continent, but Wellesley's troops were nearly routed by rockets in India a few years back. Emmet found an old Indian hand to manufacture them for him. They're not terribly accurate in battle, but they make a big bang. Set those alight, and Emmet's storehouse will go up like fireworks on the king's birthday."

Geoff looked as though he rather enjoyed the prospect.

"That could be hard to explain to the neighbors," said Letty.

"And to the night watchmen, and to the guards quartered at the castle. It might even draw General Fox back from his trip to the West Country." Geoff's eyes met hers, burning like an entire rocket fusillade in his enthusiasm. "Emmet will have to act quickly to salvage his plans. He'll have to go it without the French."

"What if he doesn't?" asked Letty.

"He has too much invested in this not to. He has a choice. He can act at once or abandon five years' worth of preparations. He has weapons scattered throughout the city, a volunteer army who will get bored and drift away if doesn't employ them soon, and enough incriminating documents floating about to hang twelve of him. He will act."

"When you put it that way . . . ," said Letty.

Geoff grinned at her. "Cry havoc and let slip the dogs of war!"

"I," said Miss Gwen grandly, "will blow up the depot."

"Ever since she fired on that boot manufactory in Calais, Miss Gwen has had difficulty controlling her incendiary impulses," commented Geoff, strolling round the table to rest his hand on the back of Letty's chair.

"That was you?" exclaimed Letty, very conscious of the hand resting next to her back. The back of her neck prickled with the knowledge that he was standing behind her, just out of her view. "I read about that in the papers! Weren't there pink petals scattered among the ashes?"

Miss Gwen looked pleased. "It is attention to detail that makes all the difference."

"No pink petals this time," said Geoff, from somewhere just above Letty's head. "Our best chance is to make it look like an accident. Otherwise they might go to ground, rather than bringing the rebellion forward."

"May I help?" asked Letty, tilting her head back and getting an excellent view of the underside of his chin. For a dark-haired man, he was quite well shaved; she couldn't find any spot he had missed.

Jane and Geoff exchanged a long look.

"I'll need you with me," said Jane. "You can entertain Lord Vaughn while I have a little chat with the marquise."

"I don't think Lord Vaughn finds me terribly entertaining."

"Well, do your best," said Miss Gwen dismissively. She looked pointedly at Geoff. "Wear a low bodice. Men are so easily diverted."

"Well," said Geoff, looking as innocent as a man who has just been caught staring down his wife's bodice can contrive to look. "That covers about everything, doesn't it? Given the lateness of the hour, I suggest we all seek our beds." He raised an eyebrow at Miss Gwen. "As the good Lord intended."

The clock on the mantel obligingly confirmed his observation by striking two.

Jane rose, her curls, which she had neglected to remove, bobbing coyly around her face. "You'll see Letty home, of course."

"Of course," replied Geoff, at his most bland.

"I'll call for the carriage," said Jane.

"And I," said Miss Gwen, sweeping out in Jane's wake, "shall seek my perch."

Alone once again in the little green parlor, Letty and Geoff exchanged a slightly sheepish look.

"She heard the bat comment, didn't she?" said Letty guiltily, rising to stand next to Geoff.

"She hears everything." Geoff's mind did not appear to be on Miss Gwen. "There is one thing we failed to address."

"Aside from Miss Gwen's sleeping habits?" said Letty, trying to keep her tone light and failing miserably.

Geoff frowned. "I didn't want to alarm you in front of the others, but it might be unwise for you to return to your own lodgings tonight."

"Emily's murderer," said Letty heavily, returning to earth with a thump. With all the talk of mimes and bats, it had been all too easy to forget how deadly the game they played actually was. "We don't know that he recognized me."

Geoff crossed his arms, looking about as malleable as a chunk of granite. "That is not a chance I want to take."

Feeling absurdly gratified, Letty suggested, "I could ask Jane and Miss Gwen if I could stay here, with them."

"With Miss Gwen stalking about in her nightcap? You might be scarred for life."

"Even Miss Gwen's nightcap must be preferable to the Black Tulip."

"I wouldn't wager on it." Clasping his hands behind his back, Geoff strolled to the dresser, examining a scene of Dublin Castle inexpertly painted on a lumpy piece of stoneware. "I have a better suggestion."

"What might that be?" Letty stayed where she was, rooted to the center of the room.

Geoff slowly turned from his contemplation of the domestic arts to face Letty.

"Come home," he said simply. "With me."

Chapter Twenty-three

Thursday night, wine bottle clutched in the crook of my arm, I trudged right back down Brompton Road.

I hadn't deliberately decided to revisit the site of Tuesday night's humiliation. It was pure ill luck in the form of geography. Pammy's mother lived in the Boltons. Directionally challenged as I am, the only way I knew to get there was via the South Kensington tube station, straight down Brompton Road. I suppose I could have taken a cab, but that smacked of cowardice—not to mention extravagance. A student budget doesn't run to much in the way of extras.

Passing the ill-fated Indian restaurant, I couldn't resist taking a tiny peek through the glass door. The bar area was crowded— it was just about that time of the evening—but there was no familiar tall blond braced against the bar. Not that I had expected there to be. Or that I cared. I had put that all behind me. All the flutters, all the euphoria, all the despair, all the ridiculous overanalyzing had been nothing more than a silly crush, undoubtedly brought on by boredom. As Pammy liked to keep pointing out to me, I'd been long overdue for a romantic peccadillo. Was it any surprise that my restless imagination had seized upon the first reasonably attractive man to come along?

Oh, well, I told myself soothingly. So I had behaved like an idiot. It was all over, and there was no harm done—except to my pride, and no one would ever see that but me, anyway.

Upon my return home from the Indian restaurant Tuesday night, I had plopped down at my little kitchen table in my little basement flat, and painstakingly dissected the entire course of my acquaintance with Colin. Not the bits that happened in my head, not the agonized phone staring or the gooey-eyed naming of our children, but all of the actual interactions, from our first meeting in his aunt's living room just about two weeks ago.

Had it really only been two weeks? It had. I counted, and then I counted again to make sure. Going through those two weeks, I came to the relieved conclusion that while I might know that I'd made an absolute idiot of myself over him, there was no reason for Colin to know. Aside from that slight puckering incident in the old medieval cloister, I had never said or done anything to indicate more than a friendly interest. And it had been very dark out there. He might not even have noticed. I was safe.

And I never, ever had to see him again.

I did intend to call Mrs. Selwick-Alderly. Eventually. But just because I was in contact with his aunt didn't necessarily mean bumping into Colin.

In the meantime, I was rather proud of everything I had accomplished over the past week without any Selwick intercession. True, it was their collection that had pointed me in the right direction, but the Alsworthy/Alsdale line of research was entirely my own, and it was paying off in spades.

It was nice to know something that Colin Selwick didn't.

The death of Emily Gilchrist opened all sorts of interesting possibilities. I wondered how many other raven-haired spies were roaming France and London, unremembered by commentators. And why would they? Who would read anything into—what had Geoff called it?—a chance quirk of physiognomy. That wasn't exactly the phrase (I had it in my notes, back in my little flat, backed up on three disks, just in case), but it was the same idea. I know historians aren't supposed to fall in love with their own theories, but I was head over heels about the notion of an entire band of female French agents, like a nineteenth-century *Charlie's Angels*. Only better.

It made the Pink Carnation's organization look positively humdrum.

Who, then, was the Black Tulip? Mr. Throtwottle was the obvious choice, but given all the women running about dressed as men, I wouldn't put it past Throtwottle to be yet another black-haired woman playing a trouser role. Noses like that didn't just grow naturally.

As for Lord Vaughn . . . Even bearing in mind the precedent of Monsieur d'Eon, there was little chance of his being a woman. But I didn't buy his complicity with Jane, any more than Geoff did. Whatever Lord Vaughn did, he did for himself, not for king or country or even the rare combination of a keen mind and pretty face.

Vaughn as spymaster? The idea had some potential. He had known the marquise for a long time . . . and there was that matter of a missing wife. The marquise? Or another black-haired agent? I had no proof, only hunches. Of all the actors concerned, Vaughn lacked motive. Related to three-quarters of the peerage of the British Isles, he had the most to lose in prestige and cold, hard cash if the French succeeded. There had been French noblemen, including Josephine Bonaparte's first husband, who had espoused the revolutionary cause, weighting ideology above their own self-interest—but that had been before the advent of the guillotine. And it just didn't seem like Vaughn.

For a time, hunched over my favorite desk in the British Library that afternoon, I had toyed with the notion of an elaborate double-fake. It would be a twist worthy of the Black Tulip if the marquise were indeed the mastermind. A truly clever spy might deliberately choose women of her own coloring to set up as decoys, like the scene at the end of *The Thomas Crown Affair*, with all those men roaming the halls of the Met in identical bowler hats.

Unfortunately, subsequent events made that theory unlikely, to say the least.

It was always disheartening when the historical record failed to comply with my pet theories. Didn't they realize that my way was much more interesting?

The farther down Brompton Road I went, the more deserted it got. It was a cold, damp night, with a chill that bit through to the bone, the sort of night that must have sent the early Britons huddling around the fires in their huts, concluding that blue paint was no substitute for good, strong wool. It made me understand why the Pilgrims had taken ship to the New World. Forget the Lower School textbook stuff about religious freedom; they were probably just yearning for a beach. Tropical sand, some palm trees, sunshine . . . Instead, they got turkeys and Wal-Mart. And religious freedom, so I guess it wasn't a total loss in the end.

Wet leaves caked the ground, plastering themselves damply to the bottom of my shoes. They squelched eerily underfoot, like some watery monster out of the late-late-night movie. In honor of Pammy's mother, I had abandoned my habitual knee-high boots for a pair of pointy-toed pumps. In the flimsy shoes, my feet felt alarmingly open to the elements. But one didn't tread on Pammy's mother's carpets in boots, even if they were Jimmy Choos.

Reaching the end of the road, I turned in to the quiet crescent where Pammy's mother had lived since her remove from New York. It was an exclusive enclave of thirty Victorian mansions, all discreetly tucked away behind high white walls, bristling with enough alarm systems and security cameras to stock Fort Knox.

Pammy's mother had never worked in all the time I had

known them, but she had made something of a career out of marrying well. Hubby Number One, the starter husband, had been long gone by the time I arrived on the scene, and therefore of little interest. Hubby Number Two had provided Pammy and a not-inconsiderable chunk of his legendary art collection, the latter in reparation for having had the poor taste to take up with a younger model—before officially initiating divorce proceedings with Pammy's mother. It was Hubby Number Three (after her American adventure, Pammy's mother had switched back to her own countrymen) who had contributed the house in the Boltons, along with a charming little property in Dorset, where Pammy's mother presided in the summer months, much in the manner of Marie Antoinette playing milkmaid at Le Petite Trianon.

As far as I knew, there was no Number Four on the radar screen just yet, but general wisdom (i.e., Pammy and my mother) held that it was just a matter of time.

Letting myself in through the gate, I waved at the security camera and started up the walk toward the front door, discreetly set back among tastefully landscaped topiaries. In the dark and wet, the shrubs looked like hulking beasts guarding the door, a Cerberus for either side. But the drawing room windows were golden with light, and even through the closed door I could hear the muted residue of bubbly chatter.

American chatter. I felt an unaccustomed swell of fondness for my compatriots. At home, I pined after things English like a parrot for the fjords, but after a few months of England—and Englishmen—there was something rather nice about a cacophony of brash American voices butchering the language as only we know how.

All in all, I was feeling decidedly sanguine as I bounced up the three steps to the front door. Pammy's mother wasn't exactly the warm, motherly sort, but there was the comfort that came of having known her for absolutely ever (or since I was five, which amounted to much the same thing). She was a known quantity.

After dealing with strangers, there's a lot to be said for that. Once you've gotten Marshmallow Fluff all over someone's Prada bag, there's not much else that can go wrong.

Relinquishing my raincoat and bottle to the maid who opened the door, I ventured into the drawing room. It wasn't a big room, but it was cleverly arranged to provide the illusion of space, papered in textured pale blue and hung with Pammy's father's guilt offerings: one Degas, two Monets, and a smattering of lesser impressionists. His Renoirs were in the back parlor, which was paneled in Victorian walnut (original to the house) and as darkly traditional as the front room was airy, linked to the decorating scheme by the use of the same shade of blue in the accents on the upholstery.

I could see Mrs. Harrington holding court on a sand-and-blue sofa in the front room, chatting with a couple I didn't know, but whose voices marked them as fellow refugees on foreign shores. We were going to be just shy of twenty for dinner, Pammy had told me, and it looked like the gang was mostly here. The crowd seemed fairly well split between Pammy's friends and her mother's, a nice sample of the American expat community in various stages of development.

Pammy's mother's friends were of the banker-and-wife variety, men in suits or blazers with wives about a third of their bulk and/or age, with shoes even pointier than mine. As for Pammy's friends, only one guy sported a blazer. It was constructed of orange velvet with elaborate piping, and boasted a faux flower in the buttonhole. I had no doubt that, if asked, he would refer to it as ironic.

A bar had been set up in the back room, appropriately located beneath a painting of a frowsy Parisian barmaid, a depiction made acceptable for the drawing room with time and a famous name to sanctify it. I spotted Pammy there, wearing a belted sweater with fur bristling five inches deep from her collar and the hem of her skirt. Knowing Pammy, the animal-skin theme was probably in honor of Thanksgiving. I was just glad she hadn't insisted everyone arrive dressed in tasteful ensembles of wampum and turkey feathers.

Waving at her, I started across the room—and stopped short when I saw just who was standing by the bar next to her.

Oh, no. No, no, no. She wouldn't.

She had.

Next to me, I could hear orange blazer man drawling, "An ironic reconstruction of an iconic representation . . ."

All the I's and R's blurred in my ears into one general buzz. Maybe my ears were going. More to the point, maybe my eyes were going.

No such luck.

Detaching herself from her companions, Pammy bounded across the room, arms flung wide, a miraculous feat of balance considering the nearly full glass in one hand. "Ellie!"

I wasn't hallucinating. What I was, was the victim of an interfering, intermeddling—

"Pammy!" Flinging my arms around her, I muttered, "I could kill you. What is he doing here?"

I have to give Pammy some points; she didn't try to pretend that she had no idea what I meant.

Instead, she smiled a big cat-and-canary grin, glancing over her shoulder at Colin, who was chatting with a couple of Pammy's work friends and looking unfairly dishy. "Well, if Mustafa won't come to the mountain . . ."

"That's Mohammed," I said through clenched teeth.

Pammy waved a hand. "Whatever."

"I'm not interested."

"Sure you're not."

"I'm not!" I insisted.

"Oh, go have a drink, Ellie. It will put you in a better mood."

"Who said I was in a bad mood?"

Pammy held up a hand, palm out. "You are just so lucky we've been friends for twenty years."

"Twenty-one," I muttered after Pammy's departing back. She never had been any good at math.

Not like it really made a difference. But in those twenty-one years, I was pretty sure that I'd put up with just as much from her as she had from me. More. I added tonight's party to the balance against her. She owed me at least a year of good behavior for that one.

She might at least have warned me.

Pammy aside, I wouldn't have minded a drink, just to have something in my hands. A drink, held debonairly aloft, goes a long way to inspiring social confidence. It's as much the pose as the contents. Combine it with a tinkling laugh and an appropriately rapt expression and, after a while, even I might be fooled.

But Colin was standing at the bar, like a linebacker guarding a goalpost, or whatever it is that linebackers guard.

Right, I told myself. This was it. Just to prove that he didn't mean anything to me at all, I was going to walk right up there and say hi, just as I would to any other random person on whom I had never had the teeny-tiniest hint of a crush.

"Hi!" I said brightly, following it up with a little wave. "How *are* you?"

Okay, maybe I was overdoing the gushing bit.

"I'm fine," said Colin. No gushing there. His entire demeanor gave a whole new meaning to the word "chill." "You?"

"Vodka tonic, please," I instructed the man behind the bar. Pammy's mother only allows drinks with a clear base, for the sake of her carpets. It's a long-established policy, dating back to their days in New York. Pammy and I were only allowed to have Coca-Cola in the kitchen and den. This, by the way, was in effect even before the Marshmallow Fluff episode.

"I'm doing well," I said over my shoulder to Colin. "Same old, same old."

The bartender fumbled with the tonic bottle, one of those funny little half-sized bottles, rather than the big, plastic ones we have at home. It was empty. Kneeling, the bartender started scavenging under the table.

Colin propped an elbow against the table. "You didn't bring Jay."

Jay? Oh, right. "He went home for Thanksgiving."

"And didn't take you?"

Under the table, the bartender's progress was marked by the clink of glass and crackle of cardboard. I was half tempted to tap him on the shoulder and tell him to give up already; I would just take my vodka straight. Anything so that I could take my glass and go.

"You know how it is," I said, trying not to peer too visibly over the edge of the table. "I had work to do."

"Hard on you." He didn't sound terribly sympathetic.

"I'll live." I accepted my long-awaited glass from the bartender, and smiled a stiff social smile at Colin. "I really should go say hi to Pammy's mother. Good talking to you."

"You, too." Colin raised his glass a fraction of an inch in farewell.

"Later, then. Bye-eee!"

Yes, I actually said "bye-eee." There is no accounting for what the brain will produce under stress.

Since I really did have to say hi to Pammy's mother, I wandered in that direction, wondering how I had contrived to sound quite so moronic in all of three or four sentences.

I glanced back over my shoulder at Colin, who was not glancing at me.

How dared he ignore me when I was working so hard at ignoring him? It was downright ungentlemanly of him.

Oh, wait. It wasn't supposed to matter anymore. I didn't care what Colin Selwick thought of me. I took a sip of my vodka tonic. Heavy on the vodka, light on the tonic, it tasted a bit like window cleaner (not that I've ever tasted window cleaner, but I imagine it has the same astringent properties). Drink any more of that, and not only would I not remember that I was supposed to be totally indifferent to Colin Selwick, I wouldn't be capable of coherent thought at all. Feeling my lips go numb from that one small sip, I deposited the glass discreetly on a small table next to an unnaturally lush potted plant and went to exchange hellos with Pammy's mother.

Mrs. Harrington was still holding court on the small sofa in the front room, her ash-blond hair cut in a neat shoulder-length bob, brushed to the shiny patina of the Bombay chest in the hall. Her face, with its retroussé nose and wide cheekbones, was more piquant than pretty, clear illustration while I was growing up that grooming and charm get you much farther than raw good looks.

Pammy was going to look just like her in another twenty years or so. I could see it happening already, although Pammy would vehemently deny it.

"Hi, Mrs. Harrington!" Under the influence of old habit, my voice went up half an octave into schoolgirl sweetness. "Thank you for having me here tonight."

"Eloise!" Mrs. Harrington lifted her cheek to be kissed. After so many years in the States, her accent was neither recognizably American nor English, but faltered somewhere in between. "We couldn't leave you alone for Thanksgiving."

"Mom and Dad send their love."

"How is your sister?"

"Enjoying college."

Mrs. Harrington narrowed her eyes shrewdly. "Not too much, I hope."

"You know Jillian," I said, with a grin. "But somehow she always pulls through in the end. I don't know how she does it."

Mrs. Harrington wagged a finger at me. "It's those Kelly brains. I don't know how Pammy would have gotten through algebra without you."

Well, that much was true.

I made modest noises of negation, anyway. It was part of the ritual, a strophe and antistrophe of compliment and demurral as stylized and immutable as the recitation of the litany, with Mrs. Harrington's Chanel No. 5 taking the place of incense.

The amenities having been observed, she smiled and gestured to someone standing behind me. "Do come over! Don't be shy."

The word "shy" should have tipped me off. Most of Pammy's friends don't answer to that description. Like her, they tend to be the self-assured product of a transatlantic education. There was only one of Pammy's circle I could think of to whom the adjective applied.

Stepping aside, I made room in front of the couch for Colin's sister.

Serena didn't look anything like her brother. Where Colin was big and blond and tanned—like the worst sort of Abercrombie ad, I thought disagreeably—Serena invited trite and mawkish analogies straight out of Victorian children's literature, phrases on the order of "as delicate as a woodland fawn." She shared Colin's hazel eyes, but in her narrow, high-cheekboned face, they had the wistful cast of a Pre-Raphaelite Lady of Shallot gazing through her casement window at faerie lands forlorn. Her skin was as pale as Colin's was browned, and her hair was a sleek chestnut that vindicated all the conditioner manufacturers' claims about their products.

Under her shiny hair, Serena's face seemed even paler than usual, the hollows under her eyes more pronounced. In contrast to the bright raspberry of her pashmina, her skin had a sickly cast to it that suggested a lack of food, or sleep, or both.

Pammy had mentioned a bad breakup in the not so distant past, but I wondered if there was more to it than that. The wrists protruding from under her pashmina were as brittle as the winter-bare twigs outside the drawing room window.

"Eloise"—Mrs. Harrington's voice recalled me to the conversation—"have you met Serena Selwick? She was at St. Paul's with Pammy."

Not only did I know Serena, I had held her head over a toilet bowl during a sudden bout of food poisoning. That sort of thing enhanced acquaintance in a hurry. It was also not the sort of story one related to one's friend's mother right before the consumption of large quantities of food.

"We've met," I said instead, leaning in to brush a kiss across the air next to Serena's cheek. "It's good to see you again."

Serena brushed her already immaculate hair back into place in a habitual gesture. "I'm sorry I missed you in Sussex."

Sussex. Scene of my ignoble crush. I was glad Serena hadn't been there to witness me making eyes at her brother. For all her timidity—and that perfect hair—I rather liked Serena.

I just made a face, and said, "I'm sure you had much better things to do in London. I was mostly holed up in the archive all weekend, anyway."

"Colin felt awful about having to run off like that."

I shrugged. "Not a biggie. It was very nice of him to let me come at such short notice in the first place."

"And, of course, he had excellent reason for leaving," put in Mrs. Harrington.

Did he? I looked at her in surprise. What was I missing?

"I hope your mother is mending nicely," she said to Serena. "I was so concerned."

Mending? Concerned?

Serena nodded earnestly. "Thank you. It was very kind of you to send flowers."

"It was the least I could do."

Like a gallumping lummox, I barged into the conversation. "Has your mother been ill?"

"Didn't Colin tell you?" Serena looked genuinely surprised. "I had thought, when he left . . ."

I shook my head in negation and tried to arrange my features into a proper expression of polite concern. I was beginning to wish I had held on to that vodka. Tendrils of apprehension unfolded in my stomach like the vines of a killer jungle plant.

"Serena's mother was in an auto accident," Mrs. Harrington filled in for her. "In Venice, wasn't it?"

"Siena."

"Oh, dear," I said. Anything else seemed entirely inadequate. "I'm so sorry."

"It was just bruises," Serena hastened to assure me. "And a broken rib."

"Oh, dear," I repeated numbly. "How awful."

"Those are the sorts of phone calls," said Mrs. Harrington, her eyes going automatically to Pammy, entertaining a crowd of coworkers across the room, "that one never wants to get."

"I can't even begin to imagine," I said.

Only I could.

We had just come in from that crazy drinks party at Donwell Abbey when Colin's mobile had rung. I remembered the moment distinctly. He had taken one look at the number, wished me an abrupt good-night, and hared off. At the time I had assumed it was simply because he didn't want anything more to do with me.

"I couldn't go, but Colin caught the first flight he could find. He stayed the week with her." Serena fingered the fringe of her pashmina, her bowed head an eloquent expression of guilt.

She wasn't the only one feeling guilty.

It must have been about six hours after the phone call that Colin had found me in the library and asked if I could be ready to leave in fifteen minutes. That intervening time took new shape in my imagination. I could picture Colin hunched over the computer, cell phone crammed against one ear, veering back and forth between making travel plans, keeping tabs on events in the hospital, and updating an anxious Serena. All alone in the middle of the night, with his mother lying injured in a foreign country and the minutes ticking inexorably away, while he was stuck in Sussex with a snippy houseguest.

I felt like pond scum.

"I'm sure your mother must have understood." I patted her shoulder clumsily. "That must have given you great peace of mind, to know that Colin was there with her."

I was the bacteria that lurked beneath pond scum. No self-respecting pond scum would have anything to do with me.

I'd been so wrapped in my own self-centered mantle of wounded ego that it had never occurred to me that something might be genuinely wrong. Something real, and life-threatening, and frightening. Something that had nothing to do with me, or aborted flirtations, or silly crushes.

I tried to imagine how I would react if I heard that my mother was injured—possibly badly—in a foreign country. Even the thought of it made me jittery.

"But she's better now?" I pressed.

"Much," said Serena resolutely. "And her husband is there with her."

Not "my father." Just "her husband." It had never occurred to me to ask about Colin's family situation. I suppose if I had thought about it at all, I would have just assumed that he had sprung fully formed out of Selwick Hall, like Minerva from Jove's head.

"Where is Colin?" I asked, craning my neck toward the bar.

I had a vague notion of . . . I don't know. Expressing my sympathies? Apologizing? It was nothing that coherent, more a generalized sense of wanting to make amends, although for precisely what, I couldn't say. After all, I couldn't very well apologize to Colin for being pissy with him because I thought he had snubbed me if a) he hadn't realized that I was being pissy, and b) he had no idea that I'd thought he had snubbed me. It was all a huge muddle.

He wasn't at the bar anymore, and I didn't see him in any of the small knots of people clustered around the front room. It didn't matter; I would have plenty of time over the multicourse Thanksgiving dinner to make up for past behavior by being punctiliously pleasant. I would be a model of grace and charm. Well, charm at least.

"There he is!" Serena, who had been scanning the room, looking for her brother, nodded toward the arched doorway that led into the front hall. As I watched, Colin's broad back disappeared into the hallway that had been conscripted as a cloakroom. "He's just leaving."

Chapter Twenty-four

*C*ome *home with me.*

Geoff's words hung suspended in the air between them, as real a presence as the pattern of green vines twining beneath their feet, and just as knotty. Letty would have liked to know just what he meant by "with." Such a simple little preposition, and yet so fraught with possible meaning. At least, it might be fraught. Or it might not. And there was the problem in a nutshell. They were friends again, certainly, after their little spat a mere two hours before. But whether they were anything more . . .

"I don't even know where home is. Your home, I mean."

Geoff's long fingers rested comfortably against the edge of the dresser, but his eyes were fixed quite steadily on her. Unreadable, as always. There were distinct disadvantages to being married to a master spy.

"At present, a place on loan from a chap who's in London for the Season. You'll be quite safe there."

"But what about Lord Vaughn? If he knows we're married . . ."

Geoff's cheeks creased with sudden amusement. "All the more reason that he wouldn't look for you there."

"True."

"Then we're agreed?"

She hadn't moved and Geoff's hand still rested casually against the dresser, but the space between them suddenly felt a great deal smaller.

"Geoffrey?" Jane's curls poked around the edge of the door, hovering about five and a half feet up the doorjamb, as though the door had suddenly sprouted a beard. The rest of Jane followed more slowly.

"The carriage is waiting downstairs," she said, standing just within the doorway. "Letty, you do know that you are welcome to stay here?"

"That's quite all right." Letty kept her voice carefully neutral, and didn't look at Geoff. "I've made other arrangements."

Jane's eyes crinkled. "I rather thought you might." Gesturing them to the stairs with the poise of a well-practiced hostess, she added, "I will expect you here tomorrow at half-three. We can discuss costuming then."

"Costuming?" Letty couldn't quite keep the trepidation out of her voice.

"We can't very well call on Lord Vaughn as ourselves," Jane said matter-of-factly. "People might talk."

"Which selves?" asked Letty.

"Either," replied Geoff. His hand lingered on the small of her back as he helped her into the carriage, burning into her back like a brand. His voice was warm and amused beside her ear. "Unless you've developed some others recently you haven't mentioned yet?"

"I'm considering it," Letty said, and felt, more than heard, his faint chuckle as he boosted her into her seat.

"Tomorrow," said Jane cheerfully, retreating to the front steps and waving as the carriage door clicked closed.

Settling down into the seat next to her, Geoff spread out across it with the ineffable ability of the male to occupy as much space as possible, legs stretched out in front of him and one arm spanning the back of the seat.

Letty's shoulder blades prickled from proximity. Trying not to be too obvious about it, she glanced sideways to where his fingers rested just past her shoulder. Not touching her. Not trying to touch her. Just there, with nothing to indicate whether it was an intentional arm or an accidental arm.

She was being ridiculous. An arm wasn't accidental; it was an appendage, and it had to go somewhere. That somewhere just happened to be right behind her back. Short of folding his hands in his lap like a convent schoolgirl, where else was he supposed to put it?

"—urm-grmm?"

"I beg your pardon?" Letty realized that her husband had been speaking and she hadn't heard a word of it.

"I asked what it is you dislike about costuming." Geoff raised his favorite eyebrow. "Or is it the playacting you object to?"

His sleeve brushed her hair, sending a little chill down her spine. Letty spoke hastily to cover her inadvertent reaction. "It's not the playacting itself that I object to. It's the being bad at it."

"You haven't done too badly so far."

Letty matched his eyebrow and raised him one, radiating skepticism.

"What made you decide to travel as Mrs. Alsdale?"

His arm had definitely moved; Letty was quite sure of it. She was so busy tracking the progress of his fingers in relation to her shoulder that it took her a moment to recall herself.

"Pride," she said, wincing at the memory. "Pure, unadulterated pride."

"Pride?" Geoff shifted to look her full in the face, his knee brushing her skirts.

"It goeth before a fall," provided Letty brightly, smoothing down her skirts.

Geoff eyed her keenly, the sway of the carriage lamp sending light shifting back and forth across the clean lines of his face.

"Why pride?"

Letty wriggled a bit to avoid an imaginary lump in the seat cushion. "I didn't want anyone to know we were traveling separately. There had been enough talk about our marriage already. . . . I didn't want to provide more grist for the gossip mills."

"So you became Mrs. Alsdale."

"Not exactly the most inventive of aliases," she said, in a tone designed to repel further discussion.

"The more effective ones seldom are," replied Geoff, accepting the implicit rebuff. "The closer to your own name, the more likely you are to remember to answer to it."

"How do you explain Mr. Throtwottle, then?" said Letty, leaping gratefully on the change of subject.

Geoff sighed. "There are exceptions to every rule. Of course, we may yet find that there is a large and thriving family of Throtwottles somewhere."

Letty had an image of a large flock of geese cackling their way across Salisbury Plain. "But you don't think so."

"No."

"You still believe Lord Vaughn is working for them, don't you?"

"I believe the only person Vaughn works for is Vaughn," Geoff countered. "He could be playing a double game, serving both sides as it pleases him."

"But why?" asked Letty. "What does he get out of it?"

"Power," said Geoff simply. "An escape from ennui. An intellectual challenge. Any number of reasons. And Vaughn, I suspect, isn't overly troubled by the dictates of conscience."

Letty's memory conjured the image of Vaughn, standing above his cousin's coffin. Like the silver he favored, he was cold logic and pure will, unalloyed by pesky questions of morality. Her father's library ran to such books, abjurations to men to fling aside the toils of religion and superstition and let pure reason reign, but never before had Letty seen that philosophy so neatly encapsulated in human form. She didn't like it.

Letty glanced at her husband, who was gazing abstractedly out the window, caught in his own reverie of tulips and treachery. There was certainly no lack of science there, no dearth of reason or logic, but in Geoff, they were tempered by something else, some leavening instinct of humanity. Responsibility, maybe. Conscience. A recognition of human frailty, including his own. It wasn't the sort of quality her father's books could parse or quantify; it couldn't be broken down into its component parts and twisted into a theorem; it just was. It was the sort of rock-deep decency that had made him honor his obligation to marry a girl of no fortune or family because the circumstance required it— even when he thought she had manufactured that circumstance herself. It was the very quality Mary had been depending on when she persuaded him into eloping.

Letty couldn't imagine Vaughn acting similarly in a comparable circumstance; his view would most likely be that any girl fool enough to find herself in such a damning situation deserved anything society chose to throw at her.

The sound of the horses' hooves changed as the carriage rattled from Capel Street onto the bridge that spanned the Liffey. In the water below, the reflection of the carriage lamps looked like the watchtowers of a drowned city.

Letty shivered with a chill that was only partly caused by the nippy night air. Something about the sight of the still water, frosted with lamplight, sent a wash of cold straight through to her bones. Reaching automatically for her wrap, Letty realized it wasn't there. In her precipitous departure, she had left it in their box in the theater. At the time, she had been quite uncomfortably warm, largely with rage.

Next to her, Geoff shifted in his seat. "Are you cold?"

Letty rubbed her hands over her arms, feeling gooseflesh against her fingertips. "A bit."

"Here." That was quite definitely an intentional arm reaching across her back, drawing her closer. Even through the material of his coat, she could feel the heat radiating from his skin, better than a hearth on a winter's day.

"It's not fair," murmured Letty, succumbing to the warmth of him. "You get so many more layers."

Geoff sneezed on a strand of her hair. Brushing it aside, he settled her more comfortably against his side. "Talk to me of unfair at noon, when you are comfortable and cool in your muslin, and I am broiling among my layers."

"You can borrow my sunshade," Letty offered, pressing the back of her hand against a yawn. "And fan."

"That will do wonders for my reputation." Geoff's chest shifted under her ear as he spoke; Letty could feel the vibration of it before she heard the words.

"Mm-hmm," agreed Letty absently, more interested in his warmth than his words. His jacket was softer than she would have thought against her cheek, not scratchy at all. There were no fobs or stickpins or buttons to poke at her, no lumpy braid or other ornament, just the ends of his cravat tickling the base of her nose.

Letty burrowed farther into Geoff's sleeve, away from the starched linen, curiously content and overwhelmingly sleepy.

"Comfortable?" Geoff asked.

"Mm-hmm." Letty fought gravity in the matter of her eyelids, and lost miserably.

Between the rocking motion of the carriage and the welcoming warmth of Geoff's body, Letty's mind drifted off among the jumbled events of the past few days. Black tulips and gilded railings and Emily lying crumpled on the ground . . . Vaughn, exchanging meaningful looks with Jane in the crypt of Saint

Werburgh's. What if Jane were wrong? What if Vaughn had
been the one to murder Emily? All that black hair, black like
Mary's, spread around her on the ground. Mary drifted wraith-
like through Letty's memory. *Who asked you to interfere?*

Letty's hands were cold, and bloody as Lady Macbeth's. She
had interfered because she wanted to, and the worst of it was that
she wasn't sorry. Letty snuggled closer to Geoff, watching bemusedly as Mary turned into Vaughn, who danced a gavotte
with Mrs. Ponsonby through an echoing hall composed of giant
flowers, all carved of stone. The flowers were singing, a soft,
humming song that rocked back and forth, back and forth. . . .

Though he was caught up in his own plots and plans for the
following day, Geoff wasn't so distracted that he didn't notice
when Letty's breath lapsed into the slow exhalations of slumber.
He was, he realized, disturbingly aware when it came to her. He
could have pinpointed the exact moment that she drifted off to
sleep, recited from memory the location of each of her freckles,
and repeated, verbatim, the bulk of their earlier conversation. Especially the bit about pride.

Glancing down, Geoff couldn't see her face at all, just a confusion of hair, lightly limned by the carriage lamp, punctuated by
the hint of a freckled nose. Against the dark fabric of her skirts,
something green gleamed greasily in the uneven light, like a
murky pond with sunlight skating over it.

Geoff touched a finger lightly to the central stone, remembering, as through a glass darkly, the resentment that had roiled
through him when he had placed it on her finger nearly a month
ago. It seemed a very long time ago, a tale told about someone
else. A very rash, selfish, and decidedly blind someone else, Geoff
thought, resting his chin on the top of her head. Her hair smelled
pleasantly of chamomile, like the old herb garden at Sibley Court
in summer.

They would have to find something more appropriate for her
when they returned to London. Aside from being ugly in itself,

the Pinchingdale betrothal ring was far too heavy for Letty's hand. The stone spanned all the way from the base of her finger to the knuckle, too large for the delicate bones of her finger. A smattering of freckles testified that someone had been out without her gloves, and the paler mark of an old scar showed along the side of her thumb. Instead of the fashionable oval, her palm was nearly square. The sturdy shape was belied by the fineness of the bones that composed it, vulnerability masked beneath a shield of capability. Beneath the weight of the emerald ring, her hand seemed disconcertingly delicate.

He had never thought of her as particularly young or small before, but sleeping, she seemed smaller, softer. The top of her head rested just against his breastbone, nestled against him as trustingly as a child's.

The rest of her, however, did not feel the least bit childlike. If he hadn't feared waking her, Geoff would have squirmed as far to the other side of the carriage as possible. Instead, he nobly gritted his teeth and tried to recall the personal dossiers of every French spy currently resident in London. In alphabetical order.

He had only made it as far as "Carre, Jean" when the carriage drew up before a secluded cul-de-sac. Trying to jar her as little as possible, Geoff eased an arm beneath Letty's knees. Carefully maneuvering her dangling legs around the doorframe, he carried her out of the carriage, painstakingly navigating the folding steps.

Letty stirred as he started down the walkway to the house. Raising her head, she peered bemusedly down at the ground, as if trying to figure out how she had come to be dangling in midair.

"I can walk," she said fuzzily, squirming a bit.

"Are you sure?" Geoff made no move to relinquish her. "I'm perfectly happy to carry you."

Pressing her eyes together, Letty stifled a yawn with the back of her fist and nodded. "I can manage."

She effected her descent by the simple expedient of linking her arms around Geoff's neck, turning sideways, and sliding down, inch by agonizing inch. Agonizing for Geoff, that was. Letty, groggily rubbing the sleep out of her eyes, seemed entirely unaware of the distress she was inflicting.

She gaped at the vista in front of her. "Good heavens. Where are we?"

Geoff held out an arm to steady her. "Home. At least, for the moment."

The house in front of her looked as out of place among the orderly rows of red brick as a camel caravan outside Dublin Castle. It was scarcely larger than a garden folly, a miniature fantasy of a house that billowed out of its own private bower of flowering plants. In the light of the torchieres, the gleaming white stone had a ghostly, insubstantial glow to it, as though at any moment the house might tremble and blow away like a silk scarf on the night breeze. The shape of the building added to the sense of movement; the building was all curls and curves, from the rounded arches of the fanlight to the bay windows that undulated from the walls of the first floor. The whole was surmounted by a whimsical dome, more suited to the pleasure palace of a Baghdad caliph than an island marooned in a chilly northern sea.

Geoff opened the door with a key as ornately curved as the oval shape of the entrance hall. To either side, Letty saw doll-sized salons opening off, one upholstered in a ravaged red reminiscent of depictions of Pompeii, painted with murals representing the sack of an unfortunate city. The women—and they were all women—appeared to be fleeing in a considerable state of upset and undress. Letty could only assume the men had been away with the vanquished army, hopefully somewhat more clothed, although the statues that flanked either side of the staircase, ebony blackamoors lifting gilded torches, were as bare as their counterparts on the wall.

"You must be tired." Geoff hustled Letty up the stairs before she could peer into the second salon.

"Not anymore." Letty craned her neck back to try to get a better look at the truly peculiar bas-relief that arched above the bedroom door. Geoff hastily ushered Letty inside before she could attain more than a muddled impression of a very enthusiastic game of leap frog in fine Grecian style.

Looking increasingly ill at ease, her husband set his candelabrum down on a marble-topped table supported by two very playful caryatids who made Letty's pectoral development look positively anemic.

She was beginning to have her doubts about the sort of establishment to which Geoff had brought her, especially when she spied the open book on the bedside table. Bound in gilt-edged leather, it had the sort of richly illuminated illustrations one generally associated with medieval manuscripts. From the looks of it, Letty doubted the monks would approve.

Geoff slapped the cover closed, but not before Letty caught a glimpse of two people entwined in a way that challenged all the known laws of gravity.

"The owner is very fond of . . . philosophy," prevaricated Geoff.

Letty reached for the book. "That didn't look like Aristotle to me."

"Aristotle explored the motions of heavenly bodies." Geoff whisked the volume neatly into a drawer and slammed it shut.

"Not those sorts of heavenly bodies," said Letty emphatically, nodding toward the drawer. "There was nothing celestial about it."

"Well, actually . . . never mind." Geoff shook his head. "I don't know what I was about to say."

Letty wandered in a bemused circle around the room, her eyes roving over the furnishings. It would be an understatement to say she had never seen anything quite like it before. She had never even imagined anything like it. An immense bed dominated the center of the room, as much with its opulence as with its size. Simpering golden Cupids supported a demi-canopy of gold-shot pink gauze. Yards of pink silk billowed across the bed, tufted and trimmed in yet more gold. All that pink made Letty's eyes ache.

Directly above was the dome she had spied from outside. In the daytime, inserts of tinted glass would cast colored shadows across the bed. Letty could only imagine how the yellow and blue and green would clash with the pink coverlet. Or how the colors would reflect off the skin of anyone lying on the bed, pillowed in pink and lit by the stained glass.

Her cheeks turning pinker than the coverlet, Letty tilted her head back and conspicuously busied herself examining the dome. Above the glass, inscribed on the underside of the dome, the gods held court at Olympus, in the style of domes the world over. Departing from the usual hierarchy, this dome was dedicated to Aphrodite rather than Zeus.

Aphrodite appeared to be having a simply marvelous time.

"Whose house is this?" demanded Letty.

Geoff stuck both hands in his pockets with the look of a man determined to brazen it out. "It belongs to a friend of mine."

Letty cast him a quick look.

"Not that sort of friend," Geoff amended. "A chap I went to Eton with keeps this house for his lady friends."

"Hmm," said Letty noncommittally. Given the nature of the decorations, she suspected that the term "lady" was singularly inapt.

Geoff moved to block a porcelain clock, which featured an amorous shepherd and his lass, enjoying the sorts of pastoral pleasures at which poets only dared hint. Given the plethora of equally objectionable items, the action was singularly ineffectual.

"Since the house isn't currently occupied," Geoff explained

rapidly, "I asked if I could borrow it. It's set well back from the street, and the servants are generously paid to look the other way."

That brought Letty to a halt. Pausing in front of a small marble statue, she stared over her shoulder at Geoff. "Your friend probably thought . . ."

"There's no probably about it."

Letty's face flared with sudden color. "So, all the servants must think . . ."

"Yes."

"Oh." Letty sank down on the bed, an endearingly prim figure in her simple black dress against the billowing opulence of pink silk that surrounded her. She rubbed her forehead with the heel of one hand. "I do seem to be having a varied career recently."

Geoff's conscience dealt him another uncomfortable blow. Now, he supposed, was as good a time as any to begin apologizing for all the manifold wrongs he had visited upon her. It was a matter of pure justice, he assured himself, not an attempt to get his wife into bed.

Well, not entirely.

"I am sorry," said Geoff, joining her on the pink coverlet. The feather tick sagged obligingly.

"It's really not all that bad," remarked Letty, cocking her head to inspect the pattern of cavorting deities on the ceiling. A sudden stiltedness betrayed her awareness of their new proximity, but she didn't pull away. "As long as one avoids the pink."

"The pink?" Was that shorthand for "Carnation"? Letty's way of telling him that a damaged reputation was manageable but spies were not? Funny, Geoff had thought that was the bit Letty minded least of the whole affair.

"The coverlet," Letty elucidated. "The large and very bright object on which you happen to be sitting." She patted it in illustration.

"Oh, right." That made his second botched apology of the evening. "That was intended as more of a blanket apology."

Letty's blue eyes crinkled. "As in this blanket?"

Despite himself, the corners of Geoff's mouth turned up. "That's not what I meant, and you know it."

Averting her eyes, Letty gave a little shake of her head. "I've given up trying to figure out what you mean."

"I'll just have to make myself plainer, then." Tipping Letty's chin up, Geoff looked her straight in the eye. "I'm sorry. I'm sorry about that idiotic remark earlier. I'm sorry for having plunged you into all of this. I'm sorry—"

"Don't." Reaching up, Letty stopped his mouth with her hand. "Please."

The last thing she wanted was to be an object of pity, or, even worse, remorse. No one liked a hair shirt. They might believe it was good for them, but that didn't mean they actually enjoyed wearing it.

But that was only the smallest part of it. Letty couldn't have quite put it into words, but she knew, with agitated certainty, that going over the past would be the worst possible thing they could do, no matter how generous an impulse drove the enterprise. Any discussion of the past would invariably come back to Mary. And once Mary entered the conversation . . . how could he help but resent Letty?

"We don't need to go through all this again," Letty insisted.

Pressing a kiss to her palm, Geoff removed her restraining hand, holding it just below his chin. "I misjudged you. Horribly."

"That was all I wanted to hear," Letty lied, lacing her fingers through his. "Truly."

It wasn't, of course. But it would have to do.

"Shall we start again?" asked Geoff, his keen gray eyes intent on Letty.

Chapter Twenty-five

Letty took in the familiar, lean lines of his face; the small creases on either side of his eyes, even in repose; the flexible quirk of his thin lips; all the infinitesimal, indefinable details that had become so familiar over the past few weeks, and which she had studied covertly across the length of London's ballrooms long before that. Whatever reservations she might have paled in comparison.

"We never did have a wedding night," she ventured.

"A lamentable oversight," Geoff agreed, solemnly enough, but there was a curious light in his eyes that sent a corresponding current straight through Letty.

His free hand was already moving through her hair, freeing it of its remaining three pins. The pins didn't make a sound as they fell, muffled by the thickly woven carpet. The last heavy coil gave way, brushing across Letty's back as it slid down.

"Shall we call this a belated one?" Letty asked, her voice strangely thick to her own ears. Geoff's hands were on her shoulders, burning through the sleeves of her gown.

"You can call it anything you like." Sweeping aside the clinging strands of hair, Geoff kissed the side of her neck. "Your hair smells like chamomile. And lemons."

"The lemon is for my freckles," Letty confessed breathlessly, distracted by the gentle brush of his fingers where his lips had been. She was having a very hard time focusing on what she was saying. "It's supposed to bleach them off over time."

Geoff turned his attentions to the other side of her neck, and Letty wondered if it was possible to simply dissolve into the coverlet in a blob of pink goo. "How long have you been trying to bleach them?"

"Since I was twelve," Letty admitted, wrinkling her nose.

Geoff lightly kissed the offending appendage. "I like your freckles."

Letty shook her head at him. "No one will ever write an ode to a freckle. It just isn't done."

"You certainly don't want *me* to," said Geoff, with a sudden boyish grin. "My odes are terrible and my sonnets are worse."

"I know. Mary showed me that last poem, the one that began—" Letty broke off, wishing she hadn't said anything.

"'O peerless jewel in Albion's crown'?" Geoff recited resignedly, banishing Mary's ghost as smoothly and deliberately as though the awkward moment had never been. "Is there anyone in London who hasn't seen that blasted poem?"

"I've read them all," declared Letty giddily. "Every last one."

"Oh, no." Geoff's head dropped in mock shame.

"Every heroic couplet. Every deathless stanza."

"You don't want to do that," Geoff warned.

Oh, but she did.

"'O Muse! O Fates! O Love Divine!'"

Letty abandoned her pose as Geoff began stalking her across the breadth of the pink bedspread. Scooting hastily backward, Letty declaimed, "'Lend strength to my . . .'"

"Right." Geoff pounced.

Rolling out of the way of Geoff's hands, Letty managed to

gasp out, "'. . . enmetered line!'" just before she found herself caught up and rolled across several yards of pink satin coverlet, in breathless, laughing confusion. They fished up on the far side of the bed, with Geoff propped up on his elbows over her. Letty's dress was decidedly worse for the escapade, and she had hair in her mouth. Making a face, Letty swiped ineffectually at it.

"Serves you right," said Geoff smugly, grinning down at her. "Mocking my poetry like that."

"You wrote it." Letty's blue eyes glinted mischievously up at him. "Don't worry. Percy Ponsonby thought it was quite good."

"Ouch." It wasn't a very convincing complaint, since his mind was otherwise engaged in the complicated engineering dilemma of how to work the buttons down Letty's back free of their moorings while she was lying on them. Any man to come up with a mathematical theorem to explain that great quandary of nature would surely win the respect not only of his peers but of posterity.

Perhaps if he rolled her just a little bit to the right . . .

"Oh, it gets better!" It certainly did. The shift in angle worked as smoothly as anything devised by Newton, exposing a whole row of buttons ripe for the plucking. Or, rather, the unplucking. Geoff eased the first one free. "He called it 'corking good verse.'"

"Corking?" Geoff paused in his unbuttoning and cast Letty an incredulous look. "Is that even a word?"

Letty shrugged, which had the beneficial effect of shaking an extra button free of its casing. "I don't know; you're the poet."

"Someone ought to cork Percy Ponsonby," declared Geoff absently, thinking mostly of buttons.

Letty's face went stiff, and she lurched upright so abruptly that her dress slid drunkenly off one shoulder. As Letty grabbed for it, the impact of Geoff's mistake thudded home. Since Percy was the one who had found them . . . Damn. Cursing himself for his carelessness, Geoff hastened to make amends.

"Not that," he said softly, cupping Letty's face in both hands. "I didn't mean that."

For a moment, Letty's lips parted as though to speak. Whatever she might have said, she thought better of it. Instead, she leaned forward and pressed her lips to Geoff's with a determination that might have meant that she believed him, or might equally well have meant that she didn't. Geoff was vaguely aware that he ought to inquire, but what with one thing and another, his body deemed external considerations irrelevant.

Geoff's hands slid to where her dress gaped invitingly, narrowing to a point at the base of her spine. His hands roamed over the exposed area, the fine fabric of her chemise bunching beneath his fingers. "Is there a hem to this?" he asked huskily, his lips barely leaving hers.

"It would be a little odd if it hadn't," began Letty, but her philosophical meditations on the finite nature of fabric ended in an indrawn breath. Geoff had found the edge of the chemise all by himself, and was involved in exploring under it.

The sensation of her husband's ungloved hands stroking the length of her spine made their previous kisses seem practically proper in comparison. There was something more than a little decadent about sitting side by side, in the glare of a dozen candles, fully clothed except for the secret caress of his hands against her bare back, hidden from view by the specious propriety of her gown. In a mirror of the movement of his hands on her back, Geoff's tongue slid across her lips. Driven by pure instinct, Letty leaned into the kiss, matching his tongue with hers. There was nothing delicate or courtly about the kiss; it was an openmouthed expression of pure passion, the sort that might have persuaded Lancelot to forsake his allegiance to Arthur, or Helen to run off with Paris.

"For that," commented Geoff hoarsely, when they could speak again, "I'll even forgive your mocking my verse."

"For that," replied Letty cheekily, "I'll even forgive you writing it."

Their eyes locked, glittering with heightened awareness. Geoff could feel a cockeyed grin tugging at the corners of his mouth, echoed by an answering expression on Letty's face, the same sort of expression he had seen on agents before they set out on a particularly exciting mission, flush with high spirits and ready to dare the devil himself. But no agent he had ever known had looked anything like Letty. With her color heightened, and her gown slipping from one shoulder, she looked like a Renaissance painter's depiction of Susanna bathing, all pink curves and unconscious sensuality.

Geoff drew in his breath at the sight.

When he spoke, it was with a certain amount of difficulty. "This is your last chance. If you want me to sleep on the divan, tell me now."

She couldn't choose the divan. It might be fitting punishment for his sins, but he wasn't sure he could survive it.

Letty ran her tongue over her lips in a gesture that was nearly Geoff's undoing.

"I couldn't make you sleep on the divan," she said breathlessly, her eyes never leaving Geoff's. "It's short. You're tall."

Geoff favored her with a decidedly rakish smile. "How fortunate."

"For the divan?"

"For me."

His hands slid over her shoulders, drawing the sleeves of her gown with them. He paused by the same freckle that had taunted him on their wedding day, perched on one dimpled collarbone. Bending over, Geoff pressed his lips to the spot, following it down to another tiny brown dot, conveniently placed just above the swell of Letty's breast, a whisper away from the deep pink barely veiled by her chemise.

"I told you I liked your freckles."

Letty's hands clutched at Geoff's hair as he eased the fabric aside for better access.

"I don't think that's a freckle," gasped Letty.

"Does it matter?" inquired Geoff, doing his best to make sure it didn't.

His tongue circled the rosy skin of her breast, closing in narrowing spirals around the tender nub.

"No."

Letty had lost all interest in semantic distinctions. She didn't care what they called it as long as he didn't stop whatever it was that he was doing.

"I thought not."

Letty shivered as his breath coasted over her dampened skin.

His lips closed and tugged, sending little quivers jolting through her. The fabric of her chemise bunched beneath her breast, pushing it into prominence and magnifying the sensation. Letty squirmed restlessly, arching away from the pressure—or toward it, she wasn't quite sure which.

"Mmph," she said, which Geoff correctly interpreted as, "Do go on."

"Let's get you out of these clothes," murmured Geoff, reaching for the edge of her chemise.

Letty was only too happy to oblige, lifting her arms obediently in the air as he drew the garment off over them. In the strange pink room, with Aphrodite beaming down from above—and various nymphs far less clad than Letty—it was hard to feel self-conscious. At least, until her husband's gaze replaced the chemise, with an unmistakable appreciation that sent delirious warmth creeping across Letty's skin. Resisting the urge to fold her arms across her chest, she scooted forward instead, closing the gap between them.

"What about you?" she asked hastily, tugging at his cravat. "You're wearing far more than me."

"An excellent point." Shrugging out of his coat, Geoff let his nimble fingers make short work of a cravat that had taken half an hour to tie. The white fabric joined Letty's chemise on the carpet, rapidly followed by his waistcoat.

As Geoff tore his loose shirt off over his head, Letty wriggled her loosened dress down over her hips, kicking it off the edge of the bed. She stilled, reverting to awkwardness as she realized that Geoff's shirt was off his head and he was staring rather fixedly. At her.

Suddenly self-conscious, Letty scooted back along the pink satin coverlet, trying to put as much space between them as possible. Geoff's eyes followed.

He shook his head. "You look . . ."

With rapidly sinking spirits, Letty wished she had thought to blow out the candles. She knew how she looked. She was too short, too plump, too round . . . just *too*. Too everything. Nothing like Mary's perfect willowy elegance. The sight of her unclothed was probably enough to kill any tender feelings Geoff might have had for her—at least until she was discreetly swathed in a gown again.

Biting her lip, Letty grabbed for the edge of the sheet. "You don't need to say it."

". . . unbelievable." He didn't sound disgusted, just dazed. His hand reached out to still Letty's before she could drag the covers across her legs. "And incredibly alluring."

"Alluring?" Letty was quite sure she must have misheard.

His hands moved up her arms, stretching them up over her head. "Sensual. Seductive. Desirable."

It was so ridiculous that Letty produced a shaky laugh. "I think you have the wrong person. Or the wrong words. Or both."

"No." Geoff gazed down at her, his gray eyes as steady as Gibraltar. "They're both just right."

There was nothing Letty could say to that, not without sounding churlish. But Geoff correctly read the slight tightening of her lips, and the way her eyes slid away from his.

"You really have no idea, have you?"

Letty bristled. "I have a mirror. And eyes."

"And no idea how to use either," muttered Geoff, before realizing that probably wasn't quite fair of him.

He looked down into her flushed face, framed with its tangle of hair that alternated between copper and gold in the candlelight, and knew that no number of compliments would convince her. With her sturdy common sense, she would write them off as pure flummery. To a certain extent, she would be right. She would never be a beauty by the accepted standards. Pretty, yes. Even lovely. But she lacked the stateliness and symmetry society demanded of its chosen goddesses.

She made up for it, in Geoff's opinion, with something far more valuable, something that went past the mere prettiness of her features, a candid appeal that her more conventionally beautiful counterparts lacked. Even her sister. It was, Geoff realized, the difference between admiration and genuine desire. One might admire a well-carved statue, but it would be deuced uncomfortable to cuddle up with at night.

He also realized that there was no way to impress any of that upon Letty. Especially, he thought guiltily, not after he had done his part to reinforce her belief that she came a poor second.

Other methods of conviction would have to be found.

"Right." He raised one brow in an unspoken challenge. His voice dropped seductively. "Then I'll just have to show you."

"Show me what?" Letty asked warily.

His breath was warm against her ear. "Just how desirable I find you."

His tongue traced the delicate shape of her ear, eroding Letty's defenses, forestalling the tart comment just on the tip of her tongue.

"Like this . . ."

His lips slid down her throat to her collarbone, while his hands explored the shape of her waist and the curve of her hips, tracing them as reverently as any sculptor shaping his masterpiece.

"... and this ..."

He followed the line of her cleavage down to her breasts, taking his time, lavishing attention on each one in turn, making Letty feel as pampered and desired as any sultan's favorite houri.

By the time his lips moved lower, Letty was having difficulty remembering what they had argued about in the first place.

"... and this."

The words were barely a breath of air, scarcely audible, skimming along the coppery curls at the join of her thighs.

"Oh," said Letty inadequately, only the word seemed to have attained several extra syllables. She hadn't known—she hadn't thought—Her fingers tugged at Geoff's dark hair as she gasped, her breathing coming raggedly through her lips. Above, Aphrodite beamed contentedly down. Letty's back arched as her husband's clever tongue plied bits of her body she hadn't known existed, twisting and turning in a complicated form of torture that had her begging him to stop ... and not to stop ... and several less coherent pleas that scarcely registered in her own ears and didn't mean anything at all, as a series of painfully pleasurable tremors overtook her, reducing her from murmurs to moans.

Rapidly divesting himself of his breeches, Geoff rejoined Letty on the pink satin coverlet. "Convinced yet?" he asked huskily, as Letty wrapped her arms around his neck, pressing up against him in a way that wore his already tattered self-control to mere shreds.

"Mmm," said Letty, running her hands along Geoff's chest in a way that rendered questions and answers entirely immaterial.

Her mouth sought his in a kiss that was part gratitude, part raw passion. She twined her arms and legs around him in an instinctive need to press closer, to feel him against her, skin to skin, from her shoulders all the way down to her toes. Her bare leg slid between his, and she felt the muscles in the arms wrapped around her go taut as corded iron.

Emulating what he had done for her, she pressed her lips to the base of his neck, thrilling at the way his body trembled at the touch.

"Letty." Geoff barely managed to force out the two syllables of her name. Her breasts were flattened against his chest, her nipples rubbing against him with every moan, every movement. Her scent filled his nostrils, drowning his senses. Using every ounce of will remaining to him, trying very hard to go slowly, he stroked gently between the moist curls at her thighs, and felt her quiver in response. With a clumsy movement, she nudged closer to him, instinctively trying to aid him.

Geoff's arms tightened around her in a convulsive embrace. His breath came out in a ragged laugh. "I don't deserve you."

"I know," murmured Letty indistinctly, pressing closer as he carefully positioned himself between her legs. "But you can—"

The rest of the sentence was lost, her fingers biting into his back as he entered her. There was a slight soreness, but it scarcely seemed to matter, not when Geoff was kissing her as though it were the last thing that mattered in the world, and she could feel a delightful tension beginning to build at the base of her stomach. Threading her fingers through his hair, Letty gave herself up to the spiral of sensation, locking her legs tightly around him as he cried out his release.

Together, they lay there, damp, disheveled, and entirely content. Opening her eyes, Letty saw the gilded nymphs and satyrs dancing along the wall through a happy haze. They, she felt quite sure, would approve.

Rolling them both sideways, Geoff brushed back the damp hair from her brow and somewhat haphazardly kissed her temple. "Thank you," he said simply, adding, with a crooked grin, "Happy wedding night. Somewhat belated."

"But worth waiting for," decreed Letty, spoiling the effect with a yawn. She cuddled sleepily against Geoff. So they were truly married now, she mused fuzzily. It didn't seem quite real, any more than anything else had since that night in High Holborn, but at the moment she was too deliciously exhausted to fret about it.

"Tired?" Geoff ruined his otherwise ideal pose as pillow by speaking.

Oh, well, a man had to have some faults, Letty concluded generously.

"A bit," she admitted, scooting to the side as Geoff extracted the coverlet from beneath her legs so it could be used for its proper purpose. He draped it over her before scooting down next to her, rearranging her hair so he wouldn't accidentally tug on it during the night.

"Mm-hmm," agreed Geoff, leaning over her to blow out the candles, and dropping an absentminded kiss to her lips in passing. There was something husbandly about the very inattention of it.

Perhaps they might really be married after all.

Letty drifted off into slumber with a smile on her face.

Chapter Twenty-six

Sunlight glistened off the glass sides of the vial, casting faint smudges of red, yellow, and blue along the pale skin of Letty's wrist. Letty gave the glass vial a diagnostic shake and watched sludgy liquid slosh sullenly from one side to the other, coating the glass with a reddish-brown film and smudging her rainbow to shadow.

Letty thrust the vial back at Geoff. "I just don't see the point of it."

Geoff closed her fingers back around the glass, covering them with his own. "It's only as a last recourse."

Even through two pairs of gloves, the pressure of his hand sent a weakening wave of warmth through her, fraught with memory.

Letty made a concerted effort to keep her mind on the matter at hand. "It's not much of a recourse, is it? Even if I manage to get Vaughn to drink something *and* empty the potion into the glass without his seeing it, I can't imagine it will take effect immediately."

"True." Geoff's fingers tightened momentarily around Letty's before letting go. "But it should at least slow him down. Just take it."

"All right." It seemed easier to accede than argue.

Letty tucked the vial neatly into her reticule, along with a pair of razor-sharp embroidery scissors, a paper of pins, a large paperweight, and a whistle—in case she needed to summon help and found herself unable to muster a suitably loud scream. Letty's demonstration, over the breakfast table, of just how loudly she could scream had resulted in the breakage of several pieces of china and permanent damage to the nerves of more than one housemaid, but had done nothing at all to deter her husband from weighing her down with a motley arsenal of largely useless items.

Even though she really couldn't see what she was going to do with a paper of straight pins—threaten Vaughn with refitting his waistcoats? Perpetrate indignities upon the cut of his coat?— Letty felt a foolish glow as she regarded the jumbled pile in her reticule. A paper of pins and a vial of sleeping potion might not exactly be love poetry, but in their own way they were a far more practical expression of affection. The pen might be mightier than the sword in the poet's parlance, but a sharp point and a loud whistle were far more effective.

Letty fingered the tin whistle fondly before pulling the strings of the reticule tightly shut.

The little bag bulged alarmingly.

"This is all likely unnecessary," said Letty.

"Likely," agreed Geoff, leaning back in his seat and propping one booted ankle on top of the opposite knee.

"If Vaughn is playing a double game, it should be in his interest to maintain his connection with Jane. And he can't maintain his connection with Jane if he attacks me."

"If Jane questions the marquise, Vaughn may be driven to desperate action."

"Vaughn?" Letty made a face. "It's hard to imagine him driven to desperation by anything less dire than dereliction on the part of his tailor."

Geoff grinned, but his amusement was fleeting.

"People thought the same about Percy Blakeney."

"Who was on our side," said Letty.

Geoff crossed his arms and looked down at her. "How does that prove anything at all?"

"It doesn't," said Letty. "But I was hoping you wouldn't notice."

The sheer audacity of it tore a ragged laugh out of Geoff.

"Well, I had to say something. It would be awful for your ego if you got to have the last word all the time."

"Duly chastened," acknowledged Geoff. "But I do get the last word on this. I'm not going to let you go into a potentially dangerous situation unprepared."

With his arms folded and his brows drawn together over the thin bridge of his nose, he exuded determination. The shadow of hair darkening his jaw emphasized the precise planes of his face, lending him a vaguely rakish air, like a Renaissance adventurer or a pirate king, ruthless, accustomed to command.

It was rather nice to have all that determination exerted on her behalf. It made her feel special. Valued. As though he would actually care if something happened to her.

"After all," Geoff finished matter-of-factly, "you are my responsibility."

Letty's warm glow vanished as abruptly as the rainbow refracted through the glass. Responsibility. What a loathsome word. From "responsibility," it was only a short step to "burden," and no one liked a burden. One shouldered burdens; one didn't lavish affection on them. She should know. For a guilty moment, she wondered whether any of her family had ever realized that.

Geoff was looking at her quizzically, clearly waiting for either acquiescence or argument.

If she was a burden, the least she could be was an entertaining one. Letty groped for her earlier bantering tone. "I'm not the one playing with explosives."

"Not yet, at any rate." Reaching into his waistcoat, Geoff drew out a long, thin object. To Letty's startled eyes, it seemed to go on forever. With a flourish, Geoff reversed his grip and presented it to her, handle first.

The handle wasn't unattractive. Chased with silver, the wood had been styled in a graceful curve, polished to the sheen of fine furniture. But no amount of ornament could disguise the deadly purpose of the long steel shaft embedded in the wooden stock, or the curious curved flintlock that arched like a diving mermaid along the top.

Letty made no move to take it. She just stared at it.

"It is a firearm," Geoff said helpfully, pressing the handle into her palm.

"I am aware of that." Letty let the piece dangle between thumb and forefinger as she regarded it dubiously. Despite growing up in the country, she hadn't had much to do with guns. Her father wasn't a hunting man. "It's not . . ."

"Loaded? No."

Relieved, Letty peered down the little hole in the middle. "Then what am I supposed to do with it? Bash Vaughn over the head with the wooden bit?"

Looking pained, Geoff took Letty's wrist and turned the pistol the other way. Even though he had emptied the bullets out himself, the sight of his wife staring down the barrel did nasty things to Geoff's nerves.

"Rule number one, never point it at yourself. Even when it's unloaded," he added, forestalling Letty's next protest.

"This isn't going to fit into my reticule," she pointed out instead, poking the muzzle of the gun into the bag in illustration. "And I'm certainly not hiding it in my bodice."

"I should hope not. I prefer your bodice the way it is." For all

that the sentiment was pleasing, there was nothing at all loverlike
about Geoff's tone. Nor should there be, Letty reminded herself.
They were preparing for a mission, not a tryst.

"Well?" asked Letty briskly. "What am I to do with it? I assume you didn't bring it along merely for its aesthetic value."

"You're not that far off the mark. Think of it as a theatrical
prop. You know it's unloaded, and I know it's unloaded, but
Vaughn won't."

"Until I pull the trigger and nothing happens."

Letty realized she was being difficult, but she couldn't seem to
help herself. Perhaps it had something to do with lack of sleep.
Fatigue and surliness generally went hand in hand, and she had
not gotten much sleep last night.

Of course, neither had he.

Letty busied herself examining the workmanship of the
flintlock.

"It shouldn't come to that," said Geoff soothingly. "You just
have to point it at him with the proper air of authority."

"Is this before or after I stick him with my embroidery scissors?"

"Here." Geoff took her hand and rearranged it around the
butt of the gun. "Point it at me."

"You must be very sure about those bullets," muttered Letty,
but she did as he said. All she had to do was point and look
steely-eyed. How hard could it be?

Held by one hand, the pistol was surprisingly heavy, ten
inches of solid steel within its innocuous wooden casing. Letty
struggled to keep the pistol level as gravity fought her grasp.
Gravity won. Her wrist shook as the muzzle began to droop,
centimeter by painful centimeter.

Geoff relieved her of the weapon, although whether it was out
of pity or because the pistol happened to be pointing straight at a
crucial part of his anatomy, Letty couldn't be sure. Letty surrep-

titiously shook out her wrist, wondering how one little part of her body could feel so much strain.

"It's heavy!" she said indignantly. It all looked so easy in the pictures in the illustrated papers.

"This was the lightest one I could find," said Geoff, leveling the pistol with one hand as though it weighed no more than a lady's fan.

"Show-off," said Letty.

Geoff looked smug.

"You want to grasp the stock with both hands to distribute the weight," he said.

He handed the gun back to her, watching critically as she tried again. Letty's arms felt stiff and awkward in the unaccustomed pose.

"Bend your elbows a bit," Geoff suggested.

Letty's arms shot back into an immediate right angle, one elbow catching Geoff in the stomach.

Geoff winced. "Not quite that much."

Easing closer, he reached around her, rearranging her hands on the stock, one slightly above the other.

"Do you feel the difference?" he asked, jiggling the barrel slightly to make her flex her arms.

"Mm-hmm." Letty's mind, admittedly, wasn't entirely on the pistol. A large part of it had wandered off along far more attractive byways having to do with the pleasant scent of Geoff's cologne, and the intriguing way his muscles moved beneath the fitted seams of his coat as he rearranged her hands on the stock.

"Now sight along the barrel." Letty lifted the pistol, and Geoff's arms went with her. She could feel his cheek brush hers as he leaned closer to inspect her aim. "And pretend to aim."

"Like this?" Letty glanced up over her shoulder.

Geoff wasn't looking at the pistol, or the imaginary target.

"Exactly like that."

Letty forgot that she was holding a heavy pistol; she forgot that her neck was twisted at an odd angle, and that she had a blister on the back of one heel.

Geoff's hands tangled in her hair, pulling her face to his for a quick, hard kiss that sent Letty's ears ringing.

The pistol dropped forgotten from her hands, landing with a thud on the floor of his carriage. In some musty corner of her mind, Letty dimly realized that it was a very good thing that the pistol had not been loaded.

Geoff drew back, his hands possessively cupping her shoulders, and stared down into her face. A slight furrow formed above his nose, and his eyes scanned hers as though he were reading a book—a book in a foreign language without a convenient translation at hand.

Letty stared right back, silently willing questions at him.

She wanted to know whether she was more than a responsibility to him. Whether, when he kissed her, he saw her—or her sister. Whether they would go on like this upon their return to England, or whether all their hard-won intimacy would dissolve as soon as they set foot on English soil, like Shakespeare's insubstantial pageants, or fairy gold smuggled into the mortal world only to turn to ash in the harsh light of day.

The door was already open, the steps down, the coachman waiting.

Leaning over, Geoff restored her fallen pistol to her, stock first, putting into the gesture what he hadn't said in words. It smacked of respect—and farewell.

"Be careful," he said simply.

And that was all.

The carriage waited until Letty had mounted the steps to the front door before trundling away down the street.

Letty stood, one hand on the knocker, watching it go, wishing she had said something else. But what? "Be careful?" There was something rather ridiculous about her telling Geoff to be careful, an amateur advising a master. Besides, it was a very poor substitute for what she really wanted to say.

"Be careful" was no substitute for "I love you."

Only one extra word, but as impossible to frame as a word-perfect recitation of the entirety of a Homeric epic. She couldn't declare her love—not only did her pride protest at the notion, but it seemed a hideous sort of imposition to thrust her love unasked on someone who couldn't feel the same way about her. How could he, when he was in love with her sister? It was as ridiculous as a Shakespeare comedy, everyone enamored of the wrong person.

And there was nothing she could do about it. Nothing, except to go on, in a staid and sensible manner, taking what pleasure she could from their companionship and camaraderie.

Much like "be careful," camaraderie made a very poor substitute for love.

"Why didn't you knock?" A pale hand reached out and whisked Letty through the door, putting a pointed period to her unproductive reverie.

"Let's get you costumed, shall we?" said Jane.

Two painful hours later, Letty stood outside Lord Vaughn's Dublin residence, tugging at her cravat.

Like the other great houses that ranged around St. Stephen's Green, Vaughn's Dublin residence was an immense edifice of stone that shone whitely in the sun, new enough that soot had not yet dimmed the luster of the facade. It might not be quite so large as the neighboring Clanwilliam House, or the Whaley mansion, but it would have made at least ten of the little brick house on Henrietta Street.

Letty wondered how Geoff was faring and whether Miss Gwen was as adept with explosive devices as she seemed to think. Sometime after six, he had said, since Emmet was supposed to be dining out, along with his senior staff, at a house in Kilmacud. They would wait till the house was largely empty, and then slip in and detonate the rockets. All perfectly simple. Unless it wasn't.

Letty went back to abusing her cravat.

"Don't fuss with it," said Jane, managing her own hat and cane with the air of one born to them. Her stride was authoritative, her demeanor lordly, and her shirt points would have made Brummell choke with envy. In short, she was the very image of a pink of the *ton*, setting out for a late-afternoon stroll prior to the evening's dissipations.

Letty glanced down at her own pantaloons. Brummell might choke, but it would be with horror, not envy. Her short, plump figure took to men's fashion about as well as Miss Gwen to humility. Her hips might be suited marvelously well to childbearing but they did nothing for the fit of her pantaloons. Her coat, cut fashionably short at waist and hip before extending behind, did little to cloak the problem. As for other unmanly protuberances, Jane had used lengths of linen to flatten her breasts and thicken her waist, lending Letty's upper half the appearance of an animated barrel of ale.

Beneath her shirt, waistcoat, and coat, she could feel the binding rubbing uncomfortably against her chest, sticky with perspiration. Although the day was mild for mid-July, Letty sweltered beneath her unaccustomed layers and thought longingly of her wardrobe full of light muslin gowns and soft kid half-boots. The stiff leather boots Jane had forced onto her legs cramped her calves and bit into the skin just above her knee every time she ventured a step.

No wonder so many gentlemen preferred to pose nonchalantly against the mantelpiece if it was this painful to move.

"Just keep your chin down," Jane advised, fluffing up Letty's cravat and straightening her shirt points. "And if anyone speaks to you, grunt."

"Grunt?"

"Like this." Jane produced a noise straight from the diaphragm, somewhere between a grumble and a growl. "It is the common masculine coin of communication."

Attempting to emulate her, Letty managed something between a squeak and a cough.

Jane sighed. "Just keep your chin down," she repeated.

"Mmph," said Letty, surreptitiously rubbing her side, where the binding was biting into her flesh.

"Not quite," said Jane, "but an improvement. A marked improvement."

Rolling her eyes, Letty clambered stiff-legged up the front steps after her, wondering how she got herself into these things. Hers was an ensemble better suited to storming a castle than a peaceful afternoon call. In addition to the boots, binding, and shirt points so starched they could be used to patch the roof, the gun tucked into her waistcoat knocked against her ribs as she moved, and the vial of potion formed a lump just inside her sleeve. The paper of pins and paperweight had remained behind, but the tin whistle was attached to her watch chain and the point of the embroidery scissors teased her palm. Fortunately, the formfitting nature of her pantaloons didn't allow for a knife strapped to her thigh, or she was sure Jane would have handed her one of those, too.

Letty was only surprised that no one had given her a small cannon to take along, just in case. She could have disguised it as a dog and wheeled it on a leash.

At the top of the steps, Jane took the knocker and let it fall with an emphatic rattle. Through the plate glass windows on either side, Letty couldn't discern the slightest sign of movement. In a house of such size, there ought to be a footman watching for visitors, ready to pop open the door. The echoes of the knock faded off across the green, unmatched by any answering noise from within.

Frowning, Jane pushed gently against the door with the head of her walking stick. The door fell easily open, revealing a polished expanse of white marble floor, and a staircase that seemed to stretch up forever, patterned on the underside with white stuccowork on a pale blue background. Following Jane, Letty ventured into the vast hall, feeling suddenly chilled. It wasn't just the eerie silence; it was the celestial cool of the endless motif of pale blue and white, like Olympus in the midst of a frost. The walls and ceiling had all been tinted the same pale blue, frosted with a design of urns and stylized acanthus leaves. The marble floor gleamed as pristinely pale as an untrodden field of snow.

"This is most unusual," murmured Jane.

Letty noticed that Jane readjusted her grip on her cane as she prowled across the hall, every step a measured act.

"Are you sure we have the right house?" Letty asked, lingering by the door. Even the sunlight seemed to shy away from entering the icy room.

"Quite sure."

Jane drew to a halt, her eyes fixed on an invisible spot on the marble floor. Invisible to Letty, at least. With one fluid movement, Jane went down on one knee, touching a gloved finger to the floor. Frowning, she rubbed her thumb and forefinger together, examining the result with all the absorption of a botanist confronted with a rare new specimen.

"Mud. And still damp. Someone—someone wearing boots," Jane amended, squinting at the marks on the floor, "walked across this hallway not long ago."

"That's not exactly remarkable in a house of this size," Letty pointed out pragmatically, reluctantly shutting the door behind her. "The staff must number in the dozens."

"This wasn't a servant," Jane said decisively, rising to her feet.

She had been about to expound further, but any explanation was cut off by a sudden clatter from a nearby room, the unmistakable sound of something fragile shattering.

"Quick," said Jane, pointing her cane like a baton. "The small salon!"

With her boots squeaking, Letty took off after her. Jane, she deduced, must have visited Lord Vaughn before; there was no way the size of the rooms could be determined from their closed doors, and Jane moved with the unerring surety of someone who knew exactly where she meant to go.

Without checking her stride, Jane flung open a pair of double doors frosted with more gleaming white stuccowork.

"Well, well," said Jane softly, coming to an abrupt halt in the doorway.

Skidding to a stop behind her—her boots were new, and the marble hall slippery—Letty leaned sideways to try to see around her. At first, all she saw were fragments of china, scattered across a pastel patterned rug. The china must have been Japanese Imari work, tinted deep red, blue, and black; the fallen fragments looked like flecks of dried blood against the paler shades of the carpet.

There, in the midst of the mess of porcelain shards, a blot stood out against the pale weave. Two blots, arms' width apart. The very pair of boots Jane had predicted in the entryway, smudged about the toe and sides with smears of mud. The boots belonged to Lord Vaughn, who stood among the bits of broken china, his face as pale and set as the plaster frieze lining the walls. Wordlessly, Jane crossed the room toward Vaughn, and Letty finally saw what her companion's body had been blocking.

On a small blue-and-yellow settee, flanked by two low chairs and a small table, reclined Teresa Ballinger, the ci-devant Marquise de Montval.

She was dressed in the stained pantaloons and ill-fitting frock coat of Augustus Ormond, her rough attire an affront to the pristine pastel perfection of the parlor. But it wasn't her clothing that had brought Jane up short.

A thin trickle of blood formed a rusty goatee beneath the marquise's lips, and her eyes were raised to the plasterwork of the ceiling in the unseeing stare of death.

Chapter Twenty-seven

It was altogether too many dead bodies for one week, as far as Letty was concerned.

Jane moved swiftly past Vaughn to kneel next to the recumbent form on the settee.

"Dead," pronounced Jane, reaching for the woman's wrist with a practiced hand. "And recently, too. Her skin is still warm."

There could be no doubt as to her identity this time. Whatever the means of death had been, it had left her face unmarred. The marquise's head was tilted back, fixed in an obsidian stare of perpetual venom in the direction of her killer. Her unruly wig had tumbled free, revealing a tight coil of black hair pinned close to her head, the severity of the style lending her an oddly chaste appearance. The combination of black hair and colorless skin had the stark simplicity of a nun's habit.

Without the hairpiece, her face looked thinner and older than it had during her appearances as Augustus. Letty could see the violet shadows in the delicate skin under her eyes, the hollows burred beneath her cheeks, the thin indentations incised between nose and lips. Along the corner of her slack lips oozed a dainty trickle of blood, as rust-red as the fragments of porcelain on the rug, and as finely drawn.

There was something repellent about the very delicacy of it. Driven by an impulse she couldn't quite explain, Letty took a corner of the dead woman's cravat and tried to wipe the blood from her face. Already drying, the rusty stain resisted removal.

Standing over the body, Letty could see what she had missed before. The silver knob protruding from the wrinkled brown cloth of the dead woman's coat was not a stickpin, but the head of a stiletto, driven with unerring precision straight into her heart. Vaughn must, realized Letty, have been standing just where she was standing, behind the settee, perfectly poised to hold the marquise still with his left hand while he drove the blade home with his right.

Rising from her position before the settee, Jane confronted Vaughn.

"Why?"

"The more apt question would be *who*."

Lord Vaughn's fingers trailed lazily around the edge of a small gilt table as he circled it, closing the space between himself and the settee. And Jane.

Sliding a hand casually into her waistcoat, Letty felt for the handle of her gun. Every movement felt painfully obvious, but Vaughn's attention was focused unwaveringly on Jane. Letty's fingers closed carefully around the wooden handle. She had, as Jane recommended, inserted the barrel into the binding wrapped around her waist at a diagonal for easier removal, but the weapon seemed to be caught on something—the binding itself, most likely.

Jane met him stare for stare, head tilted back in an age-old expression of challenge. "Not you, then."

"Do you really think it?" asked Vaughn softly, coming to a stop just in front of her. Jane did not shrink back, but from her vantage point behind the settee Letty saw Jane's fingers tighten on the head of her cane.

Letty tugged gently at the pistol and felt the wrappings tighten against her side in response. Drat. Whatever it was snagged on was caught fast. If Jane was armed, she had given no indication of it to Letty.

"The situation tells against you," Jane said, as calmly as though she were discussing the weather.

Vaughn arched an aristocratic eyebrow. "Circumstance is seldom proof."

"Aphorism," said Jane sharply, "is never answer."

"On the contrary"—Vaughn spoke softly, but there was an undertone to the simple words that made the fine hairs on Letty's arms prickle with atavistic instinct—"sometimes the truest answer lies in tergiversations."

Below her, Letty could see the eyes of the marquise, fixed in an eternal sneer. With one last, desperate pull, Letty yanked the pistol free. The fabric gave with a noise like a hundred cats sharpening their claws, drawing startled glances from the duelists on the other side of the settee.

Bracing her weapon, Letty leveled it at Lord Vaughn.

"Step away from Miss Fairley," Letty commanded, hoping that she made up in firmness of tone what she lacked in weakness of wrist.

Lord Vaughn looked as unimpressed as the marquise. But he did step away, and that, Letty reminded herself, was all that counted. Fragments of china crackled beneath his boot heel, ground to expensive dust against the weft of the carpet.

Vaughn nodded lazily toward Letty's weapon. "It's not loaded, is it?"

Letty concentrated on holding the pistol level. It was considerably harder without Geoff's hands beneath hers. "Would you care to wager your life on that point?"

Vaughn polished his quizzing glass with a corner of his cravat and examined the results. "In this instance? Yes."

Drat. It was going to have to be the sleeping potion.

"Perhaps," suggested Letty, waving the pistol in the direction of a chair suitably far away from Jane, "we should all sit down and discuss this over a nice cup of tea."

Jane glanced back at Letty over her shoulder with a quirk of the lips that suggested she knew exactly what Letty was about.

"I don't think tea will be necessary." Jane flipped her coattails and arranged herself neatly in a chair by the settee, next to the table that must have once borne the Japanese bowl. Her calm post next to the corpse presented a macabre tableau, a tea party straight out of Dante's *Inferno*.

"Indeed." Vaughn turned his back on Letty and her pistol, moving toward a table set with a decanter and set of glasses. "I could do with something stronger."

Murdering someone could have that effect on a person.

Letty kept the empty pistol trained on Vaughn as he tilted amber liquid into his glass. There was something rather comforting about holding the man at gunpoint. Even if she knew there was nothing in the gun, the weapon still provided a spurious sense of protection.

In a mockery of a toast, Vaughn raised the glass toward the trio ranged around the settee.

"Gentlemen?" Vaughn's voice was as delicately weighted with irony as a well-balanced sword. "Would you care to join me?"

"An explanation would be more to the point. Unless you have more old adages you would care to share with us?" There was an edge to Jane's voice that belied the tranquillity of her expression.

"I believe I can control myself for the moment."

Lifting the rejected glass to his lips, Vaughn drank delicately before proceeding, whether to delay or merely out of a habit of deliberation, Letty could not be sure. It was impossible to be sure of anything where Lord Vaughn was concerned.

"I entered and found the Marquise de Montval as you see her now. That is the sum total of it." Vaughn's eyes flicked almost imperceptibly toward the still form on the settee. "Teresa and I had more subtle means of causing injury to each other. We had no need for knives."

"Even the sharpest of tongues cannot do the office of steel."

Jane, thought Letty, seemed determined to out-Vaughn Lord Vaughn when it came to couching speech in obscurity. It was enough to make Letty yearn for good commonplace words of one syllable. Perhaps she should just hold up two cards, saying "yes" and "no," and demand that Vaughn point to the one that best answered the question "Did you kill the marquise?"

Knowing Lord Vaughn, he would probably find a way to point with ambiguity.

"Credit me with the common sense not to soil my own nest," said Lord Vaughn. Ambiguously.

Jane leaned back in her chair, propping one leg against the other in a studiedly masculine gesture. "That might be all the more reason to do so."

"Not," said Vaughn, "when it entails a stain on the upholstery. That fabric will be devilish hard to replace. It came from France."

Vaughn's eyes met Jane's in a way that suggested far more than a concern for interior decoration.

Letty was sure of it when Jane said, in a much milder tone, "When did you last see her alive?" For whatever reason, the interrogation had been abandoned.

"Half an hour ago?" Vaughn shrugged, as though it were of little matter, but Letty noticed that he avoided looking at the settee. A sign of guilt? Or something else?

"How would someone have entered without the servants hearing?" demanded Letty.

"You did," said Vaughn smoothly. "My cousin—no, Mrs. Alsdale, not *that* cousin. Nor"—he nodded to the couch—"that cousin."

Letty regarded him with unconcealed distaste. "Your cousins seem to experience considerable ill fortune."

"In being connected to me? In that case, it is an affliction to which a considerable portion of the peerage falls heir. My cousin Kildare, who is, I am sure you shall be relieved to hear, in the pink of health, was kind enough to afford me the use of his home. His staff, however, leaves much to be desired. The cook . . . But I digress. I returned from an invigorating visit to my tailor to find—I don't need to tell you, do I?"

"If," said Letty, leaning very heavily on the word, "your story is true, wouldn't you have crossed paths with the murderer?"

"My dear girl." Vaughn gestured expansively, snifter in one hand, quizzing glass in the other. "Look about you. The place is riddled with doors."

There was no denying the truth of that. Aside from the door to the front hall, there were doors, cleverly aligned with the plasterwork, leading off to rooms on either side. In addition to the doors, long-sashed windows offered a further means of egress. The room was above ground level, but not by much; a tall man would have no difficulty hoisting himself up on the sill, and exiting again by the same means.

"You have quite the wrong end of the stick," continued Vaughn. "There is someone who has considerably more reason than I to wish to see Teresa permanently silenced."

"And that would be?" Jane tilted her head quizzically.

"I think you know."

"It doesn't necessarily follow. Would a hunter kill his trustiest hound?"

"He would," said Vaughn, "if the hound bit him. Teresa was never good at bowing to the dictates of others." Vaughn swirled the liquid in his glass, watching its progress with as much interest as if it had been the finishing line at Newmarket. "Recently, she had taken umbrage with the activities of a lesser personage in her organization."

"Emily Gilchrist."

Letty didn't realize she had spoken the name aloud until

Vaughn's eyes met hers. He looked, she realized, surprisingly tired. Under all the bravado of his manner, fatigue lined the sides of his face and pouched beneath his eyes.

"The very one." The shadows beneath his eyes might betray him, but there was no trace of weakness in the honed cadences of his voice. "Teresa believed she needed to be removed. She broached this with her colleague. Her colleague refused."

"Ah," said Jane.

"Ah, indeed. Such a little point, to cause such a great reckoning."

A little point. Having seen the removal of Emily Gilchrist, Letty wasn't sure she could agree with Lord Vaughn's characterization of the situation. What was it that Geoff had said last night? Something about the marquise not being worthy of her sympathy. Remembering Emily's ravaged face, she found it hard to regret the great reckoning that had been wreaked on the still form on the settee.

"Teresa took it upon herself to remove Miss Gilchrist. The rest"—Vaughn waved a hand in the direction of the settee—"is pure conjecture."

"You believe this was done in retaliation, then."

"Perhaps. It might have been meant as a warning to the others. It was a matter of order. And of power. Uneasy lies the head, and all that. No ruler can brook such a blatant challenge to his authority and expect to remain long on his throne. And so, farewell, Teresa."

For someone who claimed to be uninvolved, Lord Vaughn seemed suspiciously well informed.

"By ruler," Letty asked, "do you mean the Black Tulip?"

"As you will. That name will do as well as any other. Teresa referred to her colleague only as *monseigneur*. A quaint touch, don't you think?"

"It needn't have been a literal rank," mused Jane. "In French?"

"Invariably. It is," added Vaughn, "not necessarily an indicator of his place of origin. Teresa had gone native in all things. She even took to calling herself Thérèse for a time. Or simply 'the marquise,' as if she were a piece on a chessboard with no person beneath it."

"You knew her for a long time, then," said Letty, watching Vaughn closely. A germ of an idea teased at her imagination. Vaughn's explanations all fit a little too well, fell a little too pat.

"A very long time." Vaughn smiled a crooked little smile, before adding, with a studied air of nonchalance, "Odd, isn't it, how these revolutionaries cling to their titles, despite all of their republican pretensions. Bonaparte will be naming himself emperor next."

"Might I ask," inquired Jane delicately, "why you did not see fit to bring the marquise's relations with Miss Gilchrist to my attention prior to this?"

Vaughn bowed in apology. "I was only admitted to her confidence on that score last night. Ought I to have interrupted your chaste slumbers?"

"None of us," said Jane austerely, "shall slumber properly until the matter of the Black Tulip is dealt with."

She had, realized Letty, very neatly avoided either accepting Vaughn's excuse or naming him a liar.

Vaughn turned and looked straight at the figure on the settee. There was very little spare flesh on his form, but a trick of the light made the sharp bones of his face seem even more stark than usual, as though the skin were stretched too tightly over them.

His lips twisted in what might have been mockery, or grief, or both.

" 'Sleep no more. Macbeth hath murdered sleep.' "

With an uncharacteristically abrupt gesture, he tossed back the remains of his drink. Setting the glass down heavily on the small gilt table, he said, "She wasn't supposed to be here. She had a meeting tonight, with the leaders of the rebel cause."

"Tonight?" repeated Jane. "Was it at a place called Kilmacud?"

"No. It was the name of some local saint or other. The one with the snakes."

Letty's mouth felt suddenly very dry.

"Patrick?" she asked. "As in Patrick Street?"

"The very one. Teresa had an appointment to view their armory, to make sure it would be up to snuff in time for the invasion. Tedious stuff." Vaughn flipped open a small china box and expertly deposited a smattering of snuff on the side of his wrist.

Against the lace of his sleeve, the grains looked dark as gunpowder.

Jane's face was very still. "When?"

"Six . . . half past . . . something of that order. She was to inspect, and then report back to her shadowy colleague later this evening." Conveying the snuff neatly to his nostrils, Vaughn essayed a genteel cough, indicative of extreme boredom. "That is all I know."

As one, Letty and Jane turned to the clock on the mantel. As if it knew it was being watched, the minute hand jerked awkwardly toward the Roman numeral IV, like a malingering sentry scurrying back to his post.

Twenty past six. And Geoff and Miss Gwen would still be there, caught red-handed among the kegs of gunpowder when the rebel leaders reappeared. They couldn't possibly fight their way through that many.

Jane's eyes met Letty's over the marquise's fallen form. "I need to search the marquise's belongings immediately."

She didn't add *before someone else does*, but the meaning was as clear to Letty as if she had spoken it. Whatever her arrangement with Vaughn, it didn't extend to unconditional trust. What better way to watch a potential suspect than feigning partnership? Letty approved the motivating sentiment, but if Jane wasn't able to warn Geoff, that left only one option.

On the mantel, the minute hand arched another centimeter closer to half past the hour.

"I'll go," said Letty.

"Who're you?"

The whiskey fumes hit Geoff before the words. Propping one hand against the doorjamb of the outbuilding, the watchman took an unsteady step forward, squinting at Geoff.

Geoff curved his back in a casual slouch, doing his best to look harmless. Only a yard from the back door, he had begun to hope that Emmet had left the house completely unattended. There were, after all, several other rebel caches throughout the city, and limited staff on hand to man them all.

When Geoff saw the watchman, he understood why Emmet had left him behind. Graying stubble caked the bottom half of his face, and his hands bore witness to his trade in the faint shadow of indigo that overlay his skin. Dye could be scrubbed off, but over time it left its mark, especially on the careless. McDaniels might have been a good dyer once, but his fondness for the bottle had lost him most of his custom, leaving him with tinted skin and a bellyful of bitterness against anyone he could find to blame.

Of all the members of Emmet's band, McDaniels was the least likely watchdog Geoff could imagine. Emmet must be growing careless as the big day drew nearer. A mistake.

A mistake Geoff could use.

"Byrne sent us," Geoff said confidently, hooking his thumbs in his belt. He jerked his head at Miss Gwen, similarly attired in a coarse shirt, loose vest, and baggy pants.

Despite Geoff's protests that laborers generally didn't carry parasols, Miss Gwen had refused to relinquish her chosen weapon. Geoff could only hope she was holding it discreetly behind her back, otherwise they might have some explaining to do, even to McDaniels.

"I'm Dooney and this is Burke. We're here to work on the fuses." Geoff lowered his voice to an eager whisper that could be heard three houses away. "For the *rockets*."

Either it sounded plausible to McDaniels, or he had imbibed enough that he just didn't care. With a grunt of assent, he waved Geoff on toward the house.

"Much obliged!" Geoff called back over his shoulder, and was rewarded with the slosh of liquid as McDaniels waved his bottle at him in salute.

Miss Gwen wrinkled her nose in an eloquent expression of distaste.

They slipped through the back door into the barren workroom that occupied the back of the house. There was little in it, only a few benches and some long trestle tables where the bulk of Emmet's experiments with weapon manufacture took place. Shelves lined most of the white-plastered walls, covered with a motley assortment of items, from coarse ceramic plates to a dented kettle. The ashes had been shoveled from the hearth, but not thoroughly enough. Bits of melted metal added an odd luster to the hearthstone, and a clear indicator of illicit activity. The more common smells of old meals and spilled ale were underlain by another, more acrid scent that stung Geoff's nose. The reek of sulfur was hard to hide, unless Emmet intended to pass it off as a basket of bad eggs. The hens in the coop outside would undoubtedly be deeply offended by the slur on their capacities.

Holding up a finger in warning, Geoff slid through the next door to check the front room, which had been fitted up as a sort of rough parlor. Equally empty. There was an empty plate bearing breadcrumbs and a rind of cheese, remnants of someone's hurried meal. The only sign of illicit activity was a hollow grenade shell that had rolled beneath a table, and a scattering of dark grains that were clearly not meant to be ingested, at least not if one didn't intend to fling oneself into the air and scatter body parts over a large area.

A perfunctory check revealed the upper stories to be equally empty of both human inhabitants and extraneous weaponry.

Geoff couldn't have asked for better.

There was, he thought, a basic irony in the fact that Emmet deliberately understaffed his most important depot for fear that excessive activity would draw attention to the building. That very same strategy meant that his biggest arsenal lay open, completely unprotected except for one drunken dyer, who, at this point in his nightly binge, probably couldn't tell a pig from a pike, much less a Royalist from a Republican.

"All clear," he said softly, padding back downstairs, where Miss Gwen was tapping her parasol with impatience against the scarred wooden planks of the floor.

"All very well and good, but I have made a thorough tour of the premises, and fail to see any explosive matter, except for one pitiful excuse for a grenade and some sorry grains of gunpowder. This has been a sad waste of our time."

"Ah, but that's what you were meant to think." Geoff grinned, feeling the rush of the mission run through him. "Allow me to provide explosive matter for you."

Striding toward the shelves on the wall, Geoff reached past a row of metal tankards, feeling along the brackets that held the shelves in place.

"This is hardly the time for refreshment," objected Miss Gwen.

"That's where you're wrong." Geoff found the latch he had been looking for, just behind a molding round of cheese. The whiff of it was enough to deter any less-determined seeker. "I'd say this is exactly the time."

Pressing down on a bent nail, he felt the catch give, and the entire section of shelving swung neatly back on well-oiled hinges. The door had been neatly done, built of bricks within a frame, then plastered over to resemble the adjoining wall. As an extra precaution, shelves had been bracketed to it, providing a third layer of protection. None of that, however, prevented a truly careful observer from noting that the house was a third larger on the outside than on the inside. Once that was established, it was only a matter of logical calculation to determine the location of the door.

Not to mention that Geoff had been watching through the window one night while Emmet manipulated the catch.

Propping open the door with one shoulder, Geoff gestured Miss Gwen into an Ali Baba's cave of armaments. Enough metal-tipped pikes to satisfy an entire Mongol horde were stacked along one wall, waiting to be passed out into the eager hands of volunteers. Halfway up, each boasted a small metal hinge, designed so that the pikes could be folded in two and hidden under a man's coat, ready to be pulled out when the signal was called. There were piles of blunderbusses, jumbles of pistols, barrels of gunpowder, miniature mounds of grenades, and trays strewn with sun-dried saltpeter.

All around the windowless room, weapons were ranged, weapons traditional and experimental, old weapons, new weapons, muskets and bayonets, pikes and swords, grenades and clubs, each clustered with its own kind, all awaiting the great day of liberation. It was an array designed to send the king's ministers into sheer, gibbering panic.

Miss Gwen drank in the sight with an expression of rapture reminiscent of Joan of Arc in the midst of a divine vision.

"I do hope this is satisfactory," said Geoff.

Miss Gwen made unerringly for the barrels of gunpowder. "I believe it will do."

Geoff carefully lit a glass-lined lantern and hung it just inside the door, as far away from explosive materials as he could. While the goal was to blow up the house, he preferred to wait until he was no longer in it.

Dying gloriously for the cause might be the stuff of song and legend, but he would rather accomplish his mission with a minimum of personal injury—the odd powder burn didn't really count—and head happily home to spend the evening before the hearth, Letty in one arm, a hot dish of tea in the other, trading tales of the day's adventures.

All the more reason to get the job done quickly.

"The trapdoors in the ceiling lead up to other storerooms," explained Geoff rapidly, pointing to a square hole just above Miss Gwen's head. "There are more pikes and muskets above and gunpowder on the top floor."

Geoff could see the ramifications clicking into place in Miss Gwen's keen mind. "Which means . . ."

"That each explosion will set off a successive explosion on the floor above."

It would have been uncharacteristic for Miss Gwen to express approval. "Is there enough air to feed the flames?"

Geoff indicated the outside wall, where a series of small holes had been bored in the guise of knotholes in the wood. "These rooms were designed for the potential storage of men as well as weapons. Let's get started on the rockets, shall we?"

Taking Miss Gwen by the arm, he all but dragged her over to the short stack of rockets propped against the wall. Designed to Emmet's specifications, they were all composed of iron cylinders not more than twenty inches long, with an arrowlike point at one end.

They were clumsy-looking things, and Miss Gwen eyed them askance.

"I expected something more impressive." Miss Gwen considered for a moment. "Something taller."

"Each one," said Geoff, forestalling her as she reached for the one on top, "is packed solid with a mixture of gunpowder, sulfur, and potassium nitrate."

"Hmmm," said Miss Gwen, regarding the rockets with renewed interest.

"They're meant to be tied in bunches around a central pole," Geoff explained, busily unrolling a length of twine from around his waist. "That provides the height. The pikes should be just about long enough."

That was all the instruction Miss Gwen needed. They worked swiftly and silently, grouping the rockets into bunches, securing them with thick loops of twine, and inserting fuses into the holes provided for that purpose in their bases. The only sounds in the room were the brush of rope against iron, the periodic scrape of a pike base across the floor, and the disjointed patter of mice scurrying along the baseboards.

The fuse, cotton twine coated with gunpowder, left dark flecks on their gloved fingers as they worked. The acrid smell of sulfur, stronger with the door closed, made Geoff's nose tingle and his eyes water. In the windowless room, it might have been any time from noon to midnight. The door to the back room fitted perfectly to its frame, without any cracks or chinks. The airholes bored into the wall were too small to admit any light, and they were nearly too small to admit much in the way of air. Hide the rebel leaders in there, and they were probably in greater danger of asphyxiation than discovery.

They could not have been in the room for more than ten minutes, but it felt as though they had been there for eternity, laboring among the sulfur and saltpeter in the reddish glare of the single lamp, like an engraver's etching of the horrors of the damned. It must be well after six, time enough for Letty to be at Lord Vaughn's already.

Perhaps insisting she take embroidery scissors had been a bit much.

He might as well, thought Geoff disgustedly, slicing off a piece of twine, have laden her with the sorts of magical amulets medieval peasants wore to ward off plague. They would probably be just as effective, and a great deal lighter.

Unbidden, a memory arose, of a long, paneled corridor. They kept that wing closed now. But when he was eight, Geoff had sat there, night after night, outside his father's door, crept out of bed and lurked in the hallway, standing sentry against Death. But while he slept, nodding at his post, Death had slipped past. At the time, Geoff had imagined him as a bony man in a tattered black cape, hoisting himself through the window like a burglar in the night. Unopposed, Death had slipped down the hall, through the sleeping house, and trailed his icy fingers through the nursery.

If he had stayed awake . . . If he had been more vigilant . . . Logically, he knew there was nothing he could have done. Smallpox struck where it would, and there was nothing a small boy—or even the horde of doctors that had trooped up and down the stairs of Sibley Court, shaking their gray wigs in learned resignation—could do to arrest the disease once it struck. Other than pray.

But how many accidents, how many illnesses, could be prevented through just a bit of care and planning? So Geoff had planned and he had plotted; he had charted out his friends' missions with cold-headed precision, making sure their getaway horses were always in place, their guns always primed, their information the best his spies could provide.

For the most part, he had been successful. But when he thought of Letty entering Lord Vaughn's den, all his preparations seemed as flimsy as a veil hung at the end of a sheer drop. If Lord Vaughn drew a pistol, no number of straight pins and vials of sleeping potion could stop him. It was enough to make him want to barge straight back there, carry her home, and just tie her to the bed for the next fifty years or so.

Not an unpleasant option.

Unfortunately, also not a practicable option.

Tying off the last bunch of rockets, Geoff took a professional look around the room. He had ranged the groups of rockets so that the sparks from one should light the next. With any luck, their upward passage would set off the gunpowder in the room above.

Once any sort of fire started . . . the rest would go from there, neatly wiping out a substantial part of the rebels' store of weapons. They still had the depot at Marshal Lane, piled high with cartridges, grenades, and pikes, as well as lesser hiding places on Winetavern Street, Irishtown, and Smithfield, but those alone would not be enough for a rising on the scale that Emmet had envisioned. Cartridges were all very well, but they didn't do much good unless one had the proper weapons to fire them from. And pikes, even cleverly hinged ones, were only of so much utility against trained British forces' blazing bullets.

Glancing down at the floor, Geoff noticed that the mice had already been at the sacks piled along the side of the room. The gunpowder was mostly stored in barrels, but the mice had gotten at the saltpeter, leaving a trail across the center of the room, as daintily strewn as sugar along the top of a bun.

"It can't hurt to scatter some gunpowder and saltpeter about," he commented. "The bigger the explosion, the better for our purposes."

At the words "bigger" and "explosion," Miss Gwen's eyes took on a rapacious gleam.

"I shall scatter the gunpowder." She added graciously, "You may lay the fuse."

"Charmed, I'm sure," murmured Geoff, taking the long tail of powder-flecked cotton twine and unreeling it toward the wall. One of the knotholes near the ground was large enough to thread the string through. The less distance the flame had to travel, the better. Feeding the fuse through the hole, he said, "When I see you leave the building, I'll light the fuse. Once I've done that—"

Miss Gwen struck a regal pose, chin lifted to the heavens, hand in a keg of gunpowder. "We light the sky."

"—we run like the devil," finished Geoff dryly.

"Young man," announced Miss Gwen, abandoning her tableau, "however urgent the situation, there is never the need for profanity."

Geoff forbore to argue. "When I light the match," he repeated, "run."

He left Miss Gwen neatly arranging gunpowder in the design of a large Union Jack, surmounted by the royal arms, complete with unicorn.

Outside, McDaniels appeared to have succumbed to the effects of the bottle. Propped against the outhouse wall, he was snoring fitfully; one arm wrapped protectively around the remnants of his drink, like a child with a favorite toy.

From neighboring houses, he could hear the normal noises of daily life. Hens scratching. Men scratching. Kettles clanging against the hearth. A woman's voice raised in anger. A child's agitated wail, abruptly stifled with a slap. The sound of an explosion might rattle their kettles, but the depot was set far enough back to prevent unnecessary harm to the innocent.

Geoff peered cautiously down Hanover Alley, the narrow street that abutted the back of the house on Patrick Street. With Patrick Street a popular thoroughfare, the narrow alley formed the main means of rebel access to their stronghold, a way to come and go unremarked. In the fading light of early evening, the alley drowsed in dusty quiet, undisturbed except for the sound of McDaniels's snuffling snores, and a strange, low rumbling sound coming from within the house. Tuneless and toneless as it was, it took Geoff a moment to identify the noise. Miss Gwen was humming.

He could only be glad she didn't do so more often.

Finding the tail of the fuse, masked by a clump of grass, Geoff began carefully playing it out along the side of the house, engaging in minute mental calculations. Pull the fuse too far, and there was a good chance the flame would burn out before it reached the rockets. Place the fuse too close, and none of them would make it home for supper. They needed just enough time to run like the devil. The henhouse, set close by the house, provided a convenient screen behind which to lay the end of the fuse.

"You just might want to consider finding a new nest," Geoff informed the residents, sotto voce.

The hens cackled irritably in reply. They were clearly committed to the revolutionary cause.

But they weren't cackling at him.

One hand still holding the fuse, Geoff whirled toward Patrick Street. A man pounded across the street, two agitated chickens at his heels and a pistol in his hand.

Chapter Twenty-eight

⁓

The man's other hand was engaged in trying to hold his hat on his head.

Jarred by the motion, his long hair flapped behind him, unraveling as he ran. Not just long hair. Very long hair. It flopped to the man's waist, the individual strands catching the light like a flow of spiced cider, honey-gold and flecked with nutmeg and cinnamon. Letty's hair, in fact.

Geoff's hand froze on the stock of his gun.

Suddenly, Lord Vaughn's residence seemed the height of safety, her presence there devoutly to be wished. Not only was she speeding toward enough explosive matter to blow up the entirety of Notre Dame and a few minor cathedrals besides, he really did not think she should be out in public in those pants. They hugged her hips and thighs as closely as a prostitute fondling a patron. Of all the images that could have sprung to mind, that one did little to add to Geoff's peace of mind.

Or what mind he had left. The fact that he had allowed himself to be distracted by his wife's trousers when he had a fuse in one hand and a building full of explosives behind him did not bode well for the continued viability of his mental powers.

The source of his confusion skidded to a halt in front of him in a haze of hair and feathers. Racketing to a stop, Letty tripped over an inquisitive chicken, who seemed to view the entire situation as a new form of game designed entirely for avian amusement.

Geoff grabbed her elbow to steady her, resisting the urge to grab her by both shoulders, shake her until she saw sense, and then kiss her until she couldn't see anything at all. No matter how oddly the rebels behaved, he doubted the neighbors were accustomed to seeing two men embracing by the side of the house. Although how anyone could take one look at Letty in those trousers and believe her a man . . .

No. Geoff sliced off that train of thought before it could veer into dangerous territory. He refused to fall prey to a pair of pantaloons. And he wasn't even going to think about that sliver of throat where her cravat had come undone.

"Why aren't you at Vaughn's?" he demanded, as emphatically as one could demand in a whisper. He reached out and hastily knotted the ends of her cravat together in a rough bow. "What are you doing here? It's dangerous!"

Fortunately, Letty seemed to have regained her balance, if not her breath. She panted something completely unintelligible.

"What was that?"

The fuse took advantage of his slackened grasp and promptly began trailing back toward the knothole, like a very long dog's tail. Lunging, Geoff grabbed the end before it could whisk out of reach.

"Mind on your work!" snapped Miss Gwen, from within the house.

"Rebels," panted Letty, dropping the empty pistol and clutching both hands to her aching diaphragm. The chicken, narrowly avoiding losing several tail feathers, pecked at Letty's boot in retaliation and waddled haughtily away, looking uncannily like Miss Gwen. "Meeting. Now."

"Now," Geoff repeated flatly.

The message he had intercepted had been so clear. Emmet, Allen, Dowdall, Madden, and a number of the other rebel luminaries were engaged to dine at Kilmacud with Joe Alleyburne, for an evening of pleasant conversation and plotting. Geoff had eavesdropped on such events before; they tended to go on well into the night and involve the consumption of large quantities of claret.

Clearly, tonight was the exception.

There was no hope that Letty was wrong. Down at the other end of Hanover Alley, a small cluster of men was barely perceptible, no more than flecks on a painter's palette. Geoff would wager there weren't more than six of them—which still made three too many, even if Geoff counted Letty, which he would have preferred not to. There could be no doubt as to their identity. From the not so distant distance came a snatch of a ballad, low but unmistakable.

"And you did mean now," Geoff said grimly.

Why in the hell did rebel movements always have to express themselves in song? Geoff recognized it as "The Lament of Lord Edward Fitzgerald," a lugubrious little ditty that began "Why lie ye here so pale and cold, Edward, Edward? Why ye who were so brave and bold, Edward, Edward?" and went on along that vein for the whole of thirty-eight verses, including a glowing report of Lord Edward's childhood lessons and his preference for jammy tarts at tea ("Oh, ye who liked the raspberry, Edward, Edward"), before getting on to the usual bits about bloody blades, bared breasts, and women weeping.

They had clearly been singing for quite some time; Geoff caught a fragment that ran "And when his Greek translations were due, Edward, Edward, the blank verse came out pure and true, Edward, Edward. For in the glow of Hector's shield, Edward, Edward, you saw that Eire must never yield, Edward, Edward."

One could learn to hate that name after a few verses.

The little group at the end of Hanover Alley was growing more distinct. Six men, clearly in a state of high good spirits, even if there did seem to be a small disagreement about variant endings to the twenty-third verse.

In just a few yards they would be close enough to take an interest in what was going on in their own yard. And there was very little a man could do to explain away why he just happened to be holding a fuse in one hand and a match in the other.

A hen pecked curiously at Geoff's foot, clearly mistaking it for an outré new form of feed. Rapping smartly on the wall, Geoff leaned over to speak into one of the knotholes.

"I am lighting the match," enunciated Geoff clearly. "Would you care to emerge?"

"Hmph," was all Miss Gwen said, but Geoff heard a thump that he devoutly hoped was the banging of the hidden door. For all her irritating qualities, he had no interest in immolating Miss Gwen. The blasted woman would probably come back to haunt him.

"May I help?" Letty asked, her eyes darting from the fuse to the rebels and back again.

She looked so absurdly small and vulnerable in her borrowed men's clothes. Geoff would have liked to send Letty packing, back to Jane's house, or, even better, all the way back to London. But he didn't have that luxury. Making a snap decision, Geoff held out the end of the fuse.

"Can you work a flint?"

Letty snapped to. "Of course!"

"Good. Take this." Geoff handed her the flint. Letty accepted the flint with a familiarity that boded well for her claim of competence. "The second you see Miss Gwen emerge, use it to light this." With his other hand, Geoff held out the fuse. Letty regarded the black-flecked length of twine dubiously. "Once it's lit, I want you to run, as fast as you can, down toward the church."

"What about you?"

Geoff's mouth quirked with wry humor. "With any luck, I'll be running, too."

Letty just looked at him, her blue eyes clouded with unasked questions.

Abandoning any pretense of levity, Geoff said somberly, "I'll hold them off as long as it takes to protect the fuse."

"I see," said Letty, and she did.

The need to take her into his arms was almost a physical ache. "If anything goes wrong, I want you to go straight to Jane. If anything goes wrong with Jane, go straight back to England. Understood?"

Letty nodded. Reluctantly.

Geoff could tell she was yearning to argue, and his chest swelled with an entirely unfamiliar range of emotions at her perspicacity and self-control. Nine out of ten women—nine out of ten men—would have wasted time in useless arguments. But not his Letty.

Unable to kiss her good-bye, since that really would arouse the rebels' suspicions, as well as other inconvenient organs, Geoff did the only thing he could. Under cover of the henhouse, he reached for her hand and squeezed. "I'm going to go drag Miss Gwen out of the house. The minute you see her, light the fuse."

Letty knew what she wanted to say. But since she couldn't, she went with the next best substitute, inadequate though it was.

"Be careful," she whispered, but the words were lost in a sudden burst of noise. Like an ill wish, Miss Gwen appeared, bursting forth from the back door with enough force to shake the door on its hinges. She seemed, for a moment, to hang in midair like an avenging Fury, her gray hair bristling and her parasol raised like a general's baton.

At the end of the alley, the rebels stood amazed, frozen from sheer shock.

Letty couldn't blame them.

Twisting the handle of her parasol, Miss Gwen drew out a

thin sword from the shaft. In her left hand, she braced the open purple parasol like a shield. The silk fringe bobbed merrily in the fading sunlight.

"Fire away!" cried Miss Gwen. Thrusting her sword point high in the air, she charged the astounded band of rebels.

Letty didn't need to be asked twice. Dropping to her knees behind the henhouse, she struck the flint with hands that were surprisingly steady. The metal fit familiarly into her hand, an oddly domestic counterpoint to the scent of sulfur stinging her nose and the chicken dung muddying her pantaloons. Under Letty's efforts, the tinder caught, and lit. Her heart somewhere around her cravat, Letty thrust the powdercoated fuse into the small spark and waited for it to catch flame.

Nothing happened.

The fuse wasn't taking. The flame smoldered sullenly at the very tip before winking damply out.

Fighting her rising anxiety, Letty struck the flint again, willing the metal to spark. Just on the other side of the weathered wooden structure, Miss Gwen's shrill yips of triumph and tart asides mingled with masculine oaths and grunts. They seemed to be holding their own, but how long could two hold out against six?

If there was something wrong with the fuse . . . Merciful heavens, she didn't even know what a functioning fuse was supposed to look like, much less what one was supposed to do if one wouldn't work. Those little black flecks . . . she assumed they were supposed to be there, but who knew? And the ground was damp, a damp that might have worked into the twine, inhibiting the action of the flame.

Letty worked the flint with a burst of energy born of desperation, tipping the end of the fuse to catch the flame. If the fuse wouldn't take this time, she would just have to find something else. A long spar of wood torn from the chicken coop, perhaps, and thrust through one of the larger knotholes in the wall. It might work. If the fuse didn't light, it would have to work.

The tip of the fuse caught and smoked, smoldering uncertainly against the backdrop of the muddy earth. As though through a screen, Letty could hear the pounding of booted feet against packed dirt, shouted threats and imprecations, the harsh exhalations of hard-pressed lungs, all drawing steadily nearer. It couldn't have been more than seconds, but it felt like an eternity. Cupping her hands around the red tip, she blew gently on the flame, willing it into life.

"Please," Letty breathed. "Please . . ."

Whether it was the plea or pure chemistry, the little tongue of flame gathered momentum, greedily gobbling its way down the fuse, like the fiery salamander of medieval myth.

Letty stumbled backward to her feet, watching as the flame licked toward the wall. She wanted to squeal, to cheer, to fling her hat in the air. They had done it! The fuse was lit! Giddy with triumph, Letty spun on one heel—but her cry of triumph turned to a muffled yell as someone ignominiously grabbed her about the waist from behind and hauled her painfully up into the air.

"CHARGE!" CRIED MISS GWEN, thrusting her sword parasol in the air.

Geoff caught her up halfway down the alley. "We just have to hold them long enough for the fuse to burn down to the wall," he tossed at her in a quick undertone. "No heroics."

Miss Gwen looked distinctly put out.

Putting her ire to good use, she flashed out with the point of her sword in a movement that owed more to vigor than science. Staring transfixed at the fringed purple parasol she held as a shield, her target barely had time to wrench out of her way, winning a long rent in his sleeve rather than the killing thrust Miss Gwen had intended.

"Sirrah!" snapped Miss Gwen. "Kindly stand still!"

For a moment, her opponent looked like he meant to obey. Belatedly recalling his circumstances, he scrambled for his knife, just as Geoff brought two clasped hands down on the back of his neck, sending him sprawling.

Shoving her parasol in the face of one rebel while fending off another, Miss Gwen still found the time to cast a glower in Geoff's general direction. "That one was *meant* to be mine," she complained.

"There are more than enough to go around," rejoined Geoff, ducking beneath a poorly planned punch.

Unmoved by that sensible sentiment, Miss Gwen expressed herself volubly as to the general uselessness of the male gender.

"Sharp-tongued old besom," grumbled one of the rebels. "Couldn't get a husband?"

Miss Gwen pinked him in the knee.

Leaving Miss Gwen to settle accounts with her admirer, Geoff repelled one assailant with a stiff elbow to the throat while driving his fist into the stomach of a second. The man doubled over satisfactorily, unreeling a stream of colloquial curses that mingled oddly with another noise, a cry that sounded more alto than baritone, and made Geoff's chest tighten in a way that had nothing to do with the knife blade that had just scraped stingingly across his ribs.

Dispatching the wielder of the knife—momentarily, at least—with a leg hooked beneath his knees, he heard Letty, quite definitely Letty, demanding that someone put her down, right now.

The man Geoff had tripped stumbled to his feet and staggered forward again.

"That was Letty," Geoff said shortly, finishing the man off with a blow to the head with the butt of his pistol. Four men lay groaning on the turf in various positions of pain, leaving only two to be dispatched. "Can you hold them?"

Miss Gwen ran one of the remaining two through the shoulder with her sword parasol. A grim expression of satisfaction showed on her face as he collapsed groaning at her feet.

"What are you waiting for?" she demanded, as she advanced on her final opponent.

Geoff didn't need any further urging. Sprinting down the length of the house, he called back over his shoulder, "I'm in your debt."

"Your first child, Pinchingdale!" Miss Gwen cackled.

As Geoff skidded toward Patrick Street, he could hear Miss Gwen behind him, knocking open the roof of the henhouse and urging its feathered contents onward. "Peck, my pretties! Peck! That's the way!"

It was enough to make one feel sorry for the rebels.

Geoff skidded to a stop, scanning left, then right, just in time to see Letty tumbling backward over the side of a wagon several yards away. She disappeared among a spurt of straw as the driver slapped the reins, urging his horse forward. The wagon started with a lurch that sent Letty's head, briefly visible above the slats that boxed in the sides, straight back down again.

She wasn't hurt.

Relief was rapidly replaced by rage as Geoff recognized the driver. He hadn't bothered to wear a hat, and the sun shone right down on his infamous sideburns.

Jasper had Letty.

Chapter Twenty-nine

One minute Letty was admiring her handiwork; the next she was dangling a foot off the ground.

Two large hands grasped her under the arms, yanking upward. Letty howled with indignation and pain. That grip under her arms hurt, with a throbbing pain that did not get any better when her assailant gave another concerted pull, raising her another half inch and threatening to dislocate her arms from their sockets. Letty batted ineffectually behind her, but she had failed to take into account quite how difficult it was to hit someone who had one by the armpits. Her fingers barely brushed the fabric of his sleeves.

"Let go!" Kicking out behind her, Letty's flailing foot hit wood instead of flesh, with a force that sent pain reverberating all down her leg.

Her captor took advantage of her distraction to haul her up another half foot, her backside scraping against a decidedly splintery surface. Letty's jacket snagged on a rough edge, and her captor gave an irritated grunt.

It wasn't much, but that tone of irritation was unmistakable.

Letty made a concerted effort to look behind her that resulted only in a wrenching pain in her right arm.

"Captain Pinchingdale?" she exclaimed.

"Would you be still?" Jasper demanded in aggrieved tones, as though it were perfectly unremarkable for him to be grabbing her from behind and attempting to haul her into a vehicle that seemed to be completely composed of sharp fragments of wood, all aimed at Letty's backside. "You're making this much harder."

"*I'm* making this harder?" retorted Letty incredulously. "No one asked you to grab me! Put me down *at once*."

"I'll put you down"—Jasper gave another mighty heave, bringing Letty's back into uncomfortable contact with the edge of the wagon—"once you're inside."

"You might have just asked me," Letty gritted out.

Jasper snorted. It was, Letty had to admit, a fairly accurate representation of the likelihood of her having agreed to go any-where with him. With a final heave, Letty's back scraped painfully across the edge of the wagon and she toppled over side-ways, into a scratchy substance that scraped her cheek and got up her nose. The hay smelled heavily of horse and other substances that Letty, even with her country upbringing, would really rather not have encountered quite so intimately.

Why was it that people suddenly seemed to feel an ineluctable desire to pick her up and toss her into their vehicles? Some women attracted sonnets; others collected small animals. Letty got tossed into carriages. It was a trend that had to stop.

Blowing hay out of her mouth, Letty heard the slap of reins as Jasper urged the horse into motion.

"I hadn't realized you had taken up agricultural pursuits," commented Letty, struggling to her knees as the ill-sprung wagon rocked back and forth. She had never realized before quite how slippery hay could be. Every time she managed to get a bit of pur-chase, the cart swayed, and her hand slipped out from under her.

Jasper's nostrils flared, in an expression uncommonly similar to that of the animal he was driving. The horse clearly didn't care for Jasper any more than Jasper cared for him. "I couldn't afford anything better. Thanks to our munificent Geoffrey."

Letty clawed her way up onto the bench, wincing at the ache beneath her arms. "If this is another attempt to get me to murder my husband, the answer remains no."

"Do you really think I'm that foolish?"

"Given the circumstances?" Letty didn't have to think about it. "Yes. Now that we've gotten that cleared up, I would be much obliged if you would put me back down. Right now."

"As much as it pains me to disoblige a lady, I'm afraid that won't be possible." Jasper didn't look the least bit pained. "You see, I have plans for you."

Letty had plans for herself, too. She doubted they coincided.

"Well, that's just too bad." Letty reached for the reins. "Some plans aren't meant to be."

Jasper forestalled her by the simple act of pulling a pistol from his waistband and jamming it into the region of her waist. It was much larger than the pistol Geoff had given her, sixteen inches at the least from stock to muzzle. Jasper handled it with a one-handed ease that bespoke long familiarity with the weapon.

"Sit," he commanded.

Letty sat.

"Is it loaded?" she asked hopefully.

Jasper sent her a look loaded with enough derision to stagger the Dowager Duchess of Dovedale. "What do you think?"

"I think you ought to put it down. You might hurt yourself."

"Your concern touches me deeply."

The thought of touching Jasper in any way revolted her. It did not, however, seem politic to say so while he had a gun jammed up against her spleen.

"I'm flattered that you were so determined to have our drive together, but you can let me down now." Letty favored him with a sparkling social smile that was only slightly marred by the smudges on her cheeks and the hay in her hair. "This has been simply charming, but I should be getting back before I'm missed."

"Has anyone ever told you that it's unwise to mock a man with a gun?"

"The situation has never arisen," said Letty honestly. "I would prefer to keep it that way."

It probably wasn't the wisest course to taunt a man with a gun shoved into her ribs, but Letty didn't believe Jasper would actually pull the trigger. At least, not deliberately. Jasper was a boaster and a bully, not a cold-blooded killer.

She hoped.

No, she wasn't going to let herself go down that road. If Jasper had the mettle for murder, he would have just killed Geoff outright, rather than trying to bamboozle her into doing it. Letty didn't doubt that Jasper was greedy enough and conscienceless enough to attempt to arrange the death of anyone who came between him and his tailor, but he just didn't have the backbone to do it himself, a fact for which Letty was profoundly grateful.

Letty scrounged for other explanations. The only one she could come up with was ransom money. The thought cheered Letty immensely. If he was planning to hold her for ransom, she would be far more use to Jasper alive than dead. No one paid full price for a corpse.

Perhaps if she started him talking, Jasper's grip on the weapon would relax. Once the gun was knocked out of his reach . . . well, she would deal with that bit when she got to it.

"What do you intend to do with me?"

"I thought you would never ask. Get along." Jasper impatiently slapped at the horse, which was ambling along at its own peaceful pace. With a quick look at Letty, he added, "Not you."

"Of course not." Letty folded her hands demurely in her lap and tried not to look as though she were seeking the first opportunity to whack him in the arm, steal his gun, and leap out of the wagon.

"Such a shock it will be to everyone," expatiated Jasper, waving the hand holding the gun, "when the young Viscountess Pinchingdale is found dead. On her honeymoon."

Not kidnapping, then. Jasper did seem to be taking her rejection of his advances a little too seriously. Letty wondered if she ought to have refrained from that comment about his sideburns.

"Not only dead," Jasper continued, warming to his theme, "but murdered. And by whom?"

"Preferably no one."

Jasper ignored her. "By her own husband."

"I hate to point out the flaw in your cunning plan," said Letty, squirming toward the far end of the seat, "but Geoff isn't here."

Jasper brought her to an abrupt halt by the simple expedient of thrusting the gun against her chest. "He doesn't have to be. That's the brilliance of it. It isn't necessary that our dear Geoffrey kill you—"

"How lovely."

"—simply that he be thought to kill you."

"And how do you plan to manage that? Geoff isn't exactly known for his murderous rages. No one is going to believe it."

"Oh, won't they?" Jasper looked altogether too sure of himself for Letty's liking. Even his sideburns exuded smugness. "Everyone knows our blameless Geoffrey was in love with your sister."

"Along with half the *ton*," snapped Letty. "It is not exactly an uncommon emotion where Mary is concerned."

"It is common knowledge that our Geoffrey was forced against his will to take you instead."

The way Jasper kept repeating "our Geoffrey" set her teeth on edge. Or maybe it was just the gun, poking insistently at the binding around her waist. She could feel the muzzle boring into her side, even through all the layers of fabric. For the first time,

Letty wished Jane had wrapped on more binding. And perhaps a few layers of armor.

"I could have the entire *ton* up on the stand," continued Jasper confidently, "all vouching to the fact that Geoffrey never wanted to marry you."

Letty had no doubt that Mrs. Ponsonby would be the first to testify. "That might be true, but it's no motive for murder. Otherwise you would have three-quarters of the *ton* in the dock."

"Yours was an exceptional case."

"Wouldn't you rather just kidnap me and hold me for ransom?" Letty suggested. "That way, you get an immediate influx of funds with no pesky little murder charges. You know what they say about a bird in the hand."

"That isn't a bird; it's a gull. Do you really expect me to believe that our Geoffrey would pay to have you back? He wouldn't even travel with you as man and wife." Jasper smirked. "And everyone in Dublin has seen him making up to Miss Fairley. Now there's a fine piece of flesh."

Letty wondered just what Jane would have to say about that description.

"Besides, why would I settle for a measly portion when I could have the whole? Not only the money, but the houses, the title, everything that was due me at birth."

"Due?"

"Due. It should have been mine. What right did Geoffrey have? What did he have that I didn't?"

Letty could have told him the answer to that quite easily—he had the good fortune to be born in the proper order to the proper father—but she suspected the question was intended to be rhetorical.

If Jasper wanted unfair, he should try being born a woman. That would teach him.

"Perhaps," suggested Letty, treading very carefully, "you might try discussing this with your cousin."

Jasper might be venal, but he was, unfortunately, not entirely stupid.

"Do you think I'm entirely stupid? No, the only way is to take my destiny into my own hands. And you, my dear Lady Pinchingdale, are going to help me. Once your body is found"—Jasper gloated over the reins—"I won't even have to kill him. The law will do it for me."

"I'll grant you," said Letty, "that ours has not exactly been a picture of married bliss. But that isn't enough to prove a charge of murder."

"It will be," said Jasper complacently, "when they find our Geoffrey's snuffbox beside your body. It has the letters GP quite clearly worked into the design." Jasper paused for dramatic effect before adding the pièce de résistance. "And a portrait of your sister painted on the lid."

There was very little Letty could think of to say in response to that. What was there to say? In conjunction with the rumors percolating about their marriage, the discovery of the snuffbox would be just as damning as Jasper intended it to be. With the picture of Mary simpering sweetly from the underside of the lid, it provided both evidence and motive in one convenient package.

As a peer, Geoff would be tried before the House of Lords. How many members of the peerage had seen Geoff dancing attendance on Mary? How many of them had attended their disastrous wedding? True, those of them who knew Geoff would know that he wasn't the sort to murder his wife—but what was the sort to murder one's wife? They would waggle their double chins and speak wisely of young men being driven to madness by love. Tristan and Iseult would be mentioned, and that earl, two Seasons ago, whose wits had been so weakened by amour that he had gone so far as to marry his mistress. Someone would undoubtedly quote from *Romeo and Juliet*.

There would be wagging of heads, and reminiscences over

past scandals, and the long and short of it would be that Geoff would stand condemned, hoist by his own love poetry.

Jasper wielded his whip with a self-satisfied slap.

"Bring out the black cap," he said cheerfully.

Since there didn't seem to be much point in trying to curry favor, Letty spoke as she felt. "You really are revolting."

Jasper glanced over at Letty, his handsome features arranged in a parody of sympathy. "Come, come, my dear girl, you must get some little pleasure at being the downfall of the man who ruined your reputation."

There was something fundamentally flawed with Jasper's logic, and Letty didn't have a hard time identifying just what it was. "I'd rather be ruined and live."

Jasper shook his head. "Just like a woman to reject the chance of a glorious death."

"Fine. You take death. I'll take dishonor."

"Don't worry, my dear," said Jasper, baring all his teeth. "I'll have a charming picture of you placed in the gallery of Sibley Court. I'll even tell the artist to paint out those freckles."

That did it. "If you are so keen on killing me, why haven't you just shot me already?"

"It might stain my clothes. Do you know how much this waistcoat cost?"

Letty was relieved to know that he had some scruples, even if they didn't necessarily stretch to the sanctity of human life—hers, for a start.

"Most forms of murder are messy," said Letty very seriously. "And no matter how hard you try to scrub at a bloodstain, you never really get the marks out of the fabric."

"Exactly," said Jasper. "That is why I am going to drown you in the Liffey instead."

"Are you sure you want to do that?" Letty scarcely knew what she was saying. She was too busy casting about for escape plans. She had no hope of anyone riding to the rescue. Even if Geoff, on a very rare chance, had seen Jasper carrying her off, he had the demolition of the rebel stronghold to take care of. The life of a wife—even if he was glad he knew her—ranked fairly low next to the safety of England. "Water stains silk."

"I wore wool."

Thank goodness she knew how to swim. Not well, but enough to keep her from sinking straight to the bottom. Wearing men's clothing, she stood more of a chance than she would have in skirts. She would just have to pretend to go under and swim furiously toward the other bank.

"And don't think you'll be able to swim," advised Jasper, clearly deriving great pleasure from Letty's discomfiture. "Swimming ought to be quite difficult after a blow to the head."

"Blows to the head bleed badly," countered Letty, pressing back against the side of the wagon. The vial of sleeping potion was still in her waistcoat pocket, but there was no way she could administer it. As for the whistle, she could blow until she was blue in the face; no one would hear her above the rattle of wheels, and even if they did, no one would care. That left only the embroidery scissors. Embroidery scissors. She had as much hope of storming a citadel with a thimble. "If you won't think of me, think of your waistcoat. It's too fine to mar."

With a particularly unpleasant smile, Jasper leaned forward. Reversing his grip on the gun, he raised it high above her head.

"That's a risk I'll just have to take."

LETTY WAS RIGHT; Jasper's sideburns were unbecoming.

They wouldn't be all that was unbecoming by the time Geoff was through with him. Jasper was long overdue for a damned good thrashing. Geoff charged toward his horse, before being brought up short by the realization that he hadn't brought one. Damn. He had no hope of catching them on foot. For such a rickety vehicle, Jasper's wagon was receding at an alarming pace. Ahead of him, children and livestock played in the street, carts rumbled past on their way back from market, and weary laborers trudged home from work. The throng of early traffic had slowed Jasper's progress, but it had not stopped him.

Geoff stopped a man leading a tired-looking nag. Whatever the animal's usual function was, it was not a riding horse.

"Here," said Geoff, tossing him a handful of coins without bothering to see what they were. "Buy yourself another horse."

Keeping hold of the bridle, the man tested a coin with his teeth, saying laconically, "I dunno, sir. She's a fine animal, sure and she is . . ."

Up ahead, Jasper drew something that glistened darkly in the summer sunlight before disappearing again below the level of sight.

The small form next to him went very still.

Fear such as he had never felt before froze through Geoff's veins like congealed January.

Swinging up on the surprised animal's bony back, Geoff lobbed his entire purse at the man with the precision that had made him the toast of the fourth-form cricket team. "Here. This should do."

The heavy pouch whapped the man straight in the chest. Staggering back, he released his grip on the bridle. With one swift kick, Geoff was away, guided by a single, overwhelming imperative: to catch up with his cousin and apply that gun where it would hurt the most.

"You coulda had 'er for a shilling!" floated down the street after him.

Leaning low over the nag's neck, Geoff wove around a dog-cart, a man with a wheelbarrow, and a remarkably unconcerned pig, taking a brief detour into the gutter as he skirted impatiently around a carriage that refused to grant him the right of way.

Jasper was making north, toward the river. Toward the river

and the suburbs beyond? The area to the north of the city was still largely undeveloped, a perfect place to cache an unwilling hostage, far away from the great throng of humanity, and the last place anyone would think to look. That must be what Jasper was planning to do, stow Letty away somewhere and use her as a bargaining chip for whatever his latest selfish scheme was—a commission in a better regiment, his debts paid off, his allowance increased. Jasper's desires ran along fairly predictable lines.

But that gun made Geoff nervous. Very nervous. Even if Jasper didn't actually intend to use it, the lurching of the wagon on the uneven surface of the paving stones made its going off a deadly probability. One jolt of the wagon, one inadvertent flex of the fingers . . .

Geoff was gaining, but not quickly enough.

Why in the hell hadn't he sent Jasper packing back to England the moment he had turned up in front of St. Werburgh's the week before? He ought to have shoved two months' allowance into his hand, marched him straight down to the docks, and personally supervised his removal.

He hadn't thought. He hadn't been thinking. And if he had thought, he would have assumed that the very circumstances of his union with Letty would protect her. The prospect of heirs might well spur Jasper to violent action—Jasper had been holding his creditors at bay for years on the strength of his expectancy in the Pinchingdale estate—but who was less likely to produce heirs than an unwanted wife? As far as Jasper knew, Geoff was courting the favors of Miss Gilly Fairley, which was not a course of action conducive to the begetting of legitimate heirs.

Unless Jasper had seen through the ploy. Indolent Jasper might be, vindictive and venal and selfish, but he was not without a certain raw cunning. And he had known Geoff for a very long time. Those summer holidays they had been forced to spend together at Sibley Court, "playing nicely," had left neither unscarred.

If Jasper realized that Geoff and Letty's marriage had become something more than a sham . . .

Geoff urged his horse forward, as if by the application of speed he could outrun the misbegotten images propagating through his mind.

It could all happen so quickly. A trigger pulled. A shot muffled by proximity. A limp body tossed out the side of the carriage like so many old clothes. A sea of empty words sloshed through his mind—duty, obligation, and responsibility.

None of them meant a thing next to the raw sensation of panic that washed over him at the thought of Jasper firing that gun. No more ginger hair poking him in the nose when he woke up in the morning; no more tart remarks; no more Letty. The idea of going back to England without Letty made his head echo with the very emptiness of it, as bleak and barren as the black-shrouded corridors of Sibley Court after the smallpox had swept through. Next to it, his despair at being balked of Mary was reduced to what it had been, a child crying after a toy in a window, more pique than pain. But Letty . . .

He couldn't lose her. Not now.

With an unmistakable motion, Jasper hefted his weapon, angling the solid wooden stock to come crashing down on Letty's unprotected head. Grabbing his wrist, Letty pushed back for all she was worth, but Jasper, stronger by far, was winning. Letty's arms bent back inch by painful inch, incapable of withstanding Jasper's superior force.

In the midst of it all, Jasper laughed, a great, unpleasant guffaw.

With red rage ringing through his ears, Geoff drew abreast, poised to leap from the animal's back into the back of the wagon.

The entire world exploded into chaos.

A comet of flame burst through the roof of the house on Patrick Street, seeming to set the very air on fire with a hail of fiery flecks. Horses reared and pigs squealed as debris ricocheted off the paving stones. Bent bits of metal clattered against the cobbles and carts careened into one another in blind confusion as a sulfurous cloud swept down the street, borne by the evening breeze like a whiff straight from the inner reaches of hell.

Through the screaming, crying confusion, Geoff could vaguely make out Miss Gwen, striding jauntily away from the blazing building as she neatly dusted off her parasol against her trousers.

Even the placid beast dragging Jasper's wagon did what any sensible animal would do. He bolted. Or rather, he tried to bolt. Given the three carts piled up in front of him, he didn't get terribly far, but the abrupt motion yanked the reins from between Jasper's knees and made the cart rock dangerously back and forth. The ancient slats creaked in a way that boded ill for the inhabitants.

Jasper lunged for the dangling ribbons, leaving the pistol wavering half-forgotten in his other hand.

Giving a silent cheer for Geoff and Miss Gwen, Letty seized the moment. Whipping out her embroidery scissors, she slammed the points deep into back of Jasper's hand. Howling, Jasper dropped the gun, flapping his wounded hand in the air and cursing loudly enough to drown out any number of explosions.

The weapon fell clattering to the baseboard. Letty dove for the gun. Jasper dove for Letty. The horse, meanwhile, had found a little clump of grass and was placidly engaged in munching, relieved that the maniac on the box was leaving him be for a bit.

Ha! There was the pistol, right by Jasper's boot. Letty's fingers brushed the barrel just as an agonizing pain shot through her scalp.

The gun skittered out of reach as Jasper hauled her up by the hair. Like the knell of a penny disappearing down a wishing well, Letty could hear the reverberations as the gun tumbled out the side of the wagon and clattered against the spokes of the wheel before clanking down onto the paving stones with one final, conclusory clunk.

Well, if she didn't have it, at least neither did Jasper.

Unfortunately, Jasper had other means at his disposal, means far more lethal than a dented pair of embroidery scissors. He sent Letty reeling back with one casual swipe of the back of his hand. Letty's head connected with the edge of the cart with a force that made flashes of light explode in front of her eyes, blocking all thought except for the searing reality of pain.

With some dim notion of following the way of the gun, Letty let herself slide down off the seat, and began crawling along the baseboard. The wood abraded her palms, and her head ached, throbbing front and back.

The pain made her angry.

Anger was good. Letty used it to fight back a weakening wave of dizziness. Somehow, if she could only find a way out of the cart . . .

Jasper hauled her up by the back of her collar, thrusting her back onto the seat. He shook his hand in her face, splattering blood across the grimy gray of her cravat. Clearly, he was beyond worrying about bloodstains on his waistcoat.

Jasper's lips peeled back from his teeth in a way reminiscent of wolves in fairy tales. "I'll make you sorry for this," he snarled, yanking Letty up by the cravat.

Letty clawed ineffectually at the hand holding her by the throat, gasping for breath.

"By the time I'm through with you, you'll wish you'd never seen a scissor. I'll—"

"You'll what?" a new voice demanded.

Chapter Thirty

With a low growl, little more than a rumble in the throat, Jasper dropped Letty. Letty couldn't have been more delighted.

The wagon lurched precipitately as Geoff leaped into the wagon bed, landing in a fighter's crouch in the well-used straw. Sensing the change in weight, the horse flicked its ears briefly back, before he went back to munching on his patch of grass, leaving the silly humans to their own devices.

"Would you care to repeat that—to me?" Geoff demanded, a dangerous glint in his gray eyes. "Or do you only war on women these days, Jasper?"

Slumping against the side of the wagon, Letty dragged in a labored breath, her cramped lungs sluggishly resuming work. Her cheek ached, the back of her head ached, her chest ached, but at the sight of Geoff, she could feel a wild exultation flood through her, headier than air.

Somewhat less enthused by the new addition to their party, Jasper turned slowly to face his cousin, his brows drawing together over the long Norman nose that was one of the few features they shared.

"I had other plans for you, cousin, but this will do just as well, when you and your lady wife"—nursing his bleeding hand, Jasper glowered at Letty, turning the word "lady" into the worst sort of slur—"are found dead, murdered by an anonymous footpad."

"It's so nice to find you finally pursuing a gainful occupation," replied Geoff. "But I suggest you find someone else to go bother."

"Oh, you can mock," replied Jasper. He flexed his hands as he stalked, one booted foot, then the other, up onto the wagon seat. He loomed over the box, the very image of menace. "Mock all you like. You won't be mocking—urgh!"

All his energies focused on his cousin, Jasper never saw the small form creeping purposefully along the box behind him. He didn't feel the two hands press against his back until it was too late.

Arms flailing, Jasper tumbled over the edge of the seat. With a crash that rocked the entire vehicle and sent little bits of straw spurting into the air, he landed facedown in the wagon bed.

Geoff jumped nimbly back as Jasper went sprawling at his feet.

A faint groan emerged from the straw.

"And that," said Letty distinctly, brushing off her hands, "is quite enough from you."

Geoff's eyes, alight with admiration, met Letty's over Jasper's fallen form.

"Nicely done," he said.

"Thank you." Letty regarded her handiwork with some satisfaction. "I thought so."

Jasper's bloodied face rose from the straw to glower malevolently at Letty. "My nose is broken, you—"

Geoff's foot descended heavily on Jasper's back, turning whatever the last word might have been into a loud whoosh of air. "Choose your words carefully. That's my wife you happen to be addressing."

"You should be thanking me," Jasper said thickly, spitting out blood and straw. "I was going to do you a favor. I was going to rid you of that—oof."

"Don't do me any more favors," said Geoff dryly. "Particularly not like that one."

"Hear, hear," seconded Letty, rubbing her sore throat.

At the sight of the purpling bruises on Letty's cheek and neck, an unreadable expression flickered across Geoff's face. With an almost casual air, he shifted more weight onto Jasper's back.

"It appears that you and I need to have a little chat, to prevent a recurrence of today's events. Let's just get this over with now, shall we?"

Jasper groaned.

"Good. I'm glad you agree."

Removing his foot, Geoff paced in a deliberative circle around Jasper's fallen form. Jasper's head shot up like a turtle out of its shell. He licked his bloodied lips, warily watching his cousin.

"Let me be plain," Geoff said conversationally, folding his arms and looking down his nose at his cousin. "There are a number of unpleasant things I could do to you. I could bring you up on charges of attempted murder. I could personally dismember you with Letty's embroidery scissors—yes, I believe you have encountered them already—snip by painful snip. Or"—Geoff paused, allowing that attractive image to have time to impress itself upon Jasper's imagination—"I could tell your mother."

Genuine terror flashed across Jasper's bloodied face.

"You wouldn't," he blustered.

"I will," Geoff replied implacably. "Unless—but no."

Jasper propped himself up on an elbow, watching his cousin narrowly. "No, what? What?"

"I personally vote for the embroidery scissors," put in Letty. She dangled them from one finger, just within Jasper's line of vision. "But only if I get the first snip."

"We might," Geoff suggested mildly, "be able to forgo the embroidery scissors—and your mother—if you were to go far away. Very far away."

"How far away?" asked Letty warily. No matter what Jasper

might promise now, she didn't trust him not to reappear with a wagon at the ready and a gun in hand whenever he thought he might be able to get away with it. And there was no guaranteeing that she would have her embroidery scissors in hand.

Geoff smiled at her over Jasper's recumbent form. "I hear India is lovely this time of year."

"You mean it's a malarial pit," objected Jasper, surging up out of the hay. "I won't do it."

"Won't?" Geoff didn't so much as touch Jasper, but the lash of his voice alone was enough to drive Jasper back several paces. In a voice all the more terrifying for its very calm, he went on pleasantly, "Let us be very clear on this point, cousin. If you had succeeded in harming my wife, you would be dead. Slowly. Painfully. Dead. Do you understand?"

"India. Yes. Right. Smashing place. All those . . . curries."

"Splendid." Geoff clapped Jasper on the back with cousinly bonhomie. "I was sure you would see reason."

Reason wasn't all that Geoff had on his side. He also had Jasper's arm twisted behind his back. Given that Geoff was the slighter cousin by at least a stone, it was an impressive performance. Jasper, however, was so entirely demoralized by the stinging rain of Geoff's words that he didn't even think to put up any resistance.

"Everything will be arranged for you. I'm sure your commanding officer will be more than delighted to facilitate your transfer to another regiment. Don't worry," Geoff added kindly. "We'll make quite sure whichever one it is has uniforms that meet your sartorial expectations. You needn't fear for your appearance."

Jasper nodded numbly.

"I do believe you will be needing a new valet though," Geoff went on, in the same implacably pleasant voice. "Someone will be arriving at your lodgings tonight to assume that role. He will accompany you to India—and he will make sure you stay in India. One false move, and the sideburns go."

Jasper swallowed hard.

Geoff turned to Letty. "A valet has a million small ways of enacting retribution. A nick under the chin while shaving, an overstarched collar, a seam sewn where it will rub continuously against the skin until the wearer runs mad from it. They are masters of the lesser forms of torture. I'm sure our Jasper won't do anything to displease his valet, will you, cousin?"

"No," Jasper croaked.

"Good." Geoff made no move to release his cousin's arm. "I'm glad we had this little talk. And now, dear cousin, I believe you are decidedly de trop."

Letty realized what Geoff was planning a moment before Jasper did. With a seemingly effortless movement, Geoff took his cousin by the scruff of his pants and swung him over the side of the wagon, right into the gutter. Jasper landed with a splash, cursing with enough vehemence to assure the onlookers that he was more outraged than injured.

Picking himself up, and flicking bits of refuse off his person, Jasper cast a malevolent glare over his shoulder at a pair of small children, who pointed and laughed.

"Good-bye, Jasper," called Geoff. "Don't forget to write your mother from India."

Jasper didn't bother to respond. Aiming a kick at a small dog who was exploring a tasty morsel that had attached itself to his boot, Jasper limped away, radiating indignation and refuse.

Wiping off his hands, Geoff glanced over his shoulder at Letty. "I should have done that years ago."

Letty would have liked to run to Geoff, to fling her arms around him, to cover his face with kisses, but the force of long habit held her back. That, and the echo of Jasper's jeering voice, pointing out just how much Geoff had wanted to marry another. Her own sister, in fact. Jasper was Jasper—and currently covered with muck—but that didn't change the fundamental truth of his assertions.

Clambering awkwardly down from the box, she joined Geoff in the wagon bed. Standing next to him, near enough that her sleeve brushed his, she watched Jasper's retreating form.

"Did you have to drop him on the softer side?"

"He *is* my cousin."

"He's a murderous swine," countered Letty stoutly.

Geoff looked down at her, a slight smile playing around his lips. "That, too."

That smile made Letty distinctly nervous. She took a half step back, skidding a bit in the straw. "If he had succeeded, you could have been free."

Geoff reached out to steady her, his hands cupping her elbows. "I don't want to be free," he said.

Letty's eyes searched his face for some sign of reservations, something held back. "Not in that way, you mean?"

Geoff's hands tightened on her arms. "Not at all."

Letty bit her lip. Of course, he would say that. How could he say otherwise, without making himself complicit in her attempted murder? After all, she was his responsibility, and he was bound to protect her, whether he liked it or not.

Letty knew she should just let it drop, accept his avowal in the spirit in which it was offered, and go on home, to a bath, to a debriefing, to normal life. But she was sick of being a responsibility, and she was sick of polite platitudes.

"What about Mary?" she pressed on, lifting her bruised face earnestly toward his. "It's Mary that you want, that you've always wanted. I'm not Mary—I couldn't be Mary if I tried."

"No, you couldn't," agreed Geoff, his hands sliding up her arms. "I wouldn't want you to be. You're far more precious as you are."

Letty shook her head, mutely rejecting the compliment.

"I want you," Geoff said, his eyes intent on her face in a way that made Letty feel curiously bare, all the machinery of her mind, all her thoughts and emotions, his for the taking. "Not Mary. You."

"You don't have to say that," remonstrated Letty, putting a hand against his chest to ward off further words. "I know you're trying to be kind, but—" How could she explain that it was far crueler to raise hopes that couldn't possibly be realized?

"Kind?" Comprehension kindled in Geoff's gray eyes. His lips twisted in exasperated fondness. "I'm not being kind. Mary was—" Pausing, Geoff groped for an explanation, his expression abstracted. "Mary was a young man's dream."

That was supposed to make her feel better?

Looking back down at Letty, Geoff searched for the correct words to make her understand. "Mary was a storybook illustration, a stained-glass window, an Orthodox icon. She was never real. Not like you."

"Imperfect, you mean," translated Letty.

A sudden smile transformed Geoff's thin face. "In the best of all possible ways."

Letty's nose wrinkled skeptically. "I don't think 'best' and 'imperfect' keep much company together."

"That's where you're wrong. Perfection may be admirable, but it's not very lovable."

Letty's disbelief must have shown on her face, because Geoff repeated, "Yes, lovable. I love the way all your thoughts show on your face—yes, just like that one. I love the way your hair won't stay where it's put. I love the way you wrinkle your nose when you're trying to think of something to say. I love your habit of plain speaking." He touched a finger to her nose. "And, yes, I even love your freckles. I wouldn't eliminate a single one of them, not for all the lemons in the world. There. Does that convince you?"

"You're mad," said Letty, exhibiting that laudable habit of plain speaking he so admired. "You must have hit your head. No, wait, I hit my head. That must be it. This can't be real. Not me. Not you. Not—" Letty shook her head. "No."

"Why?"

"It's too ridiculous to even contemplate. Like a fairy tale. Everyone knows the prince would never really fall in love with the beggar girl. Not in real life. The prince falls in love with the princess, and they go on living in their gilded hall, with their gilded children, in their gilded chairs."

Geoff held up his hands, spreading open his fingers. "I seem to be entirely out of gold leaf at present."

Letty shook her head, brushing away his remark.

"I used to watch you with Mary," she confessed. "I used to watch you with Mary and wish it were me."

She had never admitted it, even to herself, but it was horribly, miserably true. She had hidden it behind a screen of self-righteous judgment, telling herself it was merely that they weren't suited, or that she disapproved of Mary's methods, but that wasn't the real reason. That had never been the real reason.

She had no right to judge anyone, not her sister, not Geoff, not anyone. Not when she had channeled jealousy into spite and pretended it was for their own good. She couldn't even say with any surety that her motives for barging into their elopement were entirely pure. Guilt rose in her, like bile at the back of her throat, tainting everything it touched. That night, if she had left them alone, if she had stayed in her room, Mary would have gone off with Geoff and they would have lived happily ever after. The family reputation certainly couldn't have been more tarnished than it had been by her.

But she had interfered—not out of a pure, disinterested desire for the good of the family, but because, in a hidden little recess in the back of her heart, she had wanted Lord Pinchingdale for herself. And she had known she could never have him.

It wasn't a pleasant realization, any of it. Those people who lauded self-knowledge had clearly never tried it.

"I knew that even if she weren't there—" Letty broke off with an unhappy little laugh. "It was useless. I might as well cry for the moon. You were that far above my touch."

Geoff's brows drew together in confusion.

"Because of the title?" he asked incredulously.

For a smart man, at times he really could be very slow. The thought almost made Letty smile. Almost.

"No. Because you're you. Clever and subtle and cultured . . ." Letty waved her hands about in wordless illustration. "And I'm just plain old Letty from Hertfordshire."

Geoff's lips quirked. "Nineteen is hardly old. And if you're from Hertfordshire, so is your sister."

"Yes, but with Mary, it didn't *stick*. She looks right in a London ballroom; I don't. Your house makes me feel like King Cophetua's beggar maid."

Geoff tucked a flyaway wisp of hair back behind her ear. "You can redecorate."

"No," Letty protested, pushing irritably away. "That's not it at all."

It might be rather self-defeating to list for him all the reasons he shouldn't love her, but better that than to have him profess sentiments he couldn't really mean, that couldn't possibly survive once they left the enchanted green world of Ireland and returned to the overheated drawing rooms of London, where the spiteful whispers of their so-called friends would peck holes into any pretensions of affection he might have for her. They would return, and he would realize that she was nothing but a dowdy duckling, a glorified goose girl, stout and sturdy and utterly mundane.

Letty redoubled her efforts. "You don't understand. I'll never be sophisticated or graceful or have poems written to me. I'm not the sort of person you want at all."

Looking down into Letty's flushed face, Geoff said matter-of-factly, "Don't you think I should be the judge of that? As clever and sophisticated and whatnot as I am? Besides," he added, when Letty looked like she was about to remonstrate, "I'm not all that comfortable in a ballroom myself. And I've never had a single poem written to me. Unless you want to volunteer. Your poetic efforts could hardly be worse than mine."

Letty narrowed her eyes at him. "But you always seem so assured. So polished."

"You mean, so quiet," Geoff countered.

He waited a moment, watching her, allowing time for his words to sink in. Letty cast her memory back over the hundreds of times she had encountered him over the course of the Season, since his return from France. Her memory conjured him standing with his friends at the side of the room, leaning over Mary's chair, propping up the wall at a musicale. In every image, he was watching, observing, somewhere off on the fringes while other people laughed and danced.

"Oh," said Letty stupidly.

"I've always been more comfortable with books than people. Running off to France for years made the problem easy to avoid."

Letty felt a bit as though she had spent hours squinting at a book, trying desperately to read it, and someone had just come along and turned it right-side up. She knew, logically, this was the proper way to look at it, but her unfocused eyes were having trouble registering the words.

"So, when you came back . . ."

"I felt just as out of place as you did. So I attached myself to your sister. She made a convenient altar at which to worship. It gave me a place and a purpose, where I otherwise had none." Remembering, Geoff stared off into the air above Letty's left shoulder, lips pressed together in an uncompromising line. "I misused her badly, although that was never my intention at the time."

"No," said Letty slowly. "Of course not."

Was he saying—he did seem to be saying—that he had never really loved Mary? He couldn't mean that. His devotion to Mary had become a commonplace, like Petrarch's love for Laura or Dante's for Beatrice, a yardstick by which devotion was measured.

But it was all, Letty realized, devotion from a distance, worship from afar. She had always had her doubts as to whether Petrarch loved Laura. How could he, when he didn't know what Laura liked for breakfast, or whether she broke out in spots once a month, or had an unfortunate tendency to giggle at awkward moments?

In short, whether she was real. Letty's eyes lifted to Geoff's with new understanding, taking in the familiar features in a new way. The small lines around his gray eyes, the patient set of his mouth, the thoughtful furrow of his brow, all little imperfections that had drawn her to him from the first.

"I'm not your gilded prince with the gilded chairs, Letty," Geoff said simply. "I couldn't be if I tried."

"I wouldn't want you to be." Letty's voice felt rusty.

"I'm not particularly bold or dashing or heroic. I'm happier at my desk than in a black cloak. And I've never entirely mastered all the steps of the quadrille." He looked soberly down at her. "But what I am is yours, if you'll still have me."

It was a gesture more eloquent than a bended knee.

Somehow, Letty realized, he had turned the tables. He had taken all of her imperfections and turned them into his. He had turned his own pride inside out and offered it to her, hilt first, like a knight surrendering his sword, placing the power of refusal in her hands.

Letty was humbled by the very generosity of it. Humbled, and so filled with love that she could scarcely find the breath to express it. She didn't care if he couldn't dance the quadrille; she had no use for black cloaks; and she didn't mind if he preferred books to people so long as there was room among his books for her.

"Gladly," she said, the word choking in her throat. "So gladly."

"Warts and all?"

"Goiters, boils, and carbuncles," Letty assured him eagerly.

"I don't think we need to go quite that far. . . ." She loved the way his eyes crinkled when he smiled, the lopsided tilt of his lips, the dark shadow of his hair above his brow. "Warts are quite enough."

"And smelly straw." Letty wrinkled her nose at the odor arising from their feet. "Quite a place for a declaration of love."

Geoff's eyes moved meaningfully to her lips, in a way that made color flare up through Letty's cheeks like a whole fusillade of rockets. "We do seem to make a habit of carriages." His hands slipped around her waist, drawing her closer.

Flushed with happiness, Letty glanced around her at the splintered slats and the bloodied straw. She wouldn't have traded the dilapidated old wagon for any number of gilded reception rooms.

"I don't think you can call this a carriage," countered Letty, tilting her head back up toward Geoff. "It's really more of a cart."

Geoff lifted both his eyebrows. "Does it matter?"

Letty lifted herself up on her tiptoes and latched her arms around his neck. "No," she said honestly. "Not in the slightest."

And that was the last either of them said for quite some time.

When they had time to reflect upon it later, the Viscount and Viscountess Pinchingdale were in perfect agreement that, for certain purposes, one wheeled conveyance was quite as good as another.

Chapter Thirty-one

"Leaving?" I craned my neck in an entirely unsubtle way, but the angle of the door blocked the corridor from view. "But we haven't even had dinner yet."

I'd been counting on Colin being logy with large quantities of food before I made my approach. As a veteran of countless Thanksgiving dinners, I knew exactly how much pumpkin pie I could consume before stupor struck. A neophyte, unused to the soporific properties of turkey and stuffing, should be easy prey.

But not if he was leaving.

Blithely insensitive to atmosphere, Mrs. Harrington gave a little wave. "He had some other do to attend, he said. But Serena will be staying with us, won't you, dear?"

"Pammy was very insistent." Had that been a bit of a barb beneath the quiet cadence of Serena's voice? Probably my imagination. In the meantime, her brother was getting away.

I had to go say something to him. I didn't know if everything had been all in my head from the start; I didn't know if he had ever had the slightest bit of interest in me, or if he had realized that I had been snubbing him (even if only because I thought he was snubbing me). But I did know that if I didn't say something

I was going to spend the rest of the evening feeling awful in a way that had nothing to do with Thanksgiving bloat.

It wasn't like I was following him to Ireland, or anything.

"Will you excuse me?" I levered myself off my perch on the side of the couch so abruptly that strands of Serena's hair fluttered with the movement, rising and settling like a flock of pigeons in Trafalgar Square. "Be back in a moment."

Propelling myself toward the door, I barreled out into the hallway. It wasn't a long hallway, just a narrow rectangle that spanned the house from the front door on one end to the garden door on the other. I didn't think Colin had gone out the garden way; o'erleaping garden walls went out of fashion several centuries ago, along with lutes and codpieces. I hadn't heard the front door open and close. Although, I warned myself, it was unlikely I would have over the hum of cocktail-lubricated conversation.

There was only one other place he could be. Crossing my fingers for all I was worth, I ventured into the little spur of hallway between dining room and kitchen, a narrow space that had been commandeered as a cloakroom. Sure enough, there was Colin, pawing through a row of identical coats on a portable aluminum rack, a look of intense concentration on his face. I blessed the blandness of raincoat manufacture. Minus identifying factors like that coffee stain on the sleeve or that slightly hairy mint at the bottom of a pocket, one Burberry looks much like another. I usually identified mine by dint of an elderly movie stub in the left-hand pocket, admitting one to a 9:40 showing of *Legally Blonde*.

Colin glanced up at the click of my heels against the hardwood floors. "You're not leaving?" he asked politely.

"No, but I heard that you are." Given where we were standing, it wasn't exactly the world's most brilliant observation.

Colin whipped a Burberry off the rack. I hoped it was actually his. "I have other plans."

"Mrs. Harrington said."

This had all seemed much easier back in the living room.

Being faced with a living, breathing man intent on putting on his raincoat made matters much harder. In all the conversations I had with him in my head, he generally stayed put and listened, before responding with eloquent lines like "How right you are."

People are so much more agreeable in one's head.

"Listen," I said, taking a step forward. "I just wanted to say I'm sorry."

Colin blinked, one arm halfway into his raincoat. "What for?"

"About your mother's accident. Why didn't you say anything? I would have left right away."

"At midnight?"

"You must have cabs in Sussex. Hotels, even. I could have gone to a hotel. You really didn't have to stick around because of me. I feel awful."

"Don't." Colin's eyes crinkled at the corners, like a polar ice cap cracking. "I wasn't able to find an earlier flight."

"If you had, I hope you would have kicked me out earlier."

"Without a second thought," Colin reassured me.

"Good." I beamed at him before remembering that beaming probably wasn't appropriate when a parent was in the hospital. "She is doing better?"

"Much. It wasn't anything life-threatening to begin with, but it was someone from hospital calling, not Mum—she was out cold. All I caught was that there'd been a car accident and she was in hospital, unconscious."

"Scary," I said, making a sympathetic face.

"Her husband was away at a conference, and my Italian is purely rudimentary. Enough to ask for grappa, but when it comes to medical terms—" Colin spread his hands in an endearingly boyish gesture of bafflement.

"But they cleared it up once you got there?"

"With a great deal of pointing at the relevant phrases in an Italian-English dictionary. Once we established that she had neither gangrene nor leprosy, it went swimmingly."

"Surely there must have been someone who spoke English?"

"Probably off on coffee break," said Colin dryly. "Or just enjoying watching the English bloke make a prat of himself."

"You never know, they might have just been on strike," I provided. "I gather that's pretty much the norm over there."

"All English speakers go slow for a day?"

"It gives whole new meaning to the English-Speaking Union! Maybe that's what happened to the mimes. Being French, they went on strike, and have been doomed to communicate through hand signals ever since, like linguistic gypsies."

Don't ask me where the mimes came from. They just popped out, and once out, refused to go back.

"And the painted faces?"

"An attempt to go incognito, so people won't keep shutting them into boxes. Naturally."

"Naturally," agreed Colin, looking rather bemused. "I don't know why I didn't think of it before."

"It takes a superior intelligence. And years of painstaking observation of the mime in its natural habitat." I hoped Colin wouldn't ask what that was, since I had no idea. Every now and again, my mouth detaches from my brain, and horrible things happen. "How did we get on mimes, again?" I asked hastily.

"It all comes back to the French, somehow or other." Cinching the belt of his raincoat closed—tied, not buckled—he asked, "How is the Pink Carnation?"

"Never been better," I said cheerfully, concealing my disappointment at the signs of his imminent departure. Why wouldn't he leave? He had said he had another event to go to, and I was probably making him late as it was. "She just foiled a rebellion in Ireland."

"I had a feeling she might."

"You mean you knew about it already."

"There is that."

"But I know something you don't know."

"If it has to do with mimes, I don't need to know."

I folded my arms across my chest in exaggerated disgust. "We are just not going there again." Having dismissed the mimes, I lowered my voice dramatically. "What would you say if I told you that, rather than just one Black Tulip, there might have been an entire syndicate of them?"

"How do you mean?" Colin leaned back against the cream-painted wall as though he had no intention of going anywhere at all.

"I mean, not one, but a series of subagents, all with very pale skin and black hair. The petals of the Tulip."

"It sounds rather fantastic."

"It is," I agreed. "Only not in the way you mean."

I gave him a quick rundown on my week's archival discoveries, starting with the advent of Miss Emily Gilchrist and finishing up with the marquise's mysterious death in the parlor of Lord Vaughn.

"Aren't you a bit short on petals?" asked Colin. "It takes more than two to cover a flower."

I had to stop and count on my fingers. Surely there had to have been more dark-haired agents than just the marquise and Emily Gilchrist . . . but if there were, I hadn't found them yet.

"Of course, it's all still conjecture at this point," I said hastily. "But wouldn't it be wonderful?"

For a long moment, Colin didn't say anything at all. He just looked at me, until I could feel my damnably fair skin begin to flush under his scrutiny.

"Wonderful," he agreed, just before the pause reached epic proportions. "I'm sure Jay contributed many brilliant insights."

It took me a moment to remember who Jay was. "Don't remind me. I'm trying to blot that evening out of my memory."

"Aren't you . . . ?"

"Oh, God, no." I hastened to disabuse him of the notion. Forget the fact that I was the one who put the notion into his head in the first place. Right now, all I wanted to do was excise the whole ridiculous Jay episode and go back to where we had been a week or so ago. "I only went out with him to placate Grandma. Since he's in England and I'm in England . . . it's just easier not to argue with Grandma."

"That *is* a relief."

"Really?" I went into a full-scale head-tilt, complete with breathy voice and fluttering lashes.

"Yes. He seemed rather a git."

Damn. I couldn't argue with the analysis, but I'd been hoping for something a little more along the lines of "Darling, I wanted you for myself. I couldn't bear to see you so close to the arms of another man."

Ah, well. That's what old movies and cartons of Ben & Jerry's were for, to make up the deficiencies in real life. If this were a black-andwhite movie, I would already be clutched in his manly arms, assuring him that Jay meant nothing to me, nothing at all.

Instead, I got Pammy, wearing enough fur for any three starlets.

"Hi, you two!" she caroled, bumping into me.

I think she meant to knock me into Colin, but her aim was off. Instead, I banged my elbow into the wall with enough force to bring tears to my eyes. Subtlety personified, that's our Pammy.

"Ouch," I said.

"Sorry." Pammy didn't sound the least bit sorry. She turned her hostess smile on Colin, an uncanny mirror of her mother's, only with more of her gums showing. "Are you sure you can't stay for dinner? Really, really sure?"

"I wish I could, but I have to meet someone . . ." Colin glanced at his watch, a simple silver-framed piece with a leather band. "Five minutes ago."

"I feel bad for having kept you," I said.

"Haven't we already had this discussion?"

"Do you have a date?" Pammy overrode both of us.

"You could say that." I did my best to keep my facial muscles in proper order, rather than drooping like a sad clown. An unmarried, heterosexual male—a tall, cute, unmarried heterosexual male—couldn't possibly be single. I should have expected that he'd be seeing someone, even if it were only an early-days, casual-dating sort of thing. "With my friend Martin."

Right. Martin. Relief flooded in, followed by doubt. Wait—did this mean he wasn't straight, after all?

He *was* suspiciously well groomed for a straight man. His dark blond hair exuded a clean shampoo smell, and that was definitely aftershave I had scented as I banged into the wall next to him. True, his clothes tended toward the outdoorsy, but that might just be an affectation, like those gay-straight men who affected deep interest in tools and car parts. He had said she could call it a date. . . .

I was officially resigning from the human race. It was all just too much trouble.

"Martin," pressed Pammy. "As in Martin?"

What else could Martin stand for?

"Well, have fun!" I broke in before Pammy could embarrass herself further. Or embarrass me. As I knew from the sixth-grade dances, Pammy is, and has always been, largely embarrassment-proof. Mom's theory is that it comes from having an unsettled home life.

"Thanks. I'm not sure how much fun it will be, though. Martin's girlfriend chucked him last week."

Not gay, then. At least, Martin wasn't. As for Colin, the jury was still out. On just about everything. My personal jury is notoriously indecisive.

"Poor Martin." Pammy allowed a moment for mourning before following up with, "Is he cute?"

"What about your I-banker?" I demanded.

Pammy made a face. "He's being transferred to their Hong Kong office."

"Ah," I said wisely.

"Ah?" inquired Colin.

"Absence makes the heart go wander," I explained.

Colin looked quizzically at Pammy. "His, or yours?"

"Both," replied Pammy emphatically.

Across the coatrack, Colin's and my eyes locked in shared amusement.

I hastily looked away.

"Aren't you late?" I asked, nudging Pammy ahead of me out of the hallway to clear the way. "It seems cruel to keep poor Martin waiting. He'll think you've abandoned him, too."

"Call him and invite him over!" Pammy tossed back over her shoulder as I propelled her into the front hall. "The best way to get over a breakup is to get out there again. Right, Ellie? You can't just let him stay at home and mope. Or he might not have another date for, like, a year."

"At least let the guy have a decent mourning period," I remonstrated. "It takes a while to get over a breakup."

"Only if you *let* it take a while. It's all about positive thinking."

"And cosmos?" That had been Pammy's last breakup prescription. Take four cosmos, go out clubbing, and call her in the morning.

"I don't think he's in the mood for new people," said Colin tactfully. "But, thank you."

"Another time, then. We could all do drinks." I could see the Machiavellian wheels in Pammy's head churning up images of potential double dates.

"Won't you be seeing someone else by the time the mourning period is over?"

"I like to keep a backup list," said Pammy blithely. "You never know when they might come in handy."

"Like understudies," I explained to Colin, as the three of us filtered out into the front hall. "She keeps them in the wings in case the principal is unable to go on."

"Or sent to Hong Kong?"

"Happens all the time."

"Isn't it time to call your understudy in from the wings? Now that Jay has been sent back to grandmother?"

I glanced back up over my shoulder at him, turning down the corners of my mouth in feigned regret. "I'm not nearly as well organized as Pammy. My backstage is totally empty."

"That will never do." I couldn't see his face, but I could hear the amusement in his voice. "You need to restock."

"I haven't really had time to set up any auditions." The stage analogy wasn't entirely inapt; my heart was beating as though I were walking a tightrope as I paused next to the front door and turned to face him. "Except the hideous Jay one, and you saw how that one turned out."

"You ought to get back out there."

"Hear, hear!" said Pammy. "I've been telling her that for *ages*."

"Thanks, Pams."

Colin paused with one hand on the doorknob, and glanced casually down at me. "What are you doing Saturday night?"

I was supposed to be having dinner with Pammy. A swift kick from Pammy informed me that our plans were officially off.

"Nothing."

"Dinner?"

"One of my favorite meals."

"How does eight sound?"

Like a host of celestial angels singing. "Like an excellent time for dinner."

Next to me, I could feel Pammy bristling with repressed commentary.

"Brilliant," said Colin.

That had all happened a little too fast for me.

Did I have a date with Colin? Or was that just an abstract inquiry into the desirability of eight o'clock as a dining hour? It wasn't the sort of thing one could ask without looking really, really stupid.

Besides, Colin was busy thanking Pammy for a lovely evening, and Pammy was smirking in a way usually reserved for successful fairy godmothers. Any moment now she was going to sprout a tutu and start singing "Bibbidi-Bobbidi-Boo."

The niceties disposed of, Colin poked his head around the door one last time. "Till Saturday, then."

"Don't forget your audition materials!" I twinkled.

Fortunately, the door was already swinging shut, placing three inches of good, solid oak between Colin and my silly comments.

I really hoped he hadn't heard that.

I lowered my head to my clenched hands. "Audition materials. Oh, God. I didn't."

Pammy snickered. "It could have been worse. At least you didn't say his audition *piece*."

"Pammy!"

"Do you think it's a long audition piece?"

I whacked Pammy on the arm. "That's not what I meant. We're just having dinner."

Pammy waggled her eyebrows. "Dinner, eh?"

"Oh, Pams." Overflowing with joy to the world and goodwill toward men, I gave her a quick hug. "Thanks."

"You're welcome." Pammy patted my back complacently. "Now who's making fun of Mustafa and the mountain?"

I didn't even bother to correct her. I was too happy. She could have all the Mustafas she wanted.

"I have a *date*."

"Uh-huh," said Pammy benignly.

"With Colin."

"That's him."

"I have a date with Colin."

Pammy slipped an arm through mine and began propelling

me back toward the living room. "Okay, we got that. But you can't just get complacent. You have to think about the important things. Like, what you're going to wear."

Dinner. Saturday. Eight o'clock. It all sounded pretty incontrovertibly date-ish. Even allowing for transatlantic cultural differences, "Saturday" and "date" tend to be synonymous.

I had a date with Colin! A real date with Colin!

From the kitchen wafted the unmistakable scents of roasting turkey and yams swimming in syrup. Warm, homey smells vested with a wealth of good feelings, like lemon polish and clean linen. A deep feeling of contentment welled within me, the sort you have when you're very little, and the sun is shining, and your parents suggest ice cream without your even having to wheedle for it. All was right with the world. I had a whole new angle for my dissertation, turkey and American accents for Thanksgiving, and a date with a handsome Englishman on Saturday. A man who didn't confuse the Pimpernel with pumpernickel. Life couldn't get much better than this, not for all the Jimmy Choos in China.

With a little smile, I remembered the compositions we had to write each November in Lower School. They invariably began, "I have reason to be thankful because . . ." At the time, it usually had a lot to do with My Little Pony and naturally curly hair, with the occasional pious reference to loving parents thrown in for ballast.

Thinking of Colin, I sent a heartfelt message of gratitude out to all those turkeys who had perished to make Thanksgiving possible.

"I know!" exclaimed Pammy. "I have the most adorable little yak-skin corset!"

"No yak skin," I said.

Even gratitude only goes so far.

Historical Note

Truth can be very convenient for fiction. The events in Ireland in 1803 make a colorful story without any additional embellishment. After a brief exile in France, Robert Emmet and other veterans of the rising of 1798 returned to Dublin to plot a new insurrection. Stockpiling weapons in various depots around the city, Emmet planned to launch an attack on key centers of power within the city, to be coordinated with risings elsewhere in Ireland, and possibly a French invasion.

At six thirty in the evening on July sixteenth, all those plans quite literally went up in smoke. An explosion at the Patrick Street depot forced the hands of the insurgents. Faced with a choice of acting quickly or abandoning the enterprise, they moved the date of the rising up to July twenty-third, far earlier than intended. As Ruán O'Donnell sums it up, "The stark choice facing Emmet and the other commanders was to launch a Dublin-centered rebellion without delay or to hold out in the hope that the French would invade Ireland or England as expected in August/September."

Without a full muster of men, without aid from France, the rebellion was practically over before it began. As Emmet's biographer Patrick Geoghegan recounts, "As daylight faded on the evening of 23 July, Emmet waited for the rebels to arrive at the main depot. . . . He expected two thousand men to appear. Eighty turned up. Worse, before assembling, most of them had been to the Yellow Bottle public house. . . ." The rebel units did manage to hold positions on Thomas Street and James Street for nearly two hours, but the planned attack on Dublin Castle never occurred and the evening ended in rout and riot. Emmet fled to the Wicklow Mountains. Along with twenty other rebel leaders, he was apprehended and executed, dying a martyr for his cause.

The historical record of the rebellion is so rich that it was a wrench not to be able to use everything. One of my favorite tidbits was the use of hurling societies (not to be confused with curling, which is a different sort of sport entirely) as a screen for military maneuvers, with the hurling stick standing in for a musket or pike. Sadly, I couldn't think of any excuse for proper young ladies like Letty and Jane being allowed anywhere near the Donnybrook hurling club. But even with hurling out of the picture, there were plenty of details that I was able to press into service. The rebel depots, with their warren of secret rooms and hidden hordes of weapons, were a novelist's dream, and the explosion at Patrick Street simply begged for a role in the story. The rockets, designed as a variant on those used in India, were Emmet's innovation, not mine, and did indeed lead to the fatal explosion at Patrick Street.

There are several discrepancies in the various versions of the explosion at the Patrick Street depot—although nothing to suggest that the incident was anything other than an accident. By all accounts, some of the men had been experimenting with fuses for the rockets, and a moment of carelessness (and possibly inebriation) led to the resulting explosion. Once outside that basic frame, the stories start to vary. Since two of Emmet's men placed the blame on a dyer named George McDaniels, accusing him of working on the rockets while sloshed, I decided to keep him on in the role of scapegoat, placing him on the scene as the drunken watchman.

Historians also squabble over whether Emmet genuinely wished to secure aid from France or whether he preferred, as a powerful symbolic statement, to have Ireland liberated by Irishmen. For the purposes of this book, I went with the former theory, largely because it made tying in the antics of French spies that much easier. Emmet's brother, Thomas Addis, did meet several times with General Berthier, Bonaparte's minister of war, to discuss the loan of French troops, and there is some evidence to suggest that the rebel leaders anticipated a French invasion in late August or early September. For anyone interested in reading more about the rising of 1803, I recommend two excellent biographies of Emmet, both rich in detail but very different in their historiographical slants: Patrick M. Geoghegan's *Robert Emmet: A Life*, and Ruán O'Donnell's *Robert Emmet and the Rising of 1803*.

Those familiar with Dublin may notice some changes in the landscape. There would be no chance these days of anyone tripping over a body backstage in the Crow Street Theatre; it has been superseded by a warehouse and offices. The building was already, as a contemporary put it, being "pulled to pieces by installments" as early as the 1820s. For those who are curious, pictures of the theater and the principal performers can be found in T. J. Walsh's *Opera in Dublin, 1798–1820: Frederick Jones and the Crow Street Theatre*. St. Werburgh's survived far better than the Crow Street Theatre, but at the cost of a few appendages; it lost its steeple in 1810 and its tower in 1836. Patrick Street, home to the ill-fated rebel depot, has undergone even more of a transformation. Lauding the complete overhaul of the area, a 1905 travel guide describes its former state with unveiled distaste as "one of the most squalid, disreputable, and dilapidated in the city. It was intersected by a network of narrow streets and alleys, which were overhung by hundreds of rickety and unsanitary dwellings." It was that world, the vanished nineteenth-century landscape of narrow streets and rickety dwellings, that I strove to re-create, rather than the polished Patrick Street of today.

THE DECEPTION OF THE

Emerald Ring

OR LORD VAUGHN TAKES UMBRAGE!

Lauren Willig

AUTHOR'S NOTE

A year ago, as I was working on *The Deception of the Emerald Ring*, I came across a wonderful mystery novel by Kasey Michaels, in which an author suddenly discovers that one of her characters, a supercilious Regency gentleman, has come to life right in the middle of her living room. My first reaction was: "Oh, dear, where on earth am I going to house Lord Vaughn?"

Of all my characters, Lord Vaughn, having already hijacked the plots of two books, seemed the most likely to show up unannounced in my tiny studio apartment, raise a disdainful eyebrow, and ask what my servants had been doing to let the place get into such a disgraceful state. I had a feeling he wasn't going to be too happy sleeping on the air mattress on my living room floor, and would be even less happy with the concept of washing his own dishes. Fortunately, Lord Vaughn decided to postpone his visit (I'm convinced it was the dishwashing that put him off), but he did have a few comments (otherwise known as complaints) to make upon the publication of this third book in the Pink Carnation chronicles.

A CONVERSATION
WITH LAUREN WILLIG

Q. My dear girl, I really must object to the premise of this absurd farce in which you appear to have embroiled me. Elopements are decidedly passé.

A. If you must blame anyone for the elopement plot, blame Georgette Heyer. During my research year in London, I used to sneak Heyer books into the British Library to read over lunch in the BL Cafeteria. The English editions were conveniently small and compact, perfect for propping up against a bowl of watery soup, and it made for a nice break from peering at crabbed seventeenth-century handwriting all day. At the time, I was midway through writing *The Secret History of the Pink Carnation*. Geoff—and his infatuation with the unsuitable Mary Alsworthy—had already been introduced into the plot, and I had been rather absentmindedly wondering how I was going to extract him from that tangle.

Geoff, like so many men I knew in grad school, is entirely at home with a complicated theorem or an abstruse idea, but completely at a loss with the opposite sex. Having so little experience with women, Geoff cherishes romanticized notions of love with a capital L. Having his father and two younger siblings carried away by smallpox when he was eight, Geoff grew up in cold marble rooms, with a mother more interested in her maladies than in her sole surviving son. Like Miles, the closest Geoff came to a true family life was with the Uppingtons. But, unlike Miles, Geoff never let himself be entirely drawn into their family circle. In short, Geoff lacked any notion of what it was like to be truly close to someone, leaving him easy prey for the machinations of a Mary Alsworthy.

I'll never forget the day in the BL cafeteria when I propped open Georgette Heyer's *Devil's Cub*, and encountered the perfect solution to Geoff's problem. For those non-Heyer readers out there, in *Devil's Cub*, the sensible older sister interferes with her flighty younger sister's elopement with a bored rake, and finds herself carried off in her sister's stead. Geoff couldn't be more unlike the amoral hero of *Devil's Cub* (who certainly didn't have marriage on his mind), but the basic idea caught my imagination. If Geoff wouldn't seek out the right sort of woman on his own, I would fling her into his path in a way he couldn't ignore—by putting her in his carriage at midnight in her sister's place. Being an honorable sort, Geoff couldn't possibly refuse to marry her. Good-bye, Mary Alsworthy, and hello, *Emerald Ring*. . . .

Q. Carrying off chits of girls in carriages is one thing, but was it necessary to export me to Ireland for your literary whims? I had an engagement to attend a house party in Norfolk when I found myself arbitrarily whisked off across the Irish Sea. One would think it could at least have waited until the Irish Season in December when there would be decent entertainment to be had.

A. I give you a whole rebellion to play with, and you claim there was no decent entertainment? There's just no pleasing some characters. And, no, Lord Vaughn, it couldn't have waited till December for the simple reason that the Irish Rising of 1803 occurred in July.

I first stumbled across the Rising of 1803 in 2002, in the midst of a bitter-cold Cambridge winter. At the time, I was an overeager third-year graduate student teaching a class on the Second British Empire (1783–1945), desperately trying to stay one step ahead of my students, all of whom seemed to know more about Ireland and India than I did. As I burned the midnight oil, reading up on rebellions and revolutions, murders and mutinies, I came upon one of Ireland's lesser-known risings: the tale of Robert Emmett and the Irish Rising of 1803. The Irish Rebellion had it all: hidden identities, smoky taverns, dark alleyways, secret negotiations with the French, smuggled explosives. I knew, then and there, that it had to form the backbone of my third book. Admittedly, at that point I still hadn't even finished my first book, and I had no idea when, if ever, I was going to make it all the way to a third, but the Irish Rebellion was just too perfect to miss out on.

Fate appeared to agree. When a good friend got married that spring, the postparty to the rehearsal dinner was held at a bar. As we approached, a wooden sign creaking in the May breeze caught my attention. An oddly familiar picture of a dapper man in white cravat and black frock coat, his hair cut short and combed forward over his forehead was painted on it. The name of the bar, of course, was Robert Emmett's. The rest, as they say, is history.

Q. I have been credibly informed that you have so sunk in your social station as to take a situation in a solicitor's office. I trust this ill-advised foray into employment will not result in any delinquency in the penning of my chronicles.

A. First of all, they're not your chronicles. It's the Pink Carnation series, not the Lord Vaughn Show. One trembles to think what the Lord Vaughn show might entail. No, please, don't tell me.

It is true that I have another life outside the Pink Carnation books, as an associate at a large New York law firm. It all happened in a rather roundabout way. Way back when, during my research year in London, it finally dawned on me that the academic job market is just as bad as everyone says. Since I didn't much fancy the idea of starving in a garret by the light of a single candle—and even decent garrets are pretty hard to come by these days—I fell back on the last refuge of the liberal arts major: law school. One month into law school, I got the call that every fledgling author dreams of: suddenly, I had a book contract and a legal career (and an unwritten dissertation, but I try not to think about that bit). Once I was getting that legal education, it seemed a waste not to put it to use. So here I am, associate by week, novelist by weekend.

Although the two may seem very different, I find that my day job as a lawyer and my weekend job as an author feed into each other nicely. On weekdays, I wake up at seven, put on my suit and pearls, traipse into the office, plunk myself down at a desk, and drink too much coffee. On weekends, I wake up at seven, put on ancient plaid pants and a shirt with holes in the seams, traipse across my living room, plunk myself down at a desk . . . and drink too much coffee. See?

On a more serious note, having a day job does have an unexpectedly beneficial impact on my writing, even aside from the ability to pay my rent (*see* garret, *above*). I've always found that one of the great drawbacks of the writing life is that, while one is purporting to purvey truths about humanity, one doesn't interact much with humanity. Dialogue and characterization become increasingly based upon other authors' fictional worlds rather than the actual ebb and flow of life beyond one's apartment doors. At the workplace, on the other hand, character quirks and overheard bits of dialogue are as plentiful as the coffee splotches on the pantry floor. Gainful employment also tends to increase efficiency. As a lawyer, I know that when something needs to be done, it needs to be done now. "But I'm waiting for my muse!" is never an acceptable answer someone is waiting for a document (which begs the interesting question: Is there a Muse of Legal Writing? And, if so, where has she been hiding all this time?). Since I have a very bad tendency to procrastinate when left to myself for long periods of time, being put through the professional equivalent of boot camp on the weekdays does wonderful things for my production of prose on the weekends.

Q. I find myself in want of a mistress. If one must continue in this series, one expects at the very least to be provided with the basic amenities.

A. My dear Lord Vaughn, I fear you mistake yourself. The proper phrase is "in want of a wife." Trust me. You shan't be in want of one for long. In fact, you may be getting a bit more than you bargained for there!

QUESTIONS
FOR DISCUSSION

1. Do the modern and the historical characters play off each other in *The Deception of the Emerald Ring*? Did you feel that the modern-day London story line helped frame the historical novel within the book? Were you more interested in Colin and Eloise's romance or the romance between Letty and Geoff? Were there similarities in their romances? What were the differences between them?

2. What does the book's title mean? How does "deception" play a purpose in the novel? Who do you believe was the most deceiving character in this novel?

3. Did you feel sympathetic to Mary when Letty and Geoff were forced into marriage, even though Letty felt she was saving her sister from self-destruction? Do you feel that Mary deserves her own romantic adventure?

4. Who was the most fascinating spy to you and why? Who was the most surprising? Who was the most cunning?

5. Do you think Lord Vaughn is good or evil? How did the snake imagery and his recitation of *Paradise Lost* in *The Masque of the Black Tulip* affect your perception of him?

6. How would you compare the heroes in each book: Richard in *The Secret History of the Pink Carnation,* Miles in *The Masque of the Black Tulip*, and Geoff in *The Deception of the Emerald Ring*? How would you compare the heroines: Amy, Henrietta, and Letty?

7. Like her modern-day heroine, Eloise, Lauren has spent more than six years working on a graduate degree in English history. What did you think of her historical details? What did you think of her perspective on history?

8. Out of all three of the Pink Carnation books, which character would you choose to take out for a cup of coffee or tea?

From talented and imaginative author Lauren Willig comes the fourth installment in the popular and bestselling Pink Carnation series, available in hardcover from Dutton. Read on for a sneak preview. . . .

Mary Alsworthy is a bona fide beauty, courted by multitudes of men looking to buy her affection with a title or two. She thought she had secured her future . . . until her best suitor ran off with her sister.

Lord Vaughn has better things to do than engage in affairs of the heart, but when the Pink Carnation calls you to duty, you must act for your country. Someone needs to infiltrate the deadly Black Tulip's inner circle to help save England from a French invasion, and rumor has it that he has taken a liking to dark-haired, fair-skinned beauties . . . not unlike Miss Alsworthy. Vaughn recruits Mary, and perhaps flirts with her a bit, to convince her to help the Pink Carnation in exchange for enough funds to secure her new Season without help from her sister's new husband, her former love interest, or her disenchanted family. Mary is no clueless beauty and is far more skilled than Vaughn was prepared for to outsmart the deadliest spies, and far too magnificent for him to ignore. . . .

Even as the spies battle it out in Napoleonic France, we meet our modern-day heroine and hero, Eloise Kelly and Colin Selwick, once again, as they continue their romance and adventures in London. . . .

"I come here tonight as emissary."

"From a flower-named spy." Mary didn't bother to keep the skepticism out of her voice.

The only flowery spy at Sibley Court, as far as Mary knew, was Lord Richard Selwick, the spy formerly known as the Purple Gentian. The likelihood of his seeking her out for anything—other than a good gloat—was nonexistent. Lord Richard had all but ordered fireworks in celebration when he discovered that his best friend had escaped from her clutches (his words, not hers) and married her younger sister instead.

"What does our esteemed Purple Gentian want of me?" Mary asked.

"Oh, it's not the"—Vaughn coughed discreetly, as though the name came with difficulty to his tongue—"the Purple Gentian for whom I happen to be acting."

"Oh?" said Mary acidly. "Have we been honored with the presence of other flowers? A Roving Rosebud, perhaps?"

Vaughn spread his hands wide. "Ridiculous, isn't it? But the most ridiculous tales are often the truest."

"Unless one were to deliberately invent a ridiculous tale, trusting that others might follow that reasoning."

"Why would I go to the bother of such invention? Unless . . . Oh no. Oh no, no, no." Vaughn chuckled, a rich, full sound that resonated along the vaulted ceiling.

To her horror, Mary felt the color rise in her cheeks. With anger, she assured herself. She never blushed—and certainly not for the likes of Lord Vaughn.

The lines around Vaughn's eyes deepened with sardonic amusement. "You didn't truly believe . . . You and I? No, no, and no again."

"I find myself exceedingly relieved," Mary said stiffly, "to find that we are once again in agreement."

Vaughn wasn't the least bit fooled. He smiled lazily. "My dear, if I had wished to arrange an assignation, I would hardly have been so clumsy as to leave you in any doubt of my intentions. This matter is purely business."

"But whose business is it, then?" Mary challenged. "Why didn't they contact me directly?"

"My dear girl, if you were meant to know, why do you think our friend would have sent me?"

"I find it even less likely that you would agree to play errand boy, my lord."

Vaughn refused to be baited. He contemplated the serpentine head of his cane, twisting it so that the fangs glinted in the light. "I prefer 'go-between'. So much less menial."

"Whatever you choose to call it, you still haven't explained why."

"Wouldn't you rather know *what*?" Vaughn inquired lightly. "I should think the substance of my communication ought to interest you more than my motivations, which are of no concern to anyone at all, other than myself."

"Aren't they?" asked Mary, but left it at that. Vaughn's tone might have been casual, but there was a fine edge of steel beneath that forbade further inquiry. "All right, then. What does your Roving Rosebud want of me?"

Vaughn winced. "A better name, I should think. No, no, don't bother. It will do for present. My friend seeks your assistance in the removal of a particular thorn. A thorn called the Black Tulip."

Mary took great pleasure in saying, "You are mixing your horticultural metaphors, my lord. Am I meant to know who this unusually thorny Tulip is?"

"If any of us knew who it actually was, there would be no need to enlist you." Having scored his retaliatory point, Vaughn went on. "The Black Tulip is the nom de guerre of a spy in the employ of the French government. He started off, in the usual way of such creatures, by leaving arch notes in inconvenient places. Along the way, however, he developed an irritating habit of skewering English agents. The, ahem, Rosebud would like to see him removed."

"And you want me to bring you his head on a platter?" Mary made no effort to hide her derision.

"Metaphorically speaking. I gather that the platter is optional these days." Vaughn paused to admire the effect of his rings before adding, "You have, shall we say, certain attributes that would be most advantageous to the goal in question."

Men had admired Mary's attributes before. This was, however, one of the more ingenious stories she had been presented with.

"You must think I am very green," she said gently.

"Oh, not so very green." Lord Vaughn's eyes danced silver. "Just a trifle chartreuse around the edges."

"Inebriating?"

"Unschooled."

That would teach her to fish for compliments from Lord Vaughn. "Not so unschooled as to believe that any spy would seek me out to serve as his personal assassin."

"Ah, that explains it." Lord Vaughn's understanding smile was a miracle of polite derision. "Your role would be merely a—how shall I put this?—a decorative one. You do have some experience in that field, I believe. Your services are required not as assassin, but as bait."

Well, that certainly put her in her place. Mary raised a brow. "Weren't there any other convenient worms to hand?"

"None so well-suited as you." Oh, bother, she had walked right into that one. Before Mary could come up with a suitably cutting rejoinder about snakes and their habits, Vaughn went on. "The Black Tulip has a curious conceit. He makes it a point to employ women with your particular coloring. They are"—Vaughn paused for good effect before delivering the pièce de résistance—"the petals of the Tulip."

"How poetic. And how entirely absurd."

"My dear girl, the whole lot of them is absurd, from the Purple Wonder in the other room to every fop in London who pins a carnation to his hat and tells his friends he's turned hero. Nonetheless, they still manage to cause a good deal of bother."

Torchlight slashed in a jagged angle across Vaughn's face, slicing across his nose, leaving his eyes in shadow. In the orange light, the lines around his mouth seemed more deeply graven than usual.

"A very great deal of bother," he repeated.

Despite herself, Mary's attention was caught. The improbable tale of rosebuds and tulips might have been nothing more than a polished line of patter, designed to capitalize on the current craze for gentleman spies. But a man didn't feign that sort of bitterness. Not a man like Vaughn, at any rate. To acknowledge pain was to acknowledge that one was capable of sustaining a wound—in short, that one was capable of deeper feeling. It wasn't in Vaughn's style. Or, for that matter, in hers.

"And so," said Mary, "you introduce the bait."

"The Tulip," explained Vaughn, "is currently running rather

short of petals. Unless his habits have changed, the Black Tulip will be in want of fresh recruits. Women of your coloring are rare in this part of the world. Hence my errand tonight."

"I see." Mary took a small turn about the corridor. The train of her dress whispered along the floor behind her, dragging with it a decade's worth of dust, undoubtedly turning her hem as murky as her musings. "You do realize that this is all highly irregular."

"To say the least," Vaughn agreed calmly. "There's no need to rush to a decision. Take some time to think about my proposition. Mull it over in the deepest depths of your maidenly bosom. I would, however, advise against unburdening yourself to your friends."

Mary nearly smiled at that. "Friends." Ha. Her "friends" had been the first to claw her reputation to shreds when word of Geoffrey's defection exploded through the *ton*.

That was one lesson one learned quickly on the bloody battlefield of Almack's. Confidantes were a luxury a clever woman could ill afford. To confide in others was to invite betrayal.

Mary lifted her chin. "I keep my own counsel."

"A wise choice. Should you accept, your duties will be minimal. There is, of course, the appeal of *patria* to be considered," Vaughn added as an afterthought. "Rule Britannia and pass the mutton."

Vaughn had obviously never tasted mutton. If he had, he wouldn't joke about it. "How could one help but be swayed by such a rousing appeal?"

"Spoken like a true and loving daughter of our scepter'd isle."

"I can do no better than to model myself on you."

"Alas for England." There was something oddly engaging about the way his mouth twisted up at one corner in self-mockery. "Sharper than a serpent's tooth. . . . There is something else, however, that might quicken your filial piety."

"What could possibly move me more than mutton?"

Beneath their heavy lids, Vaughn's pale eyes glinted with pleasurable anticipation, like those of an experienced card player about to lay down a winning hand. "Something we haven't yet discussed. The small matter of remuneration."

Mary schooled her face to stillness, but she wasn't quick enough. Whatever Vaughn was looking for, he found it. His tone was insufferably smug as he added, "You will be paid. Handsomely."

Crossing his arms, he leaned back against a bust of the sixth Baron Pinchingdale and waited for her assent, the silver threads on his cuffs winking insolently in the torchlight.

He looked so vilely sure of himself—so vilely sure of her! So he thought that was all it would take to get her to say yes, did he? All he needed to do was dangle a few pieces of gold in front of the venal little creature and watch her jump.

Well, she wasn't going to jump for him. Not for an unspecified sum, at any rate. He'd have to do rather better than that. Striking her most stately attitude, Mary raked her sapphire gaze across Vaughn's face with royal scorn.

"An amusing proposition, my lord, but I'm afraid you will simply have to ask elsewhere." Without waiting for his reaction, she turned on one heel, using the sweep of her long skirt to good effect. "I cannot imagine any recompense you might offer that would be of any interest to me."

Basking in self-satisfaction, Mary swished regally down the long corridor, giving Vaughn an excellent view of her elegant back and graceful carriage. Ha! There really was nothing quite like a good exit.

Except, perhaps, for a good last word. Vaughn's amused voice snaked after her as she sailed imperiously down the gallery: "Can't you? I can. . . ."

Photo by John Earle

About the Author

The author of three previous Pink Carnation novels, **Lauren Willig** received a degree in English history from the Harvard history department and a JD from Harvard Law, where she graduated magna cum laude. A first-year associate in litigation, she lives in New York City, where she is hard at work on the fourth book in the Pink Carnation series.